Breaking Wind

Aaron Abilene

Published by Syphon Creative, 2024.

This is a work of fiction. Similarities to real people, places, or events are entirely coincidental.

BREAKING WIND

First edition. April 9, 2024.

ISBN: 979-8224709793

Written by Aaron Abilene.

Also by Aaron Abilene

505
505: Resurrection

Balls
Dead Awake

Carnival Game
Full Moon Howl
Donovan
Shades of Z

Deadeye
Deadeye & Friends
Cowboys Vs Aliens

Ferris
Life in Prescott

Afterlife in Love

Island

Paradise Island

The Lost Island

The Lost Island 2

The Lost Island 3

The Island 2

Pandemic

Pandemic

Prototype

The Compound

Slacker

Slacker 2

Slacker: Dead Man Walkin'

Texas

A Vampire in Texas

Thomas

Quarantine
Contagion
Eradication
Isolation
Immune
Pathogen

Virus
Raising Hell

Zombie Bride
Zombie Bride
Zombie Bride 2
Zombie Bride 3

Standalone
The Victims of Pinocchio
A Christmas Nightmare
Pain
Fat Jesus
A Zombie's Revenge
505
The Headhunter
Crash
Tranq
The Island
Dog
The Quiet Man

Joe Superhero
Feral
Good Guys
Devil Child of Texas
Romeo and Juliet and Zombies
The Gamer
Becoming Alpha
Dead West
Small Town Blues
Shades of Z: Redux
The Gift of Death
Killer Claus
Skarred
Home Sweet Home
Alligator Allan
10 Days
Army of The Dumbest Dead
Kid
The Cult of Stupid
9 Time Felon
Slater
Bad Review: Hannah Dies
Me Again
Maurice and Me
Breaking Wind
The Family Business
Lazy Boyz
Sparkles The Vampire Clown
She's Psycho
Vicious Cycle
Romeo and Juliet: True Love Conquers All
Hunting Sarah
Random Acts of Stupidity

Born Killer
The Abducted
Graham Hiney
Zartan
The Firsts in Life

Breaking Wind

Written by Aaron Abilene

Ben, a man whose ambition had long ago been devoured by the couch cushions he perpetually indented, lounged in his disheveled living room amidst a fortress of takeout boxes and fantasy novels with dog-eared pages. His fingers, slick with the residue of salt and oil, danced lazily across the crumbs that dotted his stained sweatshirt—a tapestry of his recent culinary adventures. His hair, an unkempt thicket of unwashed tangles, lay plastered to his forehead. In his mind, the grand tales of heroism and valor were always accompanied by the thought, 'That sounds like effort,' swiftly followed by the comforting embrace of apathy.

"Another day, another lack of dollar," Ben muttered to himself, reaching for a half-empty soda can, its contents flat and warm. He tipped it back, grimacing at the syrupy aftertaste. "If only writing didn't require actual writing."

As he reclined further, his thoughts drifted to Oak Isle—his would-be magnum opus—if he ever managed to get past the first few paragraphs. The land of Oak Isle was as lush and vibrant as his apartment was dingy and gray. Towering mountains pierced the sky like jagged teeth, their snowy caps glinting in the sun's brilliant caress. The forests teemed with creatures of old lore; faeries with gossamer wings flickered between ancient oaks, and unicorns grazed on verdant hills, their coats shimmering with an ethereal glow under the moonlight.

"Probably smells better than here, too," he quipped, casting a disdainful glance at a particularly menacing pile of laundry.

Imagining himself within the fantastical realm brought a rare spark of motivation. He envisioned walking along the meandering paths, each lined with emerald ferns and whispering willows that swayed with secrets. A dragon, majestic and terrifying, soared above, casting a shadow that swept across the land like a passing thought.

"Could make a great scene... if I ever got to it," Ben sighed, the fleeting burst of inspiration dissipating as quickly as it came. He pushed himself up, sending empty snack wrappers fluttering to the floor like defeated soldiers.

"Alright, alright," he huffed, shuffling towards his cluttered desk where a blank document awaited him. "Let's give this world-building nonsense another shot." He paused, his finger hovering over the keyboard, the cursor blinking mockingly. "After a snack. World-building is hungry work."

He ambled back to the kitchen, the creak of the floorboards beneath his weight serving as a reluctant drumroll for his return to the pantry. As he foraged for something resembling food, his mind wandered, unbidden, back to the splendor of Oak Isle.

"Maybe just one more daydream," he conceded with a grin, embracing the familiar comfort of procrastination. "After all, what's a fantasy without a little embellishment?"

Ben's fingers drummed atop the faux-wood veneer of his kitchen table, echoing faintly in the silence of his cramped apartment. The rhythmic tap-tap-tapping was drowned out by the sudden whirlwind of a dream that descended upon him, as sudden and ferocious as an Oak Isle tempest.

"By the unwashed socks of Eldritch!" Ben exclaimed, startling himself awake from the dream where he had been a bystander in a world both ludicrously ornate and outrageously alive. The table was now littered with crumpled pages covered in doodles of fantastical creatures and landscapes, evidence of his subconscious creative spree.

"Ah," he mused with a smirk, "the elusive muse visits the most when one is teetering on the precipice of slumber."

In the hazy realm of near-sleep, Ben had envisioned the grand tapestry of Oak Isle unfurled before him. At the center of this whimsical land stood three preposterous pillars of rulership: the Queen, resplendent in her gown of shimmering moonbeams, the Dwarf King, whose beard bristled with the pride of a thousand ancestral axes, and the Gay King, flamboyantly adorned in colors that put the very rainbows of Oak Isle to shame.

"Subjects!" boomed the Queen, her voice echoing against the towering trees, "Let it be known that our lands shall thrive under my benevolent gaze!"

"Crivens!" bellowed the Dwarf King, his voice as rough as the mountain stone. "And let it never be forgotten, we'll hew our destiny with stout hearts and sturdy hands!"

"Darlings," cooed the Gay King, twirling a lock of his perfectly coiffed hair, "Under my rule, we shall ensure that every feast ends with a fabulous ball!"

"Indeed, a queer trio they may seem," Ben chuckled, scribbling notes with a newfound fervor. "But such is the stuff of legends—or at least, bestsellers."

Their distinct personalities were ripe for comedy; the Queen's haughty demeanor, the Dwarf King's stubborn practicality, and the Gay King's extravagant flair. They were like mismatched pieces of a puzzle that somehow fit together in the grand design of Oak Isle.

"Conflict," Ben muttered to himself, envisioning the Queen rolling her eyes at the Dwarf King's insistence on turning their castle's grand hall into a forge. "The very heart of narrative!"

"Excuse me, your Stoniness," the Queen would say with a snide tilt of her head, "but I'd rather not have my tapestries reeking of soot and sweat."

"Ye'd prefer them smelling like lavender and lilac, eh?" the Dwarf King would retort, a gruff laugh erupting from his chest. "Might as well invite the goblins for tea!"

"Boys, boys, please," the Gay King would interject, silencing them with a raised hand bedecked in dazzling jewels. "There's nothing that can't be solved with a touch of style and a dash of panache."

"Panache, he says," Ben sniggered, imagining the Dwarf King's flabbergasted expression. "As if one could smelt iron with a flick of a feathered boa."

Ben leaned back, feeling an odd sense of accomplishment mingling with his usual lethargy. His characters were coming to life, and with them, the seeds of a story that could—just maybe—rival the classics of epic fantasy comedy.

"Tomorrow," Ben declared with a resolve that surprised even him, "I shall begin in earnest. For tonight, I've danced with inspiration, and she's a fickle partner."

"Besides," he added, eyeing the cheese-stained wrapper of his midnight snack, "a bard must keep his strength up. Adventure awaits after all... in due time."

The wedding of the Queen and Dwarf King was an affair more ostentatious than any festival Oak Isle had ever seen. Banners in every shade imaginable hung from the branches of ancient trees, their leaves whispering secrets to the winds as if they too were gossiping about the unlikely union.

"By the gods, it's like a rainbow vomited all over the forest," Ben muttered, his eyes wide at the sight of silk streamers entwined with strings of glittering gems that dangled from the boughs. The air was thick with the scent of roasting meats and sweet perfumes, a cacophony of fragrances that battled for dominance.

"Would you look at those centaurs?" he whispered to himself, watching half-horse, half-human creatures prance by, their manes braided with flowers that sparkled with dew. "If only I could make my words prance like that."

"Careful, sir," came a voice from behind, as a fairy with wings like shards of stained glass zipped past his ear, almost colliding with his head. "Wouldn't want to end up with a hoof print on your manuscript."

"Manuscript?" Ben scoffed quietly, patting the empty satchel slung over his shoulder. "More like a collection of blank pages."

"Excuse me, out of the way!" A troop of gnomes scurried by, carrying a gargantuan cake adorned with icing sculptures of the bridal couple. The Queen, poised and elegant even in marzipan form, looked down upon her dwarven counterpart, who seemed to be scowling at the sugary indignity of his effigy.

"Ah, the sweet taste of compromise," Ben chuckled, scribbling the scene into his mental notebook.

"Would you just behold the splendor, my dear fellow?" a passing elf exclaimed, draped in a cloak so bright it might have been woven from sunlight itself. "The joining of two great powers!"

"Great powers and greater egos," Ben replied under his breath, taking in the uneasy glances exchanged between elves and dwarves, neither particularly pleased by the alliance, but all bedecked in finery that made peacocks seem drab.

"Oi! Clear the path for the bride!" a voice boomed, and the crowd parted like the sea before a prow. The Queen glided forth, her gown a cascade of diamonds and moonbeams, each step a silent decree of her regal grace. The Dwarf King clomped alongside her, his beard intricately braided with golden threads, though his expression suggested he'd rather face a dragon bare-fisted than partake in this pageantry.

"Smile, Your Stoniness, it's your wedding day!" Ben snorted, imagining the Dwarf King's internal monologue filled with grumbles about the weight of his ceremonial armor.

"Could've done with less metal and more ale," the Dwarf King probably would've said, had he not been too busy maintaining whatever semblance of dignity he could muster.

"Look lively, Ben!" an imaginary voice rang in his head, one he attributed to the Gay King, master of ceremonies and advocate of extravagance. "There's inspiration to be plucked like fruit from these very boughs!"

And indeed, Ben couldn't help but agree. Each character was a story waiting to burst forth, each glance an unspoken narrative. As the ceremony commenced and vows were exchanged with all the enthusiasm of a rehearsed play, Ben's thoughts raced.

"Imagine the tales," he mused, "that spring from such a spectacle."

"From today, our kingdoms are one!" the Queen announced, voice clear as crystal.

"Indeed," grumbled the Dwarf King, his 'I do' sounding more like an 'I suppose.'

"May we find strength in unity," the Queen continued, casting a sidelong glance at her new husband that spoke volumes of the political chess game ahead.

"Strength, and a good deal of patience," Ben added silently, already penning the dialogue in the grand epic of comedy unfolding within his mind's eye.

"Let the feast begin!" the Gay King declared, and the assembly erupted into cheers and applause, a ruckus that set the stage for revelry and perhaps, a hint of chaos to come.

"Feast," Ben thought with a grin, eyeing the mountains of food. "Now there's something I can get behind."

As the first dishes were served and the music swelled, Ben took his place among the throngs, invisible yet observant, ready to weave the night's folly into the fabric of his burgeoning tale.

The grand hall of Oak Isle thrummed with the harmonies of lutes and laughter, a cacophony of celebration that could make the very heavens envious. Ben, nestled between the shadows and the shimmering light, watched as the newlywed Queen and Dwarf King approached the high table, their union an elaborate tapestry of reluctant smiles and political necessity.

"Your Highness," simpered the Gay King, his voice like honeyed wine, "the stars themselves envy your radiance tonight."

"Flattery, dear King," the Queen replied with a practiced smile, her gaze sharp enough to slice through the thickest armor. "We should focus on the stars aligning for our kingdoms, rather than my countenance."

"Ah," chuckled the Dwarf King, his short stature in no way diminishing the gravitas of his presence, "but what's a night without a bit of stargazing?" His beard, a cascade of braided silver, glittered almost as much as his eyes did with hidden mirth.

From the shadows emerged the Queen's loyal advisor, Seraphine, her robes whispering secrets against the marble floor. She leaned in, her voice a low murmur only for royal ears. "Your grace, the eastern lords look restless. Perhaps a reassuring word?"

"Restless or simply inebriated?" the Queen quipped, though she nodded subtly, acknowledging the wisdom in Seraphine's caution.

"Perhaps both," Seraphine conceded with the hint of a smile.

Nearby, a burst of laughter erupted as the Dwarf King's court jester, a sprightly figure named Jinks, cartwheeled into view, bells jangling with each acrobatic feat. "My liege!" he called out, pausing to bow dramatically before the Dwarf King, "I've just returned from the future! It appears you grow taller each year of your reign!"

"Is that so?" the King said dryly, tapping his fingers on the armrest of his stone-carved throne. "And here I thought my only growth would be in the breadth of my treasury."

"Ah, but sire," Jinks tittered with a mischievous twinkle in his eye, "riches do not compare to the height of ambition!"

Ben chuckled to himself, scribbling mental notes about Jinks' jests. The jester understood the delicate art of using humor to dispel tension—a skill Ben was keen to employ in his own writing.

"Dear Kings," the Queen interjected, raising her glass, her voice commanding the room's attention. "May we find more than convenience in this alliance. May we indeed reach new heights—of prosperity, of peace, and perhaps even genuine fondness."

"Here, here," the crowd echoed, glasses raised in a symphony of crystal clinking.

"Mayhaps fondness will come with time," the Gay King declared, winking at the Dwarf King, who merely grunted in response, the corners of his mouth twitching ever so slightly.

"Time," the Queen mused aloud, "is the most cunning of thieves, stealing away moments of discord and leaving behind only what truly matters."

"Like dessert?" Jinks piped up, gesturing towards the towering confections being wheeled in, eliciting chuckles from the crowd.

"Indeed," the Queen laughed, a rare sound that seemed to make the air sparkle. "Dessert, above all else."

Ben observed the trio, their interactions layered with complexity and humor. He saw through the veneer of royalty to the individuals beneath—each playing their part in this grand charade, yet each so vividly alive. As Ben continued to watch, he couldn't help but feel a connection to these figments of his imagination, their lives unfurling before him in a spectacle of light and shadow.

"Every joke a truth wrapped in a giggle," he murmured to himself, the words a mantra for the story he was destined to tell.

Ben, garbed in a tunic that was a shade too snug around his middle, ambled through the throng of wedding guests with the grace of a befuddled bear. His fingers, glossy with the grease of roasted pheasant, fumbled for a goblet of wine from a passing tray. In a motion that could only be described as disastrously overzealous, he brought the goblet to his lips, but not before it collided with the elbow of a particularly animated elf discussing the aerodynamics of pixie flight.

"Good heavens!" Ben exclaimed as the ruby liquid cascaded down the front of his already-stretched tunic, mapping out a new river across the fabric. He blinked at the stain, imagining it as the Crimson River of Sorrow from his nascent novel, where the Queen once wept for her lost love.

"Ah, looks like you've been christened by the Wine Sprite himself!" chortled a rotund gnome, who had witnessed the debacle from a nearby table laden with candied fruits and spiced nuts.

"Indeed," Ben said, attempting to dab away the stain with a handkerchief that seemed to smear rather than clean. "Perhaps I should take it as an auspicious sign."

"Or a cue to avoid further refreshments," the gnome quipped, his belly shaking with laughter.

"Or that," Ben conceded, the corners of his mouth twitching into a reluctant smile.

His attention was soon captured by the energetic strains of music that filled the hall, prompting guests to flock to the dance floor. Before Ben could retreat to the safety of a shadowed corner, a sprite with eyes like polished emeralds seized him by the hand. "Come, sir! Dance with me!"

"Uh, I'm not quite—" But his protest was lost in the whirlwind of movement as the sprite twirled him onto the dance floor. She moved with the fluidity of wind over water, while Ben stumbled like pebbles in a storm drain. Giggles bubbled up from the onlookers as the sprite led Ben in a dance that was more akin to a comedic performance than a display of elegance.

"Left foot, right foot... No, your other right!" the sprite coached, her mirth infectious.

"Apologies," Ben huffed, out of breath yet oddly exhilarated. "I seem to have two left feet today."

"Every day, you mean?" she teased, spinning him once more before releasing him to collapse into a nearby chair.

Catching his breath, Ben watched the festivities unfold with a newfound appreciation. He envisioned the Dwarf King, his stone-like exterior cracking as he attempted to match the Queen's graceful steps, and the Gay King, laughing heartily as he swept partner after partner off their feet.

As he observed, Ben's mind was ablaze with the vibrant tapestry of Oak Isle's inhabitants—bejeweled dresses shimmering like sunlit lakes, jesters performing acrobatics that defied the laws of physics, and the air itself ripe with the scent of magic and merriment. He saw his characters come to life in every misstep and twirl, in every chuckle and cheer.

"Such vibrancy," Ben whispered to himself, the words tingling on his tongue. "Such chaos and charm. This world, my world, is alive."

He scribbled notes onto a napkin, each word a promise to capture the spirit of this enchanting realm. Ben, in his stained tunic and panting from exertion, was no longer just an observer. He was the creator, the chronicler of an epic tale that begged to be told—one humorous misadventure at a time.

Ben felt the weight of his napkin-scribed destiny as he watched the Queen, her voice dripping with honeyed sarcasm, sidle up to the Dwarf King.

"Darling, you do realize that dancing requires movement, not just... vibrating in place?" she asked, barely suppressing a giggle.

"Movement, eh?" the Dwarf King grumbled, his stony face betraying the hint of a smile. "I thought I was doing an imitation of your cooking—full of unexpected jerks and quite unsettling."

The Gay King, ever the flamboyant peacemaker, swept in with a flourish of his cape. "Now, now, let's not be hasty! The night is young, and so are the chances of me stepping on both your feet if we don't find some rhythm soon."

Their laughter echoed through the hall, weaving around Ben like tendrils of a spell, pulling him deeper into the world he had conjured from the depths of his reluctant imagination.

"Watch closely, Ben," he muttered to himself. "This is fodder for your masterpiece." He sipped at his drink, noting how the characters' barbs were more affectionate than cutting, like dancers in a verbal waltz.

"Your Majesty," piped up the Queen's advisor, a twinkle in his eyes betraying his stoic facade, "perhaps a demonstration of your famed diplomatic footwork could inspire our noble guests?"

"Ah, but where would the fun be in that?" the Queen retorted with exaggerated distress. "If my feet move too swiftly, I fear my dear Dwarf King might turn to stone permanently in awe!"

"Stone? Aye, but gold would suit me better, considering the dowry I've been promised!" the Dwarf King shot back, earning a chorus of chuckles from the surrounding courtiers.

Ben scribbled another note on the napkin, his hand cramping but his spirit soaring. These characters—his characters—were alive with wit and whimsy.

"Where there's laughter, there's life," Ben whispered, his previously dormant passion for writing flaring like a torch in the night.

As the festivities reached their crescendo, a sudden hush fell upon the room. The music skittered to a stop, the jesters paused mid-flip, and all eyes turned to the grand doors at the end of the hall. They creaked open ominously, revealing nothing but darkness beyond.

"Perhaps it's the dramatic entrance of an uninvited guest," suggested the Queen's advisor, his words hanging in the air like a challenge.

"Or the beginning of a tale most intriguing," murmured the Gay King, his usual mirth replaced by a spark of curiosity.

"Or," Ben thought, his heartbeat quickening, "the perfect cliffhanger to end a chapter."

With a gulp of excitement laced with fear, Ben realized that the world he had dreamed into existence was taking on a life of its own—a life that now beckoned him into its shadows and mysteries. He clutched the napkin, his notes suddenly feeling like a map to a treasure that everyone—characters and creator alike—was destined to seek.

The cavernous maw of the cave exhaled a sulfurous breath as the Dragon Lady unfurled herself from the bowels of the earth, her emergence a choreography of deliberate power. Sunlight dared to glance off her opalescent scales, creating an aurora of menacing beauty over her massive form. The iridescent display was a stark contrast to the churning darkness that began to swallow Oak Isle's skies, an ominous tapestry woven by her very presence.

"By the whiskers of the Great Catterwaul," muttered Sir Reginald Fumblefoot, his knees knocking together like a pair of castanets at a skeleton's dance party. "She's... she's rather large, isn't she?"

"Large?" echoed Dame Agnes Snorkel, clutching her bosom as if that could protect her from dragonfire. "She's a bloomin' catastrophe with wings!"

Indeed, the villagers scattered like ants beneath a magnifying glass, their frantic cries harmonizing with the low rumble of the earth—the Dragon Lady's personal percussionists. Their homes, once sturdy and reassuring, now seemed no more protective than paper lanterns in a tempest.

"Would you look at that?" Reginald's eyes were saucers of awe. "Even the ground's doing a jig for her."

"More like a death rattle," Agnes retorted, eyeing the nearest cellar door. "I'd say it's high time we practice our underground etiquette."

As the Dragon Lady stretched her colossal wings, an eclipse took form above them, casting Oak Isle into premature twilight. Chickens squawked in confusion, believing night had come to steal away their evening worm hunt, and the cows lowed in despair, already mourning the light.

"Darkness at teatime," Reginald mused aloud, his thoughts as scattered as the fleeing townsfolk. "Mum always said tea without sunshine is like a knight without armor—"

"Utterly useless," Agnes finished for him, her gaze never leaving the serpentine silhouette now slicing through the darkened heavens. "And speaking of knights without armor..."

"Oi!" Reginald feigned offense, though the tremor in his voice betrayed him. "I'll have you know my armor is merely... undergoing strategic ventilation modifications."

"Strategic ventilation..." Agnes snorted, but her laughter died in her throat as the Dragon Lady's shadow passed over them. "We need a plan, Reggie. A good one."

"Right." Reginald swallowed, his throat as dry as the humor he was known for. "Perhaps a strongly worded letter? Dragons respect bureaucracy, don't they?"

"Only as much as they respect bite-sized buffoons," Agnes shot back, her eyes narrowing at the winged terror. "No, we need something with teeth."

"Teeth, huh?" Reginald scratched his head. "Well, I did bring my dentures today—"

"Your wit may be sharp, but it won't cut dragon scales, you daft halberd." Agnes sighed, then her face brightened with a manic sort of inspiration. "But perhaps... Yes! That's it!"

"Care to share with the class, oh enlightened one?" Reginald asked, the sarcasm dripping like honey from his tongue.

"Dragon Lady meets Dragon Slayer." Agnes grinned, a glint of madness sparking in her eyes. "Or at least, the closest thing we've got to one."

"Which would be...?" Reginald prompted, dreading the answer.

"Us, Reggie." Her grin widened. "Us."

Beyond the trembling shadows of Oak Isle, where moonlight feared to tread, the wolves prowled. Their sleek forms glided through the underbrush, as silent as death's whisper, yet their presence was announced by a cacophony of howls that tore through the night like a dagger through silk. At their forefront, the Wolf King moved with a calculated grace that belied his savage nature. His eyes, aglow with lupine cunning, scanned the dark expanse for signs of weakness, for the land itself seemed to recoil at the passage of his pack.

"Would you listen to that?" Reginald muttered, his gaze fixated on the treeline from which the dissonant chorus emanated. "Sounds like someone's throwing a canine opera. And we're uninvited."

Agnes shivered, not from the chill in the air but from the creeping dread that clung to her skin. "They're gathering," she whispered, her voice barely rising above the howling. "The wolves and the Dragon Lady... it can't be a coincidence."

"Coincidence, fate, or particularly nasty bit of bad luck, it doesn't change the fact that we're out here, in the proverbial open buffet." Reginald's attempt at levity faltered, his eyes darting nervously between the sky and the forest.

"Reggie, focus!" Agnes snapped, her fingers tightening around the hilt of her sword. "We've faced worse than oversized lizards and flea-ridden furballs."

"Ah, but have we faced them together, at the same time, with nothing but our wits and your grumpy disposition?" he retorted, his laughter forced and hollow.

"Quiet! They'll hear us." Agnes pressed herself against the rough bark of a tree, peering into the darkness. She could feel the pulsating energy of fear that throbbed in the air, a tangible force that made her heart race and her mind whirl.

"Let them come," she said, though whether it was bravado or genuine courage, even she couldn't tell. "We'll give them a show they won't forget."

"Right. A show." Reginald nodded, although his pale face suggested he'd prefer an audience of none. "But just so we're clear, if things go south, I'm fully prepared to make a heroic retreat."

"Retreat isn't in my vocabulary, Reggie." Agnes's voice was steel. "Now, let's find a vantage point. If we're to stand any chance, we need to see them before they see us."

"Agreed. I always say, 'better to look down on your problems than have them breathing down your neck.'" He followed her lead, his boots crunching softly on the forest floor.

"Your words of wisdom never cease to amaze me," Agnes said dryly, casting a glance at the stars that flickered feebly above. "Now come on. The night grows darker, and our foes grow bolder."

"Then let's not keep our unruly guests waiting." Reginald straightened, trying to match Agnes's determination. "After all, it's not every day you get to crash a party held by a Dragon Lady and the Wolf King."

"Indeed," Agnes replied, her eyes reflecting the faint light of resolve. "It's going to be one hell of a soirée."

The air in Oak Isle had become a stew of dread, simmering with every passing moment. The ground beneath their feet seemed to hum with a warning as the people scurried like ants whose hill had been kicked. Agnes watched through narrowed eyes as villagers fortified their homes with whatever they could—barricading doors with furniture and boarding windows with planks that had seen better days.

"Sharpen your pitchforks, reinforce your spirits! Brace yourselves for the dragon's scorn," bellowed the town crier, his voice cracking under the strain of impending doom.

"Perhaps we should also reinforce our undergarments," muttered Reginald, fumbling with the strap of a leather cuirass that was evidently made for someone two sizes smaller. "I have a feeling we'll need it."

Agnes couldn't help but snort at the image. She tightened the grip on her sword, the cold metal a solid reassurance against the warm tremor of fear in her belly. 'If laughter is the best medicine, will it cure the terror of facing down mythical beasts?' she mused, her inner thoughts tinged with gallows humor.

"Reggie, I swear, if you don't stop fussing with that armor and help me look out for those fiends, I'll feed you to them myself!" she threatened lightly, though her gaze remained vigilant, scanning the dark treeline.

"Ah, tough love. How it warms my heart and chills my spine all at once," he said, giving up on the cuirass and drawing his own blade—a weapon with more ornamental flair than practicality.

"Remember, folks, dragons are attracted to shiny objects," called out an old man from his window, squinting at Reginald's glimmering sword. "You're practically a walking buffet!"

"Very helpful, Bernard! Thank you!" Reginald shouted back, sarcasm dripping thicker than the evening fog.

Agnes smirked, but her attention snapped back as a low growl rolled across the fields. Her pulse quickened. 'This is no laughing matter,' she reminded herself. 'But if you can't laugh in the face of death, when can you?'

"Keep your wits about you, Reggie," she whispered, her voice steady despite her racing heart. "We'll need more than quips and shiny trinkets to survive the night."

"Agreed," he replied, trying to embody the bravado he so clearly lacked. "And should we survive, I'm thinking of starting a new career. Comedy seems safer, doesn't it?"

"Only if you're funny," Agnes quipped, peering into the darkness. 'Humor in the shadow of fear; perhaps that's our truest shield,' she thought, steeling herself for what was to come. The tension in Oak Isle was a living thing, gripping each villager with icy fingers, yet here they stood, jesting at the jaws of chaos.

"Let's hope our laughter reaches morning light," she murmured, not sure who she was trying to reassure—Reginald or herself.

Agnes watched, her heart sinking in time with the sun, as the Dragon Lady's breath leaked into the world like ink in water. The once-lush fields of Oak Isle curled and blackened beneath her gaze, the emerald blades of grass shriveling to ashen wisps. A shiver ran down Agnes's spine as a rose bush beside her trembled, petals withering to dust, leaving behind thorny skeletons—a grim echo of the island's fate.

"Looks like she's got the Midas touch if Midas was a gardener of doom," Reginald quipped, his voice falling flat against the backdrop of decay.

"More like a compost enthusiast," Agnes retorted, but the humor tasted bitter on her tongue. With each step the Dragon Lady took, the verdant vitality of Oak Isle succumbed to a wintry blight, casting shadows upon shadows until even the bravest of souls doubted whether daylight had ever graced their land.

"Behold, nature's least favorite landscaper," Reginald muttered, clutching his sword as though it offered warmth against the chill of encroaching darkness.

Amidst the dying light, the Wolf King prowled, his silhouette a ghostly wraith against the bleakness. His pack moved as one, a fluid shadow across the desecrated earth, their eyes gleaming with a predatory intelligence that sent shudders through the villagers' bones. They were silent, save for the occasional symphony of howls that seemed to mock the disquieted hearts of Oak Isle.

"Ah, the serenade of fluffy nightmares," said Agnes, her attempt at levity clashing with the gravity of their plight. "Perhaps they're just misunderstood vocal artists."

"Or perhaps they're rehearsing for 'Oak Isle's Got Talent,'" Reginald added, his chuckle hollow against the crescendo of lupine cries.

"Whatever they are, they're cunning... and they're close," Agnes whispered, her eyes scanning the treeline where the wolves disappeared and reappeared like phantoms teasing the eye.

"Marvelous," Reginald sighed. "Now we've got stealthy singers. Next, they'll be juggling fireballs or doing card tricks."

"Let's not give them any ideas," Agnes said, gripping her own weapon tighter. 'The Dragon Lady may scorch the earth, but it's the wolves who will dance among the cinders,' she thought, dread coiling in her gut.

"Imagine," Reginald mused, his voice a notch too high, betraying his fear, "a dragon that burns your house down and a pack of wolves clever enough to pickpocket you while they do it."

"Small mercies," Agnes breathed out, trying not to envision such a scene. "At least we'd be too charred to notice the theft."

As night enveloped what remained of the day, Agnes could feel the Dragon Lady's oppressive force vying with the sly menace of the Wolf King. There was a destructive elegance to their terror, a dance of dark power and darker intellect, and it left the people of Oak Isle trapped in a reluctant audience, watching the prelude to their potential demise.

"Shall we take bets on which fright gets us first?" Reginald asked, attempting to smirk but only managing a grimace.

"Call me an optimist, but I'm betting on sheer dumb luck," said Agnes, hoping her smile looked more convincing than it felt.

"Then let's hope Lady Luck hasn't fled with the rest of the fauna," Reginald quipped, gazing out at the bleak expanse before them.

"Or joined the wolves' choir," Agnes added, her laughter a touch maniacal. 'Because if there's one thing more terrifying than our current predicament, it's the idea of luck singing soprano.'

As the last light died and darkness claimed dominion over Oak Isle, the Dragon Lady's destruction intertwined with the Wolf King's guile, weaving a tapestry of fear that would hang heavy over the land until dawn—if dawn dared return.

"Alright, listen up!" Agnes clapped her hands together, the sound echoing off the stone walls of the makeshift war room they'd assembled in Oak Isle's stoutest tavern. "We've got a fire-breathing diva on one hand, and a fur-coated mafia on the other. It's time to get creative or get crispy—and I don't know about you lot, but I'm not ready to be today's roast."

Reginald, who had been half-heartedly sharpening a sword that looked as though it had seen better days during the reign of some long-forgotten king, looked up. "I've always fancied myself more of a medium-rare," he quipped.

"Quiet in the peanut gallery," Agnes shot back, rolling out a map of the isle on a large oak table. The once colorful chart now seemed drained of life, much like the land it represented. "Here's the plan: we're going to set traps for those wolves—something involving meat pies laced with sleeping draughts."

"Because nothing says 'welcome' like a drugged dessert," Reginald chuckled, earning him a glare from Agnes.

"Meanwhile, we'll need archers stationed at strategic points. Any sign of scales or smoke, and we rain down a hailstorm of arrows," she continued, pointing to the cliffs that overlooked the darkening forests.

"Great, so we either drug our problems away or poke them full of holes. What could possibly go wrong?" Reginald muttered under his breath.

"Did I mention the fireproof shields?" Agnes asked, ignoring his sarcasm. "We've got the blacksmith working overtime. Every house will have one by dawn."

"Fireproof shields? Made by the same man who thought wooden armor was a stroke of genius?" Reginald raised an eyebrow.

"Desperate times, Reginald. Desperate times call for desperate—"

"Shoddy craftsmanship?" he finished for her.

"Ingenuity!" she corrected firmly, but a smile threatened to break through her stern facade.

Agnes could feel the weight of responsibility pressing on her shoulders, like the heavy cloak she'd donned against the chill of fear that had settled over Oak Isle. They were outnumbered, outmatched, and quite possibly out of their minds, but they were not out of fight.

"Tonight, we fortify. We reinforce the walls, secure the livestock, and say a little prayer to whichever deity hasn't abandoned this sorry island," she announced, her voice carrying the ring of command. "Tomorrow, we make our stand."

"Here's to hoping the Dragon Lady is allergic to iron and the Wolf King has a thing against pointy objects," Reginald said, finally standing up. He stretched, joints popping, and offered Agnes a wicked grin. "Or perhaps they'll just die laughing at our audacity."

"Laughter can be a weapon," Agnes mused, the corners of her lips twitching upward. She surveyed the room, filled with the anxious faces of her fellow islanders, their determination a flickering flame in the encroaching darkness. "If we're going to face the end, we might as well do it with a bit of style."

"Style, questionable strategies, and a dash of hope. Quite the cocktail," Reginald said, lifting an imaginary glass in a toast.

"Drink up," Agnes replied with a smile. "We've got a long night ahead of us."

The moon hung heavy in the sky, a pale spectator to the frantic preparations below. Oak Isle was alive with the sound of hammers and clanging metal, each strike a heartbeat counting down to an uncertain dawn.

"Careful with that barrel of pitch! We don't want to set ourselves ablaze before our guests arrive!" Agnes called out, her voice tinged with a laugh that didn't quite mask the tremor of fear beneath.

"Wouldn't dream of it," huffed Merek as he maneuvered the barrel into place. "Though it might be worth considering if things go... you know, dragon-shaped."

Agnes rolled her eyes, her thoughts racing like the swift undercurrent of a treacherous river. *We're preparing for a siege led by mythical beasts*, she mused wryly, *and here we are, joking about self-immolation. The bards will have a field day with this tale, assuming there's anyone left to sing it.*

"Hey, Agnes, how do you think the Dragon Lady likes her knights?" Reginald quipped from atop the ramparts, a lopsided grin on his face as he brandished a newly sharpened spear.

"Medium-rare, I'd wager," she shot back, unable to suppress a smirk. "But let's aim to disappoint her culinary tastes, shall we?"

Laughter bubbled up from the group of villagers nearby, a momentary reprieve from the stifling dread. They fortified the gate, their hands working with a fervor born of desperation. Each plank of wood, every iron bolt, was a testament to their resolve to survive the coming onslaught.

"Remember folks, no heroics," Agnes reminded them, her gaze sweeping across the determined faces. "We fight smart, we stay alive. And when in doubt, aim for the snout!"

"Or the tail!" chimed in a young boy, barely old enough to lift a sword. "I heard wolves hate that!"

"Tail it is," Agnes agreed, chuckling at the child's fierce expression. She hoisted a torch, casting shadows that danced ominously against the stone walls.

Suddenly, a distant howl cleaved through the night, sending shivers down the spines of all who heard it. Silence fell upon Oak Isle as the laughter died in their throats, replaced by the weight of reality.

"Seems the Wolf King doesn't appreciate being the butt of the joke," commented Reginald, peering into the darkness.

"Let him howl," Agnes replied, her voice steady as she extinguished the torch, plunging them into strategic darkness. "It'll be the last song he sings if we have anything to say about it."

An uneasy quiet settled over the island, punctuated only by the occasional creak of leather and the soft rustle of leaves in the wind. Agnes stood motionless, her hand resting on the hilt of her blade, her senses stretched taut as bowstrings.

And then, without warning, the earth began to tremble—a low, menacing rumble that spoke of ancient wrath stirring beneath the surface. Eyes wide, the villagers exchanged glances, their previous bravado evaporating into the charged air.

"Looks like the lady of the hour makes quite the entrance," Reginald murmured, his attempt at levity falling flat even to his own ears.

"Stay sharp," Agnes whispered, her heart pounding a frantic rhythm. "This is it."

With a deafening roar that split the heavens, a shadow unfurled from the mouth of the cave high above, blotting out the stars. The Dragon Lady had arrived, her scales glistening like a tapestry of malice woven by the night itself.

"May the gods be with us," Agnes breathed, her grip tightening around her weapon. "We're going to need all the help we can get."

The chapter closed with the villagers of Oak Isle bracing against the fury of the Dragon Lady and the cunning of the Wolf King, their fate hanging in the balance. As readers turned the page, they were left wondering: would wit and steel be enough to withstand the storm that loomed on the horizon? Or would laughter and courage fade like embers in the relentless gale of darkness?

Ben's couch, a sagging beast with stuffing peeking out like tufts of chest hair on an overweight beachgoer, groaned under his weight. His shirt, a mosaic of grease stains and salsa drips, clung to his ample belly as if afraid to let go. The living room was littered with the detritus of his latest writing binge: candy wrappers formed crinkling carpets, and half-eaten bags of chips lay abandoned, their contents spilling out like the guts of a plush toy.

Manuscripts, smeared with ketchup fingerprints and coffee rings, were strewn across the floor, each one a monument to his boundless ambition and equally expansive procrastination. He lounged there, the very picture of sloth, an emperor atop a throne of cushions, ruling over a kingdom of junk food and unfinished dreams.

"Ben, my boy, are you sitting down?" The voice crackled through Ben's cellphone, which he had almost mistaken for a chocolate bar in his sugar-induced stupor.

"Technically I've merged with the couch, so yeah," Ben replied, crumbs tumbling from his lips as he spoke. "What's up, Jerry? Did someone finally buy a copy of my book? Should I break out the off-brand champagne?"

"Sit tight, butterball! Your novel, 'The Enchanted Eclair' – it's a bestseller!" Jerry sounded like he'd just inhaled a helium balloon. "The critics are eating it up like... well, eclairs!"

"Bestseller?" Ben blinked, his brain trying to swim through the fog of disbelief. "As in, people are actually reading it? Like, other than my mom and that weird guy who thinks I'm a secret dragon?"

"Kid, you've hit the big leagues! Picture this: your face on billboards, book signings with lines longer than the wait at the Winged Unicorn Drive-thru, and movie deals! They're saying you're the next big thing since sliced bread—if that bread could shoot lightning bolts and summon armies of the dead."

"Wow..." Ben let the word hang in the air, as heavy as his last attempt to jog. A smile curled the corners of his mouth, lifting the crumbs into a brief dance before they settled back onto his stubble. "Jerry, this is... I mean, I don't even have words."

"Better find some quick, pork chop, because they want a sequel! And a third! A whole series! You're about to be richer than a goblin king in a diamond mine!"

Ben's heart thumped in his chest, a drumbeat of panic dressed as excitement. He imagined himself, not as a triumphant author, but as a knight facing a dragon, armed only with a quill. Could he really do this? Was he destined to be more than the ruler of Couch Kingdom?

"Okay, okay," Ben exhaled, puffing out his cheeks like a pufferfish preparing for battle. "Let the fantasy begin."

Ben's elation perched upon his chest like a proud falcon, its talons clutching his heart with the grip of unexpected victory. He swiveled in his chair to face the glaring white abyss of his computer screen, the cursor blinking expectantly, awaiting the torrent of words that would birth a sequel into existence. Yet, the falcon of triumph swiftly mutated into a leaden vulture of doubt, heavy on his shoulders. The screen remained as barren as the Wastelands of Procrastination he so frequently visited in his mind.

"Okay, Ben," he muttered to himself, "just write... something epic. Easy." His fingers hovered over the keyboard, an army of soldiers too petrified to charge into battle.

"Right, what about... a knight who's also a baker? No, no, that's half-baked already..." He winced at his own pun, a silent audience to his comedic misfire.

He leaned back, his office chair creaking under the weight of his uncertainty, and cast his gaze toward the ceiling, where a lonesome cobweb drifted in the stagnant air of his creativity. "How about a shape-shifting hedgehog, eh? Everyone loves hedgehogs." The idea fizzled out faster than a sparkler in a rainstorm.

"Alright, focus Ben, think big! Dragons!" His voice rose with hope, "Yes, dragons that... uh... knit! They could knit their own wings and fly away when they're done." A snort escaped him. "Oh, come on, that's just ridiculous. Since when do dragons have hobbies?"

"Perhaps a wizard then," Ben continued, his voice trembling with desperation, "one whose spells only work when he's drunk?" He shook his head, cringing at the thought of pitching such a fiasco to Jerry.

"Or maybe—" A sudden inspiration struck him, as fleeting as a comet across the night sky. "A quest for the Golden Spatula of Destiny!" But even as the words tumbled out, his excitement deflated like a sad balloon. "What would they even do with it? Flip the ultimate pancake to bring peace to the realm?"

The room seemed to contract around him, walls papered with the ghosts of discarded ideas. Each breath Ben took was thick with the musk of stale potato chips and desolation. He slumped forward, his forehead touching the cool desk, the once mighty call of adventure now a distant echo.

"Come on, you've got to give me something here, brain!" he pleaded with his traitorous mind. "Anything but a carrot-wielding elf or a vegan vampire with a sun allergy."

"Ugh, maybe I'm the vegan vampire," he groaned, "allergic to the sunlight of originality." He lifted his head, eyes squinting at the mocking cursor still blinking—blinking—blinking. The silence of the room punctuated each failed attempt at genius.

"Jerry's going to feed me to the literary wolves," Ben said, a grim chuckle escaping his lips as he envisioned himself in the Colosseum of Critics, armed with nothing but a broken pencil and a thesaurus.

"Bestseller or not, Ben my boy," he sighed, leaning into the cushioned embrace of his chair, "it seems you might just be the one-hit wonder of the fantasy world. And I don't mean the kind with magic wands."

The glow of Ben's laptop screen cast a pale light on the cluttered chaos of his living room. A half-eaten bag of cheese puffs lay defeated beside an army of empty soda cans, all standing vigil as he scrolled aimlessly through the void of the internet, searching for a spark of creativity.

"Maybe my protagonist should have a pet rock that's actually a dormant golem," Ben muttered to himself, wincing at the thought. "No, no—too Flintstones meets Tolkien."

With every click, the pit of desperation in his stomach grew. Just as he was about to surrender to another round of mind-numbing TV shows, something caught his eye—a news article tucked away amidst the pop-up ads and celebrity gossip. The headline screamed: "Dragon Lady Rises, Oak Isle Trembles!"

"Dragon Lady?" Ben raised an eyebrow, curiosity pricking at him like a splinter. He clicked on the link, devouring the words. According to the article, a fearsome sorceress with the power to command dragons had emerged from centuries of hiding, threatening to engulf Oak Isle in flames.

"Ha! That's more like it!" Ben chortled, imagining the Dragon Lady with her scaly minions. "That's some high-quality grade-A fantasy fodder right there."

His fingers danced across the keys, typing notes with newfound vigor. But as the details poured in—the isle's floating monoliths, the talking animals swearing allegiance or defiance to the dragon queen—Ben's manic energy faltered. This wasn't just fodder; it was fascination.

"Oak Isle...dragons...a sorceress with probably fantastic hair," he mused aloud. "This is it! This is what I need. Not just to write about but—to see!"

The decision crashed into him like a wave, leaving no room for second thoughts. He pushed back from his desk and stood, a man possessed. It was time to pack, time to embark on the kind of adventure he'd only ever written about. And so, with the clumsy grace of a newborn giraffe learning to walk, Ben set about stuffing his backpack.

"Let's see...socks, shirts, my lucky pen—no, wait, that ran out of ink two books ago." Ben tossed aside the useless pen. "Trail mix, flashlight, the biggest notebook I've got...and oh, band-aids! Can't forget those. Who knows what paper cuts lie ahead?"

His packing method was less 'careful consideration' and more 'whirlwind of fabric and essentials,' with each item making a dubious leap of faith into the gaping maw of his backpack.

"Okay, okay, think, Ben. You're going to a place where the animals talk. Do you bring a phrasebook? Is there a Rosetta Stone for squirrel?"

He paused, glancing around the room, its walls now stripped of their usual occupants—his clothes and various knick-knacks. The sight was enough to send a jolt of reality through him.

"Am I really doing this? Going on a quest like some sort of round-bellied Bilbo Baggins?" he thought, a pang of anxiety threading through his excitement. "What if I'm not cut out for this? What if the Dragon Lady is real and she's nothing like the book jackets make her out to be? More fire, less ladylike?"

"Stop it, Ben," he scolded himself, zipping up the overstuffed backpack with a final yank. "You need inspiration. You need to finish your series. And who knows, maybe the Dragon Lady has writer's block too. You could start a support group—Villains with Vacant Minds."

With the pack slung over one shoulder, he looked back at his apartment, a smile tugging at his lips. "Goodbye, couch," he said dramatically. "Farewell, refrigerator. Until we meet again, microwave. Adventure calls, and it doesn't do takeout."

Ben stepped out of his door, the weight of his backpack a solid reminder of the journey ahead. "Oak Isle, here I come. Let's hope they're ready for a little less conversation and a little more action."

"Also, please don't let the trolls have a taste for struggling authors," he added under his breath as he shut the door behind him.

Ben paused at the threshold of his apartment, a fortress of comfort and procrastination. Above him, the light fixture—caked in dust and the corpses of long-dead moths—seemed to flicker a dramatic farewell. He snorted at its theatrics.

"Right, then," he muttered, stepping out into the hallway that smelled faintly of cabbage and broken dreams. "To glory, or whatever."

He lumbered down the stairs, each step creaking under protest from his weight and the overloaded backpack. Passing Mrs. Gribble's door, he couldn't help but announce, "Off to slay dragons, Mrs. Gribble! Keep my potted plant alive, would you?"

"Mad as a bag of cats, that one," he heard her grumble from behind the peephole.

"Cheerio, then!" Ben called out cheerfully, pushing against the heavy front door. A gust of wind greeted him, ruffling his unkempt hair—an auspicious start to an unlikely quest.

"Alright, Oak Isle. Prepare to be dazzled by my middling athleticism and questionable survival skills," he mused as he trudged toward the docks where his journey would truly begin.

Hours later, as land gave way to gently rolling waves, Ben leaned on the ship's railing, watching the horizon expand. The sea air filled his lungs with a freshness that was foreign after years of recycled air and stale snacks. His stomach churned—not from seasickness, but from a cocktail of dread and excitement.

"Oak Isle ahead!" shouted the captain, a burly man whose beard seemed to contain entire ecosystems.

"Land ho!" Ben echoed weakly, squinting at the sight before him. It was nothing like the world he'd left behind.

Floating islands hovered above the sea like mischievous sprites, tethered to the water by cascading waterfalls that defied all logic. A flock of seagulls circled overhead, their squawks forming coherent insults.

"Outta the way, tubby! Fresh fish comin' through!" one bird jeered, causing Ben to frown.

"Rude," he huffed, shaking his head. "And they say Canadians are polite..."

"Welcome to Oak Isle, where animals don't hold back their opinions," the captain chuckled, clapping a hand on Ben's shoulder with a force that nearly sent him overboard.

"Appreciated, Captain Obvious," Ben retorted but couldn't suppress a grin. This place was ludicrous, absurd, and utterly fascinating.

Stepping off the gangplank onto solid ground—or what passed for it in this bewildering place—Ben's knees wobbled like jelly. A cat sauntered past, its tail high and eyes judging.

"Lost, butterball?" it purred, circling him with a disdain only a feline could muster.

"Hardly," Ben shot back, straightening up. "I'm on a quest of great importance."

"Sure you are," the cat drawled before darting away, leaving Ben to marvel at the absurdity of being sassed by a talking animal.

"Note to self: include sardonic house pets in next book... if I survive this madness," he thought, shaking his head in disbelief.

With a deep breath, Ben looked ahead, adjusting the straps of his backpack. The fantastical landscape of Oak Isle stretched before him, daring him to step forward into his own story—a tale that was bound to be filled with more blunders than bravery.

"Alright, Ben," he murmured to himself. "Time to find your muse, or at the very least, not get eaten by the wildlife."

Taking a tentative step forward, he couldn't help but feel that the real adventure was just beginning.

The path ahead wound upwards, spiraling into the clouds like a stairway for giants. Ben's first challenge loomed before him: the mountain pass of Gargantu, known less for its height and more for its surly gatekeeper—a troll named Grindar whose reputation for bad temper was eclipsed only by his notorious lack of hygiene.

"Right," Ben huffed, hands on hips as he surveyed the ascent. "Just think of it as an extreme workout. No pain, no... whatever it is I'm supposed to get out of this."

"Who trespasses on the realm of Grindar?" boomed a voice from above.

"Name's Ben. A novelist on a quest for inspiration. And passage."

"Novelist, eh?" The troll emerged from a cave, his thick brows knitting together. "What good are words against the might of Grindar?"

"Words are mightier than the sword, or so they say," Ben quipped, eyeing the troll's club that looked suspiciously like a tree trunk.

"Ha! You'll not weave your wordy magic on me. None shall pass without besting me in a challenge."

"Alright, Grindar, let's make it interesting then." Ben patted his belly, which had already started sweating at the thought of physical exertion. "How about a battle of wits?"

"Fine!" Grindar grunted, scratching his matted beard. "Answer me riddle, and you may pass. Fail, and you become part of my rock collection."

"Hit me with your best shot."

"Riddle me this: What is so fragile that saying its name breaks it?"

"Silence!" Ben exclaimed with a triumphant smirk.

"Curse your sharp mind!" Grindar growled, stepping aside begrudgingly. "Pass, wordsmith, but know the forest beyond is filled with tricks more vexing than my riddles."

"Thanks for the heads-up. And the new material," Ben replied, nodding at the troll as he trudged past, wondering if trolls had royalties.

Beyond the mountain pass, the landscape changed dramatically. Trees, impossibly tall and dense, formed a canopy that seemed to swallow the sky. The air was thick with the sound of laughter—not the joyful kind, but the sort that sends shivers down one's spine.

"Great," Ben muttered. "From grumpy trolls to giggling greenery."

"Who said we're greenery?" tittered a voice, followed by a shower of sparkles.

"Fairies!" Ben's eyes widened as a dozen tiny, winged creatures appeared, flitting around his head. "I've heard of you lot. Cute, helpful, guiding lost travelers..."

"Wrong!" one fairy snickered, yanking the strap of Ben's backpack.

"Hey!" Ben swatted at them, tripping over a root and tumbling to the ground with a thud.

"Oof! Not the 'falling' inspiration I was looking for," he groaned, pushing himself up just in time to dodge a barrage of acorns.

"Come now, big man," another fairy taunted. "Dance for us!"

"Fine," Ben sighed, standing up. "You want a dance? I'll show you a dance."

With surprisingly nimble feet for a man of his girth, Ben began an impromptu jig, arms flailing and legs kicking. The fairies were taken aback, their mischievous smirks giving way to delight.

"Look at him go!" one exclaimed, clapping her tiny hands.

"More, more!" chorused the others.

"Okay, okay, encore's over," Ben panted after a minute, using the distraction to snatch his backpack back. "Now, would you kindly point me towards the lair of the Dragon Lady?"

"Follow the moon's shadow when night falls," a fairy instructed, still giggling. "But beware, human. The forest watches—and it has quite the sense of humor."

"Fantastic," Ben said, sarcasm dripping like the sweat down his brow. "A laughing forest. What's next, singing stones?"

"Wouldn't you like to know?" the fairies sang in unison before disappearing in a puff of glitter, leaving Ben alone once more.

"Note to self," Ben thought as he ventured deeper into the woods, "never trust anything under a foot tall and sparkling. Also, invest in better cardio when—or if—I make it home."

Ben's thighs chafed with every step, his breath came out in laborious huffs that fogged up the evening air. The moon's shadow crept along the forest floor like an ethereal serpent, leading him deeper into the realm of whispered myths and forgotten secrets.

"Great. I'm playing follow-the-leader with a celestial body," Ben muttered to himself. "Why couldn't it have been follow the bread crumbs? At least then, I'd have something to snack on."

As he trudged on, the trees seemed to bow conspiratorially over his path, their limbs creaking with barely concealed laughter. The forest was indeed watching, possibly waiting for another chance to trip him up. But Ben had developed a begrudging respect for the capricious woods. It reminded him of his own unpredictable muse—when she bothered to show up, that is.

"Come on, Benny boy, you're not just a one-hit-wonder," he encouraged himself. "You've got... well, at least two or three good ideas left in you."

Suddenly, his foot caught on a root—or at least, what he hoped was a root—and sent him sprawling forward with a gracelessness that would make a boulder seem balletic. He face-planted with an oof that echoed off unseen walls. Groaning, Ben lifted his head to find himself at the mouth of a hidden cave, its entrance veiled by trailing ivy and shadows that seemed almost solid.

"Since when did my life become a series of pratfalls?" Ben complained aloud, pushing himself up and dusting clods of earth from his shirt. "Well, let's see what this cave has to hide. A dragon's lair map, perhaps?"

He ventured inside, the light from the entrance rapidly swallowed by the gloom. After several minutes of fumbling progression and whispered curses, his hand brushed against something that crackled. Squinting in the dimness, Ben discovered a parchment, aged and brittle, pinned under a stone.

"Jackpot!" he exclaimed, snatching up the paper. Unfurling it revealed a meticulously drawn map, complete with a large 'X' marking a spot not too far from the ominous symbol of a dragon. "Oh, this is too cliché. Even I wouldn't write this."

His elation waned as the reality of his situation settled in like a thick fog. "So, Dragon Lady, we meet at last—well, geographically speaking." He traced the path with his sausage-like finger. "Through the Whispering Gorge, skirting the Grinners' Den... This looks like the itinerary from hell."

With the map as his guide, Ben exited the cave, clutching the paper like a lifeline. His determination grew with each step, even as thorny vines seemed to reach out to snag him, and roots appeared to shift beneath his feet.

"Alright, universe, I get it! I'm out of shape and you're having a great time reminding me," he grumbled. "But guess what? I've dealt with worse. I've survived scathing book reviews, and I've battled the blank page. This quest? It's just another plot twist in the epic saga of Ben the Bestselling Author."

His resolve hardened, and he focused on the image of the Dragon Lady. She represented more than just a foe to be vanquished; she was the embodiment of every doubt that ever plagued his creative mind. Overcoming her meant proving to himself that he was more than a one-hit-wonder, more than just a guy who got lucky.

"Time to earn that sequel," he said, half to himself, half to the ever-present forest around him. The map fluttered in his hand, as if eager to lead him onward. And so, through brambles that tugged at his clothes and over streams that laughed at his clumsy crossings, Ben forged ahead. Each obstacle was but a stepping stone, each setback a verse in the ballad of his unexpected journey.

"Bring it on, Oak Isle," Ben declared to the night, a wild grin splitting his face. "This wanna-be author's got some new material, and it's going to be epic."

The trees thinned as Ben approached a clearing where the jagged silhouette of a towering castle stabbed at the twilight sky. Its blackened ramparts seethed with a malevolent aura, and even the wind seemed to hold its breath, fearful of what lay within. A shiver danced down Ben's spine—not from the chill but from the realization that this was it: the lair of the Dragon Lady.

"Looks like the kind of place that would have 'Abandon all hope, ye who enter here' written on the doormat," Ben muttered, his voice a mix of apprehension and dry humor. He could already picture the TripAdvisor review: "One star. Would not visit again. Too dragon-y."

He stepped forward, gravel crunching beneath his sneakers—a sound monstrously loud in the oppressive silence that clung to the outskirts of the lair. The castle loomed, its twisted spires clawing at the heavens like the fingers of a drowned witch reaching for salvation.

"Here goes nothing," he declared to no one in particular, attempting to inject bravado into his quivering knees. His hand dove into his backpack, rummaging past half-eaten bags of chips and crumpled fantasy novels until it emerged triumphantly brandishing the flashlight he had almost forgotten to pack.

"Alright, Dragon Lady, I hope you're ready for some literary critique because I've got a few choice words about your home decor," he said as he clicked on the flashlight, the beam cutting through the encroaching dusk.

Ben's heart hammered against his ribs like a desperate prisoner, each beat a percussive prelude to the danger ahead. He swallowed the lump forming in his throat and reminded himself that he had faced worse foes—like the time he'd been cornered by a mob of angry fanfiction writers after he'd publicly denounced their favorite trope.

"Let's add 'trespassing in an evil sorceress's lair' to my resume, shall we?" he mused, the idea oddly comforting.

Taking a deep breath, Ben felt the weight of his undertaking settle upon him, a cloak woven from threads of fear and excitement. He tried to imagine himself as the heroes from his books, but instead of noble steeds and gleaming armor, he had a second-hand backpack and a witty repertoire at his disposal.

"Okay, dragon. I've dealt with Twitter trolls before, how bad can a real one be?" he whispered to himself, though the joke did little to ease the knot of nerves in his stomach.

With one last look at the purpling sky, Ben stepped over the threshold, the darkness enveloping him like the pages of a book closing around its protagonist. The musty scent of ancient secrets mingled with the tang of sulfur greeted him—an olfactory assault that made him long for the artificial citrus of his apartment's air freshener.

And there, in the heart of the shadows, something stirred. Something immense. Something that promised an encounter worth every word he would later pen. Whether he would live to tell the tale, however, remained to be seen.

"Showtime," Ben said, his voice barely above a whisper, as he ventured deeper into the gloom. The map, now a crumpled testament to his journey, rested securely in his pocket. If legends were to be believed, soon he would come face to face with the Dragon Lady herself.

"Hope she doesn't mind autographs."

The dim light from the lair's entrance dwindled rapidly as Ben advanced, the soles of his worn sneakers scraping against the jagged rock beneath him. His heart drummed a rhythm of impending doom—or was it opportunity?—echoing off the cavern walls. Each step felt like he was wading through the thick syrup of his own anxiety.

"Okay, Ben," he muttered to himself, "you've written about stuff like this. Pretend it's just another chapter." But deep down, he knew there was no backspace key in this story.

A rumble shook the ground, sending pebbles dancing across the floor. Ben paused, squinting into the abyss. He could make out the faintest glow in the distance, a beacon beckoning him towards his fate or folly. His breath caught in his throat; he stifled a cough that threatened to betray his presence.

"Probably just the central heating," he quipped to the darkness, wishing his jokes could illuminate the path ahead.

He rounded a corner, and there it was: an expanse of cavern that stretched upward into obscurity. Stalactites hung like daggers from the ceiling, and the light emerged from an array of crystals, bathing the chamber in an otherworldly glow. It was as if he'd walked onto the set of a high-budget fantasy film, except the danger here was all too real.

"Interior decorating by Tolkien," Ben mused aloud, trying to keep his spirits up. A cascade of laughter bubbled up inside him, absurdity mixing with terror. "I'm either going to slay a dragon or get a wicked case of vitamin D deficiency."

His gaze settled on what appeared to be a throne fashioned from interwoven branches and glowing stones. It sat empty but felt full of menace. Ben could almost hear the Dragon Lady's voice echoing through the cavern, though she remained unseen.

"Come out, come out, wherever you are," he called, the words sounding braver than he felt.

There was a hiss, like the release of steam, and a shadow shifted behind the throne. Ben's pulse quickened; his mind raced—should he run, hide, or perhaps engage in witty banter? The strategies of his fictional heroes seemed impractical now that his own skin was on the line.

"Note to self," he thought, "never write a scene where the protagonist has to do... whatever it is I'm about to do."

The air grew warmer, heavier, as if charged with expectation. Then, a voice, sibilant and commanding, filled the chamber. "Who dares enter my sanctum seeking audience?"

"Benjamin Fiddlesticks, ma'am," he replied, his voice steady despite the tremor in his knees. "Bestselling author and... um, occasional adventurer."

"Ah," the voice purred, laced with intrigue, "the weaver of tales. Have you come to entertain me, Benjamin Fiddlesticks, or to end me?"

"Entertain, definitely entertain," Ben assured quickly, hands raised in a gesture of peace—or surrender. "Though, if things go well, maybe we can talk about a book deal?"

Silence fell once more, thick enough to smother his hopes of a peaceful resolution. Ben swallowed hard, the taste of fear acrid on his tongue. Then, suddenly, two luminous eyes snapped open within the darkness behind the throne, fixating on him with predatory interest.

"Cliffhanger," he whispered to himself, knowing his readers would forgive him for such a trope—it was, after all, quite literally his current predicament.

As those eyes began to advance, reflecting a future uncertain, the chapter closed, leaving readers to wonder whether Ben's wit would be enough to charm a dragon or if his next title would be posthumously released.

"By the crooked teeth of the Cavernous Chasm," Ben muttered, reflecting on the peculiar path that had led him to this precise moment. It seemed like only yesterday he was a mere apprentice to the bumbling yet beloved wizard, Master Thaddeus. But fate, with its twisted sense of humor, had unceremoniously thrust upon him the mantle of 'Chosen One' after Thaddeus's most unfortunate experiment with an exploding potion—may his eyebrows rest in peace.

Oak Isle, an enchanted forest where trees whispered secrets and shadows danced at the edge of sight, had become more than a backdrop to Ben's newfound destiny; it was a living labyrinth filled with both wonder and peril. With Master Thaddeus gone, guidance was as scarce as a dragon's dieting tips. Thus, driven by an insatiable need for mentorship and a smidgen of desperation, Ben sought the wisdom of Elara, a sorceress whose reputation was as wild as the forest itself.

"Seriously, a secret meeting spot?" Ben couldn't help but quip aloud as he navigated through the maze of verdant chaos. "Why not just a cozy tavern or, I don't know, anywhere without carnivorous plants!"

The forest, however, seemed to chuckle in the rustling leaves, guiding him to a secluded grove that felt like stepping into a forgotten world. Ancient trees formed a cathedral-like canopy, their interlocking branches veiling the sky. Sunbeams pierced through the foliage, casting dappled light onto moss-covered stones that glowed with an ethereal luster. In the heart of the grove, a crystal-clear pond mirrored the heavens, and around it, vibrant flowers hummed with life, each petal pulsating with magic.

"Okay, this place is admittedly impressive," Ben conceded, his fingers tracing the air as if trying to capture the magic that lingered like perfume.

"Benjamin Teller, I presume?" A voice echoed within the grove, rich and melodious.

"Um, y-yes! That would be me," Ben stammered, swiveling around to spot the source. "Geez, do you always greet people like they're about to be ambushed by an illusionary choir?"

"Only those who seek my tutelage."

"Right, well, I'm here. In this very normal, not-at-all-intimidating magical garden of yours." Ben's hands fumbled with the strap of his satchel as he tried to appear nonchalant. "So, about that guidance and inspiration you're supposedly famous for..."

"Patience, young one. Mastery over magic is not dispensed like candy from a street vendor."

"Good, because I've had quite enough sweets to last me a lifetime." Ben's gaze wandered, taking in the surreal beauty of the grove. "What with all the enchanted gingerbread golems Master Thaddeus loved creating."

"Your journey has barely begun," the voice continued, resonating with the serenity of the grove. "And the road ahead is fraught with challenges that only a clear mind and a tutored hand can overcome."

"Right, challenges, clear mind, got it. But does it come with instructions? Maybe a manual? I tend to do better with visual aids."

The grove seemed to pulse with laughter, a gentle reminder that Oak Isle never took itself too seriously, even when cloaked in mystery. And so, amid the enchantment of the sacred grove, Ben waited, poised on the cusp of the unknown, yearning for the wisdom that only Elara could bestow.

Ben shifted uncomfortably, the weight of his destiny pressing down upon him like a lead cloak. In the heart of the secluded grove, nature bowed in silent reverence to the figure that materialized before him. Elara stood shrouded in mystery, her robes cascading around her like a waterfall of midnight silk, laced with threads of silver that shimmered with each subtle movement. Her eyes glowed like twin sapphires, alight with an ethereal flame that illuminated the grove's ancient secrets.

"Are those... battery-operated?" Ben quipped, pointing at her luminous gaze, his skepticism a shield against the awe threatening to crack his casual facade.

"Child of irony," Elara responded, her voice a melody harmonizing with the rustle of leaves, "the only power I harness is that which flows from the ley lines of Oak Isle itself."

"Of course, ley lines. Why didn't I think of that? Maybe because I'm not a walking spellbook!" Ben muttered under his breath, taking a tentative step forward. His mind churned with doubts and curiosities, the former trying to overshadow the latter.

"Your wit is as sharp as a griffon's talon," Elara observed, a ghost of a smile playing on her lips, "but it will take more than clever words to master the arcane arts."

"Fantastic, I'll add 'griffon manicurist' to my resume." Ben's attempt at humor veiled his fascination with the enigmatic sorceress. He couldn't help but marvel at the air of power that clung to her like a second skin, making the very atmosphere around her thrum with potential.

"Come closer, Ben," Elara beckoned, her hand gesturing fluidly as if she were conducting an orchestra of fireflies. "You must shed your disbelief to clothe yourself in wisdom."

"Disbelief is my favorite outfit, though. It goes with everything," he quipped again, stepping into the clearing where moonlight danced across Elara's figure, casting otherworldly shadows.

"Let me guess, you're going to turn me into a newt if I don't play along?"

"Only if you fail to learn the lessons I offer. And newts have quite the regenerative capabilities," she retorted, a spark of mischief in her glowing eyes.

"Great, that's reassuring. I've always wanted to grow a tail," Ben said, his tone laced with sarcasm. Yet behind the jest, his heart raced with anticipation. Here was the mentor who could unveil the arcane mysteries he so desperately sought. He took a deep breath, readying himself for whatever outlandish training methods Elara might employ. His hands ceased their fidgeting, steadied by the resolve to embrace the ludicrous, the fantastical, and the terrifying realm of magic that awaited his command.

"Prepare yourself, Ben of Oak Isle," Elara announced, her voice resonating with a gravity that set the forest abuzz. "For your tutelage under the stars begins now."

"Under the stars, huh? Does this involve constellations, or should I brace myself for another round of cryptic riddles?" Ben asked, half-expecting a star to drop down and smack him on the head for insolence.

"Only time will reveal the path forward," Elara replied, her silhouette blurring slightly as if she were part of the night itself. "But fear not, for the cosmos has a sense of humor too."

"Perfect," Ben sighed, rolling his eyes skyward. "The cosmos and I are going to get along just fine."

Ben watched, his skepticism waning like the crescent moon above, as Elara's form coalesced from the shadows of the grove. Her robes seemed to drink in the starlight, exuding an ethereal luminescence that made the very air around her shimmer.

"Observe," Elara commanded lightly, her voice tinged with amusement. She extended a slender hand, palm facing the midnight sky.

Ben stiffened, expecting some parlor trick or sleight of hand. Instead, fire erupted from her fingertips, not with the ferocity of destruction but in a dance of creation. The flames swirled into a fiery orb, casting flickering light across their faces. It hovered above her palm, a sun miniature in its grandeur.

"Whoa," Ben managed, his mouth agape. His mind raced to comprehend the spectacle, and he chuckled nervously. "Is it too late to get marshmallows?"

"Your levity is noted, but this is merely a prelude," she said, smirking at his jest. With a graceful motion, Elara sent the fireball arcing through the trees, where it dissipated harmlessly against the bark of an ancient oak.

"Show-off," Ben muttered under his breath, secretly impressed.

"Would you prefer a more... uplifting demonstration?" Elara's eyes twinkled mischievously. She then whispered an incantation, and the ground beneath Ben's feet began to tremble.

"Hey, what are you—"

Before he could finish his protest, Ben found himself floating, his body rising effortlessly off the forest floor. He flailed for a moment, arms pinwheeling as if swimming through the air would help. "Put me down!" he yelled, half-terrified, half-delighted by the sensation.

"Magic is not just about power, Ben. It's grace, control," Elara said, lowering him gently back to earth. "It's also about knowing when to let go." Her laughter was like wind chimes in a gentle breeze, harmonizing with the rustle of leaves around them.

"Easy for you to say, you're not the one being yo-yoed!" Ben retorted, brushing dirt from his trousers, though a grin betrayed his exhilaration.

"Ben, my role as your mentor transcends mere spectacle," Elara said, her tone shifting to a solemn timbre. "The Dragon Lady's shadow looms over Oak Isle. Your heart is brave, but without guidance, bravery alone will lead you to folly."

"Guidance, huh?" Ben crossed his arms, trying to look unfazed. "And how exactly can you guide this 'brave heart' to victory?"

"By teaching you the essence of magic itself. By helping you unlock the latent powers within you." Elara swept her arm across the grove, as if presenting the world itself. "You have potential, Ben. Together, we will hone it to confront the darkness that threatens our home."

"Potential, right." Ben scoffed playfully, yet deep down, something stirred—a glimmer of hope, a spark of possibility. "Guess I'm in good hands, or should I say, good spells?"

"Indeed," Elara replied, a warm smile gracing her lips. "But remember, the path ahead is fraught with peril and peppered with... unexpected turns."

"Unexpected turns?" Ben quirked an eyebrow. "With you? Never saw that coming."

"Ah, but that is the beauty of our journey, young apprentice." Elara's eyes danced with mirth. "Now, come. There is much to learn, and time waits for no man, nor sorceress."

"Lead the way, O Wise and Powerful Mentor," Ben declared, giving an exaggerated bow. "I'm ready to be dazzled, educated, and possibly turned into a newt."

"Only if absolutely necessary," Elara assured him, her laughter echoing through the grove as they set off into the heart of the enchanted forest, toward destiny's uncertain embrace.

The forest hummed with ancient secrets, its whispers curling around Ben like a familiar shroud as he followed Elara deeper into the secluded grove. The sorceress moved with an otherworldly grace, her robes trailing behind her like tendrils of mist, and her eyes reflecting the faint iridescence of the magical canopy above.

"Behold," Elara proclaimed, spreading her arms wide as if to embrace the very air. "Oak Isle teems with wonders unseen by mundane eyes."

"Like invisible fairies or bashful goblins?" Ben asked, his voice laced with a hint of jest.

"More than that, dear Ben. Creatures of legend and lore. Take the Whispersprites, for instance," Elara explained, pointing to a cluster of ethereal lights flitting about a tree hollow. "They are the scribes of the forest, recording every leaf's rustling tale."

"Whispersprites? Do they speak in library voices too?" Ben mused, his thoughts tickled by the absurdity of scribing sprites. He could already picture the tiny creatures shushing each other over the noise of a falling acorn.

"Your humor is your shield, young one," Elara chided gently, then twirled her fingers, conjuring a miniature cyclone that danced upon her palm. "But let us focus. These spells," she said, nodding at the swirling air, "are but a whisper of what you will command."

"Right. Because a whispering mini-tornado is exactly what I'll need against the Dragon Lady." Ben watched, intrigued despite himself as the cyclone dissipated into a shower of sparkles.

"Patience," Elara counseled. "For now, watch closely." Her hands moved through the air, weaving an intricate pattern. Suddenly, the ground trembled, and from the dirt rose a crystalline artifact pulsating with energy—the Heartstone of Eldwyn.

"Wow, that's not something you see every day," Ben admitted, eyes widening at the sight. "What's it do? Besides look pretty and possibly induce seizures?"

"It channels the latent magic within one's soul. Here, try to lift it with your mind," Elara suggested, her tone a mixture of challenge and encouragement.

"Sure, because telekinesis is totally in my wheelhouse," Ben quipped, focusing on the stone. He squinted, grunting with effort, but the stone remained indifferent to his mental prods.

"Visualize the connection, like a rope of light between your heart and the stone," Elara instructed, her own aura shimmering with the flow of her power.

"Rope of light, got it," Ben muttered, picturing a luminous lasso because, why not? To his astonishment, the stone quivered, rising a whole inch before clattering back down. "Holy... did you see that?"

"Progress!" Elara exclaimed, clapping her hands in delight. "You're tapping into the wellspring of your potential, however uncoordinated it may be."

"Hey, 'uncoordinated' is my middle name. But I'm all for tapping into wellsprings, especially if it means getting one-up on scaly fire-breathers," Ben retorted, rubbing his hands together with mock determination.

"Indeed," Elara said, her smile broadening. "With each spell you master, the closer we get to saving Oak Isle from its fiery fate. Now, once more, but this time, imagine the rope is made of sturdier stuff—say, the resolve to triumph."

"Resolve rope, coming up," Ben replied, embracing the ludicrousness of his task. As he focused on the Heartstone, he felt something deep within him stir—a force waiting to be unleashed. And as the stone levitated higher, Ben couldn't help but laugh.

"Elara, you might just make a mage out of me yet."

"Or at the very least, an entertaining novice," Elara teased, her glowing eyes sparkling with pride.

"Entertaining's my specialty," Ben shot back, his newfound confidence blooming like a firework as the Heartstone spun in mid-air. "Now, about turning things into frogs..."

"Let's save the amphibian transformations for another day, shall we?" Elara suggested, amusement clear in her voice.

"Fair enough, O Wise and Powerful Mentor," Ben conceded, his heart racing with anticipation for the next lesson in this wild, unpredictable symphony of magic.

Ben gripped the Wand of Wending Winds, his knuckles turning as white as the first frost of winter. Elara stood a few paces away, her arms folded across her chest, her expression unreadable as the ancient oaks that encircled them.

"Remember, it's about finesse, not force," she reminded him, her voice as calm as still water.

"Right, finesse," Ben muttered to himself. "I'm all about that finesse." He swished the wand with an extravagant flourish that he hoped looked wizardly. Instead of a gentle breeze, a torrential gust erupted from the tip, sending leaves swirling like dancers in a mad waltz.

"Oops," Ben exclaimed, ducking as a particularly aggressive twig shot past his ear. "Bit stronger than I intended!"

"Clearly," Elara said, though a smile tugged at the edges of her lips. "Control is key, Ben. You must be the eye of the storm, not its raging periphery."

"Eye of the storm. Got it," he replied, shaking out his stiff limbs. The wand felt alive in his hand, vibrating with pent-up zephyrs. He took a deep breath and tried again, this time whispering to the forces within the wand. The result was a soft puff of air that barely ruffled the feathers of a nearby crow.

"Better," Elara encouraged. "But you're holding back. Magic is an extension of your will. Own it."

Ben nodded, sweat beading at his brow despite the coolness of the grove. He could feel Elara's gaze on him, heavy with expectation. He focused, imagining the wind as an ally, a friend. With a flick of the wrist, he beckoned to the invisible currents. A gentle breeze caressed their faces, and Ben couldn't help but beam.

"Ah! There it is!" he cheered, triumphant.

"Indeed," Elara agreed, stepping closer. "You have the raw talent, Ben. But magic also requires patience and discipline."

"Patience I can do," Ben said, wiping his forehead with a sleeve. "Discipline might require some work."

"Work we shall do," Elara replied, her eyes gleaming with the promise of challenge. "Now, let's move on to the Orb of Illumination."

The orb sat upon a pedestal, looking innocuous enough, but Ben had learned looks could be deceiving when it came to magical artifacts. He reached out tentatively, brushing his fingers against its surface. It began to glow—a warm, inviting light.

"Nice and easy," Elara instructed. "Picture the light spreading, reaching into every shadow."

"Like butter on warm bread," Ben visualized, and the orb obeyed, its luminescence stretching outwards.

"Except without the crumbs," Elara added dryly. "See? When you are calm and deliberate, the magic responds."

"Feels weird, being calm," Ben admitted, watching the orb's light play across the grove. "Usually, I'm more of a 'leap before you look' kind of guy."

"Leaping without looking can be exhilarating," Elara said with a nod. "But it won't defeat the Dragon Lady or save Oak Isle."

"True," Ben acknowledged. "But hey, if I keep acing these baby steps, who knows? I might just leap and land on my feet next time."

"Or on something less forgiving," Elara teased, but her eyes held respect. "Stay diligent, Ben. Your journey has only begun."

Ben eyed the myriad of artifacts and spellbooks surrounding them. Each one was a mystery, a puzzle piece to mastering the arcane. And with Elara by his side, Ben felt the stirrings of what might have been pride—or perhaps it was the first spark of true belief in himself.

"Alright, Elara," Ben said, a determined glint in his eye. "Let's see what other kinds of trouble I can conjure up with a little guidance."

"Trouble?" Elara echoed, her mouth quirking upwards. "No, Ben. Let's see what kind of hero you can conjure up instead."

"Hero," Ben tested the word, liking how it sounded. "Yeah, I think I could get used to that."

"Ribbit."

Ben blinked. Once, twice. The world loomed large and green around him, and he was staring at Elara's boots—her very tall boots from his new, rather damp perspective. Panic fluttered in his chest until Elara's melodic laughter trickled down to him.

"Ah, so you've discovered the Frog's Perspective spell," she said, amusement lacing her voice. "An interesting choice for a beginner."

"Ribbit," Ben tried again, his voice a croak. He meant to say, 'This was not what I intended,' but the words were lost in translation. His tongue flicked out, tasting the air, betraying his human intent with decidedly frog-like behavior.

"Focus, Ben," Elara instructed, squatting to become level with his new amphibious form. "Reverse the spell. Remember, it's about intention, not just incantation."

"Ri—no, wait, I've got this." Concentrating, Ben willed himself back into his human shape. There was a moment of vertigo, a ripple through reality, and then he was standing, albeit unsteadily, on two feet again.

"Ah, that's better," he said, shaking out his limbs which felt entirely too long after his stint as a frog. "I'm beginning to think magic has a sense of humor."

"Magic is a reflection of us," Elara replied, offering him a hand up. "It seems your inner self is quite... ribbiting."

"Ha, ha," Ben rolled his eyes, but there was no bite to it. Elara's puns were growing on him, like moss—or like warts, if he wasn't careful.

"Let's try something simpler," Elara suggested, leading him toward a clear space away from the spellbooks and artifacts. "Conjure a light—just a small orb."

"Right," Ben said, nodding. He closed his eyes, envisioning the glow, feeling for that strange tug inside him that seemed to connect to the world's hidden threads. "Lux."

A soft orb of light appeared above his palm, bobbing gently. He grinned, triumphant, until he noticed the flicker of movement beside it. A tiny, mischievous sprite had materialized, its gossamer wings beating rapidly.

"Oops," he muttered as the sprite stuck out its tongue at him before darting towards Elara, who waved it away with an indulgent smile.

"Your control is improving, but focus is key," she said. "Sprites are attracted to stray magic like moths to flame."

"Guess I'm still a bit of a stray magic buffet," Ben admitted, watching as the sprite playfully dodged Elara's attempts to shoo it away.

"Control will come with time," Elara assured him, finally capturing the sprite within a shimmering bubble of magic and sending it off into the forest. "For now, let's work on precision."

"Precision," Ben echoed, squaring his shoulders. He turned to face a row of targets Elara had conjured. "Simple enough."

"Remember," Elara said, "magic isn't just about power. It's about intention, clarity, and finesse."

"Intention, clarity, finesse," Ben repeated like a mantra. He raised his hands, focusing on one target. "Ignis."

A jet of flame shot from his fingertips, narrow and controlled. It struck the center of the target, which smoldered and burned with a satisfying crispness.

"Excellent!" Elara clapped her hands, her glowing eyes bright with pride.

"Yeah?" Ben couldn't help the wide grin splitting his face. The frustration of his past failures seemed a distant memory compared to this moment of triumph.

"Absolutely," Elara confirmed. "You're learning to weave your will into the fabric of magic itself."

"Maybe I won't always be the guy who turns himself into a frog," Ben mused aloud, a chuckle bubbling up from deep within. "Or maybe I'll be the greatest frog-mage the world has ever seen."

"Either way," Elara said with a wink, "you'll be extraordinary."

The sun dipped below the horizon, painting the sky with streaks of crimson and gold as Elara and Ben stood at the edge of the grove, their silhouettes etched against the twilight. The air itself seemed to hum with the anticipation of their impending quest.

"Think of it, Ben," Elara said, her voice a melodic chime that harmonized with the evening song of crickets. "Ahead of us lies a journey fraught with perils and wonders beyond your wildest dreams."

Ben's gaze followed the path winding out of the grove, the shadows of the trees stretching long and twisted like the very mysteries they were about to unravel. "I feel like I've been stuffed into a minstrel's tale," he mused, his mind racing with images of fire-breathing dragons and spells that could turn the tide of fate.

"An apt feeling," Elara replied, adjusting the intricate silver clasp that held her robe closed. "For every hero must start somewhere, and this—" she gestured grandly to the forest around them "—is our beginning."

"Right, the beginning," Ben chuckled. He flexed his fingers, still tingling from the raw magic he'd harnessed earlier. It was both exhilarating and terrifying. "Just hope it doesn't end with me being a permanent fixture in some frog pond."

"Your wit will be as much a weapon as your spells," Elara quipped, a wry smile dancing on her lips. She began to stride forward, her robes whispering secrets against the fallen leaves.

Ben took a deep breath and followed, his boots crunching on the path. His mind swirled with the incantations Elara had taught him, each word a thread in the tapestry of power he was learning to weave. 'Intention, clarity, finesse,' he reminded himself. 'Don't forget finesse, or you'll be dining on flies tonight.'

"Remember, Ben," Elara called back to him, her glowing eyes catching the last light of day. "The Dragon Lady is cunning, with a heart forged in the deepest shadow. She will not yield easily to our cause."

"Let her come," Ben responded with bravado he only half-felt. "I've got a few tricks up my sleeve now. Like... like turning her minions into toads!" He winced at the image of an army of amphibians hopping madly around Oak Isle.

"Ah, yes," Elara laughed, her voice ringing through the forest. "The fearsome Toad Conjurer of Oak Isle. Bards shall sing of your exploits for ages to come."

"Hey, frogs are serious business," Ben shot back, unable to suppress his own laughter. The sound echoed, mingling with the rustle of leaves and the distant call of nocturnal creatures.

As night fully embraced the world around them, the first stars emerged, pinpricks of destiny against the darkening canvas. Ben glanced at the twinkling lights and felt a surge of determination. 'This is no jest,' he thought. 'There's a real chance to change things—to save Oak Isle.'

Elara paused, sensing his resolve. "Together, we will face terrors untold and laugh in the face of danger," she proclaimed, her hand resting on the hilt of a dagger that glimmered with enchantments. "Are you ready, Ben?"

"Ready as I'll ever be," he affirmed, squaring his shoulders. "After all, who else is going to keep the local frog population in check?"

"Then let us step into legend," Elara declared, and together they walked into the embrace of the enchanted forest, the night alive with the promise of adventure and the echo of their shared laughter.

The moon now sat high, a great silver medallion pinned against the night as Ben and Elara made their way through the labyrinthine paths of Oak Isle. The trees, ancient and wise, whispered secrets in a language only the wind seemed to understand. Fireflies danced around them like tiny lanterns guiding their steps, their light reflecting off the dew-kissed leaves.

"Ever ridden a Griffin, Ben?" Elara asked, her voice laced with mischief as she sidestepped a particularly aggressive fern that seemed intent on tripping her.

"Can't say I have," Ben replied, swatting away a low-hanging branch with more bravado than necessary. "Do they have seatbelts?"

"Only if you conjure them," Elara retorted, eyes twinkling with unspoken laughter. Her robe billowed behind her like a sail caught in a tempest, as if she were navigating more than just the forest floor.

Ben's mind whirled with thoughts, a chaotic tapestry of excitement and anxiety. 'I'm actually doing this,' he mused. 'Training with a sorceress, cracking jokes about mythical creatures, preparing to take on a Dragon Lady. Ma would have a fit if she could see me now.'

"Here's a spell for courage," Elara said suddenly, floating a few inches above ground—showing off, no doubt. She sketched something in the air with her finger, and a warm, golden glow enveloped Ben. It felt like being wrapped in a blanket fresh from the sun.

"Feels... tingly," Ben remarked, trying not to sound too impressed. "Is it supposed to smell like cinnamon?"

"Side effect," Elara shrugged, drifting back down. "Or maybe I just had pastries on my mind."

"Ah, the well-known Cinnamon Courage Concoction," Ben jested, puffing out his chest exaggeratedly. "For heroes with a sweet tooth!"

"Quiet, or I'll turn you into a pastry," Elara threatened, but her eyes sparkled with humor, softening the threat into nothing more than a playful jab.

They continued onward, the forest giving way to clearings and then closing in again, a dance of shadows and moonlight. With each step, Ben's confidence grew, fed by Elara's encouragement and the strange, wonderful sense of power that coursed through him. He began to move with more purpose, his strides longer, his gaze steadier.

"Elara," Ben started, breaking the comfortable silence, "what did you do before becoming a mentor? Were you, like, an adventurer or something?"

"Or something," she replied cryptically, a knowing smile playing on her lips. "Let's just say I've had my share of escapades."

"Understood. Say no more," Ben nodded solemnly. "Your mysterious past shall remain your own. For now."

"Smart boy," she praised, her laughter echoing around them like a spell of joy. "But remember, even the most enigmatic sorceresses need allies. And you, Ben, are proving to be quite the companion."

"Companion, confidant, and frog whisperer," Ben declared, a grin spreading across his face. "At your service."

The path ahead opened up to reveal a cliffside overlooking the vast expanse of the island, the sea shimmering below, a mirror to the heavens. Ben stepped forward, the edge beckoning, and took a deep breath, filling his lungs with the crisp, salty air.

"Look at that view," he said, awe coloring his words. "It's like the world's reminding us there's so much left to fight for."

"Indeed," Elara agreed, standing beside him. "And fight we shall."

Ben turned to her, a fierce resolve in his eyes. 'This is it,' he thought. 'My moment to make a difference.' The fear that had once gripped his heart was now a distant memory, replaced by a determination as unwavering as the ocean itself.

"Tomorrow, we confront our fate," Ben proclaimed, louder than he intended, his voice carrying over the cliffs. "And we'll do it with fireballs and cinnamon-scented courage!"

"Perhaps less of the fireballs near the cliffs," Elara suggested wryly. "Wouldn't want to singe your newfound bravery."

"Of course," Ben chuckled. "Safety first. Then heroism."

As the pair turned back to the forest, Ben felt a surge of energy, a readiness to embrace whatever lay ahead. With Elara by his side, he wasn't just prepared—he was eager. The chapter of his life as an ordinary man had ended; a new one, filled with spells, laughter, and the promise of legend, was just beginning.

The moon hung in the sky like a lethargic silver coin, barely shedding enough light to reveal the grotesque tableau unfolding around Ben and Elara. The pair stood back-to-back, circled by an eclectic mix of shambling zombies, slavering werewolves, and haughty vampires, all eerily illuminated by the malignant glow emanating from Zalathor, the undead Necromancer who orchestrated this symphony of horror.

"Elara," Ben whispered, his voice deadpan despite their dire circumstances, "do you ever feel like we're in some kind of twisted petting zoo? Because I'm pretty sure that zombie just tried to nibble my arm affectionately."

"Focus, Ben!" Elara hissed, her eyes darting between the encroaching horde. "Remember your training with the Arcane Arts: pointy end goes into the other man... or creature."

"Right." He nodded solemnly, then winked at her. "At least if we don't make it, I won't have to endure another one of your wind summoning lectures."

As they assessed their grim situation, Ben couldn't help but marvel at how perfectly terrible their timing was. Here they were, trapped in what could only be described as the worst possible blind date setup, and he had yet to perfect his most impressive spell - 'Ben's Brilliant Ballad of Blasting'.

"Ok, strategy," Ben mumbled, more to himself than to Elara. His gaze fell on the undead throng, noting the way the vampires preened and the werewolves salivated. "We can't let them pen us in. Werewolves take the lead - nasty biters, those. Vampires will hang back; they're arrogant enough to think themselves above a brawl until it's time for a dramatic entrance."

"Right. And Zalathor?" Elara's voice was steady, but Ben caught the flicker of concern in her eyes.

"Ah, yes, the puppet master." He cracked his knuckles exaggeratedly. "He's the key. Cut off the head and the body will flounder. Metaphorically speaking, of course. In reality, we might just get a bunch of headless zombies, which is both less threatening and more comical."

"Ben!" she snapped, though a smile threatened the corners of her lips. "We stand together. Your magic, my sorcery. We can do this."

"Agreed," he replied with a confident grin. "Let's show these undead monstrosities the true meaning of 'power couple.' After all, what's a few dozen supernatural beings when you've got style, panache, and questionable judgment on your side?"

"Questionable?" Elara raised an eyebrow, feigning insult.

"Okay, okay, impeccably poor judgment. Happy now?"

"Ecstatic," she retorted, rolling her eyes. But Ben saw the determination set in her stance, the spark of defiance in her expression. They were two against an army, but they had each other – and a shared belief that they could turn the tide of this battle.

"Alright," Ben said, taking a deep breath and feeling the thrum of magic coursing through his veins. "Let's dance with death and hope she's got two left feet."

"Charming," Elara replied, brandishing her wand with a flourish. "But I prefer to lead."

"Shield up!" Ben cried, thrusting his hands forward as if pushing against an unseen force. A shimmering dome of iridescent light sprouted from the earth, encasing him and Elara in a bubble of magical protection. The horde's gnashing and howling crescendoed into a cacophonous symphony of frustrated hunger as they collided with the barrier.

"Nice trick," Elara quipped, her voice steady despite the undead circus clawing inches from her face. "Now watch this." She raised her wand skyward, swirling it in a dramatic arc. A tempest responded to her command, a gust of wind so powerful it seemed to rip the very breath from the ghouls' lungs—or whatever served as lungs for the undead.

"Whoo! Go, Elara! Blow them away!" Ben cheered, watching with gleeful amazement as zombies tumbled backward like leaves in an autumn gust. The werewolves fared slightly better, their claws digging into the dirt, but even they staggered under the relentless wind.

"Keep your head in the game, Ben," she shouted back, not taking her eyes off the snarling mass being held at bay. "Your turn!"

"Right, pyrotechnics!" He focused intently, recalling the incantations he had practiced, words that once felt foreign now tumbling out with surprising ease. Fingers splayed, palms outward, he summoned the primal energy of fire. "Incendio maxima!"

With a flick of his wrists, fireballs burst forth, arcing through the air like comets. Each one found its mark, engulfing zombies in flames that burned unnatural flesh but somehow left the grass beneath untouched. "Ha! Take that, you shambling barbecues!"

"Focus on precision, not theatrics!" Elara chided between concentrated blasts of her own, though she couldn't help but smirk at Ben's unbridled enthusiasm.

"Sorry, sorry," he muttered to himself, still grinning. "But come on, who doesn't love a little showmanship with their sorcery?"

As another wave of creatures pressed forward, Ben's fingers danced with electricity—a private lightning storm at his command. "Fulminis!" he bellowed. Bolts of lightning zigzagged from his fingertips, crackling through the air with a sound like the world splitting open. Vampires recoiled from the light, flesh charring, while werewolves yelped in pain.

"Is that precise enough for you?" Ben called over the roar of his own power, a wild gleam in his eyes.

"Better," Elara conceded, though internally she was impressed by his growing mastery of magic. Together, they were a destructive ballet, their movements synchronized not by practice but by necessity and a shared will to survive.

"Remember," she yelled as they fought, "aim for the heart or the head! It's the only way to put these nasties down for good!"

"Got it!" Ben replied, already targeting the next onslaught. "But, Elara, just so you know, I'm definitely more of a 'heart' guy than a 'head' guy!"

"Ugh, Ben. Keep your bad puns for after we survive, please!" Despite the dire situation, she couldn't suppress a chuckle. It was either laugh or scream, and laughter packed more of a punch.

"Deal!" Ben shouted back, laughing too. "Just promise me there'll be an 'after'!"

"Promise!" And with that, they turned their attention back to the battle, their magic weaving an intricate tapestry of destruction as they wrote their survival story—one spell at a time.

Ben, his heart thundering like a war drum in his chest, let out a feral cry that would have made any barbarian proud. With the enchanted blade in hand—a glowing beacon of defiance—he charged into the thick of decayed flesh and fur. His sword carved arcs of silver light, severing limbs that fell to the ground with sickening thuds.

"Take that, you undead fashion disasters!" Ben hollered, as his blade met the rotting carcass of a zombie, cleaving it in twain. He couldn't help but grin at the absurdity; he'd just bisected a corpse wearing what looked like half a tuxedo. "What's the matter? No time to change after the apocalypse prom?"

"Less commentary, more evisceration!" Elara's voice cut through the chaos, her tone sharp as the ice shards she was hurling from her outstretched hands—magical projectiles that speared through ghouls with deadly precision.

"Got it, coach!" Ben quipped, ducking as a werewolf lunged, snapping its jaws where his head had been moments before. He rolled, feeling the rush of wind as a claw swiped above him. The beast was fast, but Ben's reflexes were faster, honed by fear and an overwhelming desire not to become werewolf chow.

I never thought I'd be grateful for all those dodgeball games in P.E., he mused, springing back up and delivering a swift uppercut with his sword, sending the creature's head flying like a gruesome cork from a champagne bottle.

"Behind you!" Elara's warning came just in time. Ben pivoted on his heel, parrying a vampire's lunge with a move that felt oddly like a dance step. If there was ever a time to cha-cha, it's while avoiding being drained by Dracula's distant cousin, he thought with a grim sort of amusement.

"Can't touch this!" he sang out, almost giddy with adrenaline as he danced away from death's grasp once again.

"Focus, Ben!" Elara admonished, though her words were softened by the glow of healing magic that enveloped him, stitching together the cuts and scrapes sustained in the melee. "And for heaven's sake, stop quoting old Earth songs during battle!"

"Sorry, can't help it! They're catchy and strangely appropriate," Ben replied, grinning as he felt the warmth of Elara's magic invigorating his limbs.

The undead horde pressed in, relentless, but Ben found himself moving with a fluidity he didn't know he possessed. The sword seemed to sing in his hands, guiding him to strike true and fast. Each movement was punctuated by Elara's incantations, her spells flashing brightly against the night sky, providing a rhythm to their desperate fight.

"Elara, when we get out of this—" Ben started, dodging another swipe, "—remind me to thank you for being the best backup a guy could ask for!"

"Only if you remind me to find you a new hobby that doesn't involve near-death experiences!" Elara shot back, a laugh bubbling up despite the dire situation.

"Deal!" Ben exclaimed, as he swung his sword in a wide arc, dispersing a group of skeletons that crumbled under the force of his enchanted blade.

"Also, dinner's on you!" Elara called out, her voice tinged with mirth amidst the mayhem.

"Of course! But it might be takeaway from 'Necromancer's Nosh' at this rate!" Ben retorted, imagining a macabre menu featuring 'finger food' that was quite literal.

Together, they fought, their banter a lifeline in the darkness, their courage a beacon as they stood against the night's horrors, each spell and strike a testament to their indomitable spirit.

"Elara, we need to trim the fat from the herd," Ben said, swiping his sword through a vampire's shadow as it recoiled from the light of his blade. "Zalathor's the puppet master. Let's cut some strings."

"Agreed." Elara nodded, her staff humming with energy. "I'll aim for his phylactery. Without it, he's about as menacing as a one-legged troll in a butt-kicking contest."

"Strategically speaking, that's oddly specific, but let's not quibble over details." Ben grinned, watching as Elara's hands danced, weaving spells that crackled in the air.

"Focus!" she snapped, though her eyes twinkled with shared excitement. "Now!"

Together, they launched a volley of attacks at Zalathor. Ben felt his magic surge, pulsing through him with the rhythm of a war drum. His thoughts raced - if they were successful, Zalathor would be reduced to nothing more than a spooky tale told by overly dramatic bards.

"Your focus on me is flattering, but futile!" Zalathor's voice boomed, echoing off the twisted trees surrounding them. With a sweep of his gnarled staff, he beckoned forth a new wave of terror. Skeletal warriors, clad in rusted armor and wielding swords that hadn't seen a whetstone in centuries, emerged from the earth, clattering like a morbid wind chime convention.

"Great, he's called in the boney brigade," Ben muttered, parrying a skeleton's attack. "New plan! Keep at Zalathor, I'll handle the calcium club."

"Try to keep up, then!" Elara called out, her laughter ringing clear even as she dodged a skeletal swipe. "Remember, ribs are not just for eating!"

"Who knew osteoporosis could be so aggressive?" Ben thought, ducking beneath a skeleton's blade and allowing himself a brief moment to marvel at the absurdity of their predicament. The sheer ludicrousness of battling a legion of undead with a companion who wielded wit as sharply as her magic made him almost, strangely, happy.

"Ben! Less thinking, more slashing!" Elara shouted, lobbing a fireball past his ear, singeing the tips of his hair.

"Right, because who needs eyebrows?" he yelled back, leaping forward and cleaving a path through the bone soldiers. He couldn't help but imagine these skeletons at a livelier time, perhaps as farmers or awkward court dancers. Now, they were just another obstacle, and he was the insurmountable force determined to reclaim their borrowed time.

"Keep your eye on the prize, Elara" he reminded himself, catching her glance as she unleashed a torrent of arcane energy towards the dark sorcerer. Their silent agreement was clear - Zalathor had to fall.

In the heat of the fray, with skeletal warriors clashing and snarling ghouls advancing, Ben's mind raced for a distraction worthy of Zalathor's vile attention. The necromancer's eyes, dark as voids, were locked onto Elara, his fingers weaving an incantation that would surely spell disaster.

"Hey, bonehead!" Ben shouted, conjuring a burst of vibrant sparks to erupt overhead, a kaleidoscope of fiery blooms that sizzled and popped like a celestial carnival. "Ever seen the Fourth of July? No? Well, here's a sneak peek!"

Elara seized the moment—the Necromancer's gaze fixated on the pyrotechnics—with her staff glowing ominously. She thrust it forward, murmuring an ancient incantation that coiled around Zalathor like spectral vines. His limbs froze mid-gesture, his mouth agape in silent fury.

"Nice one, Elara! I guess he's really... stuck on you now," Ben quipped, barely dodging a werewolf's slavering jaws. He twirled his sword, dispatching the creature with a flourish that sent its head rolling comically aside, eyes still wide in surprise.

"Keep the puns coming, Ben," Elara said, her voice steady despite the exhaustion that clawed at her edges. "I'm sure they're just dying to hear more."

"Death by bad jokes—has a certain ring to it, doesn't it?" he retorted, sending a fireball into a cluster of zombies that erupted into a comedic display of flailing limbs and charred torsos.

"More like a death knell," she laughed, flicking a lightning bolt from her fingertips that sizzled through the air, striking down a vampire in a puff of smoke and leaving behind a pair of smoldering boots.

Ben couldn't help but admire Elara's poise under pressure. Her spells were precise, deadly, and delivered with the grace of a ballerina wielding a bazooka. Together, they danced through the battlefield, their movements synchronized in a deadly ballet.

"Time for the grand finale!" Ben bellowed, leaping high into the air. Underneath him, the undead surged like a grotesque tide. He plunged down, sword first, into the heart of the horde. Each swing of his enchanted blade was a conductor's baton orchestrating a symphony of destruction.

"Try not to hog all the spotlight!" Elara chided, conjuring a whirlwind that swept up the remaining creatures and spun them until they unraveled like old yarn. "Some of us enjoy the occasional solo."

"Then by all means," Ben grunted, parrying a zombie's clumsy lunge, "take the stage!"

"Thought you'd never ask," Elara said playfully, calling forth a radiant orb that hovered above her palm. With a dramatic flourish, she released it, and the orb exploded outward in a blinding flash, vaporizing any undead unfortunate enough to be caught in its path.

"Encore! Encore!" Ben cheered, panting from the exertion, his humor masking the adrenaline-fueled tremor in his voice. They stood back-to-back now, surveying the thinning ranks of their foes.

"Let's wrap this up," Elara said, her tone fierce yet tinged with the same exhilarating rush Ben felt. "I've got plans later, and they don't include being ghoul fodder."

"Right there with you," Ben agreed, his magic crackling at his fingertips, ready for whatever came next. This battle had been a test—one they wouldn't fail. Not today. Not ever.

The field of battle was a morass of shadows and chaos, but amidst the tumultuous dance of death, Ben spotted the crumpled form of

Zalathor. The Necromancer's breath came in ragged hisses, his eyes flickering with the fading embers of his dark power.

"Elara!" Ben bellowed over the din, pointing towards their fallen adversary. "It's time for the grand finale!"

"Music to my ears!" Elara replied, her cloak billowing dramatically as she stepped over a werewolf whose snarls had turned to whimpers. With a twirl of her staff, she summoned a cascade of sparks that showered over them like a curtain call.

Together, they raced to Zalathor's side, their weapons at the ready. Ben raised his enchanted sword, its blade shimmering with a light so bright it seemed to mock the very darkness it cleaved through. Elara chanted an incantation, her voice rising above the clamor, a crescendo that sought the final note of this deadly score.

"Here's a twist ending for you, Zalathor!" Ben shouted, thrusting his sword downward. The blade pierced the Necromancer's heart with a satisfying squelch, while Elara's spell wrapped around their foe like a serpentine embrace, squeezing the last vestiges of his vile essence.

A shockwave rippled across the battlefield, and the undead host faltered. Zombies stumbled mid-shamble, werewolves froze with fangs bared, vampires' eyes dimmed from malevolent red to lifeless gray. As one, they crumbled like brittle statues, bones clattering to the ground and turning to dust that the wind eagerly swept away.

"Talk about losing your support base," Elara quipped, wiping necrotic ichor from her brow with a grimace.

"Show's over, folks!" Ben exclaimed, sheathing his sword with a flourish. He surveyed the desolation around them, feeling a curious mix of elation and exhaustion. They had won, but at what cost? His muscles ached, and he could feel the weight of each spell he'd cast pressing down on him like an invisible burden.

"Elara, remind me to never cross you," Ben said with a weary chuckle. "Your spellcasting is... terrifyingly effective."

"Flattery will get you everywhere, darling." Elara grinned, leaning heavily on her staff. "But let's not make a habit out of these near-death experiences, agreed?"

"Agreed," Ben murmured, his thoughts drifting to the journey ahead. Oak Isle needed them, and this was merely the first of many horrors they would face. A shiver ran down his spine—not from fear, but from the anticipation of challenges yet to come. They were a team now, bound by magic, wit, and a shared destiny.

"Come on," Elara said, breaking into his reverie. "Let's find somewhere less... apocalyptic to rest. I hear the next town has a tavern with the most divine apple cider."

"Lead the way," Ben replied, a smile tugging at the corner of his mouth. Victory was sweet, but the promise of cider and a moment's peace was sweeter still.

"Besides," he added under his breath, "I've always been partial to happy endings."

Ben squatted low, his back pressed against the rough bark of an ancient oak that seemed to whisper the secrets of Oak Isle through its leaves. Every rustle spoke of impending doom, every snapped twig a testament to the urgency of his quest. In the shadow-dappled forest, his mind was a battleground where hope and despair clashed in equal measure.

"An army of one is no army at all," he murmured, plucking a blade of grass and shredding it with nervous fingers. "Especially when facing a dragon with more mood swings than a troll in love."

He'd need allies—fierce, unyielding, and preferably not terrified of imminent incineration. His gaze drifted across the clearing to where Lila stood, her bowstring taut, her eyes narrowed with hawk-like precision.

"Watch closely, Ben," she called out, her voice laced with confidence as if she could hit a target blindfolded and hopping on one leg. "I'm going to show you why they call me Lila 'Bullseye' Greenleaf."

"Is it because you have a knack for hitting bull's noses?" Ben quipped, unable to help himself.

The arrow whistled through the air, a thin streak of inevitability that kissed the wind before embedding itself dead center in the target—a poor scarecrow sporting a pot for a helmet and a rather shocked expression painted onto its sackcloth face.

"More like I've never met a bull I couldn't charm with an arrow between its eyes," Lila retorted, smirking as she fluidly notched another arrow. With a flick of her wrist, the second arrow split the first in two, sending bits of straw and pride alike into the air. "And I didn't even ruin his pot-helmet. What's my prize?"

"Remind me never to wear a hat around you," Ben said, clapping slowly, the sound punctuating his appreciation and concern. "Your prize, should you choose to accept it, is a chance to help save the world—and hopefully not perforate me in the process."

"Saving the world comes with the job description," Lila replied nonchalantly, already scanning the treeline for her next victim. "Perforating you... that's just a bonus, depending on how often you make that troll joke."

Ben chuckled, the sound bittersweet as he considered the road ahead. The Dragon Lady was no laughing matter, and while humor could lighten their spirits, it wouldn't shield them from her flames. He needed Lila, not just for her aim, which was admittedly legendary, but for the lightness she brought to the grim tapestry of their quest.

"Alright, Lila 'Bullseye' Greenleaf," he said, stepping into the clearing, the determination etched on his features. "Let's talk strategy. And maybe work on a nickname for you that doesn't involve any form of livestock."

The clang of steel rang out like a chorus of angry church bells, and Ben found himself ducking as a broadsword whistled through the air where his head had been moments before. He turned to face the source of the near decapitation and saw Roran in the thick of combat, a whirlwind of muscle and fury.

"Roran the Relentless," Ben thought, an involuntary smirk creeping across his face despite the danger. The man's sword carved through the air with the grace of a dancer and the impact of a battering ram. His opponents—a pair of unfortunate training dummies—were taking an absolute beating, their straw innards spilling onto the ground like the world's saddest harvest.

"Ha!" Roran bellowed, driving his blade through the chest of one dummy so forcefully that it exploded into a cloud of straw and rags. "That's for doubting my mother's beef stew!"

"Your enemies quake in their boots at the mention of soup spoons, I'm sure," Ben said, stepping clear of the debris.

"Ah, Ben!" Roran grinned, yanking his sword free and resting it on his shoulder as if it weighed no more than a twig. "Come to admire my handiwork?"

"More like avoid being part of it," Ben quipped, brushing a stray piece of straw from his hair. "But I'd be lying if I said I wasn't impressed. Your strength would give a mountain pause—and likely reshape its geography."

"Then let's hope this Dragon Lady has a sense of humor about her topography," Roran laughed, the sound booming across the field.

"Speaking of which..." Ben hesitated, scratching the back of his neck. "I actually came to talk to you about—"

"About Lila?" Roran interrupted, not missing a beat. "I saw you two. Don't think I can't spot a budding alliance when I see one."

"Right," Ben said, relieved he didn't have to explain further. "She could shoot the wings off a fly, and we could use someone with her precision."

"Indeed," Roran agreed, nodding. "And what of me, then? What role does this humble servant of the blade play in your grand scheme?"

Ben met Roran's gaze, his eyes serious despite the levity that always seemed to dance around the edges of their conversations. "We need your strength, Roran. Your courage. I've seen you stare down beasts thrice your size without a flicker of fear. But more than that, I need someone who can stand firm when everything else is falling apart."

"Say no more!" Roran boomed, puffing out his chest. "You had me at 'we need your strength.' The rest was just flattery."

"Flattery?" Ben raised an eyebrow. "I don't flatter. I speak only the dire truth. And the truth is, we won't survive this without you."

"Then consider my sword yours," Roran said, clapping Ben on the shoulder with a force that nearly sent him sprawling. "To victory, or a glorious end!"

"Preferably victory," Ben muttered under his breath, steadying himself. "Glorious ends are overrated."

In the shadow of a crumbling watchtower, where vines clung to stone like desperate lovers, Ben sought out Roran. The warrior was a solitary silhouette against the dusk, his sword plunging and rising in a dance with imagined adversaries.

"Practicing for a phantom war?" Ben called out, crossing the distance between them with measured steps.

"Every battle begins in the mind," Roran replied without pausing, his blade whistling through the air. He executed a flawless spin, dispatching a horde of invisible foes. "What brings you to my humble field of valor?"

"Your mind might be ready, but I've come to enlist more than your imagination," Ben said, dodging an errant swing that suggested Roran's 'phantom war' was perilously inclusive.

"Enlist away," Roran grinned, finally stilling his sword. "Though I must warn you, I don't come cheap."

"Good thing we're not paying in coin, then," Ben retorted. "We need your arm, Roran. Oak Isle faces a threat unlike any before – the Dragon Lady stirs in her volcanic nest, and her wrath will scorch the land unless we stop her."

"Ah, dragons!" Roran exclaimed, eyes alight. "Finally, an enemy worthy of my steel! And what makes you think I'm the man for this fiery task?"

"Because when darkness falls over the land, your blade always finds the light," Ben said earnestly, locking eyes with the warrior. "Plus, Lila's already on board. Her arrows alone won't keep the flames at bay."

"Ah, Lila, the sharpshooter!" Roran chuckled. "Her aim is true, but it's the quiver of my heart she pierces most accurately. Very well, count me in."

As the evening crept forward, the trio gathered around a fire that crackled like the harbinger of the inferno they sought to extinguish. Roran regaled them with exaggerated tales of his heroic deeds, each more implausible than the last, while Lila rolled her eyes so hard Ben feared they might dislodge.

"And then," Roran boomed, gesturing wildly, "I wrestled the sea serpent with nothing but my bear hands!"

"Your 'bare' hands?" Lila corrected, one eyebrow arched to the heavens.

"Did I say bare? I meant bear. I had bear hands at the time. A minor enchantment," Roran clarified, puffing out his chest.

"Of course," Ben interjected, suppressing a chuckle. "Who doesn't have a pair of bear hands lying around for aquatic emergencies?"

"Exactly!" Roran roared with laughter, clinking his cup against Ben's. "You understand me, friend."

"Either way," Lila interjected, "let's hope those 'bear' hands are ready for dragon scales."

"Dragon scales, pah!" Roran dismissed with a wave. "I'll turn them into fine armor once we've vanquished the beast!"

"Optimism or madness?" Ben mused aloud, though he couldn't help but admire Roran's indomitable spirit.

"Both, I reckon," Lila quipped, her smirk belying the respect that flickered in her gaze.

"Indeed," Ben agreed, feeling the bonds of camaraderie weaving tighter around their little fellowship. "To victory, then, with our bear-handed warrior, our eagle-eyed archer, and... whatever it is I do."

"Plan, worry, and occasionally trip over roots," Roran supplied helpfully, earning a snort from Lila.

"Essential skills for any leader," Ben admitted with a grin. As the laughter died down, replaced by the comfortable silence of shared purpose, Ben knew that despite the peril ahead, he wouldn't face it alone. With these two by his side, the quest felt a touch less daunting, the night a shade less dark.

The crisp morning air was alive with the sound of steel clashing against steel, punctuated by the occasional twang of a bowstring. Ben watched Lila move through the trees like water—fluid and unerring. Each arrow she loosed found its mark on the makeshift targets hanging from the branches, each one emblazoned with a crudely drawn dragon that bore an uncanny resemblance to a plump cat with wings.

"Ha! Take that, you winged feline fiend!" Lila exclaimed triumphantly as another arrow pierced the center of a target.

"Excellent shot, Lila," Ben praised, his tone earnest though his eyes danced with mirth. "Those 'dragons' won't know what hit them."

"Nor will the real ones, once I'm through," she retorted with a wink, already nocking another arrow.

Roran's laughter rumbled like a distant storm as he hefted his sword, muscles bulging beneath his tunic as if they were trying to escape confinement. He faced off against a straw dummy armored in old pots and pans, giving it a fierce glare that would have sent a lesser opponent fleeing for the hills.

"Feel the wrath of Roran Stormblade!" he bellowed, charging the hapless figure with the gusto of a bull in a crockery shop. His sword swung down with the force of an avalanche, cleaving through air and straw with equal ferocity. Pots clanged and flew; straw snowed down upon him like victory confetti.

"Stormblade, indeed," Ben murmured to himself, scribbling mental notes on Roran's technique. "I suppose we won't be needing stealth with you around."

"Stealth is for those who fear to be seen!" Roran declared, raising his sword high. "I want our foes to quake at the sight of me!"

"Quake with laughter, perhaps," Ben quipped, but there was no denying Roran's effectiveness. Fearlessness could be as potent a weapon as the sharpest blade.

"Your turn, Ben," Lila called out, her voice teasing. "Show us the legendary footwork of the Tripping Tactician."

"Ah, my reputation precedes me." Ben grinned, drawing his own sword—a more modest affair compared to Roran's behemoth of a blade—and approached a dummy of his own. With deliberate care, he executed a series of strikes, each paired with a dance-like step.

"Careful now," Roran teased from the sidelines. "Don't hurt yourself with all that fancy stepping."

"Mock all you like," Ben retorted, panting slightly from the exertion. "But when we're neck-deep in dragon breath, you'll thank the stars for my tripping prowess."

"Only if it trips the dragon," Lila quipped, firing another arrow that zipped past Ben close enough to flutter his hair.

"Point taken," Ben conceded with a chuckle, sheathing his sword. "Shall we strategize?"

"Indeed," Lila agreed, joining them with a handful of arrows still ready for action. "So, oh great Tripping Tactician, what's our brilliant plan?"

"Simple," Ben started, spreading out a rough map on the ground between them. "We exploit our strengths. Lila, your aim will provide cover and keep the Dragon Lady's minions at bay."

"Turning them into pincushions, got it," Lila said, nodding.

"Roran, your strength will be our breakthrough. You'll cut a path straight to her lair."

"Like wheat before the scythe," Roran boomed, striking a heroic pose.

"Exactly. And I," Ben continued, tapping the map where a treacherous mountain pass zigzagged toward their ultimate goal, "will ensure we navigate this maze without becoming hopelessly lost or dragon snacks."

"Sounds flawless," Roran said, sarcasm dripping from his words like honey from a spoon.

"Flawless? No," Ben admitted, locking eyes with each of them in turn. "But together, we might just be formidable enough to pull this off."

"Formidable and fabulous," Lila added with a flourish, twirling an arrow between her fingers.

"Then it's settled," Ben said, standing up and brushing dirt from his knees. "We train until dusk, rest, and at dawn... we face our destiny."

"Or trip over it," Roran added, a wide grin splitting his face.

"Either way," Ben concluded, his heart lighter than it had been in ages, "we face it together."

With renewed vigor, the trio resumed their training, the sounds of their laughter mingling with the clatter of weapons—three comrades bound by purpose and the promise of the adventure that lay ahead.

The late afternoon sun dipped below the jagged peaks, casting long shadows across the clearing where Ben and his newfound allies rested, their breaths forming puffs of mist in the cool air. They sat in a rough circle, their backs to a large boulder that had become an impromptu dining table, strewn with remnants of bread and cheese.

"Your eye," Ben began, nodding towards Lila as he peeled an apple with his dagger, "it's sharper than the wit of a court jester. How did you come to be such a marksman?"

"Markswoman," Lila corrected with a smirk, plucking the apple slice from the blade's tip. "And it was either learn to shoot or get eaten by wolves in the Darkened Woods. I chose the former."

"Smart choice," Roran chuckled, his massive form sprawled on the grass, absently polishing his greatsword. "I once wrestled a wolf for my dinner. It was a good fight; tenderized the meat nicely."

"Roran, your muscle is only matched by your appetite," Ben mused, tossing apple slices to his companions. "It's a marvel how you turn every battle into a feast."

"Feasting keeps my strength up. And speaking of strength," Roran said, rising to his feet in one fluid motion, "who else here can cleave a goblin in two with a single swing?"

"Thankfully, no one," Ben replied, stealing a glance at Lila who rolled her eyes dramatically. "You're our battering ram, Roran. Without you, we'd be hard-pressed to break through enemy lines."

"Ah, but without your cunning, Ben, we'd likely march straight into a dragon's den thinking it was a tavern," Lila quipped, shooting an arrow into a tree knot fifty paces away without looking.

"True," Ben acknowledged, a thoughtful expression crossing his face. "My strategic mind has saved more hides than a tanner's guild."

"See? We're like a well-oiled catapult," Lila said, stretching her legs. "Each with our own role to play."

"Except when the catapult flings us into trouble," Roran added, grinning. "Remember the Cavern of Echoing Sorrows? I still have an echo in my left ear from all the screaming."

"Ah, yes," Ben laughed. "When Lila's arrow ricocheted off three walls and disarmed the sorcerer. You couldn't plan that kind of shot."

"Pure skill," Lila retorted, winking at Ben. "As for your 'strategic retreat' that turned into an accidental ambush on their reinforcements—"

"Impeccably timed," Ben cut in, his eyes twinkling. "And let's not forget Roran's heroic leap over the chasm. I thought you were a goner."

"Ha! The look on your faces!" Roran boomed. "But there's no chasm wide enough to keep me from a good brawl."

"Or from the feast afterward," Ben quipped, earning a hearty laugh from Roran and an amused snort from Lila.

"Speaking of feasts," Lila began, pulling out another arrow, "let's make sure this next one's in celebration, not commiseration."

"Agreed," Ben said, standing up as the first stars appeared in the twilight sky. "For Oak Isle, for glory, and for the stories we'll tell thereafter!"

"Stories that will echo through the ages!" Roran exclaimed, lifting his sword high.

"Or at least until the next round of ale," Lila added, shouldering her bow.

"Either way," Ben concluded, his heart buoyant despite the weight of their quest, "we write them together."

The moon hung low, swollen and ripe as a blister on the night's canvas. Its light silvered the edges of the forest, turning every leaf and twig into a shard of quiet radiance. Ben squatted beside a small fire that crackled with an air of secrecy, casting furtive glances at his new comrades.

"Remember," Ben said, poking at the flames, "stealth is paramount. We strike under cover of darkness, like—"

"Like a trio of lovesick owls wooing the indifferent night?" Lila suggested, her eyebrow arched with mischief.

"More like shadows with purpose," Ben corrected, but his lips curled in spite of himself.

"Shadows that snore, perhaps," Roran chimed in, stretching his massive arms. "I heard you last night, Ben. Thought it was a dragon's growl."

"Strategic breathing," Ben retorted, "keeps the enemy confused."

Lila chuckled, nocking an arrow to her bow with practiced ease. "Does it now? And here I was thinking we were trying not to alert the entire realm to our presence."

"Ah, but that's where you're wrong," Ben shot back, smirking. "It's all about misdirection." He pointed a finger skyward. "You let them think you're there, when really—" He jabbed a finger toward the underbrush.

"Ben, the only thing you're directing is my will to live straight off a cliff," Roran joked, his laughter booming through the trees like thunder flirting with the horizon.

"Ha! You'd need a cliff twice as steep to support that legendary girth of yours," Ben quipped, earning a playful glare from the warrior.

"Careful, Ben," Lila warned, her voice laced with mock severity, "or he might sit on you. That'd be one strategy the Dragon Lady wouldn't see coming."

"True," Ben mused, "but let's stick to the plan where we all survive, shall we?"

"Survival," Roran grunted, his face suddenly solemn, "is not guaranteed for those who insult Roran's honor—or his cooking."

"Speaking of which," Lila interjected, eyeing the provisions they had packed for their journey, "if your stew tonight is anything like last time, survival's looking pretty bleak."

"Blasphemy!" Roran declared, his hands clutching his heart as if mortally wounded. "My stew is a culinary masterpiece!"

"Masterpiece or master crime?" Ben teased, dodging a playful swipe from the warrior.

"Enough," Lila laughed, standing and brushing off her tunic. "We have a Dragon Lady to confront, not each other's cooking."

"Right you are," Ben agreed, rising to join her. His mind wove through the threads of their mission, tying together the humor, the camaraderie, and the unspoken fears that danced on the edge of their banter. Each jest, a shield against the darkness ahead; each laugh, armor fortifying their resolve.

"Then it's settled," Roran said, grabbing his shield and sword with a clang of metal. "We embark upon this quest with full bellies and light hearts."

"May our aim be true, our blades swift, and our jokes even swifter," Lila added, her eyes sparkling like twin stars caught in the tapestry of night.

"Agreed," Ben said, feeling the knot of anxiety in his chest loosen ever so slightly. "For Oak Isle, for its people, and for the punchlines yet to come."

Together, they stepped away from the dying embers of their campfire, letting the cloak of night swallow them whole. As the last ember flickered out, the trio melted into the shadowy embrace of the forest, three figures bound by fate, laughter, and the unyielding desire to pen their own legend.

The morning sun, a brash orange eye in the sky, watched as Ben and his motley crew of would-be saviors set forth on their latest escapade. With their previous haunt now but a speck on the horizon, they faced Oak Isle, a land whispered to hold wonders enough to make even the cynics sing.

"By the hairy toes of the Ancient Dwarves, look at that!" Roran exclaimed, pointing towards a copse of trees that twinkled as if bedecked with stars. The leaves were a kaleidoscope of colors, some transparent, others shimmering with a light that seemed to come from within.

"Must be the famed Crystalwoods," Elara chimed in, her eyes alight with the kind of excitement that came from encountering footnotes in dusty tomes. "Legend said they'd sparkle more than my future crown."

"Your humility astounds me, as always," Ben retorted dryly, leading the way with a map that looked suspiciously like it was drawn by a drunk gnome.

"Guys! Do you think there's something edible around here? I could eat a whole dragon right now," Lila quipped, her stomach rumbling louder than thunder over the Emerald Cliffs.

"Only if you fancy a mouthful of crystal berries. They'll turn your tongue into a prism for a week!" Roran chuckled, ducking as a low-hanging branch, glittering and sharp as a witch's promise, reached out for his hair.

"Could be a new fashion trend," Ben mused, his thoughts wandering to the endless possibilities this land held. 'Oak Isle, a place where even the flora flirts with the extraordinary. What secrets do you cradle in your heart?' he pondered, squinting at the foliage that seemed to dance and laugh in the gentle breeze.

"Careful not to wander off; we might have to rescue you from a sentient vine or a ticklish tree," Elara admonished, her gaze fixed on the horizon where mountains rose like the backs of slumbering dragons. 'Would finding the Staff of Tomorrow be as simple as plucking a flower from these woods?' she wondered.

"Or worse, you'll trip over your own feet and fall face-first into a fairy ring," Lila added with a snicker. "You'll come out a century later, still hopeless with directions and sporting a beard longer than Roran's tales."

"Ha! As if any beard could match the epic sagas I carry in my whiskers," Roran boasted, running a hand through his impressive facial hair, which he claimed was an archive of their adventures.

"Speaking of directions," Ben interjected, bringing their focus back to the parchment in his hands. "This path here should lead us straight to the—"

"Let me guess, to the heart of temptation and probable doom?" Elara cut in, a smirk playing on her lips.

"Exactly! Where's your sense of adventure?" Ben shot back, his spirit buoyed by the untamed beauty around them.

"Left it back with the last horde of goblins we encountered—the ones with the particularly nasty dental issues," Roran said, shuddering at the memory.

"Keep your wits about you," Ben warned, though his tone betrayed his own enthusiasm. "We're treading on mysteries older than Roran's jokes."

"Impossible!" Lila laughed, her voice joining the symphony of this strange, fantastical landscape.

As they ventured deeper, even the air seemed to thrum with anticipation, carrying whispers of magic and old, old stories waiting to be unraveled by the brave or the foolish. Perhaps, Ben considered with a grin, they were a bit of both.

The group pressed on, the air thick with an aroma of moss and ancient stone. Each breath seemed to fill their lungs with the dust of bygone centuries as they wove through the colossal trunks of trees that stood like sentinels guarding secrets of the past. The landscape was a tapestry of green, embroidered with flowers that shimmered in hues not found in any natural spectrum, each petal glinting as if woven with threads of pure moonlight.

"By the stars, would you look at that?" Lila's voice cut through the verdant quiet, her eyes wide with wonder. She pointed towards a crumbling archway, half-eaten by ivy, its stones whispering tales of grandeur and decay.

"Ruins!" Ben exclaimed, his gaze tracing the weathered contours of what must have been a citadel of immense power. "Elara, do you feel it? The thrumming in the air?"

"Thrumming or grumbling," Elara replied, her hand inching towards the hilt of her sword, "either way, something doesn't want us here."

"Or perhaps," Roran chimed in, stepping closer to examine a bas-relief depicting a figure with an otherworldly grace, "it's been waiting for just us."

"Waiting to trap us, more likely," said Ben, squinting at the shadows dancing within the ruins' embrace. Yet, he couldn't shake off the thrill of discovery, the lure of untold stories etched into every stone.

"Traps are merely puzzles with higher stakes," Lila mused, her fingers grazing over a glyph that glowed faintly under her touch.

"Higher stakes? I'm game!" Ben declared, his pulse quickening. He could almost hear the call of the unknown guiding them forward, the promise of adventure too potent to resist.

"Shh! Someone's here," Elara hissed, drawing her blade with a ring that sang of readiness and steel.

From the shadows, a figure emerged, wrapped in robes that shifted color with each step, as if woven from the essence of the forest itself. The mysterious guardian's eyes were hidden beneath a hood, yet their gaze was palpable, piercing through the veils of secrecy that shrouded this place.

"Travelers bold, seekers of lore, why disturb the silence of yore?" The voice was both ancient and ageless, demanding and droll.

"Bold is our middle name," Ben quipped, then winced at his own bravado. "Actually, we seek the Staff of Tomorrow. Any chance you've seen it lying around?"

"Found in jest, lost in earnest. To find what you seek, unveil the serpent." The words slithered around them like a riddle wrapped in enigma, topped with a generous dollop of mystery.

"Unveil the serpent?" Lila echoed, arching an eyebrow. "Is that metaphorical or should we be worried about actual snakes?"

"Metaphors and serpents oft intertwine," the guardian replied cryptically, a barely perceptible smile tugging at the corners of their lips. "Beware the enemy in the dark, for they march towards the morrow's spark."

"Enemy in the dark?" Roran pondered aloud, scratching his beard thoughtfully. "I'd prefer them in the light, much easier to punch."

"Thank you, wise... person," Elara said with a respectful nod. "We'll heed your words."

"Guardian of shadows, guide of fate, remember this: hesitate and it's too late," the figure intoned before melting back into the ruins, leaving behind only the echo of their laughter.

"Too late for what?" Ben muttered. His thoughts churned like a sea storm; they needed to find the Staff before their unseen adversary. But first, they had to decipher the guardian's cryptic counsel. "Unveil the serpent" indeed.

"Let's not dawdle then," said Lila, determination lighting her features. "Adventure waits for no one!"

Ben grinned despite the uncertainty ahead. They were deep in the heart of a comedy of perils, but together, they would turn the page on destiny's tantalizing tale.

The mist-shrouded path wound upward, a serpentine coil through the dense thicket of the Whispering Woods. The trees were ancient, their gnarled roots clawing at the earth like the hands of the long-forgotten dead, and their leaves whispered secrets to the wind – or possibly insults, Ben wasn't fluent in foliage.

"Are these trees getting grabbier, or is it just me?" Elara muttered, swatting away an overly affectionate branch. Her sword, Evergleam, dangled at her hip, its blade singing softly as if itching for action.

"Reminds me of my Aunt Gertrude's hugs. Clingy, with a hint of doom," Roran quipped, ducking as a low-hanging limb tried to tousle his hair.

"Stay sharp," Ben warned, eyes darting as he led them forward. "These woods are thick with more than just tree sap."

"Ha! Thick with tree sap," Lila chuckled, her lilting voice dancing on the edge of hysteria. "You're a poet, Ben. And here I thought your talents lay exclusively in brooding."

"Brooding is an art form. Plus, it's good for the complexion," Ben shot back, his usual stoic expression betraying a twitch of amusement.

"Guys, focus," Elara said sternly, though her lips curled into a smile. "We've got more important things to worry about than Ben's skincare routine."

"Like that!" Lila pointed towards a bramble-covered clearing where the undergrowth rustled ominously. A pair of yellow eyes blinked open within the thicket, followed by another set, and another, until the foliage seemed alive with watchful gazes.

"Ah, the welcoming committee," Roran deadpanned, readying his fists which, Ben noted, were roughly the size of small hams.

"Those are Snarklebeasts," Ben said, his mind reeling through the bestiary of lore he'd studied. "They're not known for their hospitality or their table manners."

"Snarklebeasts? Who names these creatures? A bored bard with a rhyming dictionary?" Lila mused, nocking an arrow to her bow with graceful precision.

"Let's try not to become dinner theater," Elara suggested, drawing Evergleam, which hummed with anticipation.

"Or worse, brunch," Roran added, flexing his shoulders like a bear preparing to tussle.

"Remember, they're more afraid of us than we—never mind, that's a lie. They're definitely not afraid of us," Ben conceded as the largest Snarklebeast leapt from the shadows, fangs bared.

"Here comes cuddles!" Roran bellowed, meeting the beast head-on with a thunderous punch that sent it reeling back into the bushes.

"Nice right hook!" Lila called out, loosing arrows in a dazzling display that would have made any circus performer weep with envy.

"Thanks! I call it 'The Roran Welcome'!" he replied, grinning amidst the chaos.

"Less chatting, more splatting!" Elara shouted, her blade whirling in arcs of silver light, severing vines and fending off snapping jaws.

Ben found himself back-to-back with Elara, his own sword, Night's Sigh, a blur of dark steel. "Remember when we dreamed of adventure?" he asked over the din of battle.

"Vividly," she panted, parrying a lunge. "This beats paperwork and court politics any day."

"Even with the imminent threat of being devoured?"

"Especially then," Elara grinned fiercely.

"Watch out!" Lila cried, as a Snarklebeast bigger than its brethren emerged, drooling with malicious intent.

"Ah, the grande finale," Ben sighed, feeling a strange surge of excitement. Adrenaline, fear, or perhaps the thrill of the unknown, he couldn't tell.

"Time to make a big beastie regret skipping breakfast," Roran declared, charging with a roar that would've made the mountains reconsider their stability.

"Ben, I don't know if we'll survive this," Elara confessed between strikes, "but there's no one else I'd rather have by my side."

"Likewise," Ben replied, heart hammering. "Let's show them that we're the nightmare lurking in the woods."

"Agreed," Elara nodded, and together they turned to face the onslaught, their laughter mingling with the roars of the Snarklebeasts.

It was absurd, it was terrifying, it was exhilarating. It was adventure – raw and untamed, like the land itself. And as they fought, united in purpose, Ben realized that this motley crew had become more than just allies. They were friends, bound by the kind of camaraderie that could only be forged in the heat of shared peril.

"Alright, team," Ben declared, slashing down another vine. "Let's carve a path out of this comedy of errors!"

"Right behind you, Captain Broody!" Lila cheered, as an arrow found its mark.

"Lead the way!" Elara echoed, her laughter ringing clear as Evergleam cleaved through shadow and snarl alike.

"Adventure waits for no one," Roran whooped, a Snarklebeast tumbling behind him. "But it sure does put up a fight!"

The afterglow of their recent skirmish still etched on their faces, Ben led the way, his boots crunching over a carpet of ancient bones that whispered secrets of old. The ruins rose before them like the skeletal remains of a long-dead titan, its hollowed eyes peering into their very souls.

"Would you look at this place?" Lila's voice echoed off the weathered stones, her eyes wide with childlike wonder. "It's like history had a party and forgot to clean up!"

"History doesn't throw parties, Lila," Roran muttered, adjusting the grip on his axe. "It throws wars."

"Then let's hope we're not the after-dinner entertainment," Elara chimed in, running her fingers along the cryptic engravings that danced across the ruin's surface.

"Speaking of dinner..." Ben began, but a sudden shift beneath his feet cut him short. The ground swallowed them whole as they plummeted downward, landing in a heap amidst a cloud of dust and curses.

"Next time," Ben grumbled, spitting out a mouthful of cobwebs, "I'm packing a cushion."

"Or a parachute!" Lila added with a snort.

"Quiet," Elara hissed. "We're not alone."

Their eyes adjusted to the darkness, revealing a chamber shrouded in mystery, lined with shelves teeming with scrolls and artifacts that hummed with ancient power.

"By the stars," Ben breathed, his fingers tracing the spine of a tome that seemed to vibrate under his touch. "These texts... they could change everything."

"Change is good," Lila piped up, poking suspiciously at a skull with two sets of teeth. "Unless it involves more teeth."

"Focus," Elara snapped, her eyes scanning the parchment spread before them. "This speaks of the Staff of Tomorrow. It's closer than we thought, and if the enemy..."

Her voice trailed off as realization dawned upon her, her gaze locking onto Ben's. "They're moving faster than us."

"Of course they are," Roran growled. "Evil never lingers over breakfast."

"Then we can't dawdle over jokes," Ben said, his tone sobering. "If they get their hands on the Staff—"

"End of the world, yada yada," Lila interjected. "We get it. Less reading, more raiding!"

"Agreed." Elara closed the scroll with a decisive snap. "We've got to beat them to it."

"Wait," Ben paused, a gnawing doubt nibbling at his resolve. "Are we ready for this? What if—"

"What if the sky falls?" Elara retorted, her hand finding his. "Then we'll just have to catch it, won't we?"

"Or at least break its fall with our heads," Roran quipped, shouldering his axe with a grin.

"Right," Ben affirmed, the weight of destiny pressing down on him like a leaden cloak. "For Oak Isle, for us, for the bloody sky—let's find that Staff."

"Before breakfast," Lila added helpfully, and together they stepped deeper into the shadowy heart of the ruins, where fate awaited with open jaws.

The air in the ancient ruins was thick with the scent of time-worn stone and a palpable sense of anticipation. As they ventured deeper, the flickering light from Roran's torch fell upon an unexpected figure—a creature both bizarre and wondrous. It was small, with emerald skin that shimmered like morning dew and eyes as wide and luminous as full moons.

"Whoa," Lila gasped, her hand inching towards her blade. "Is that a—"

"Keepling," the creature piped up before anyone could finish, its voice a melodic chirp. "Pleased to meet your acquaintance, I'm Twindle."

"Sounds like a snack," Roran mumbled, eyeing Twindle skeptically.

"Or a dance move," Ben added thoughtfully, his mind racing with the implications of this new ally. Could it be a trap? Yet something in Twindle's gaze beckoned trust.

"Neither!" Twindle huffed. "I am the guardian of these here corridors. And you lot look more turned around than a cyclone in a square dance."

"Speak for yourself," Elara retorted, but her stance softened. "We seek the Staff of Tomorrow."

"Ah, yep, that's a popular one lately," Twindle nodded sagely. "Follow me, but mind your noggin. This place is older than Roran's sense of humor."

"Hey!" Roran protested, but Twindle had already darted ahead, leading them through a labyrinth of passageways.

"Remember, red stones in the floor mean safety," Twindle called back. "Step on black, and you're in for a whack!"

"Got it. Red, good. Black, bad," Lila repeated to herself, though her eyes were on the lookout for anything that glittered and wasn't nailed down.

"Feels like we're stuck in some giant's game of checkers," Ben muttered under his breath, following the Keepling's instructions closely.

"More like chess. And I hate being a pawn," Elara whispered back, her hand gripping his for reassurance. Together, they navigated the treacherous path, their hearts hammering in unison.

As they progressed, the group encountered a massive door etched with runes that glowed faintly in the torchlight. Before it stood a pedestal with three levers, each adorned with a cryptic symbol.

"Fantastic," Lila groaned. "What is this, the entrance exam for wizard school?"

"Only if failure means getting squished," Roran said, pointing upwards where large, menacing spikes loomed on the ceiling.

"Think, people," Elara urged. "The symbols... They must correspond to the stories in the texts we found."

"Of course!" Ben exclaimed, his eyes lighting up. "See, the hawk represents cunning, the bear strength, and the fish—"

"Is dinner?" Roran interjected, earning an elbow nudge from Lila.

"Adaptability," Elara finished, ignoring the interruption. "We need all three to get through this."

"Right." Ben nodded, stepping forward. He grasped the lever with the hawk symbol, feeling the weight of centuries beneath his fingers. "On three?"

"Wait, hold on," Lila said, her brows knitting together. "Doesn't the story say the hawk flies highest at dawn? Maybe it's about timing!"

"Brilliant, Lila!" Ben praised, waiting for just a moment before pulling the lever. The door rumbled open, revealing the path onward.

"Would you look at that," Roran chuckled. "Brains and brawn."

"Mostly brains," Elara quipped, shooting him a playful smirk.

"Let's not celebrate yet," Ben cautioned, his thoughts swirling with possibilities. What other challenges lay ahead? And would their newfound knowledge prove enough?

"Staff of Tomorrow, here we come," Twindle cheered, hopping excitedly. "Told ya I was helpful!"

"Indeed," Ben agreed, a grin spreading across his face despite the tension. "Lead the way, Twindle."

"Next time, we bring a Keepling-sized hamster wheel," Roran suggested, following the others into the newly-revealed passageway.

"Or a dictionary," Lila added with a wink. "For when he starts making up words again."

"Ha-ha," Ben said dryly, his thoughts already on the next puzzle. But deep down, he couldn't deny the thrill of the adventure, the camaraderie among them, and the hope that, against all odds, they might actually win this madcap race.

The walls of the hidden sanctuary loomed before them, an ancient monolith whispering secrets into the ears of time. Vines clung to the stone like desperate lovers, and the air hummed with a melody of forgotten magic. Ben's heart thumped against his ribcage—this was it, the cradle of their hopes and fears.

"Okay," he huffed, squinting at the ominous structure. "We go in, we get the Staff, we get out. Piece of cake."

"Piece of cake?" Elara arched an eyebrow, her armor glinting in the dappled light that filtered through the canopy. "Ben, that 'piece of cake' looks like it could hide a thousand ways to die."

"Only a thousand?" Roran quipped, but his usual bravado waned under the weight of the sanctuary's silent judgement.

"More like a treacherous tiramisu," Lila muttered, eyeing the overgrown entrance warily.

"Enough with the dessert metaphors!" Ben snapped, feeling the gravity of their quest press down on him. "Look, I know it's risky, but we've come too far to back down now."

"Risky is an understatement," Elara countered, crossing her arms. "You're not thinking straight. We should wait, observe—"

"Wait? The enemy won't be taking a tea break, Elara!" Ben's voice rose, echoing off the stones. "Every second we waste, they get closer to the Staff!"

"Your impatience could lead us into a trap," she shot back, her eyes blazing with a fire that matched his own. "We need strategy, not recklessness."

"Guys, guys!" Twindle interjected, hopping between them, his small form barely reaching their knees. "Maybe you both have... um, goodish points?"

"Goodish isn't a word, Twindle," Ben grunted, but he couldn't help a half-smile at the creature's attempt to mediate.

"Neither is cakemisu, but here we are," Lila said, earning a snort from Roran.

"Enough!" Ben bellowed, more loudly than he intended. Silence fell over the group, and for a moment, all that remained was the wind's haunting lullaby.

"Sorry," Ben sighed, running a hand through his hair. "I just... I'm scared, okay? If we fail..."

"We won't," Elara said softly, the anger fading from her voice. "But we have to be smart about this. Together."

"Fine," Ben conceded. "Together."

Cautiously, they approached the sanctuary's entrance, the air growing colder as if welcoming them into the embrace of the abyss. They slipped inside, shadows clinging to their every step.

"Ominous much?" Lila whispered, her voice bouncing around the chamber.

"Shh!" Roran hissed as something stirred in the darkness ahead.

From the shadows, figures emerged, eyes gleaming with malice. Soldiers of the enemy, their armor etched with curses and lined with the bones of the fallen.

"Looks like the welcome committee's here," Ben joked weakly, drawing his sword with a metallic ring.

"Didn't even bring a fruit basket," Roran added, readying his axe.

"Guess we're not getting past without a fight," Elara stated, the blade in her hand reflecting her resolve.

"Remember, hit them with your pointy end," Lila reminded them, drawing her own weapon—an elegant rapier that had seen its share of battles.

"Pointy end, got it," Ben replied, rolling his eyes. He glanced at his friends, their faces set in grim determination. "Let's show these boneheads why they should've stayed buried."

"Staff of Tomorrow," Elara breathed, her eyes locked on the unseen prize, "here we come."

"Or the death of today," Lila added cheerfully.

"Could do without the pessimism," Ben said, but there was no time for further banter as the enemy charged.

"Bring it on, skelebrutes!" Roran roared, swinging his axe with reckless abandon.

"Reckless" might have been Ben's middle name, but right now, he was grateful for Roran's version of it. Each member of their mismatched family fought with a fervor born of desperation and hope—a dangerous cocktail that fueled their dance with death. And as steel clashed against cursed bone, Ben knew one thing for certain: they'd either leave with the Staff of Tomorrow or not at all.

"Ha! Missed me by a hair, you bumbling bag of bones!" Ben taunted as he ducked under a wild swing from one of the skeletal warriors. With a flourish, he drove his sword into its ribcage, the clatter of bones like a macabre xylophone solo accompanying their deadly waltz.

"Ben, less talking, more stabbing!" Elara shouted, slicing through another adversary with precision that would've made a surgeon envious. "We don't have all eternity—just them!"

"Details, details," Ben shot back, his heart pounding a rhythm akin to a drumbeat in a bard's most raucous tune. He could feel the weight of destiny pressing down on them, and though he'd never admit it aloud, doubt nibbled at the edges of his bravado.

"Hey, ugly!" Lila called out, her rapier a silver streak as she parried and thrust. "You're so old, when you were young, the Dead Sea was just getting sick!"

"Comedy and carnage, Lila? You're multitasking!" Roran grunted, cleaving a skeleton in twain, bone fragments flying like grotesque confetti.

"Got to keep the morale up," she quipped, punctuating her jest with a swift riposte that sent a skull spinning.

"Rally around the Staff!" Ben yelled, spotting the artifact atop an altar. Its crystalline structure pulsed with an inner light, a beacon amongst the chaos. He charged forward, sidestepping a swipe and elbowing a skeleton in its hollow chest, sending it crashing into its companions.

"Cover me!" Elara commanded, dashing behind Ben to secure the staff. Their eyes met for a moment, a silent understanding passing between them—for all their disagreements, they were united in purpose.

"Got it!" she exclaimed, snatching the Staff of Tomorrow, its power thrumming through her veins.

"Time to leg it!" Roran announced, as if they needed the reminder. They turned as one, the enemy's relentless horde like a tidal wave of malice at their heels.

"Left corridor, I saw a way out!" Lila directed, her memory a lifeline in the labyrinthine sanctuary.

"Brilliant, let's not get trapped in a dead end with the dead!" Ben quipped, his humor a thin veneer over the clawing fear of capture—or worse.

"Careful, the floor looks—" Elara began, but her warning came too late as Ben's foot found a loose tile, triggering a spray of darts from the walls.

"Trap designer must be a hit at parties," Ben grumbled, weaving through the deadly projectiles with the grace of a drunken pixie.

They dashed through twisting corridors, the echoes of their pursuers a grim chorus urging them forward. Every shadow seemed alive, every whisper of wind a threat. The weight of history pressed upon them, the forgotten stories of this place yearning for a voice.

"Almost there... can see the exit!" Elara panted, her determination a flame refusing to be snuffed out.

"Right behind you," Ben assured, though his lungs burned with the effort.

"Less encouraging, more running!" Roran bellowed from the rear, his axe now a makeshift shield warding off the relentless assault.

"Sunlight!" Lila cried out as they burst forth from the dank confines of the sanctuary into the blinding embrace of day.

"Keep moving!" Elara urged, clutching the Staff tightly. "They won't stop until we're either out of reach or dead!"

"Opting for out of reach, personally!" Ben added, casting a glance over his shoulder to see the skeletal army spilling out into the daylight, their pursuit undeterred by the transition from shadow to sun.

"Into the woods!" Lila directed, pointing to the dense forest that promised cover—and hopefully, safety.

"Never a dull moment with you lot," Ben thought, his legs pumping, his mind racing, and his heart daring to hope that maybe, just maybe, they'd live to joke about this day.

The forest loomed like a wall of gnarled, grinning sentinels, their leafy arms beckoning the exhausted adventurers into a verdant maze. Branches clawed and leaves whispered as Ben led the charge, his hair plastered to his forehead in a most unflattering manner.

"Left or right?" Roran huffed, his axe now an unwelcome companion whose weight he could no longer romanticize.

"Whichever way the skeletons aren't!" Lila retorted, ducking as a low-hanging branch seemed to take a swipe at her.

"Great strategy," Ben said, rolling his eyes skyward. "Let's just ask them nicely to point us in the direction of 'Not Here.'"

"Ben, focus!" Elara snapped, her grip on the Staff of Tomorrow so tight it seemed to glow with indignation. "We need to—"

Her words were cut off by a thunderous crack overhead. A massive tree, ancient and indignant at being disturbed, chose that moment to shed one of its limbs. The bough descended like the sword of an angry deity, aiming straight for them.

"Move!" Ben shouted, diving to the side, his thoughts a jumbled mess of 'not today, death!' and 'did I leave the oven on?'

There was a cacophony of splintering wood and the rush of air as the limb crashed where they had been seconds earlier. They scrambled to their feet, the noise undoubtedly drawing their pursuers closer.

"Nothing like a deadly game of timber to raise the spirits," Ben quipped, brushing dirt from his clothes while casting a wary glance behind.

"Your humor is going to be the death of us," Elara said through gritted teeth.

"Better my humor than those bone-janglers!"

"Quiet!" Roran growled. "I hear something..."

They froze, the only sounds their ragged breaths and the distant, relentless rattling of the skeletal horde. Then, from deeper within the woods, a melodic hum floated on the wind—a tune both haunting and somehow... taunting?

"Is that... singing?" Lila asked, bafflement clear in her voice.

"Probably just the wind," Ben replied, though his gut knotted with the suspicion that winds didn't usually carry a tune unless they were whistling through skulls.

"Wind doesn't sound that off-key," Elara muttered, squinting into the dark heart of the forest.

"Whatever it is, it's better than what's behind us," Ben reasoned, gesturing for them to press on.

"Into the creepy singing forest it is, then," Lila sighed, stepping over the fallen limb with an athlete's grace.

"Could be a trap," Elara warned.

"Could be an ally," Ben countered, ever the optimist. "Besides, we've handled traps before."

"Handled, nearly died to—semantics," Roran added helpfully.

They moved deeper into the forest, the eerie song growing louder. Ben couldn't shake the feeling that each note was laced with a silent, mocking laughter—as if the very trees knew secrets they could not fathom.

"Are we seriously following a sinister lullaby?" Lila asked, her voice barely above a whisper.

"Got any better ideas? I'm all ears—literally, this foliage has done something unspeakable to my hair," Ben complained.

"Shh!" Elara hissed.

They came to an abrupt halt as the forest opened up into a clearing bathed in an ethereal light. And there, in the center, stood a figure cloaked in shadows, its presence as commanding as it was chilling. The humming ceased abruptly, replaced by the suspenseful silence of anticipation.

"Welcome," the figure spoke, its voice a blend of silk and steel. "You are late."

"Late for what?" Ben blurted out, his heart hammering against his ribs as he clutched a stitch in his side.

"Late for the end... or perhaps, the beginning," the figure answered, and with a flourish of its cloak, vanished into the nothingness from whence it came.

"Brilliant," Ben gasped, trying to catch his breath and make sense of the sight. "Now we've got vanishing welcoming committees."

"Who was that?" Lila asked, wide-eyed.

"New friend? Old enemy? Enthusiastic party planner?" Ben suggested, but uncertainty gnawed at him. Their journey had taken a turn into the surreal, and the weight of the Staff in Elara's hands felt suddenly heavier, fraught with unknown consequence.

"Doesn't matter," Elara stated, resolve hardening her features. "We have to keep moving."

"Agreed," Roran nodded, peering back the way they'd come. "They're close."

"Anyone else feel like we're part of some grand cosmic joke?" Ben mused aloud, but inside, the flicker of fear was kindling into a flame.

"Only every second of the day," Lila replied with a wry smile.

"Then let's not disappoint our audience," Ben said, and with a nod from Elara, they stepped forward into the clearing and beyond, toward an uncertain destiny that lay shrouded in the forest's embrace.

"Remember, folks," Ben added, as the first arrow whistled past his ear from the darkness ahead, "the trick is to laugh in the face of danger—right before you run from it."

"Running seems good!" Elara agreed, and they sprinted across the clearing, the echo of pursuit and the thrill of the unknown propelling them onward as the chapter closed with their fate hanging in the balance, leaving the reader to wonder: What happens next?

Ben's boots sank into the spongy earth of the Forest of Shadows, each step squelching as if the ground itself was reluctant to release them. Lila, ever light on her feet, seemed to dance beside him, her cloak fluttering like a wayward shadow.

"Remind me again why the Descendant of Eclipse is hiding in a forest that feels like walking through a swamp?" Ben grumbled, trying to shake off a clinging vine that had taken a particular liking to his ankle.

"Because," Lila said with a grin that was all mischief, "even ancient beings of immense power enjoy a good game of hide and seek. And this—" she twirled, arms outstretched, "—is their preferred playground."

"Fantastic," he said dryly, finally freeing himself from the tenacious plant life. "Next time, let's seek someone who enjoys sunbathing on a beach instead."

"Where's the fun in that?" Lila laughed, hopping over a gnarled root that Ben was certain had not been there a second ago.

"Fun is not the term I'd use for this excursion," Ben muttered, but he couldn't help a smile creeping onto his lips. If the truth were told, he relished the thrill of adventure almost as much as she did.

"Admit it, you love the mud," Lila teased, her eyes twinkling like two stars caught in the twilight canopy above.

"Only when it's in a wrestling pit, and I'm winning," Ben retorted, ducking under a low-hanging branch that seemed to have the malevolent intent of decapitating him.

"Keep dreaming, Ben. In your case, the mud would be pinning you down within seconds," she said with a playful nudge that sent him stumbling into a suspiciously giggling bush.

"Ah, so the mighty warrior reveals her strategy: distract with banter, then push into carnivorous foliage. Devious."

"Only the best for you," Lila replied, her laughter echoing through the trees.

As they journeyed deeper into the heart of darkness, the air grew thicker, and the sense of foreboding crept up Ben's spine like ivy. He shook it off, focusing on the here and now, on the bond forming between them, solid and real as the ground beneath their feet.

"Seriously though," Ben said, casting a glance at the ethereal gloom around them, "do you think the Descendant will just... pop out and say hello?"

"Who knows? They might throw us a 'welcome' party." Lila made air quotes with her fingers before continuing. "With ghostly streamers and phantom cupcakes."

"Phantom cupcakes?" Ben echoed, skepticism lacing his tone. "Are those anything like invisible sandwiches? Because I'm starving, and I'll gladly take either at this point."

"Trust me, the only thing you'll be eating here are your words," she quipped, dodging another playful swipe from Ben.

"Ha, ha," he deadpanned, though inwardly, Ben felt an unexpected warmth at their exchange. The camaraderie was new but undeniable, like finding a piece of a puzzle he hadn't known was missing.

"Careful, my friend," Lila said, her voice suddenly taking on a serious note as they approached a part of the forest where the shadows deepened, and even the air seemed hesitant to enter. "The Forest of Shadows is full of tricks and treats. It's going to take more than our wits to find the Descendant."

"Good thing we've got your charm to fall back on then," Ben shot back, only half-joking.

"Charm, wit, and your brawn. We're practically unstoppable," she agreed with a confident nod.

"Unstoppable," Ben repeated, allowing the word to roll off his tongue like a spell, fortifying him against the encroaching darkness. With a shared look of determination, they ventured forward, side by side, into the unknown, their laughter the only light in the enveloping dark.

The gnarled roots of an ancient oak provided a temporary respite for Ben and Lila, their faces speckled with the dappling light that filtered through the dense canopy overhead. They sat, backs against the rough bark, as if it were the only thing anchoring them to reality in the ever-twisting Forest of Shadows.

"Ever wonder if the trees are laughing at us?" Ben mused aloud, tearing off a chunk of his meager rations, eyes tracing the intricate dance of sunlight and shadow.

"Only when you speak," Lila retorted with a smirk, her gaze not leaving the small, flickering fire they'd managed to coax to life between them. "But honestly? I'm more worried about what's hiding in the dark."

"Ah, the insecurities of the mighty Lila," Ben said, voice laden with mock surprise as he chewed thoughtfully. "What could possibly make your heart quiver in such hallowed grounds?"

"Same as you, I suppose," she replied, her tone losing its playful edge. "Fear of failure. Of not being strong enough to protect those I care about..." Her words hung between them, a confessional whispered to the wind.

Ben felt a pang of something akin to guilt. "I worry that my sword arm won't be quick enough," he confessed, matching her vulnerability. "That my jokes will one day fall flat."

"Perish the thought," Lila chuckled, though the twinkle in her eyes was tinged with compassion. "We're quite the pair, aren't we? A would-be knight afraid of being unfunny, and a sorceress who fears the dark."

"Yet here we sit, jesting in the jaws of jeopardy," Ben said, his lips curving into a smile that didn't quite reach his eyes.

"Jesting is our shield, Ben," Lila said, resting her hand momentarily atop his. "And perhaps... it's also our sword."

Their reprieve was short-lived, however, as the path forward soon beckoned—a treacherous mountain pass that snaked through the heart of the looming peaks like the spine of some slumbering dragon.

"Looks like we've got quite the climb," Lila observed, squinting up at the jagged rocks that loomed like silent sentinels above them.

"Nothing like a morning scramble to get the blood pumping," Ben quipped, though his mind raced with potential perils hidden amongst the crags.

As they ascended, each foothold was a precarious dance with gravity, each handhold a fleeting promise of safety. The mountain seemed to groan beneath their weight, a grudging host to their unwelcome intrusion.

"Watch out for—" Lila began, just as a loose stone betrayed Ben's grasp, sending him sliding down a few heart-stopping inches before he regained his balance.

"Loose rocks?" he finished for her, grinning sheepishly. "You might have mentioned those sooner."

"Consider it payback for every bad pun you've inflicted upon me," she retorted, but her concern was evident in the way her eyes tracked his every move thereafter.

Their ascent was further complicated by the sudden appearance of goblins—small, wiry creatures with eyes like coal and grins full of malice. They emerged from crevices and shadows, brandishing tiny, wicked blades and chittering in a language that sounded suspiciously like insults.

"Seems we've wandered into a goblin gala," Ben said, drawing his sword with a flourish that bordered on the dramatic.

"Crashers, no less," Lila added, her fingers weaving patterns in the air, tendrils of magic ready to spring forth.

"Shall we dance?" Ben asked, lunging forward to parry a swipe from the nearest goblin.

"Thought you'd never ask," Lila replied, releasing a burst of energy that sent a ripple of force through the ranks of their pint-sized adversaries.

Together, they whirled and fought, a symphony of steel and sorcery against the discordant cacophony of goblin shrieks. It was chaos dressed in the guise of a ballroom blitz, punctuated by Ben's irreverent commentary and Lila's incandescent spells.

"Any chance these guys know the two-step?" Ben joked, ducking as a goblin sailed overhead, courtesy of Lila's telekinetic shove.

"More likely to step on your toes," Lila called back, dispatching another with a well-placed bolt of lightning.

Eventually, the goblins retreated, leaving behind only the echo of their retreat and the heavy breaths of two weary travelers. Ben and Lila shared a look—one that spoke of battles endured and friendship forged in the flicker of forge-forged steel and flame-wrought magic.

"Next time," Ben panted, "let's take the scenic route."

"Agreed," Lila replied, though they both knew their journey held no promise of ease. But for now, they pressed forward, side by side, their laughter once again the torch that lit their way.

The Forest of Shadows was a wretched hive of twisted trees and trickster winds, where the sunlight filtered through the canopy in mocking patterns, as if to highlight the dangers that lurked in every shadow. Lila's boots squelched in the mossy undergrowth while Ben scythed away brambles with a blade that glinted like a sliver of captured moonlight.

"Ever get the feeling the forest is laughing at us?" Lila asked, flicking a violet slug from her shoulder with a grimace.

"Only when you talk," Ben quipped, but his smile didn't quite reach his eyes. It was clear; they were both on edge, the weight of their quest heavy on their shoulders.

"Ben, wait." Lila's hand shot out, seizing his arm. "I need to say something."

He paused, turning back to face her, brow arched inquisitively. She took a deep breath, the words tumbling out in a rush. "Back there, with those goblins... I've never seen anyone fight like that. You move like a storybook hero, only... real. It's like you're dancing with danger."

A rosy hue bloomed across Ben's cheeks, spreading to the tips of his ears. "Dancing, huh? I guess that makes you my partner then. Though I must admit, your version of 'leading' involves a lot more lightning bolts."

Lila chuckled, but her eyes stayed locked on his, earnest and shining. "I'm serious, Ben. Your courage... it's kind of amazing."

"Comes with the territory," he said, rubbing the back of his neck, clearly uncomfortable with the praise. "Let's keep moving. This forest isn't getting any friendlier."

Progress was slow, the terrain determined to hinder them at every step. Suddenly, the earth gave way beneath their feet. They tumbled downward, a blur of limbs and startled yelps, before landing in a heap on the damp floor of a hidden cave.

"Great," Ben groaned, disentangling himself from Lila. "Trapped in a cave. There's a new experience for the memoirs."

"Could be worse," Lila mused, trying to sound optimistic as she conjured a small orb of light. "We could be trapped in a cave with goblins."

"Thanks for not jinxing us," Ben said, offering her a hand up. They scanned their surroundings, the orb casting long shadows against the walls.

"Looks like we have two options," Lila pointed out. "That narrow crevice there or the tunnel with the ominous breeze."

"Ominous breeze has a certain allure, don't you think?" Ben's eyes twinkled mischievously.

"Only to a madman," Lila retorted, though she couldn't suppress a grin.

"Madman it is, then," Ben declared. He approached the tunnel, a hand trailing along the wall. "Besides, what's life without a bit of—"

"Ben, don't say adventure. That's how people end up cursed, or worse, in epic ballads."

"Was going to say a stiff breeze, actually," he said, deadpan.

"Sure you were."

They edged forward, Ben leading the way with exaggerated caution, each footstep a pantomime of stealth. Lila followed, her chuckles punctuating the silence.

"Stop, stop!" she gasped between laughs. "If we die here, I don't want my ghost still laughing at your ridiculous—"

"Shh," Ben interrupted, suddenly serious. "Do you hear that?"

"Please don't say goblin war drums."

"No... it sounds like... running water?"

"Water means an exit," Lila said, hope infusing her words.

"Or an underground river ready to sweep us off our feet. Not quite the dance I had in mind." Despite his words, Ben's lips curled into a hopeful smile.

"Lead the way, O fearless dancer," Lila said, nudging him forward with a teasing smirk.

"Only because you asked so nicely," he replied, stepping toward the sound with renewed determination.

Together, they navigated the darkness, the cave's secrets unfolding before them, their laughter and jests echoing off the ancient stone—a duet of bravery and banter.

The cave's breath was cool and moist, a whisper of mist that danced upon their skin as they inched closer to the sound of rushing water. Ben, with his torch held high, squinted into the darkness, while Lila, her hand bracing against the slick cave wall, kept a watchful eye on their rear. The light flickered, casting erratic shadows that cavorted across the uneven ground.

"Careful," Ben muttered, his voice barely above the water's din. "Floor's as treacherous as a politician's promise."

"Ah, but unlike a politician, the cave can't pretend it didn't try to trip you," Lila quipped, her eyes sparkling with mirth even in the dim light.

Their laughter mingled with the subterranean echoes, a harmony of delight that seemed out of place in the shadowy depths. Side by side, they navigated the narrowing path, their shoulders brushing more frequently now.

"Watch your step, there's a—"

"Got it!" Lila interjected, her foot slipping nevertheless, sending a shower of pebbles skittering into the abyss.

Instinctively, Ben reached out, his hand encircling her arm, steadying her. Their gazes locked, a moment suspended in time, where the cascade of the waterfall seemed to fade into silence. His thumb brushed against her skin—a touch feather-light, yet charged with an unspoken connection. The warmth of his hand seeped through the fabric of her sleeve, igniting a trail of goosebumps.

"Thanks," she murmured, her voice swallowed by the intimate proximity of their faces.

"Anytime," he replied, the corners of his mouth hitching up in an almost shy smile.

As they regained their footing, the cave opened up, revealing a breathtaking sight that stole the very air from their lungs. A waterfall cascaded down in a veil of liquid silver, moonbeams filtering through a crevice above to dance upon the surface. It was as if the stars themselves had descended to frolic in this hidden sanctum.

"By the beard of the Ancient Dwarf King," Ben exclaimed, "that's... that's actually beautiful."

"Looks like the universe took a paintbrush to the night sky and just... went wild," Lila said, her eyes wide with wonder.

They settled on a moss-covered boulder, side by side, their legs dangling over the edge. The spray from the waterfall kissed their faces, a refreshing contrast to the musty cave air they'd grown accustomed to.

"Never thought I'd find something like this here," Lila confessed, her gaze fixed on the undulating water.

"Oak Isle keeps its secrets well," Ben said, leaning back on his hands, his face turned upward to where the moonlight played hide and seek with the cavern's stalactites. "But sometimes, it shares them with those who wander long enough."

"Are we still wanderers if our feet know the taste of every stone?" she pondered aloud, tilting her head to catch his eye.

"More like connoisseurs of chaos," Ben chuckled, meeting her gaze. "Someday, we'll look back at this madness and laugh."

"Or write a strongly worded complaint to the universe for excessive plot twists," she added, grinning.

"Wouldn't be our story without them," he replied with a wink.

In the serene glow of the grotto, their laughter rose up to the heavens, declaring their resilience—a pair of hearts defiant in the face of destiny's labyrinthine design.

The night descended upon Oak Isle like a black velvet cloak draped over the world, embroidered with a menagerie of glinting stars. Ben and Lila, their spirits buoyed by the beauty they'd witnessed in the grotto, ventured further into the unknown, where the shadows stretched long and twisted like gnarled fingers beckoning them deeper into the dark.

"Ben," Lila whispered, her voice quivering like a violin string in the wind, "Do you ever get the feeling we're not alone?"

"Only every second since we stepped foot in this Forest of Overly Dramatic Entrances," he muttered, peering into the gloom. His hand rested on the hilt of his sword—a blade that had seen more action than a bard's lute at a tavern sing-along.

"Ah, good. It's not just my stomach then," she said, patting her belly as if to calm an unruly pet within. "It keeps doing flips, and I don't think it's from your cooking."

"Hey! My stew has been described as 'unexpectedly survivable,'" he retorted, puffing out his chest.

"By whom? A troll with no taste buds?" Her laughter tinkled in the darkness, a sound so pure it could make an ogre blush.

"Ha ha," Ben mocked, rolling his eyes, but his lips curled into a smile. He couldn't help but bask in the warmth of her mirth—even in the midst of peril, she was a torch in the fog.

Their playful banter was cut short by a rustling noise that erupted from the underbrush. Lila's hand flew to her mouth, stifling a gasp, as a beast sprung forth—a creature with more teeth than the Royal Tax Code had loopholes.

"Look out!" Ben roared, pushing Lila behind him with a strength borne of sudden adrenaline and perhaps one too many heroic ballads. The beast lunged, jaws snapping with the enthusiasm of a tax collector scenting coin, but Ben's blade sang its deadly song, cleaving the air between them.

"Back, ye fanged accountant!" he bellowed, parrying with a flourish that would've made a dramatist swoon. The creature recoiled, apparently reconsidering its dietary choices as it retreated into the brush, leaving behind nothing but the echo of its growls and the sharp scent of thwarted hunger.

"Your heroics are showing," Lila said, her voice soft but edged with awe as she touched his arm, her fingers lingering just a moment longer than necessary.

"Can't have anything happen to my favorite comedic relief," he quipped, though his heart hammered like a war drum in his chest.

"Right, because you'd be lost without someone to insult your cooking," she replied, batting her eyelashes exaggeratedly. But her eyes held a depth of gratitude that far surpassed her jests.

"Exactly," he said, feeling a warmth spread through him that had nothing to do with the danger they'd just faced. It was a different kind of peril altogether—the sort that came with the intertwining of souls.

They continued onward, the forest finally opening up to reveal a clearing bathed in the ethereal glow of moonlight. The sky above was an ocean of darkness dotted with celestial pearls, and the air was so crisp it felt as though one could shatter it with a whisper.

"Would you look at that," Lila breathed, her gaze locked onto the heavens above. She seemed to drink in the sight, as if it were nourishment for her very being.

"Stars... countless stories waiting to be told," Ben murmured, his own eyes fixed on the celestial tapestry. And there, beneath the watchful eyes of the universe, something shifted—a tectonic movement of the heart.

"Ben," she said, turning toward him, her expression illuminated by the silver luminescence, "I—"

"Shh," he interrupted, closing the distance between them with a few measured steps. "Some things don't need words."

Her breath caught as he cupped her face gently, his thumbs tracing the outline of her cheeks with a tenderness that belied his warrior's hands. Then, in a moment as fleeting and eternal as a shooting star, their lips met, igniting a fire that no darkness could extinguish.

The kiss was a clash of laughter and longing, a melding of spirits that danced together in the light of a thousand distant suns. Ben's mind raced with thoughts louder than any battle cry—of how right it felt, how every adventure paled in comparison to the journey of her lips against his.

"Ben," she whispered against his mouth, her words a caress that stoked the flames higher.

"Lila," he replied, voice thick with emotion, "Whatever comes next, we face it together."

"Like a pair of valiant idiots."

"Exactly." And the world fell away, leaving only two hearts beating as one beneath the grand tapestry of the stars.

The dawn chorus was in full swing as the first hints of sunlight began to nudge the darkness aside. A symphony of chirps and tweets crescendoed around the hidden grove where Ben and Lila lay entwined, a tangle of limbs beneath the canopy of whispering leaves. The previous night's grand celestial display had faded to memory, but the magic it had woven between them lingered like the sweet scent of the morning dew.

"Ben... your arm is dead," Lila mumbled, her voice a raspy lullaby against his chest.

"Ah, the noble sacrifice of the romantic embrace," Ben replied with mock solemnity, wiggling his fingers to bring life back into his limb. "A small price to pay for such unparalleled comfort."

"Unparalleled discomfort, you mean," she retorted playfully, extricating herself from his hold with exaggerated care. "I think I have the imprint of your belt buckle on my cheek."

"Perhaps we should consider a softer means of protection then," he quipped, sitting up and stretching his arms with exaggerated gusto. "Feather-stuffed armor, for instance."

"Only if you're ready to be plucked by every passing hawk," she teased, standing and brushing off remnants of leaves and moss. "Though, I suppose it would add a new meaning to 'flying colors.'"

"Ha! Always ready with a quip, aren't you, Lila?" Ben chuckled, his eyes tracing the curve of her smile. He admired her quick wit as much as her swift blade—both were sharp and unyielding.

"Comes with the territory of being enchanting," she said, offering him a hand to help him up. "Come on, we've dallied enough. The Descendant of Eclipse won't wait forever."

"Right," Ben agreed, clasping her hand and allowing the warmth of her touch to permeate his being. "No rest for the wicked or the lovestruck."

"Or those cursed with both," Lila added, her grin as bright as the dawning day.

"Indeed." Ben gazed upon her, his heart swelling with a newfound resolve. Their union had forged an alliance stronger than any steel, a bond that would fuel their determination to fulfill their quest. "We move forward together, my valiant shield maiden."

"Shield maiden? Oh, please." Lila rolled her eyes. "If anything, I'm saving your hide more often."

"True," he conceded with a laugh. "My daring damsel in defense."

"Much better." She nodded approvingly, leading the way as they packed their scant belongings and prepared to depart. "Now, let's see about escaping this Forest of Shadows before it decides we make a good permanent addition to its décor."

"Agreed," Ben said, following her lead. His thoughts danced a precarious jig between anticipation for the challenges ahead and the echo of last night's passion. "Though, I must say, I wouldn't mind being stuck with you."

"Flatterer," she tossed over her shoulder, her laughter mingling with the sounds of the waking forest.

"Only stating facts," he called back, the lightness in his tone belying the depth of his emotion.

As they stepped out into the filtered light, the forest seemed less menacing, the path ahead less daunting. Together they would face whatever trials awaited, their love a beacon guiding them through the darkest depths of Oak Isle. For now, the adventure continued, and with each other, they were ready for anything—even if it meant battling goblins with feathered armor.

The ground trembled beneath them as the formidable enemy emerged from the tainted mists of the Forest of Shadows—a gargantuan troll with tusks like the bowsprits of a sunken ship, and a hide so thick it seemed woven from despair itself. Ben, his heart drumming a battle-hymn in his chest, flashed Lila a grin that was equal parts foolhardy courage and unspoken promise.

"Remember when you said you saved my hide more often?" he quipped, unsheathing his sword with a flourish that caught the dappled sunlight. "Wouldn't happen to be up for an encore, would you?"

"Only if you keep up your end of the duet," Lila retorted, twirling her twin daggers with a showman's flair. Her eyes sparkled with the thrill of the impending clash. "Let's make this a performance to remember."

Their banter hung in the air, a momentary shield against the overwhelming might that lumbered towards them. Ben felt a surge of love for this fierce woman beside him, even as he braced for impact. Together, they charged, their feet pounding the earth in rhythm with their racing pulses.

"Left flank, darling!" Lila called out, her voice lilting above the roar of the troll.

"Already there!" he shouted back, darting to position himself. His sword met the calloused skin of the beast, a laughable scratch against a mountainous foe. But it was a distraction, one that allowed

Lila the precious seconds she needed to find a crevice in the creature's armor.

"Your turn!" Ben hollered, rolling away from a massive fist that cratered the ground where he'd stood mere moments ago.

"Watch and learn!" Lila's voice was a melody of determination as she vaulted onto the troll's back, her daggers finding purchase in the supple flesh behind its gnarled ear.

Ben could only marvel at her grace under pressure, her movements a dance of death designed for an audience of one. He knew then, with a certainty that ran deeper than the roots of the Forest of Shadows, that their bond was unbreakable. Love had forged them stronger, together they were unstoppable.

"Fall, you great brute!" Lila cried triumphantly, her blades singing through sinew and bone.

With a shuddering groan that seemed to echo the sorrow of the forest, the troll collapsed, its monumental frame shivering the earth. Ben rushed to Lila's side, helping her down from the fallen behemoth. Their hands clasped, slick with the proof of their victory, and in that clasp was a language of trust that words could never capture.

"Quite the duet we make," Ben said, his breathless laughter mingling with hers.

"Indeed," Lila agreed, wiping a smear of troll blood from her cheek with a thumb. "I daresay the bards will clamor to sing of our exploits."

"Or run screaming from the terror of our tale," he added, the absurdity of their situation sparking another bout of laughter between them.

As they turned to face each other, the world around them faded—an island of two hearts beating as one amidst a sea of shadow. Their shared victory bound them closer still, not just in triumph over a monstrous adversary, but in the unspoken depth of feeling that thrummed between them. It was a silent anthem of unity that promised no darkness, no enemy, no fate could ever rend them asunder.

"Shall we continue, my valiant shield maiden?" Ben asked, his tone teasing yet tender.

"Lead on, my daring damsel in defense," Lila replied, her smile brighter than any treasure they might find at journey's end.

And with a shared nod, they stepped forward, their laughter echoing through the once-ominous trees, a beacon of light in the Forest of Shadows.

The air hung heavy with the scent of victory—a curious blend of singed monster hide and the invigorating freshness of new life. Beneath a canopy woven from the twisted limbs of ancient trees, Ben and Lila found themselves in a small clearing, illuminated by the ethereal glow of fireflies engaged in their nightly dance. The forest, once a cacophony of danger, now seemed to be holding its breath, listening for the whispers of triumph that clung to our heroes like the finest silken cloak.

"Ah, Lila," Ben sighed dramatically, sprawling onto a moss-covered boulder, "we've bested beasts most foul, scaled cliffs unclimbable, and yet here we are, merely grappling with our own grandeur."

"Grapple away," Lila quipped as she joined him on the stone, her armor clinking merrily. "But if your 'grandeur' expands any further, we'll need a bigger rock."

Their laughter mingled with the rustling leaves and the distant hoots of an owl who clearly had no appreciation for comedic timing. In the aftermath of battle, their spirits soared higher than the treetops, unburdened by the weight of what was and what might never be again.

"Ben, my dear delusional knight," Lila began, her eyes twinkling like stars caught in a net of mirth, "promise me something."

"Anything," he declared, puffing out his chest in mock solemnity. "For you, I'd wrestle a dragon wearing nothing but a smile."

"Let's save that spectacle for a day lacking in entertainment," she said, her smile softening into something genuine and warm. "Promise me that no matter the peril, the ridiculousness of our quest, or the inevitability of goblin pranks, we will always find a moment like this... together."

Ben's heart drummed a playful rhythm, one that echoed her sentiment with every beat. "I vow it," he proclaimed. "By the power vested in me by absolutely no one at all, I swear to stand by your side through curses, through chaos, and—should fate be so cruel—through another round of those blasted enchanted riddles."

"Good," Lila nodded, her gaze locking onto his with an intensity that could melt diamond—or at least make it really uncomfortable. "Because, Ben, without your unwavering presence, who would I have to ridicule for being overly dramatic?"

"Ah, but who would exaggerate your modest achievements into the legends they deserve to become?" he countered, waggling a finger adorned with a ring that had once belonged to a particularly fashionable troll.

"Fair point," she conceded, leaning in closer until the heat of their shared laughter warmed the space between them. "It appears we're stuck with each other, then, for better or worse."

"Mostly better, I'd wager," Ben murmured, the corners of his eyes crinkling with delight. "Though I must admit, the thought of enduring your terrible navigation skills for eternity does give me pause."

"Terrible navigation? How dare you, sir!" Lila gasped, though the sparkle in her eyes betrayed her feigned outrage. "I'll have you know I've led us exactly where we intended to go... eventually."

"Eventually is the best kind of venture," Ben agreed, his heart swelling with a fondness that transcended the folly of their banter.

In that quiet moment, surrounded by the beauty of Oak Isle and the lingering echoes of their laughter, they made a silent pledge to each other. They would forge ahead, with hope as their compass and their bond as their beacon. No challenge too great, no joke too small, for together they were more than mere adventurers—they were a force to be reckoned with, wrapped in the absurd glory of their epic tale.

The grand hall of the Dragon Lady, a cavernous space where shadows flickered like the ghostly dance of long-forgotten spirits, was alive with the symphony of clinking armor and the hushed whispers of anxious warriors. At its heart stood Zalathor, a man whose reputation for loyalty had been as unyielding as the mythical steel from which his sword was forged.

"Friends," he began, voice dripping with a honeyed duplicity that would've made a siren envious, "I have gathered you under the pretext of strategy, but I fear my true agenda is far more... entrepreneurial."

Gasps echoed off the stone walls, rebounding like startled bats in the night. The Dragon Lady, her eyes narrowing to slits that could slice through deceit, regarded Zalathor with a mix of shock and indignation.

"Zalathor, what jest is this?" she demanded, her voice a thunderclap against the tense silence.

"Jest? Oh no, my dear lady," Zalathor chuckled, the sound sinister as a graveyard at midnight. "I am deadly serious. You see, your enemies offered me a kingdom, and who am I to refuse such a gracious gift?"

"Traitor!" one knight bellowed, his insult as subtle as an ogre in a porcelain shop.

"Et tu, Zalathor?" another murmured, shaking his head. "And here we thought you merely collected knives for their aesthetic value."

"Alas, sometimes they're for plunging into one's back," Zalathor quipped with a twirl of his mustache.

Panic bloomed like a poisonous flower among the ranks. Warriors shuffled uneasily, their gazes darting about as if betrayal might be contagious. One paladin accidentally impaled his own foot on a decorative lance in his flustered state, hopping on one leg while cursing in ancient tongues.

"Steady, comrades!" the Dragon Lady commanded, though her voice betrayed the sting of Zalathor's treachery. "We cannot let this... court jester turned Judas undo us."

"Indeed, how can we focus on our task when our so-called brother has decided to play hopscotch over to the dark side?" a mage quipped, his attempt at levity falling flat as a pancake in an abyss.

"Dark side, light side," Zalathor mused, twirling his blade with the flourish of a circus performer. "Why must we label things? I prefer 'the opportunistic side,' rolls off the tongue, don't you think?"

"Rolls off the tongue?! You'll be rolling heads if we don't keep ours about us!" the youngest of the heroes shouted, his voice a squeaky toy amidst the clamor.

"Silence!" The Dragon Lady's command cut through the chaos. "We must not succumb to disorder!"

"Too late for that, I'm afraid," Zalathor said with a smirk, stepping backward toward the shadow-draped exit. "You'll find disarray suits you. Chaos is the new black, after all."

"Someone catch him before he turns our fates into a punchline!" another snapped, but Zalathor was already melting into the darkness beyond, his laughter lingering like the scent of brimstone.

"Curse his sudden but inevitable betrayal," grumbled a dwarf warrior, his beard bristling with irritation. "Now, how do we clean up this comedic catastrophe?"

"First," the Dragon Lady said, rallying the troops with a fire in her eyes that rivaled her namesake, "we compose ourselves. Then, we compose a plan to drag Zalathor back by his jesting jowls."

And with that decree, the heroes endeavored to stitch their frayed nerves back together, their unity tested but not yet torn asunder.

As the echo of Zalathor's mocking laughter faded into the abyss, a cacophony of clamoring voices rose like a tempest among the heroes. The Dragon Lady's once-commanding presence seemed to shrink as confusion reigned, her crimson scales catching the flicker of torchlight with less brilliance.

"Maps! We need the maps!" barked the dwarven warrior, his stout fingers fumbling through a mass of parchments that now resembled the aftermath of a toddler's tantrum. "Zalathor had his greasy mitts on 'em last!"

"Useless as a one-legged unicorn in a butt-kicking contest," muttered the youngest hero under his breath, though loud enough for all to hear. His gaze darted helplessly from face to face, seeking some semblance of order that was slipping away like sand through an hourglass.

"Perhaps," mused the Dragon Lady, her voice tinged with frustration, "we could navigate by the stars? Or does anyone here speak bird? Maybe they've seen our treacherous jester skulking about."

"Speak bird?" squawked the mage, his long robe tangling between his legs as he spun in circles, trying to catch a glimpse of anything that might resemble a plan. "Brilliant idea! Let's all flap our arms and hope to fly while we're at it!"

"Enough!" The youngest hero slammed his fist onto the table, rattan armor rattling with the force. "We're spiraling like a gryphon caught in a whirlwind. We must anchor ourselves in strategy, not sarcasm."

"Strategy, he says," huffed the dwarf, finally extracting a crinkled map from the pile. "If only our minds were as sharp as our blades."

"Or as pointed as your beard," quipped the mage, unable to resist the jab even amidst the turmoil.

"Silence!" Her demand pierced the bickering like a spear through chainmail. "We assemble anew, lest Zalathor's deceit be our undoing."

The heroes edged around the war table, its surface now a battleground of scrolls and ink pots. They watched as the Dragon Lady traced her claw along a jagged mountain range etched upon the map.

"Here," she declared, "the valley of shadows. If our enemy seeks to cloak himself in darkness, then so shall we."

"Blend with the night, strike with the dawn," whispered the youngest hero, a spark of clarity igniting within him. "He won't expect us to mirror his tactics."

"Ah, mirroring—like a mime, but with swords," the mage chuckled, earning him a glare from the rest.

"Let's not get ahead of ourselves," cautioned the dwarf. "First, we figure out who holds which end of the stick—and make sure it's not the pointy one aimed at our own feet."

"Agreed," the Dragon Lady concluded, her tail swishing with renewed determination. "We shall divide and conquer, each to their strengths. Some will seek intelligence on Zalathor's whereabouts; others will prepare to rescue Lila and Roran."

"Divide and conquer," repeated the youngest hero, feeling the weight of their task. "For unity in division is our only path to victory."

"Unity in division," mused the mage, scratching his head. "Sounds like something my ex-wife would say."

"Focus," growled the dwarf, rolling the map and tucking it under his arm. "We have a snake to catch—and I don't mean the legless kind."

Together, they turned toward the ominous threshold that had swallowed their traitorous ally, sobered by the road ahead yet steadied by the promise of retribution. With the first step taken, the chaos wrought by Zalathor's betrayal began to morph into a plan—a plan etched in resolve and sealed with a shared, if wary, chuckle.

The chamber echoed with the clinks and clangs of armor as the heroes settled into an uneasy circle. Shifty eyes darted about, seeking a place to rest, but found none amongst the faces reflecting betrayal's sting.

"Would you look at us?" bellowed the dwarf, his voice ricocheting off stone walls like a rogue pinball. "We're eyeing each other as if we've got daggers for dinner!"

"Perhaps because one of us might," retorted the Dragon Lady, her scales shimmering with a distrust that was as cold as it was colorful. Her tail thumped the ground in a rhythmic cadence of annoyance.

"Preposterous!" exclaimed the youngest hero, posturing like a peacock in a gust of wind. "We are companions, bound by—"

"Bound by what, youthful naiveté?" interrupted the mage, twirling his mustache as if it were the key to unlocking the riddle of their woes. "Zalathor played us like a lute at a bard's convention!"

"Enough!" The main character, Sir Reginald the Bold, felt his stomach knot tighter than the gordian tangle of their current predicament. His mind raced, thoughts pinballing between anger, disbelief, and the gnawing realization that they stood on the precipice of infighting. 'I must be the glue,' he thought. 'The sticky, somewhat overcooked porridge that keeps this motley breakfast together.'

"Friends! Comrades! Lend me your earlobes!" Sir Reginald declared, drawing curious glances and a few raised eyebrows. "We cannot let Zalathor's treachery divide us. He has sown seeds of doubt, yes, but we shall not water them with the tears of suspicion!"

"Easy for you to say," growled the dwarf, arms folded across his chest like a miser guarding his coin purse. "You didn't train with the snake."

"True," agreed the Dragon Lady, her nostrils flaring so wide they could have housed small families of field mice. "But Sir Reginald speaks sense. We must uproot these seeds before they sprout into a forest of folly."

"Forest of folly..." murmured the mage, scratching his chin. "Sounds like a dreadful place. Full of philosophers and tax collectors, no doubt."

"Let's focus on our strategy," Sir Reginald urged, trying to steer the ship of their conversation away from the iceberg of irrelevance. "We know Zalathor's moves are as predictable as a two-headed coin. Let us flip the script!"

"Flip the script?" The youngest hero's head tilted, puzzled. "Is that some form of acrobatics? Because I'm quite limber—"

"Metaphorically, lad." Sir Reginald sighed, resisting the urge to facepalm. "We adjust our plan. Adapt. Improvise!"

"Ah, improvise," said the mage with a glint in his eye. "Like when I accidentally turned my familiar into a hat. Quite stylish, though impractical..."

"Adapt and improvise," repeated the Dragon Lady, nodding sagaciously. "We must become the unpredictable ones. Shift our tactics like shadows in a flickering candlelight."

"Shadows don't carry swords," quipped the dwarf, but there was a spark of understanding in his eyes.

"Then let's be shadows with swords!" declared Sir Reginald, his enthusiasm inflating like a hot air balloon in a heatwave. 'By the whiskers of the Great Lion,' he thought, feeling a surge of inspiration, 'we might just carve victory from this tempest of turmoil.'

The chamber, lit only by the eerie glow of enchanted torches that danced like frenzied sprites, thrummed with an electric tension. Sir

Reginald stood at the head of the council table, a slab of ancient oak that bore the scars of a thousand strategy meetings. The heroes, a motley collection of valor and vengeance, huddled around it, their faces a tapestry of concern and resolve.

"Silence, ye bickering barnacles!" Sir Reginald's voice boomed like thunder rolling over the Brimstone Hills. "We're spinning in circles like a one-legged griffin!"

"Perhaps we should attack at dawn," suggested the elf, her voice as smooth as polished crystal. "Zalathor won't expect a direct assault."

"Direct assault?" scoffed the dwarf, his beard bristling like the spines on an urchin. "And be skewered before breakfast? Nay! We tunnel beneath them, erupt from the earth like wrathful moles!"

"Wrathful moles," Sir Reginald mused, trying to quell the smirk tugging at his lips. 'Now there's an image more suited for a nursery tale than a war council.'

"Stealth is our ally," whispered the rogue, cloaked in shadows despite the flicker of flames. "I can slip through their ranks, a ghost in the night."

"Right, because last time you were so stealthy, the entire garrison heard you coming," muttered the mage, rolling his eyes. "'Twas like a parade led by a flatulent dragon."

"Enough!" The Dragon Lady's command sliced through the cacophony of suggestions. "We must weave our strategies together, not tear them apart like starved wolves on a scrap of meat."

'To weave, then,' thought Sir Reginald, 'like a tapestry bearing the image of our triumph.' His heart pulsed with a warrior's rhythm, each beat a drum call to action.

"Let's combine our strengths," he proposed, a spark igniting behind his steely gaze. "A feint at dawn led by the elf, the dwarf and his kin tunneling to disrupt their rear guard while the rogue cuts a path for the mage to bring a storm of fire upon them."

"Feint, tunnel, cut, and storm..." the mage murmured, tracing arcane symbols in the air with a flourish. "It's so mad it might just work."

"Madness is the brother of genius," quipped the Dragon Lady, a smile playing on her lips.

"Then let us hope they share more than just a family resemblance," said Sir Reginald, feeling the weight of leadership heavy on his shoulders yet buoyed by the unity forming before him.

"Agreed," they all echoed, a chorus of newfound determination.

"Then it's settled," declared Sir Reginald, his chest swelling with pride. 'Out of chaos, a plan. Out of discord, harmony. And out of a comedy of errors, perhaps a victory worthy of song.'

The air in the war council tent was thick with the must of old maps and the tang of determination. Sir Reginald, his armor clinking like an overworked blacksmith's forge with every movement, stood center stage among his motley crew of valiant heroes.

"Alright, listen up!" he bellowed, his voice resonating through the canvas walls. "Zalathor's betrayal cuts deeper than a goblin's cleaver, but we've got two of our own in the viper's nest."

"Indeed," the mage chimed in, eyes flickering with the glow of his next spell. "Lila and Roran are out there, probably arguing about who gets to take credit for getting rescued first."

"Let's not forget the snake himself, Zalathor," interjected the rogue, twirling a dagger between her fingers. Her smirk was as sharp as the blade's edge. "I'd like to have a word or two with him—preferably through interpretive stabbing."

Sir Reginald nodded, a plan unfurling in his mind like a scroll slapped open by a gust of wind. "We'll split into teams. Team Rescue will swoop in for Lila and Roran. Team Spy," he said, glancing at the rogue, "will find out where that double-dealing dastard is hiding."

"Sounds simple enough," the dwarf grunted, scratching his beard. "But what if they're guarded by something big and toothy?"

"Then we'll be big and... punchy?" offered the elf, an uncertain smile beneath his leaf-shaped ears.

"Look at us," Sir Reginald thought, surveying the hopeful yet nervous faces around him. "A fellowship of the improbable, standing on the precipice of madness."

"Team Rescue, you'll have me, the Dragon Lady, and the dwarf," Sir Reginald declared, slapping a gauntleted hand on a map so forcefully it sent a few stray quills flying. "Our might and magic should be enough to shatter any chains."

"Good." The Dragon Lady stepped forward, her flowing robes leaving a trail of embers in her wake. "I still owe them a lesson in dragon etiquette. Last time, Roran tried to ride me during a battle charge."

"Team Spy will be the rogue, the elf, and the mage," continued Sir Reginald. "You're sneaky, you're quick, and you can set things on fire from a distance. A perfect trio."

"Understood," replied the elf, nodding with a grace that made even his armor seem ethereal. "We shall move like shadows under the moonlight. Silent but deadly."

"Like my uncle's cooking," the rogue added with a wink.

"Excellent," concluded Sir Reginald. "Tonight, we dine with victory or wake up with our ancestors. Preferably the former."

"Here's to hoping Zalathor hasn't grown a brain overnight," the mage muttered, sparks dancing off his fingertips as he practiced a cantrip.

"Brains are overrated," quipped Sir Reginald, a grin creasing his weathered face. "Give me heart. Give me courage. And give me a flagon of ale when this is all over. To the mission!"

"TO THE MISSION!" they roared in unison, their voices a jumbled melody of accents and octaves.

Sir Reginald could feel the rush of adrenaline, the camaraderie binding them together. They were more than just a team; they were a spectacle of heroism, ready to plunge into the mouth of chaos. With a rallying cry fit for the bards, they dispersed, each to their own daring task.

"May the gods have mercy on Zalathor," Sir Reginald whispered to himself, "for we shall have none."

Sir Reginald's gauntlet-clad hands trembled as he rolled the parchment map, its edges singed by the deceit that now burned in their midst. His eyes, once beacons of unwavering confidence, darted between his comrades, seeking some foothold of trust amidst the treacherous sands of doubt.

"Curse it," Sir Reginald muttered under his breath, his voice a gruff whisper that barely rose above the crackling of the nearby campfire. "Zalathor's treachery has turned our plans to pudding."

The elf, lithe and serene even in turmoil, leaned against an ancient oak, his bowstring taut with tension. "We have been played like lutes at a harvest festival, Sir Reginald. Our own judgment, a foe more cunning than any dragon."

"Judge not the judgment, for it's all we've got," the rogue chimed in, flipping a dagger end over end. The moonlight glinted off the blade, a fleeting dance of silver on steel. "Besides, who hasn't accidentally trusted a backstabbing wizard? Happens to the best of us."

"Right you are, my sneaky friend," Sir Reginald conceded with a heavy sigh, his heart burdened by the weight of leadership. "But can we afford such follies when Lila and Roran hang in the balance?"

"Speaking of hanging," the mage interjected, pulling a strand of his beard anxiously, "I do hope they're not actually hanging."

"Enough!" Sir Reginald barked, his voice slicing through the uncertainty like a broadsword. "We must adjust, adapt, and act. Zalathor may have taken our plan, but he shall not take our spirit!"

"Or our wits," the elf remarked, his gaze sharpening like the arrowheads in his quiver.

"Or our ale, though I suspect it's gone sour with this turn of events," the rogue added, eliciting a snort from Sir Reginald.

"Your jests may preserve our sanity yet," Sir Reginald admitted, allowing a small smile to break through his stony demeanor. He straightened, puffing out his chest with renewed determination. "Comrades, to our new mission! We shall rescue our allies and give Zalathor a lesson in loyalty!"

"Here's to hoping it's a lesson with ample explosions," the mage said, conjuring a small flame that danced upon his palm—a spark of defiance in the creeping darkness.

"Quietly, if you please," the elf reminded, nocking an arrow to his bow. "Shadows and silence are still our allies."

"Both of which are terrible conversationalists," the rogue quipped, securing his cloak. "But excellent for dramatic exits."

"Then let us make our exit, dramatic and triumphant," Sir Reginald declared, leading the way into the shrouded forest. Their footsteps were muffled by the mossy earth, each step a promise to themselves and to each other.

"Zalathor will rue the day he crossed us," Sir Reginald thought, his mind a whirlwind of strategy and suspicion. "And if not, may my sword become a plowshare, and my armor a chicken coop."

With a collective inhale of resolve and an exhale of lingering fears, they embraced the path ahead, their hearts pounding like war drums in their chests. They set forth, a motley crew of valor, humor, and sheer, unadulterated gall, ready to face whatever twisted fate awaited them in the shadow of betrayal.

Under the cloak of night, the heroes trudged through the dense ferns and twisted roots of the Enchanted Forest of Perilous Endeavors, their destination known only to the stars that winked mischievously above. Sir Reginald's armor clanked with a rhythm that would have surely irritated a stealthy assassin, but it was music to his ears—a symphony of impending justice.

"By the Elder Beards of Yore, would someone oil Sir Clanks-a-lot before he alerts every dark minion in earshot?" the rogue muttered, rolling his eyes so hard they practically echoed in the stillness.

"Your concern for my auditory discretion is heartwarming," Sir Reginald retorted, pausing to tighten a buckle that had done nothing wrong except exist. "But fear not, our foes will be too busy shielding their eyes from your garish attire to notice little old me."

"Garish? This is the latest fashion in covert operations!" the rogue protested, gesturing to his ensemble of mismatched patterns. "Camouflage, my dear knight, is an art."

"An art best left to those who understand the concept of blending in," the elf interjected, his voice smooth as the silk tunics he so favored. "Speaking of which, I recall you have a rather... explosive affinity for making things stand out, mage?"

"Explosions are an essential part of any balanced strategy," the mage quipped, twirling his staff until it hummed with arcane energy. "Like breakfast."

"Enough bickering," Sir Reginald commanded, his gaze set on the path ahead. Internally, he wrestled with the sting of Zalathor's treachery—a wound deeper than any blade could inflict. "We must focus. Our comrades depend on us, and we shall not fail them."

"Agreed," the elf said, releasing an arrow into the canopy where it found its mark with a thud, dislodging an eavesdropping squirrel spy. "Though I do wonder how many more woodland creatures we'll conscript into our service before daybreak."

"Let's hope they're all as forthcoming with intelligence as Mr. Nutkin there," the rogue replied, saluting the fallen creature.

"Forward, my friends," Sir Reginald declared, his voice laced with the iron of resolve. "Our destiny awaits, and I've heard it's terribly impatient."

As they pressed on, each member of the group entertained their private thoughts. The rogue contemplated the countless pockets he'd picked, wondering if his nimble fingers were destined for greater deeds. The elf mused on the many songs he'd yet to sing, their melodies floating like specters in the fog of uncertainty. The mage considered the countless spells at his disposal, keenly aware that their true power lay in their unexpected application. And Sir Reginald... he pondered the weight of leadership, the mantle heavy on his shoulders, yet lighter than the prospect of defeat.

"Remember, we strike with the dawn," Sir Reginald called, his voice a beacon in the darkness. "Lila and Roran will taste freedom once again, and Zalathor... the taste of retribution."

"Here's to hoping it's seasoned well," the mage shot back, a grin spreading across his face like wildfire.

"Seasoned with the salt of our enemies' tears, no doubt," the rogue added with a chuckle.

"Let's season it with victory instead," the elf suggested, his smile as sharp as his arrows.

And so, with hearts ablaze and spirits undaunted, the heroes marched on, their laughter ringing out as a challenge to the shadows that dared to dance in their wake. They moved not as four, but as one, bound by purpose, fueled by camaraderie, and utterly convinced that the pages of history awaited their indelible mark.

The chapter opened with a flourish of leaves, each one seeming to mock Ben and his band of weary travelers as they marched on. The Descendant of Eclipse was out there, somewhere beyond the gnarled roots and creeping vines that seemed all too eager to trip them at every step.

"By the hairy chin of the Great Goblin King," grumbled Sir Thorne, swiping a branch away from his face, "I swear these forests are more foul than a troll's backside after a feast."

"Feasts!" piped up Jinx, the sprightly rogue whose appetite for mischief was matched only by her hunger for food. "Now that's something I could use. My stomach's growling louder than a dragon with a toothache."

"Focus," Ben chided, though his voice was betrayed by a growl from his own empty belly. "The clues lead us here, to the Wailing Woods, not to a banquet hall. Though I'd wager my sword that the underbrush has been conspiring against us since we entered."

The forest seemed to close in around them, the shadows lengthening as if the very trees themselves bore ill will. A dense fog rolled in, bathing everything in a ghostly hue. Suddenly, the ground gave way beneath Ben's boot, and he found himself sliding down an embankment, barely catching onto a vine.

"Whoa there, Captain Graceful," teased Jinx, extending a slender hand to haul him back onto solid ground. "Wouldn't want to lose you to the mud. The stories would never let you live it down."

"Thank you," Ben said, brushing off the embarrassment along with the dirt. He pushed forward, his determination unwavering despite the mishap. This was no time for slip-ups; the fate of Oak Isle hung precariously in the balance.

The terrain grew ever more treacherous as they advanced. Rocky outcrops jutted from the earth like the jagged teeth of some slumbering beast, and each step felt like a gamble against the whims of gravity.

"Is it just me, or are these mountains getting steeper by the minute?" Sir Thorne huffed, his armor clanking melodramatically with each exaggerated step.

"Perhaps the mountains are merely rising to meet your grandeur, Sir Thorne," quipped Jinx, her eyes twinkling with mirth.

"Quiet, both of you," whispered Elara, the mage whose wisdom often cut through their banter like a knife. "There's a presence here, ancient and watchful. We must tread carefully."

Ben nodded, feeling the weight of her words settle over him like a cloak. His heart pounded with a mix of fear and excitement.

They were close now; he could sense it. The Descendant of Eclipse had to be near, hidden within the labyrinthine embrace of this dark wilderness.

"Stay sharp," he murmured, his gaze piercing through the tangled greenery. "Our destiny lies ahead, and we won't let any swamp or crag stand in our way."

"Or our own two feet, apparently," Jinx added with a wink, eliciting a rare, begrudging smile from Ben.

Their laughter mingled with the haunting whispers of the wood, a defiant melody against the symphony of dangers that lay before them. They pressed on, united in purpose and spirit, ready to face whatever trials awaited in their quest for the Descendant of Eclipse.

The verdant underbrush gave way to a clearing rimmed with towering stones, each one inscribed with runes that shimmered like fireflies caught in amber. A hush fell over the group as they approached the stone circle, the air charged with the electricity of ancient magic.

"Looks like we've hit the proverbial magical wall," Jinx announced, her hand hovering inches from the runes, feeling the thrum of power without touching.

"Indeed," Elara intoned gravely. "This is a warding circle, and no ordinary one at that. It requires a key of wit, not force."

"Great, another riddle," Sir Thorne grumbled. "I swear, if I have to hear one more 'what has roots as nobody sees'..."

"Silence!" Ben's voice was sharp, slicing through the tension. His eyes narrowed as he studied the runes, his mind racing. "It's a puzzle alright, but not just any puzzle. This one speaks of history and lore."

"Benjamin, our resident bookworm," Jinx teased, though her eyes held a glint of respect. "What dusty tome did you pry this knowledge from?"

"Quiet," Ben said, only half-irritated. "The Descendant of Eclipse was known for his love of the old tales. If we're to pass, we must prove ourselves worthy by understanding those very same stories." He stepped closer, reading aloud the words etched into the central obelisk, his voice steady:

"Born of twilight, cloaked in night,
A shadow's whisper, a waning light.
Speak my name and open the way,
Or in darkness eternal you'll stay."

"Sounds cheery," Jinx quipped, but her jest fell flat in the solemnity of the moment.

"Twilight... shadow... waning light..." Ben murmured, his thoughts tumbling over themselves like leaves in a storm. He paced the circumference of the circle, the pieces of the puzzle clicking together in his mind. "The Descendant revered the Dusk Wolf fables... Could it be that simple?"

"Out with it, boy!" Sir Thorne barked, agitation wrinkling his brow beneath his helm.

"Quiet, Thorne. Let him think," Elara whispered, though her own curiosity was a palpable thing, coiled tight within her.

Ben stopped abruptly, turning to face his companions. "Lupus Crepusculum," he declared confidently. "The Dusk Wolf, guardian of the threshold between day and night."

A collective intake of breath preceded a silence so deep it felt as though the forest itself awaited the outcome. Then, as if in response to Ben's assertion, the runes flared a brilliant gold, and the stones began to shift, grinding against each other with the sound of a thousand whispers. The path forward opened like the maw of some great beast, inviting yet ominous.

"Your love for those dusty scrolls has paid off," Jinx said, relief evident in her voice as she flashed Ben a grin.

"Let's not celebrate just yet," Ben replied, casting a wary eye on the dark passage ahead. "This is but one step closer to the Descendant. We must remain vigilant."

"Vigilance I can do," Sir Thorne said, puffing out his chest as if readying for battle. "Puzzles, less so."

"Lead the way then, brave Sir Thorne," Jinx teased, nudging the knight forward with a playful smirk.

"Very well," he sighed dramatically, stepping into the lead with an exaggerated flourish of his cape. "But let it be known that I am doing so under protest."

"Protest noted," Elara said dryly, her lips twitching in amusement.

As they ventured into the newly revealed path, Ben couldn't help but feel a swell of pride. The riddle had been a test, and he had passed. Yet, the true challenge, he knew, lay just beyond the veil of shadows that now enveloped them. With determination set in his heart and the light of knowledge as his guide, he stepped forward, ready to face whatever waited in the darkness.

The damp air of the cavernous path clung to Ben's skin like a second cloak, thick and suffocating. His breath misted in the air with each exhale, mingling with the low murmurs of his allies as they pressed forward. Their footsteps echoed, a haunting melody against the oppressive silence.

"Shh," Jinx hissed suddenly, her hand shooting out to halt Sir Thorne mid-stride, whose armor clanked in protest. The sound of his grumbling was swallowed by the shadows.

"Enemies ahead," she whispered, eyes narrowing at the flickering torchlight that spilled around a distant bend.

"Or perhaps it's a welcome party?" Sir Thorne offered, a hopeful lilt in his voice betrayed by the grim set of his jaw.

"Only if you consider being skewered by dark enchantments 'welcoming,'" Elara quipped, shifting her stance into one ready for combat.

"Right," Ben muttered, flexing his fingers to ward off the creeping numbness. He could feel the thrum of adrenaline coursing through him—a warrior's call he never knew slumbered within.

As they rounded the corner, a grotesque tableau unveiled itself: a phalanx of goblin soldiers, their beady red eyes glinting with malice. They wielded jagged blades that seemed to thirst for the light.

"Ah, just as I suspected!" Sir Thorne bellowed, brandishing his sword with an enthusiasm that bordered on theatrical. "A skirmish to spice up the evening!"

"Stay sharp," Ben cautioned, pulling a short blade from his belt—a token from his days sifting through ancient armories for knowledge, now a weapon in his uncertain grip.

"Sharp is my middle name!" Jinx declared, launching a dagger from her fingertips that whistled as it found its mark in a goblin's chest.

The fray erupted with the chaos of clashing steel and guttural cries. Ben ducked beneath a wild swing, feeling the wind of the blade rather than seeing it. His heart hammered, but his mind was eerily clear, recalling every scroll on combat tactics he'd ever studied.

"Remember, aim for their—" he started, only to be interrupted by Sir Thorne.

"Underbellies! Yes, we know, lad! It's Goblin Slaying 101!"

"Actually, I was going to say knees," Ben corrected, pivoting to drive his blade into the joint of an oncoming assailant. The goblin screeched, collapsing in a heap.

"Knees, underbellies, all squishy bits are fair game!" Jinx cheered, somersaulting over another enemy to deliver a swift kick that sent teeth flying.

"Delightful imagery, Jinx," Elara remarked dryly, her staff glowing as she conjured a shield that deflected a volley of arrows.

"Thanks! I try!" Jinx replied, flashing a grin before resuming her deadly dance.

Ben parried another strike, the motion more fluid than he expected. Perhaps there was merit to those long hours of practice when he should have been deciphering cryptic texts. With a twist and a thrust, he disarmed another foe, the goblin's eyes widening in shock before it slunk away, whimpering.

"Ha! Look at you, Ben!" Sir Thorne roared approvingly, cleaving a path through their adversaries. "You've got the heart of a lion and the grace of a—well, something decidedly more graceful than a lion!"

"Maybe a panther," Ben suggested with a breathless laugh, ducking another blow and counterattacking with newfound confidence.

"Exactly! A scholarly panther with a penchant for ancient riddles!" Jinx added, winking at him as she dispatched another goblin.

"Let us not forget why we fight!" Elara's voice cut through the din, grounding them. "For Oak Isle, for the Descendant of Eclipse, for hope!"

"Right," Ben affirmed, his resolve hardening like forged steel. With each goblin that fell, with each comrade's life he protected, the weight of their quest anchored in his soul. He was no longer simply a seeker of lost knowledge. He was a defender, a warrior joined in battle with those who would stand against darkness.

And as the last of the enemy scattered, fleeing back into the inky depths from which they came, Ben stood tall amidst his comrades, panting and victorious. They exchanged weary smiles, their bond solidified in shared triumph.

"Nicely done, team," Ben said, his chest swelling with pride and a touch of disbelief at the metamorphosis he had undergone. "Onward, to the Descendant of Eclipse!"

"Spoken like a true hero," Jinx teased, elbowing him gently.

"Indeed," Sir Thorne agreed, clapping Ben on the shoulder with enough force to stagger him. "Let's hope this Descendant appreciates the flair with which we dispatch his foes."

"Flair and panthers," Ben chuckled, sheathing his blade. "Who could resist?"

"Let's find out," Elara said, leading them onward with a smile that held the promise of further adventures and the allure of destiny beckoning just beyond their reach.

Ben's boots squelched in the mud, each step a symphony of slops and slurps that seemed to mock their progress. The sun had dipped below the horizon hours ago, leaving them to navigate the treacherous terrain by the unreliable flicker of Jinx's enchanted fireflies.

"Are we sure this is the right way?" Ben muttered, more to himself than his companions. He could scarcely see a foot in front of him, let alone the fabled signs leading to the Descendant of Eclipse. "We've been walking for hours and, aside from an impressive collection of blisters, we have nothing to show for it."

"Right path?" Jinx quipped, bounding over a particularly large puddle with a grace that made Ben scowl. "Oh, darling, the right path is whichever one leads to victory or at least a tavern with a decent stew."

"Jinx, focus," Elara chided gently, though her eyes sparkled with shared amusement. "Ben, you have the map Elara gave you, right?"

"Map?" Ben echoed, patting down his pockets frantically until he produced a crumpled piece of parchment that looked as if it had survived a dragon's digestive tract. "Ah, yes. This... treasure."

"Let me see that," Sir Thorne said, leaning over Ben's shoulder with a grunt. "You're holding it upside down, lad."

"Of course, I am," Ben sighed, flipping the map and squinting at the indecipherable squiggles that passed for directions. "Because today wasn't challenging enough."

"Chin up, Ben!" Elara encouraged, her hand finding its way to his arm. "Remember why we're on this quest. The Descendant of Eclipse holds the key to saving Oak Isle. We can't give up now."

"Elara's right. Besides," Sir Thorne added, puffing out his chest, "we've bested swamp goblins and scaled Mount Gloom. A bit of murky navigation won't defeat us."

"Indeed," Jinx chimed in, executing a theatrical bow. "We are the most extraordinary band of misfits this side of the Enchanted Chasm. Now, lead on, our fearless, albeit directionally-challenged, captain!"

A smile tugged at the corner of Ben's mouth despite the uncertainty coiling in his gut. "Fearless captain? You lot are delusional."

"Delusion keeps life spicy!" Jinx exclaimed, throwing his arms wide as if embracing the very concept.

"Spicy like the time you tried to charm a basilisk with a mating dance?" Sir Thorne teased, earning a round of laughter from the group.

"Hey, it worked, didn't it?" Jinx retorted, grinning. "Mostly."

"Mostly," they all echoed, shaking their heads.

"Alright, alright," Ben conceded, the warmth of camaraderie bolstering his resolve. "If we're to face deadly creatures and worse cooking, then it's together. For Oak Isle."

"Lead the way, Captain 'Upside-Down Map,'" Elara winked, nudging him forward.

"Captain 'Upside-Down Map' it is," Ben declared, stepping boldly into the unknown, his doubts momentarily quenched by the laughter of his friends echoing through the murky darkness.

The rustle of leaves and the soft squelch of damp earth underfoot accompanied Ben and his motley crew as they approached what appeared to be an ordinary glade. Yet, Elara's keen eyes caught the faint shimmer in the air, a distortion that set her nerves on edge.

"Ben," she whispered, her hand instinctively reaching for the hilt of her dagger, "do you see it? The barrier?"

"See it?" Jinx piped up, squinting dramatically. "I could dance a jig on the darn thing!"

"Quiet, Jinx," Sir Thorne admonished with a gruff hiss. "This is no time for your theatrics."

"Indeed, Sir Thorne," Ben said, his gaze locked onto the glimmering veil before them. "This barrier... Elara, is it like the one you showed me in the Crystal Forest?"

"Similar," she replied, nodding gravely. "But this one hums with a power far more ancient. I suspect it's tied directly to the Descendant of Eclipse himself."

"Great," Ben muttered under his breath. "Ancient, powerful barriers. Just what we needed."

"Ben, remember the incantation I taught you?" Elara asked, drawing closer to him. "The one that unravels magics?"

"Ah, yes. 'Magic born from darkest night, unravel now beneath my sight,'" he recited, the words feeling strange and potent on his tongue.

"More like 'magic born from an old man's back hair,'" Jinx snorted.

"Focus!" Ben snapped, his palms beginning to sweat. He stepped forward, extending his hands toward the barrier. Closing his eyes, he concentrated on the incantation, channeling every ounce of determination into his voice. "Magic born from darkest night, unravel now beneath my sight!"

The air thickened around them, the atmosphere crackling with unseen energy. A low thrumming noise began to resonate, growing louder until it filled the entire glade. The barrier's shimmer intensified, pulsating with a rhythm that matched Ben's heartbeat.

"Is it supposed to do that?" Sir Thorne queried, gripping his sword tighter.

"Probably not," Ben admitted, opening one eye to peek at the spectacle he was causing. "But it's definitely doing something."

"Keep going, Ben!" Elara encouraged, her eyes wide with anticipation. "It's weakening!"

"Magic born from darkest night, unravel now beneath my sight!" Ben repeated, louder this time, his voice cracking with effort. His mind whirled with Elara's lessons, each word imbued with the magic she had painstakingly taught him.

Suddenly, the barrier let out a sound akin to a balloon deflating at a jester's party. With a final flicker, it dissolved into a myriad of sparkling motes, fading into the ether. Ben stumbled forward, nearly face-planting into the newly-revealed path.

"Ha!" Jinx exclaimed, clapping Ben on the back. "You did it! Didn't even need the old man's back hair after all!"

"Jinx, you are insufferable," Elara sighed, but there was relief in her eyes.

"Insufferably charming, you mean," Jinx winked.

"Still, well done, Ben," Sir Thorne rumbled, offering a rare smile. "Seems you've got more magic in your pinky than most have in their whole body."

"Let's just hope it's enough for whatever lies ahead," Ben said, steeling himself as he led the way through the now-open path.

"Whatever it is, we'll face it together," Elara said firmly, her hand brushing against his. "For Oak Isle."

"For Oak Isle," they echoed, stepping into the unknown with a camaraderie that could face down any dark magic or ancient being—perhaps even the Descendant of Eclipse himself.

The chamber beyond the shattered barrier was a cathedral of shadows and whispers. Torches flickered along the walls, casting an eerie dance of light that seemed to avoid the figure seated upon a throne wrought from obsidian. There, in a pool of darkness that defied the very notion of illumination, sat the Descendant of Eclipse.

His form was both there and not, like a specter caught between realms. He was clothed in robes that drank in the light, and his eyes were twin orbs of fathomless silver, reflecting the weight of eons.

"Who dares disturb my ancient slumber?" The voice that emanated from the enigmatic figure was resonant, imbued with the timbre of rolling thunder but carrying the softness of a secret.

"Uh, hi! I'm Ben," Ben started, waving awkwardly as if he'd just bumped into a stranger at a tavern. "Big fan of your work. Love what you've done with the place—very... shadowy."

"Ben," Elara hissed under her breath, "perhaps a little more gravitas?"

"Right, sorry." Ben cleared his throat, stepping forward with a boldness that surprised even himself. "Great Descendant of Eclipse, we have traveled through realms fraught with peril to seek your wisdom and aid. Oak Isle is in dire straits, besieged by forces of darkness that threaten to consume it whole."

"Ah, the exuberance of youth," the Descendant mused, his tone suggesting a smile unseen beneath the hood of his robe. "Tell me, young Ben, why should I stir from my solitude to meddle in the affairs of mortals?"

"Because," Ben replied, meeting the Descendant's gaze with an intensity that belied his comic exterior, "not only is Oak Isle teetering on the brink of annihilation, but without your help, the very fabric of our world could unravel. And let's be honest, who wants to rule over a pile of cosmic dust? It's terrible for the complexion."

A flicker of amusement seemed to pass across the Descendant's face. "And what makes you think I possess the power to sway such a calamitous tide?"

"Elara has taught me much about the old ways, the magic that once coursed through this land like a heartbeat," Ben continued, his words punctuated by earnest gesticulations. "You are the living embodiment of that era, a force that can bring balance back to our world. Plus, it's been ages since you've had visitors, right? Got to be pretty lonely playing solitaire for centuries."

"Your audacity is as boundless as it is amusing," the Descendant conceded, rising from his throne with the grace of nightfall. "Very well, Ben, champion of Oak Isle. I will consider your plea."

"Brilliant!" Ben exclaimed. "Just so you know, we're all stocked up on adventure, danger, and probably some near-death experiences. It's going to be epic!"

"Silence, fool," Sir Thorne muttered, though a glimmer of respect shone in his eyes.

"Let us leave the Descendant to his thoughts," Elara suggested diplomatically, ushering Ben away from the throne.

"Of course, of course," Ben babbled, backing up with a series of exaggerated bows. "Take all the time you need. We'll just be... um, preparing for impending doom outside."

As they exited the chamber, Ben couldn't help but feel a surge of hope. Perhaps his offbeat brand of courage and his knack for persuasive banter might just be enough to save their home.

The Descendant of Eclipse stood immobile, his silhouette an eclipsing shadow against the flickering torches that lined the ancient hall. A cloak of silence settled over the chamber like a thick fog, suffocating the remnants of laughter that Ben's earlier jest had birthed. The air itself seemed to wait with bated breath for the enigmatic figure's decision.

"Surely," Ben began, breaking the stillness as he stepped forward, "you can see the urgency in our—"

"Silence." The Descendant's voice was the rustle of dead leaves, a sound that made Ben halt mid-step, his boot hovering awkwardly above the ground. "I have watched empires rise and fall through whispers and shadows. Why should I trust the fate of this age to a band of motley crusaders?"

Ben's mouth felt suddenly dry, but he swallowed hard, pushing back the creeping doubt. He needed to connect, to present a truth so raw and undeniable that not even this ancient being could dismiss it. His allies' expectant gazes were upon him, their faith fueling his resolve.

"Because," Ben said, lowering his boot to the stone with a soft thud, meeting the Descendant's gaze squarely, "you once knew someone like us. Someone who believed in the impossible."

The Descendant's eyes, twin orbs of starless night, narrowed imperceptibly. Ben seized on the momentary flicker of curiosity.

"Alaric," he declared triumphantly, the name resonating in the silence. "The first hero of Oak Isle, the one you guided to victory when all seemed lost. We walk the path he carved, fighting not just for our home, but for the future of all lands shadowed by darkness."

A murmur ruffled through Ben's companions, each exchanging glances charged with hope and tension. The Descendant's expression remained unreadable, but there was a shift in the air, a crackling energy that suggested the walls around them were listening, remembering.

"Alaric was...a rare soul," the Descendant conceded after what felt like an eternity, his voice softening by a shade. "One whose heart was as fierce as the sun's fire."

"Exactly!" Ben exclaimed, almost tripping over his own enthusiasm. "And we're like Alaric! Well, mostly. Sir Thorne has the fierce part down, Elara's got wisdom that makes owls jealous, and me? I'm...uh, exceptionally good at not dying!"

"Your levity is ill-timed," Sir Thorne grumbled, crossing his arms, though the corners of his mouth betrayed a reluctant smile.

"Yet not unappreciated," Elara whispered, her eyes gleaming with pride at Ben's audacity.

"Think of it," Ben pressed on, spinning a tale with his hands as much as with his words. "Joining forces with the spiritual successor of your old friend, battling side by side to turn the tide against chaos. It's not every millennium you get an offer like that!"

The Descendant paused, a statue contemplating motion. In the fraught silence, Ben felt his heart hammering against his ribs, a drumbeat urging them all toward an unknown precipice.

"Very well," the Descendant finally spoke, the words falling like autumn leaves, "I will listen to the echo of the past within your voices. Convince me that Alaric's legacy lives on through you."

A collective sigh rippled through the group, a blend of relief and anticipation. Ben's grin stretched from ear to ear, his mind already racing ahead to their next grand, perilous adventure.

"Brace yourself for a tale of epic proportions," he declared, bowing with a flourish. "For we are the heroes Oak Isle needs, and our story is only just beginning."

Ben's heart thrummed a symphony of hope as he watched the Descendant of Eclipse, shrouded in ancient power, weigh their fate. The silence in the chamber was stifling, thick with the weight of eons and the heavy breaths of his companions—each daring not to disturb the momentous decision hanging like a sword above their heads.

"Alright," the Descendant said at last, each syllable a stone cast upon still waters, "I have witnessed your valor and heard the echo of Alaric in your fervent pleas. My aid is yours."

"By the hairy chin of the Great Dwarf King!" Sir Thorne erupted, his voice booming like thunder, "We did it!"

"Indeed," Elara chimed in, her amusement dancing through the air like sparks from a fire. "Alaric's legacy couldn't ask for a more... colorful continuance."

Ben could barely contain his exuberance, his mind ablaze with triumph and relief. *We've done it! We've actually convinced a living relic to join our motley crew. If only the bards could see us now!* His thoughts somersaulted through past victories and future glories.

"Let's not get ahead of ourselves," Ben interjected, trying his best to marshal the giddy parade of thoughts into order. "Our quest is far from over. Where is the Staff of Tomorrow?"

"Ah yes, the staff," the Descendant murmured, almost to himself, as if remembering a long-forgotten tune. He extended a hand, and the air shimmered like heat above a forge, revealing an intricate map that seemed to float between them. "The staff lies hidden, cloaked by spells within the Cavern of Whispers. Only those who carry the light of Alaric can hope to pierce its veil."

"Of course, the Cavern of Whispers!" Ben exclaimed, slapping his forehead in mock realization while rolling his eyes theatrically. "Why does it always have to be whispers? Why not the Cavern of Uncontrollable Giggles? I bet that's a hoot!"

"Your humor remains as questionable as your hairstyle," Sir Thorne grunted, though his eyes twinkled with mirth.

"Focus, gentlemen," Elara scolded gently, yet her lips curved in a suppressed smile. "This is but the threshold to our endeavor."

"True," Ben agreed, nodding gravely before winking at Elara. *Oh, what tales we'll tell when this is all over.* "But who needs focus when you have flair?"

"Flair won't disarm the traps nor will it charm the beasts that lurk within its shadows," the Descendant intoned. "Tread lightly, for the cavern is old, and its secrets are guarded by more than mere echoes."

"Beasts, traps, secrets—sounds like my last birthday party," Ben quipped, but his jest fell away as he studied the ethereal map. His mind raced, plotting courses, envisioning challenges. *We'll need more than jokes to navigate this labyrinth.*

"Very well," Ben said, his voice steady despite the fluttering in his chest. "To the Cavern of Whispers we go. With your guidance, Descendant, and the light of Alaric, we shall claim the Staff of Tomorrow and save Oak Isle!"

"Indeed," the Descendant affirmed, his voice a deep chord that seemed to resonate with the very stones around them. "May fortune favor your path, children of destiny."

With that, the map faded, leaving behind a resolve as tangible as the swords at their sides. They stood together, a band of unlikely heroes bound by shared purpose, their hearts alight with the promise of the quest ahead. The chapter closed on laughter and determination, setting the stage for a climax that would ring through the ages.

The evening air was thick with the scent of roasting meats and sweet mead, as Oak Isle's capital city buzzed with the revelry of an unexpected festival. Yet, amidst the cacophony of laughter and clinking mugs, a shadow darker than the night itself crept over the cobblestone streets. Zalathor, the necromancer with a penchant for dramatic entrances and even more dramatic undead minions, chose this moment of mirth to unleash a surprise attack that crashed the party like the proverbial bull in a china shop.

"By the beard of the Great Goblin King!" Ben exclaimed, spitting out a mouthful of pie as a skeletal hand burst from the earth, groping at the air like it had lost its favorite bone. His eyes widened as he witnessed a spectacle that would turn a bard's hair white – legions of the undead emerging from nowhere, turning the merry frolics into shrieks and chaos.

"Right," Ben muttered, brushing pastry crumbs off his tunic as if they were the first line of defense. "This wasn't on the evening's itinerary."

With the grace of a cat wearing boots on a slippery roof, Ben stumbled onto a crate to address his ragtag band of allies who were as ready for battle as a duck is for a desert trek. Elara wielded her staff like a maestro with a baton, except instead of music, she was preparing to conduct a symphony of spells. Roran adjusted his armor, which emitted a squeak of protest – it had been anticipating a night off.

"Listen up!" Ben bellowed, barely audible over a zombie performing what could only be described as an interpretive dance of doom. "We need barricades! I want them higher than my aunt Mabel's hairdo on her wedding day!"

They sprang into action with all the urgency of squirrels during nut harvest season. Barricades made of barrels, tables, and even a grandiose cake stand (much to the baker's dismay) sprouted across key streets like mushrooms after a rainstorm. The defenders fortified positions with anything they could get their hands on – street signs, statues, and one overly enthusiastic merchant's collection of novelty shields.

"Protect the alehouse," Ben commanded, pointing towards the establishment with the determination of a man whose priorities were impeccably ordered. "We're going to need somewhere to celebrate after we kick these boneheads back to the grave!"

His allies set about their tasks with a zeal that bordered on slapstick. A pair of twins armed with slingshots used rotten fruit as ammunition, creating a slippery gauntlet for the approaching skeletons. Meanwhile, Elara chanted incantations that made the very air sizzle with arcane energy, her focus so intense it could burn holes through logic.

"Alright, team," Ben cheered, unsheathing a sword that glinted with enchantments and a bit of leftover gravy. "Let's show these party-crashers how we do things on Oak Isle!"

And with that, the stage was set for a battle that would be sung about for ages – or at least talked about until next week's farmers' market. The defenders stood ready, their spirits undampened by the advancing horde, their faces set in expressions of fierce determination and mild indigestion. Oak Isle's capital might have been caught off guard, but its people were no strangers to rolling up their sleeves and getting their hands dirty, be it in soil or spectral ectoplasm.

"Charge!" Ben yelled, leading the charge with a war cry that sounded suspiciously like "For the love of cake, let's not die!"

The clash of steel rang through the air as Lila, with a sword in one hand and a frying pan in the other, danced a deadly ballet amidst the shambling corpses. Her blade sang as it cleaved through bone and sinew, while her cookware emitted a comical 'donk' each time it met the hollow skulls of the undead.

"Take that, you decomposing dunce!" she bellowed, flipping an omelette with a flourish before launching it like a discus at an oncoming ghoul. The egg concoction splattered across its face, momentarily blinding it before Roran's hammer sent it back to the underworld with a thud.

"Nice toss!" Roran called out, his laughter almost drowned by the cacophony of battle. He swung his mighty warhammer with the grace of a dancer and the force of a boulder tumbling down a hillside. With each blow, he turned another member of Zalathor's undead army into a pile of bones fit for a dog's dinner.

"Didn't know you had such a soft spot for my cooking," Lila quipped, ducking a clumsy swipe from a zombie whose arm fell off mid-swing. She kicked the detached limb back at its owner, turning the appendage into an impromptu projectile.

"Only when it's served with a side of vengeance," Roran replied, winking at her as he punted a skeleton into a group of its comrades, knocking them down like ghoulish bowling pins.

The defenders fought with a ferocity born of desperation and seasoned with a dash of absurdity. As the undead horde pressed on, undeterred by their losses, the warriors of Oak Isle found strength in their camaraderie and sheer stubbornness.

"Stand fast, defenders of brunch and breakfast!" Ben's voice cut through the chaos, his sword glowing with a mystical light that seemed to flicker in rhythm to the limericks he shouted with each swing. "These bone-bags don't stand a chance against our secret weapon: high spirits and higher cholesterol!"

Amidst the melee, the main characters showcased not only their martial prowess but also a knack for unconventional tactics. Roran hoisted a fellow defender onto his shoulders, allowing him to rain down arrows upon the enemy from this elevated vantage point—creating what they had dubbed the 'Human Ballista.'

Lila, ever the innovator, had rigged a series of pots and pans around the barricades, which clanged alarmingly whenever struck, creating a symphony of culinary chaos that disoriented the foes. She would then leap out from behind cover, dispatching the confused creatures with a combination of spells that smelled suspiciously of rosemary and thyme.

"Looks like we've got them in a stew now!" she exclaimed, a grin spreading across her face as she watched a zombie trip over a ladle embedded in the ground, its uncoordinated limbs flailing comically.

"Keep stirring the pot, Lila!" Ben cheered, blocking a strike with his shield before delivering a swift kick that sent the attacker flying into a makeshift cauldron of boiling oil.

The defenders might have been outnumbered, but their spirits were unyielding, bolstered by the ludicrous yet lethal nature of their resistance. They stood shoulder to shoulder, their laughter mingling with the sounds of battle, defiant in the face of the relentless onslaught. And though the undead were many, the defenders of Oak Isle were determined to let none pass, fighting for their home with every hilarious, heroic stroke.

The air crackled with sorcerous energy as Ben and Elara stood back-to-back, their hands weaving intricate patterns that glowed with arcane light. Where once Ben's fingers fumbled with the basic cantrips of a novice, they now danced confidently through the gestures of power. Elara's chants, tinged with the melody of ancient incantations, harmonized with the hum of magic in the air.

"By the frizzy beard of the Archmage!" Ben exclaimed as he conjured a vortex of wind that swept a cluster of skeletal warriors off their feet, bones clattering like a xylophone gone rogue in a gusty storm.

"May your marrow curdle, you fiendish bag of bones!" Elara countered, her voice rising to a crescendo as a beam of radiant energy shot from her fingertips, blasting through the ranks of shambling horrors like a sunbeam through morning mist.

"Take that, you undead nincompoops!" Ben crowed, as his spell transmuted a group of approaching zombies into a gaggle of bewildered ducks, quacking in befuddled dismay.

"Ben, focus! We're not running a farmyard here," Elara chided, though a smirk betrayed her amusement, even as she summoned a spectral hammer that pounded the ground, sending shockwaves through the earth that tripped up the advancing horde like toddlers on a slippery slope.

Their newfound powers collided with Zalathor's necromancy, sizzling in the air, the smell of ozone and charred feathers mingling with the tang of dark magic. Each pulse of their combined might pushed the undead back, buying precious seconds for their beleaguered comrades.

But with each spell cast, the toll on Ben and Elara grew heavier, like a comedian bearing the weight of an audience's silence. They watched as the city walls were battered by ceaseless assault, stone crumbling under the relentless siege. The groans of the injured and the cries of the dying filled the air with a grim chorus, punctuated by the occasional 'quack' of confused waterfowl.

"Elara, I never thought our end would be so... feathered," Ben gasped between incantations.

"Nor I, Ben. But if we are to be pecked to death by ducklings, let it be known we quacked up a good fight!" Elara replied, her laughter bittersweet as her eyes swept the chaos around them.

Despite their jests, the sting of loss was sharp—friends and allies fell, their bravery snuffed out by the cold hand of undeath. Roran's axe flew less frequently as fatigue set in, and Lila's pot-and-pan orchestra rang with a dirge-like quality that spoke of dwindling hope. The resolve of the defenders was tested as never before, a blade on the whetstone of despair.

Yet it was their indomitable spirit—their refusal to yield to darkness—that burned brightest. Even as tears mingled with the sweat and grime on their faces, they found strength in their camaraderie, their shared defiance against the night.

"Remember, Elara, every time one of us falls, ten shall rise!" Ben declared, rallying his fading strength.

"Then let us be the tide that sweeps away this plague!" Elara shouted, her voice a clarion call that pierced the cacophony of battle.

Together, amidst the absurdity and the tragedy, they fought on, their spells a testament to their unyielding will, their laughter a weapon as potent as any sword or spell. And though the night was long and the enemy vast, their courage would not falter—they would stand, they would fight, and they would endure until the very last quack.

In the thick of battle, where steel clashed with bone and sorcery lit the sky with arcane fire, Zalathor's macabre intelligence proved as sharp as the swords wielded by his lifeless legion. With a sinister snicker that chilled the blood of the living, he directed his undead monstrosities to swarm Oak Isle's capital from every conceivable angle. The streets became rivers of decay, coursing through the city's defenses.

"Split up!" Ben hollered, dodging a particularly toothy skeleton that seemed to have been on a liquid diet for an eternity. "Lila, take the east! Roran, guard the west! And Elara—"

"Say no more, I'll cover the skies," Elara replied, already conjuring a whirlwind that swept up zombies like leaves in an autumn gale.

"Watch out for flying ghouls!" she warned, as one particularly airborne corpse flew past Ben's head, missing by mere inches.

"Thanks for the heads-up!" Ben quipped, ducking another projectile cadaver. He then channeled his magical energies into a spell that turned the ground beneath a group of skeletons into a slippery slope, sending them cascading into each other like the world's least amusing game of dominos.

"Whoops! Looks like you fell for that one," he laughed, his humor as infectious as it was inappropriate given the circumstances.

Roran, his axe now singing a tune of defiance, found himself facing a phalanx of skeletal warriors. With a roar that echoed the ferocity of his forebears, he swung with such force that the bones burst apart in a shower of calcium confetti.

"Bone voyage!" Roran bellowed, grinning at his own pun even as he braced for the next wave.

Lila, meanwhile, had turned her culinary arsenal into implements of war. She lobbed pots filled with an explosive concoction at the encroaching horde. The resulting blasts sent zombie limbs flying, some still grasping for the defenders in a futile effort to fulfill their dark purpose.

"Soup's off!" Lila yelled, as a zombie head landed in a cauldron with a splash. "Guess that's one way to stew over your problems."

Their individual battles were fierce, but the moments of triumph ignited a spark of hope amidst the onslaught. They exploited openings in the enemy's ranks, coordinating strikes with a precision that belied the chaos surrounding them.

"Keep pushing! They've got more holes in their formation than my socks!" Ben shouted, slicing through a ghoul with a sword glowing with enchanted light.

"Any chance we can patch things up later?" Elara jested, her laughter tinged with exhaustion as she summoned a barrier of light to protect a group of retreating civilians.

"Only if you promise to darn my cloak too! It's seen better days!" Ben called back, deflecting a blow from a towering wight with a shield charm.

Through wit and will, they held the line, finding strength in their shared laughter and relentless determination. The tides of undeath ebbed and flowed, but so too did the unbreakable spirit of those who stood against the darkness, their courage as bright as the spells they wove and the jokes they told.

"Remember, folks!" Ben announced to anyone who could hear over the din of combat, "We're not just fighting for our lives; we're fighting for the punchline!"

As Ben ducked beneath the swing of a decaying giant, he couldn't help but notice how its arm detached in a comically slow arc, spinning through the air before smacking into another unsuspecting ghoul. "Heads up!" he called out with a chuckle, even as his heart pounded against his chest. The battlefield was a macabre circus, and he was starting to suspect that the clowns were winning.

"Roran, if you ever wished to practice your juggling, now's the time!" Ben yelled, lobbing a fiery spell at an advancing horde of skeletal warriors. Their bones clattered to the ground, creating a xylophone melody upon impact.

"Juggling swords or heads?" Roran retorted, swinging his mighty axe with such flair that it would've earned applause under different circumstances. His enemies fell in halves, quarters, and eighths, a practical demonstration of fractions for any onlookers with an academic interest.

"Preferably neither!" Lila quipped as she vaulted over a fallen tombstone, her blade dancing in her hand like a maestro directing a symphony of destruction. "We're not aiming for a standing ovation here, just survival!"

The sky darkened as Zalathor summoned his most dreadful lieutenants – wraiths that whispered despair and abominations that wore their grotesqueness like a badge of honor. Yet amidst the terror, the defenders' spirits remained unyieldingly buoyant.

"Ah, audience participation. How quaint," Elara observed dryly, her staff crackling with energy as she prepared a counterspell for an incoming spectral assault. Her magic lashed out, a radiant whip that sent the wraiths screeching back into the shadows.

"Remember, aim for the funny bone! It's their weakest point!" Ben shouted, his sword a blur of light as he carved through a particularly portly zombie who seemed to lose limbs as easily as a leper in a windstorm.

"Ben, I'm fairly certain they have no sense of humor to speak of!" Lila countered, dodging a swipe from a creature whose arms were far too long for its body—a design flaw she exploited by severing them mid-flail.

"Then let's introduce them to slapstick!" Roran bellowed, using an undead ogre's own club to bat away its minions like some perverse game of croquet.

As the battle raged on, the laughter began to wane, replaced by the grim reality of their situation. A towering monstrosity, stitched together from the parts of a dozen fallen beasts, loomed over the defenders, its many eyes gleaming with malevolent hunger.

"Time to make some tough cuts," Ben muttered, feeling the weight of his responsibilities clamp down like a vice. With a heavy heart, he directed a group of younger warriors toward a safer flank, knowing full well it left a weaker contingent at the main gate.

"Keep them safe, Ben. We'll hold the line," Elara said, understanding the necessity of his choice. She summoned a dome of protective light around a cluster of wounded soldiers, her expression etched with resolve.

"Divide and conquer, eh? Let's hope we're the ones doing the conquering," Roran grunted as he parried a blow from the behemoth, his muscles straining against the force.

"Conquering, stand-up routines... we're a multi-talented lot," Ben replied, the strain evident in his voice as he joined Elara at her side. Together, they stood as beacons of hope, determined to keep the darkness at bay with every incantation, every swing of the sword, and every defiant jest.

"Take heart, my friends!" Ben rallied. "For today, we fight not only with steel and sorcery but with the unbreakable will of comedy! They may take our lives, but they'll never take our punchlines!"

With a war cry that sounded suspiciously like the mating call of the northern wild hog, Ben swung his sword with an admirable – if somewhat unorthodox – flair. Beside him, Elara was a blur of motion, her fingers dancing as they wove spells that sizzled through the air, crackling with power and leaving the stench of singed undead in their wake.

"Your invasion is about as welcome as a skunk at a garden party, Zalathor!" Ben bellowed over the chaos, hacking through the arm of a skeleton that had seen better millennia. "And just as ill-advised!"

Elara, amidst casting a spell that turned an approaching ghoul's bones to jelly, couldn't help but snort at Ben's attempt to maintain their spirits through humor. "Focus, Ben! Your jokes are almost as dreadful as your fencing!"

"Ah, but both are still sharper than Zalathor's wit," he quipped back, ducking as a clawed hand swiped at him from the fog of battle.

It was then Roran's voice cut through the din, strained with exertion yet edged with excitement. "Look lively, you two! I've spotted something!"

"Spotted something? Is it the end of this madness?" Ben asked, parrying another blow.

"Better! Zalathor's minions falter whenever he pauses to gloat!" Roran cried out, dodging a spectral wraith that dissipated into mist with a disgruntled howl.

"Wait, their strength ebbs when his attention does?" Elara mused aloud, her mind racing. "Ben, Roran, that's it! His power has limits – he can't sustain his army and his arrogance at the same time!"

"Typical villain oversight," Ben said with a grin, his fatigue momentarily forgotten. "He's too busy monologuing to keep his magical plates spinning."

"Then let's test that theory," Elara declared, her eyes igniting with fierce determination. "Roran, hold his attention. The more he rambles, the weaker they get."

"Leave it to me," Roran replied, puffing out his chest. "I'll distract him with my rugged charm."

"Or your lack thereof," Ben added cheerily, as he prepared himself for what might be their only chance.

"Alright, everyone, it's showtime!" Ben announced to the beleaguered defenders. "Stick to the script—improvise if you must—but let's make this a performance to die for!"

"Or rather, not to die for," Elara corrected wryly, drawing upon her deepest reserves of power.

"Semantics," Ben winked, and together they surged forward, their laughter ringing out as they turned the tide of battle with every spell cast and blade swung, united by the spark of hope that glimmered amidst the darkness.

The ground trembled beneath their feet as Ben and his allies charged, a motley crew of gritty determination and wildly flailing weapons. Lila's sword danced like a ballerina with an attitude problem, cleaving through bone and ectoplasm with equal parts grace and ferocity. Roran, muscles bulging to the point of comedic exaggeration, bellowed challenges that echoed like the world's most aggressive opera singer.

"Come at me, ye skeletal scallywags!" he roared, flexing so hard one could swear his armor squeaked in protest.

Elara, her once pristine robes now looking like the aftermath of an unfortunate altercation with an inkwell, raised her arms high. A torrent of shimmering energy surged from her palms, weaving around her comrades like ribbons of pure defiance. "Taste the rainbow of retribution!" she shouted, a catchphrase that would have made any brand wizard proud.

"Colorful," Ben quipped, twirling the Staff of Tomorrow like a majorette with delusions of grandeur. The staff hummed, its tip crackling with anticipatory magic. "Let's paint the town red... or whatever color scares off dead people."

With a flick of his wrist and a dramatic whoosh, Ben sent a blaze of light arcing over the battlefield, momentarily blinding the undead. It was less a coordinated assault and more an interpretive dance of destruction, but it was working. Their combined might became a symphony of chaos, each note striking true against the discordant army of Zalathor.

"Less prancing, more lancing!" Elara called out, conjuring spears of light that soared like deadly shooting stars.

"Prancing is a valid combat style!" Ben protested, narrowly dodging a decomposing limb that flew past his head. "It's called tactical flamboyance!"

As the last remnants of the undead horde began to crumble like poorly baked scones, a cold silence fell upon the battlefield. Standing amidst the debris, Zalathor emerged, his cloak billowing ominously despite there being no wind. He fixed his gaze on Ben, eyes glowing with malice that could curdle milk at twenty paces.

"Ah, the puppet master himself," Ben said, rolling his shoulders back. "Ready for your final performance, Zalathor?"

"Your jests end here, whelp!" Zalathor spat, raising a hand wreathed in shadows. "I shall enjoy unmaking you."

"Unmaking me? Please, I'm a self-made man. Literally. Spent years crafting this impeccable character arc," Ben bantered, positioning the Staff of Tomorrow before him like a fencing foil.

"Enough!" Zalathor snarled, unleashing tendrils of dark energy that snaked toward Ben with lethal intent.

"Ooh, tentacles. Original," Ben mocked, sidestepping with a flourish. The Staff of Tomorrow pulsed, and he struck out, countering Zalathor's assault with a blast of golden light that illuminated the necromancer's surprised face.

"Yeowch! That's going to leave a mark," Ben cheered, ducking another shadowy swipe.

"Insolent fool! You dare mock my power?" Zalathor raged, his voice rising in octave with every syllable.

"Mock? I'm not mocking. I'm providing constructive criticism through interpretative battle!" Ben retorted, his movements a blur as he matched Zalathor blow for arcane blow.

Their duel became a spectacle of exaggerated gestures and overblown theatrics. Each clash of magic sent shockwaves rippling across the land, bending the very air with the sheer absurdity of their showdown.

"Prepare to be vanquished by the Staff of Tomorrow, which, by the way, came with a very vague instruction manual!" Ben declared, swinging with all his might.

The impact when it came was cataclysmic, a crescendo in their ludicrous concerto of combat. Zalathor's dark magic met the radiant aura of the staff, and for a moment, they were locked in a stalemate of epic proportions.

"Looks like your subscription to 'Necromancy Today' just got canceled," Ben quipped as the light overpowered the darkness, sending Zalathor staggering back, his defeat imminent.

"Impossible..." Zalathor gasped, his form beginning to waver.

"Believe it, bucko," Ben grinned, thrusting the staff forward with a final, triumphant jab. "And scene!"

As the last vestiges of Zalathor's dark magic fizzled out, Ben stood tall, panting from the exertion of their climactic duel. The necromancer's form dissipated like morning mist under the relentless sun, leaving behind only the echo of his disbelief.

"Whew! Did anyone else feel that? That was like ten back-to-back spin classes," Ben said, wiping the sweat from his brow with a dramatic flourish. He glanced at the Staff of Tomorrow, still thrumming with energy in his grasp. "Kudos to you, stick of destiny. You're getting five stars in my book."

Around him, the undead army faltered, their connection to Zalathor severed. They crumbled into piles of bones and dust, as if someone had just hit the off switch on an incredibly macabre puppet show. The defenders of Oak Isle, once besieged and beleaguered, now surged forward with renewed vigor.

"Ha! Take that, you calcium-rich creeps!" one of the soldiers cheered, kicking aside a skull that rolled comically before coming to a stop with its jaw agape, as if in its final moment it wanted to protest its untimely demise.

"Ben! You did it!" Elara called out, her voice cutting through the din of battle. She ran toward him, her robes billowing behind her like the standard of a conquering hero.

"Technically, we did it," Ben replied, opening his arms for an impending celebratory embrace. But instead of a hug, Elara slapped a 'I Defeated An Undead Army And All I Got Was This Lousy T-Shirt' over his armor. Ben looked down and chuckled. "Perfect fit!"

"Everyone, gather 'round!" Roran's booming voice commanded attention as he clambered atop a pile of defeated foes, posing as if he expected a painter to immortalize the moment. "Today, we have fought not just for our lives, but for the very soul of Oak Isle!"

The remaining forces gathered, forming a motley crew of mages, warriors, and even a few townsfolk who had taken up arms. Some were nursing wounds; others were sharing water skins or passing around loaves of slightly squashed bread. But all eyes were on Ben, the unlikely champion with a penchant for quips.

"Friends, neighbors, lend me your ears... but please, make sure to take them back afterward," Ben began, eliciting a ripple of laughter. "We've faced down darkness, danced with death, and came out with our limbs mostly intact. We did more than survive—we thrived!"

Cheers erupted, filling the air with a sense of raucous jubilation. Someone in the back started a chant, which quickly caught on: "Ben! Ben! Ben!"

"Look, I know times have been tough, scarier than a minotaur in a china shop," Ben continued, raising the staff above his head. "But if we can keep laughing in the face of fear, then there's nothing we can't conquer!"

"Here's to a future so bright, we'll need shades!" Elara added, prompting a chorus of agreement.

"May our ale be cold and our fires warm!" Roran bellowed, raising his sword in salute.

"Three cheers for Oak Isle!" a voice shouted from the crowd.

"Hip hip—"

"Hooray!"

"Hip hip—"

"Hooray!"

"Hip hip—"

"Hooray!"

And so, amid the echoes of victory and the laughter of brave souls, Oak Isle rejoiced. For in the heart of triumph, they found something greater than any spell or sword could grant—the hope of a brighter future, forged in the camaraderie of battle and sealed with the promise of peace.

The torch in Ben's hand flickered, casting elongated shadows that danced along the stone walls like mischievous spirits at a spectral ball. He'd been navigating through the labyrinthine bowels of the castle for what felt like an eternity, his sense of direction as reliable as a compass in a magnet factory. Each corridor seemed to smirk with the same stony indifference, offering no more clues than a sphinx on a vow of silence.

"Ah-ha!" Ben exclaimed, stubbing his toe against a flagstone that protruded like the overbite of an ancient troll. "Got you now, you sneaky slab of sediment!"

He knelt down, nursing his abused toe and inspecting the odd stone. With a grunt, he pushed against it, and to his surprise, the wall beside him gave way with a sound like a giant clearing its throat. Dust billowed forth, coating Ben's face and making him look like a powdered donut caught in a windstorm.

"By the saggy stockings of the Sorceress Supreme," he coughed, waving away the dust as he peered into the newly revealed chamber.

Inside, the room was a treasure trove of forgotten lore, shelves bending under the weight of scrolls so old they could apply for historical landmarks. The air smelled of mothballs and mystery, with a hint of eau de ancient librarian. Ben stepped inside, feeling like a burglar in the vault of time.

"Scrolls and scrawls, let's see what forbidden fruits you bear," Ben muttered, approaching the nearest shelf with the giddy anticipation of a child at a candied apple stand.

He unrolled the first scroll, squinting at the cryptic symbols that looked like they'd been penned by a spider high on ink. But Ben's mind was sharper than a unicorn's wit at a dragon's dinner party. He recognized these as the ancient script of Yore-ese, a language so dead that even necromancers refused to summon it.

"Let's unravel this puzzle wrapped in an enigma, swaddled in a conundrum," Ben declared, tracing the symbols with an eager finger.

As he pieced together the messages, a picture began to form—a picture clearer than a minstrel's falsetto on a silent night. The words spun a tale of deceit and power, each phrase a breadcrumb leading towards the mastermind of the rebellion.

"By the goblin king's left nostril... could it be?" Ben whispered, disbelief seasoning his voice. The cryptic messages hinted at an identity so unexpected it would make a ghost gasp.

"Whoever said knowledge is power never mentioned it comes with a side of indigestion," Ben mumbled, rolling up the scroll as realization dawned upon him like sunrise on a hangover.

This was it. The clue he needed was within these arcane writings. However, the truth was as slippery as an eel in a barrel of butter, and Ben knew he had to tread carefully, lest he become as lost in conspiracy as a needle in a haystack the size of a small village.

With a new fire kindling in his belly—one not caused by last night's questionable stew—Ben tucked the telling scroll under his arm and prepared to venture forth into the unknown. The game was afoot, and Ben was determined to win, even if it meant chasing shadows until the cows came home and asked where their supper was.

Ben's hands trembled as the final piece of the puzzle clicked into place. The chamber, once echoing with his triumphant chuckles, now seemed to mock him with silence. Each scroll lay unfurled like a tapestry of treachery, and there, inscribed in an ink that smelt faintly of cabbage, was the revelation that shattered his world: the Flatulent

King was not merely a figurehead lost in his own gaseous clouds but the maestro of mischief, the sultan of subterfuge.

"Great dragon's dentures!" Ben gasped, his voice ricocheting off the stone walls. "The Flatulent King... a mastermind? That's like finding out that a troll has been ghostwriting love sonnets!"

He could no longer stand idle while the realm teetered on the edge of a butter knife, held by the very man who farted in tune with the royal anthem. With the scroll clutched to his chest as if it were the holy grail of gossip, Ben sprinted through the corridors. His boots slapped the stones with a rhythm that sang of urgency and a touch of indigestion from the stew that still waged war within his bowels.

Bursting into the king's chambers without so much as a knock, Ben found the monarch sprawled upon his throne, a scepter in one hand and a leg of mutton in the other. The air was thick with the scent of overripe cheese and the less savory emanations of the king's namesake.

"Your flatulence!" Ben blurted out, then winced. "I mean—Your Highness! Explain yourself this instant! How could you orchestrate such chaos? You, who trips over your own royal slippers and confuses your crown for a chamber pot?"

The Flatulent King looked up, his jowly face creasing into a grin that would curdle milk. "Ah, dear Benjamin," he said with a belch that rattled the stained glass windows. "You've sniffed out my little secret."

"Little? It's as 'little' as a dragon in a dollhouse!" Ben exclaimed, waving the scroll like a flag of rebellion. "You've played us all for fools, but why? Why unleash such bedlam?"

"Bedlam?" The king chuckled, licking grease from his fingers. "My boy, this kingdom needs a good airing out. And I am just the monarch to lift the veils, or should I say... vapors of obscurity."

Ben's nostrils flared—not solely in response to the odious perfume that permeated the chamber—but with the burning need for the truth. The Flatulent King may have underestimated him, thinking him just another pawn in his game of thrones, but Ben was ready to prove that even a pawn could cross the board and become a force to be reckoned with.

Ben's hands clenched into fists, the ancient scroll crumpling under the pressure. "You call this a revelation?" he thundered, his voice cracking the heavy air like a whip. "To turn the realm inside out with your farcical coup?"

"Farce!" The Flatulent King roared with laughter, slapping his knee with such force that his royal robes flapped like sails in a storm. "No, dear Benny, it's a masterstroke! I've orchestrated the rebellion to forge a kingdom in my image—a glorious empire of unbridled freedom and... expressive release."

"Freedom?" spat Ben, incredulous. "By consorting with cutthroats and charlatans? You're tearing apart the very fabric of our society!"

"Fabric is too constrictive!" the king bellowed, releasing a resounding bout of flatulence that echoed off the chamber walls. "Imagine, Benjamin, a world where one needn't hide their true essence behind layers of pretense and perfume. A world ripe with honesty!"

"Honesty?" Ben paced furiously, his mind ablaze. "There is nothing honest about deception and manipulation! You've endangered our people, your own subjects, for what? A grand jest?"

"More than jest, boy," the king winked, a mischievous glint in his eye. "Power. The kind that makes men quake and nations kneel. And who better to wield it than a king who has been perennially underestimated because of a simple, natural bodily function?"

"Simple?" Ben guffawed, throwing his arms up in exasperation. "There's nothing 'simple' about plunging Oak Isle into chaos!"

"Chaos is but a ladder," the king quipped, leaning back on his throne with an ease that belied the gravity of his treachery. "And I intend to climb it to heights unknown, on the winds of change—and other gases."

"Your 'winds of change' reek of tyranny!" Ben retorted, his face flushed with fury. "I will not stand by while you corrupt the heart of this kingdom. I'll expose you for the power-hungry despot you are!"

"Expose me?" The king chuckled, scratching his ample belly. "Oh, my naive boy, who would believe the word of a lowly scribe against the might and right of their king? Especially when he's as endearingly pungent as I am?"

"Endearing?" Ben's voice was laced with scorn. "The only thing you endear yourself to is mockery!"

"Mockery can be powerful, you know," the king said, a conspiratorial smirk twisting his lips. "It disarms and distracts, leaving enemies ripe for the plucking—or should I say, plunking?"

"Enough of your verbal acrobatics!" Ben's eyes blazed with resolve. "I vow to bring your reign of odoriferous oppression to an end, even if I must rally the four corners of Oak Isle to do it!"

"Ah, young Ben, so full of fire and brimstone," the king sighed theatrically, waving a dismissive hand. "Do try not to burn down the castle with your fervor. It's such a bother to rebuild."

"Better to rebuild from ash than live in the stench of your betrayal," Ben declared, his heart hammering with the weight of his promise. "I will see your plots unravel, mark my words."

"Marked and noted," the king said, feigning a yawn. "Now, if you'll excuse me, I have a realm to reshape. Do close the door on your way out—it traps the heat so delightfully."

With each step away from the Flatulent King's chambers, Ben's resolve hardened like steel forged in the fires of indignation. He knew the path ahead would be fraught with peril and punctuated by the perilous pop of insurrection, but in his heart, he also knew the time for action had come. A new wind was rising, and it carried on it the scent of revolution.

Ben marched down the gloomy corridor, his cloak billowing like a storm cloud on legs. The mocking laughter of the Flatulent King echoed in his ears, igniting a firestorm of determination within him. But as he rounded a corner, he skidded to a stop, nearly colliding with an unsuspecting tapestry that depicted the king's legendary conquest of the Gassy Glens.

"Dismiss my threats, will you?" Ben muttered under his breath, his fists clenched tighter than the corset on a courtier trying to impress at the annual Harvest Ball. In the dim light, his shadow stretched across the stone floor, taking on the appearance of a vengeful spirit ready to topple tyrants.

"Mock my efforts, dare you?" He whispered to himself, the words bouncing off the walls and gaining momentum like a rolling boulder in a dwarven mine.

The Flatulent King sat upon his throne of polished whoopee cushions, a smug grin plastered on his face like a bad jester's makeup. "Oh valiant Ben," he said, twirling a ring-laden finger in the air, "Do try to amuse me more with your quaint little insurrection. It's been dreadfully boring around here."

"Your overconfidence is your weakness," Ben retorted, though he spoke to empty air—the king was long gone. A plan began to bubble up in his mind, much like the ill-timed burps that plagued the court after a feast of fizzy fairy brew.

"Proof, I need proof..." he mumbled, pacing back and forth before an armor-clad statue that seemed to judge his every step with its stoic metal gaze.

"Ah-ha!" A eureka moment struck him harder than a minstrel's lute during an accidental tavern brawl. Ben knew he needed irrefutable evidence to expose the Flatulent King's sinister schemes—something so damning that not even the most skeptical noble could deny it.

"Perhaps his royal windbag keeps a record of his own foul deeds," Ben pondered aloud, scratching his chin, which had recently begun sporting a rebellion-worthy beard.

He darted toward the royal archives—a place he knew well for its quiet corners perfect for plotting and its musty smell that reminded one of secrets long buried. If any incriminating documents existed, they would be there, nestled among the endless scrolls like a needle in a haystack made entirely of hay-shaped needles.

"Rally support, gather the proof, and let the winds of change blow through this realm," Ben proclaimed to a particularly judgmental-looking gargoyle perched above the archive's door.

"Tonight, the whispers of rebellion shall grow into a roar!" His voice carried the weight of his conviction, and somewhere deep within the castle, a rat squeaked in agreement.

With a heart full of courage and pockets devoid of evidence, Ben crept into the shadows of the archive, his mission clear. The game of thrones was afoot, and it smelled suspiciously like flatulence. But soon, the Flatulent King would find that underestimating the plucky hero named Ben was akin to ignoring a simmering pot of dragon chili—it was only a matter of time before it exploded spectacularly.

Ben slinked through the dimly lit corridors of the castle, his cloak billowing like a shadowy specter evading the light. The heavy oak door to the Flatulent King's study loomed before him, its intricate carvings mocking the solemnity of his quest. With a deft touch and a silent prayer to the gods of mischief, Ben picked the lock, the tumblers clicking into place as if they too were complicit in his rebellious act.

He slipped inside, closing the door with the gentlest of nudges, and surveyed the room. The study was a chaotic symphony of opulence and oddity—taxidermied creatures wearing monocles, bookshelves lined with volumes ranging from "Alchemy and Its Discontents" to "101 Jokes for Court Jesters" (the latter clearly well-thumbed). But Ben's focus was singular: find the evidence that would deflate the King's inflated treachery.

Candelabras threw flickering shadows across his determined face as he rummaged through drawers overstuffed with royal decrees on proper court flatulence etiquette. He upturned gilded inkwells and sifted through mounds of parchment, each inscribed with the King's looping, extravagant script that spoke of a man who surely loved the smell of his own prose.

"Where are you, you wretched little scribblings of sedition?" he muttered, tossing aside a treatise on the gastronomical perils of cabbage soup.

Then, behind a portrait of the Flatulent King himself, eyes bulging with gaseous pride, Ben discovered it—a hidden compartment. With trembling hands, he reached in and extracted a stack of secret letters bound by a ribbon that reeked of conspiracy (and a faint hint of brimstone).

His eyes scanned the first letter, the words leaping out at him with the force of a catapulted cow: plans, troop movements, alliances—all laid bare in an indigestible stew of treacherous detail. Ben's lips curled into a triumphant grin. "Got you by the royal breeches now, your windy highness," he whispered.

But fate, that capricious jester, chose this moment to play her hand. The sound of footsteps echoed down the corridor, growing louder, unhurried but purposeful. Panic's icy fingers gripped Ben's spine. He needed a hiding spot—a tapestry, perhaps? No time! With the agility of a cat—or perhaps a very quiet elephant—he dove beneath the massive desk, clutching the letters to his chest, and scarcely daring to breathe.

The door creaked open, and the footsteps entered the room. Ben's heart hammered against his ribcage, threatening to burst forth and proclaim his presence. From his vantage point, he could see the intruder's boots—polished, portentous, and predictably pompous.

"Whoever you are, tread lightly," Ben thought, stifling the urge to sneeze or laugh or cry. "For the winds are changing, and soon, the Flatulent King will be caught in the gale of his own making."

And so, there he lay, amidst dust bunnies the size of actual bunnies, awaiting the chance to turn whispered winds into a tempest of truth.

The boots stopped short of Ben's trembling hideout, and a second pair clacked against the cold stone floor. The Flatulent King's voice, ripe with the smugness of overripe cheese, wafted down to Ben's ears.

"Your Flatulence," greeted the henchman, his voice oozing obsequiousness like a slug on a salt-free diet.

"Ah, my loyal windbreaker," the king replied with a guffaw that reeked of arrogance and last night's cabbage stew. "How fairs our little uprising?"

"Like a bean-fed steed in full gallop, sire," the henchman snickered. "Oak Isle will never see it coming."

"Excellent! They'll be bowing to our gusts before they know what hit them. Remember, we strike at dawn when the air is still... and unsuspecting."

Ben's heart raced like a jester on stilts; the menace in their tone was palpable even beneath the layers of flatulence-laden banter. He clutched the letters, each word now a spark to ignite rebellion's tinder.

"Ensure the guards are silent as the grave," the king continued, "I want no whiff of our plans leaking out."

"Of course, your Gassiness. Silent as the dead air in a crypt." The henchman bowed, the creak of his leather armor squeaking like a mouse under interrogation.

As their footsteps faded into the distance, Ben exhaled slowly. It was time for an escape worthy of legend—or at least worthy of the tavern tales. Slipping from under the desk with the grace of a greased-up gnome on a slide, he scanned the room. Guards would be upon him faster than a hiccup after hot soup if he didn't move swiftly.

With all the stealth of a shadow at midnight, Ben darted toward the door and pressed his ear against the cool wood. Silence teased him from the other side. He turned the handle with a tenderness usually reserved for lovers and old wounds, eased the door open, and slipped through like a secret passed in a whisper.

Corridor stretched before him, dimly lit by flickering torches that cast long, dancing shadows. Ben hugged the wall, moving with purposeful haste. A guard rounded the corner ahead, and Ben froze like a statue cursed by a sorcerer to eternal stillness.

"Mustn't look up. Mustn't see me," Ben willed with all the mental might of a warlock in a duel of minds. The guard, oblivious to the high stakes game of hide-and-seek, ambled past, picking his teeth with the casual air of one who has never stumbled upon a clandestine intruder.

Ben crept onward, the secret letters prickling against his skin as though alive with urgency. He reached the end of the corridor where two guards stood sentry, their conversation a dull murmur of nothingness.

"Distraction," Ben muttered. With a deft flick, he tossed a coin down an intersecting hallway. It clattered, bounding with the enthusiasm of a puppy off its leash. The guards turned, perplexed, their thoughts clearly not trained for such complex events. As they shuffled off to investigate, Ben seized the moment.

He sprinted down the remaining stretch, the castle's heavy doors now in sight. Heart thundering like a drum in a bard's most rousing tune, he pushed the doors open and burst into the cool night air.

Freedom beckoned as Ben fled into the embrace of darkness, clutching the letters that held the power to unravel the Flatulent King's foul plans. Oak Isle's fate hung in the balance, and it was up to him, of all people, to tip the scales.

Ben bolted across the moonlit courtyard, his boots slapping the cobblestones with the urgency of a town crier who'd just discovered caffeine. The night air nipped at his cheeks, but he could not afford to be caressed by the chill – there was no time for such frigid flirtations.

"By the dragons' snoring nostrils," he panted, "I must gather the motley crew of misfits!" Oak Isle, that gem of a land, squirmed under the Flatulent King's odorous oppression, and Ben knew he had to be the laxative to relieve this constipated kingdom of its bloated tyrant.

He ducked into the shadowy recesses of an alleyway, the secret letters rustling in his tunic like a chorus of conspiratorial crickets. He could almost hear the whispers of rebellion hidden within the ink, urging him on. Every second squandered was a second the Flatulent King remained on his noxious throne, unleashing silent-but-deadly schemes upon the unsuspecting masses.

"Enough with the stench of treachery!" Ben declared to the night, startling a pair of courting owls. With the resolve of a knight facing a dragon with nothing but a spork and a good sense of humor, he set off toward the seedy tavern known as The Wobbly Goblin. It was there he would find the rebels, those brave souls who dared to raise their noses at the foul wind of despotism.

He navigated through the streets, avoiding the patrols with a nimbleness that would make a mountain goat write home in envy. "To arms, friends! To arms!" he practiced his rallying cry, though it came out as a whisper, for fear of waking up more than just revolutionary spirits.

As he neared the tavern, the sound of lutes played poorly and drunken laughter spilled out into the streets like ale from a bottomless mug. This was it, the den of potential heroes, each one likely nursing a grudge against the Flatulent King along with their hangovers.

"Time to turn the tides of fate," Ben murmured, squaring his shoulders. He pushed open the door to The Wobbly Goblin with a dramatic flair worthy of the grandest stage, prepared to unite a band of rebels in a most epic, if not slightly comedic, struggle for freedom.

"Listen well, ye brave but soused souls!" Ben proclaimed, standing atop a rickety table that groaned in protest. "Tonight, we plot more than mere mischief; we plot the downfall of a flatulent fiend!"

A hush fell over the crowd, tankards pausing mid-tilt, and all eyes turned to Ben – some bleary, some bloodshot, but all blazing with the fire that only the prospect of rebellion (or perhaps free drinks) could ignite.

"Who's with me?" he bellowed, brandishing the secret letters like a flag of revolution.

The tavern erupted into cheers, the uproarious kind that could start an avalanche or at least a bar brawl. Rebels leapt to their feet, raising fists and whatever else they had handy. Ben felt it then, the surge of camaraderie, the unity of purpose – and above all, the tickling beginnings of hope. The Flatulent King's days were numbered, and the count was more hilarious than anyone could have imagined.

The night air was thick with the scent of impending revolution and questionable hygiene as Ben burst from The Wobbly Goblin, a chorus of hiccups and war cries billowing behind him. His cloak flapped dramatically in the wind—a wind that also carried the distinct aroma of the Flatulent King's latest decree—reminding all too vividly why they were fighting.

"Comrades of Oak Isle," he shouted, teetering on the edge of the town square, which was not so much a square but rather an awkward trapezoid. "We stand on the cusp of destiny! A destiny that smells better than our foe's chambers after a feast of beans and cabbage!"

His motley crew—an assortment of bakers with rolling pins poised like maces, blacksmiths wielding hammers with the finesse of seasoned warriors, and even the local jesters juggling knives with more skill than sense—all rallied around him, their spirits as high as the stakes.

"Let us march," Ben declared, pointing a determined finger towards the castle that loomed ominously in the distance, its turrets silhouetted against the full moon like crooked teeth in a sinister grin. "We march to unseat the tyrant king who has reigned over us with nothing but hot air and broken promises!"

A cheer went up, echoing off the cobblestones. Ben's heart swelled with pride, and his stomach churned with nerves—or perhaps it was the dubious stew from the tavern. Either way, he was ready to lead this ragtag rebellion into the annals of history or at least into a very memorable tavern tale.

"Remember," he cried out, pausing for dramatic effect as his followers leaned in, "the Flatulent King may have the power to clear a room with a single toot, but we have the power of the people! And considerably better manners!"

With that, Ben led the charge, his boots clomping against the stone with the sort of rhythm that could inspire a dance number in a more musical world. His comrades followed suit, a cacophony of footsteps, clanging metal, and the occasional belch of determination.

As they approached the castle gates, the reality of what they were about to do settled upon them like dew on morning grass—slightly uncomfortable and unavoidably damp. Ben knew that the battle ahead would be fraught with peril, likely involving some slapstick mishaps and narrow escapes, but he also knew that the story of tonight would be told for generations—or at least until next week's ale-tasting festival.

So there Ben stood, at the forefront of an army fueled by courage and fermented beverages, ready to face the challenges ahead and expose the Flatulent King's true colors to the world. It was the beginning of a new battle, one that would test their mettle, their wits, and their capacity to withstand bad odors.

"Charge!" he bellowed, as the first chicken launched from a makeshift catapult sailed over the walls, signaling the start of a most unconventional siege. The revolution had begun, and its battle cry was a resounding, albeit comical, squawk.

The sky above Oak Isle's capital city was a dreary canvas splattered with menacing hues, but no one expected the paint to drip monsters. Ben squinted up at the heavens as if he had ordered chaos for breakfast and received an extra helping of doom. With a collective groan louder than a tavern brawl, Zalathor's undead army tore through the clouds like ragged fingernails on the soft underbelly of serenity.

"By the hairy toes of the Ancients," Ben exclaimed, dodging a particularly enthusiastic skeleton that seemed to think it could fly. It couldn't. It crashed beside him, bones clattering like a xylophone in the hands of a drunkard.

Oak Isle's denizens scattered, their screams composing a symphony of panic with undertones of 'not again' and overtones of 'we're doomed'. A chicken, caught in the frenzy, sprinted past with an urgency normally reserved for foxes. Or tax collectors.

"Alright, chums!" bellowed Ben as a zombie's arm flew by, still gripping a rather confused looking turnip. "Regroup! And someone tell me why there's a turnip involved!"

His allies—a band of misfits who'd seen more battles than a training dummy—scrambled to his side, each wearing an expression ranging from 'mildly inconvenienced' to 'outright horrified'.

"Zalathor's really outdone himself this time," muttered Elara, ducking a decapitated head that rolled with an agenda. "And I thought last week's rain of frogs was his pièce de résistance."

"Can we focus, please?" Lila snapped, as she parried a blow from an overly ambitious ghoul with her frying pan. The ghoul reeled back, evidently insulted. You don't bring a sword to a frying pan fight.

"Right," said Roran, nocking an arrow to his bow with the casual flair of a man who'd done it a thousand times, probably because he had. "Let's take stock: undead army falling from the sky, check; citizens losing their collective minds, double-check; and us, without a plan, triple-check!"

"Actually," interjected Ben, "I have half of a plan."

"Half?" echoed Elara, as she cast a spell that turned a nearby wraith into an assortment of daisies. "What kind of discount strategy is that?"

"Discount or not, we need to move!" insisted Ben, ushering them away from a collapsing bakery that belched out cookie-scented smoke. "We've got an immediate threat to face and a city to save. Also, we might want to check on the turnip situation later; it could be significant."

"Or," suggested Lila, swinging her frying pan with a gusto that would make a chef weep, "it could be just another Tuesday in Oak Isle."

Ben vaulted over a crumbling wall, narrowly missing the swipe of a skeletal hand that sought to add him to the ranks of the undead. The capital city was a macabre dance floor where the living pirouetted around death at every turn. As he landed, his boots squelched into something unpleasantly soft and suspiciously brain-like.

"Damnable necromancer!" shouted Roran, plucking an arrow from the eye socket of a decapitated skull with a flourish. "He's turned the town square into a jigsaw puzzle for the morally deceased!"

"Less complaining, more stabbing!" Elara commanded, her staff ablaze with arcane energy that crackled like a tempest in a teapot. She dispatched another wave of undead, turning them into a flock of blackbirds that promptly flew off, cawing insults at their former master.

"Listen up," Ben gasped, ducking as a zombie's head flew past – courtesy of Lila's well-aimed skillet. "If we don't deal with Zalathor now, there won't be a city left to save. Yet, if we abandon our quest for the Descendant, all this" – he gestured broadly at the pandemonium – "will be just the opening act."

"Are you suggesting we do a little column A, a little column B?" Lila quipped, using her frying pan to deflect a bone shard like a bizarre game of badminton. "Because I'm not sure we can multitask with this level of apocalyptic flair."

"Perhaps a strategic retreat is in order," Roran mused, twirling an arrow between his fingers. "Draw back, find the Descendant, grab the Staff of Tomorrow, then come back swinging?"

"Easy for you to say," Elara retorted. "Your quiver doesn't have a 'this way to the prophesied savior' arrow, does it?"

"True," Roran conceded. "But it does have a 'let's not get eaten by the ravenous dead' one."

"Ben," Lila pressed, her eyes scanning for the next reanimated offense. "You're our fearless-ish leader. What's the play?"

With the weight of Oak Isle on his shoulders, Ben chewed his lip thoughtfully. He could practically hear the tick-tock of an imaginary clock counting down their fate. "We need to stop Zalathor, yes, but without the Descendant of Eclipse... we're just bailing water out of a sinking ship with a sieve."

"Poetic," Elara said dryly, "but what's the decision?"

Ben took a deep breath, steadying his resolve. "We split up. Some stay to keep these bones rattling in their own graves, and others go for the Descendant."

"Splitting up is what people in scary stories do right before they get picked off one by one," Roran pointed out helpfully.

"Ah, but those are stories," Ben grinned, a manic glint in his eye. "This is Oak Isle, where the improbable is breakfast, and impossibility is lunch. We'll have victory for dinner... hopefully not as the main course."

The ground shook with the thunderous advance of Zalathor's legion as Ben and his motley crew of would-be saviors ducked another volley of necrotic arrows. "By the great Beard of Eldrin," Ben gasped, nearly tripping over a cobblestone that had the audacity to protrude at such an inopportune time, "this is turning into a circus act where the clowns are trying to murder us!"

"Except clowns don't usually reanimate and try to kill you... again," Lila quipped, dispatching a skeletal assailant with a jab of her staff that sent bones scattering like macabre confetti.

"Debatable," Roran muttered, slicing through the air with his twin blades, their edges singing a requiem for the recently undead.

"Enough!" Ben bellowed over the din of destruction. "We're doing less deciding and more dying here, and I'm not fond of either!"

"Then make the call, Captain Indecisive!" Elara snapped, loosing another enchanted arrow that exploded in a burst of light, momentarily illuminating her exasperated scowl.

"Fine!" Ben roared back, the very fire of the Dragon's Maw seemingly alighting his gaze. "We stand our ground! We can't let Zalathor turn this city into his personal playground of perdition!"

"Ah, so now we're playground monitors fending off the bully who happens to command an army of the damned?" Roran's tone was drier than the Desert of Despair during a particularly parched summer.

"Exactly!" Ben said, missing the sarcasm entirely. "If we don't hold the line here, there won't be an Oak Isle to save!"

"Ben's right," Lila conceded with a sigh, twirling her staff as if it were a baton in a parade celebrating their impending doom. "We might be chasing legends and prophecies, but the people here are real, and they need us now."

"Thank you, Lila! Finally, some sense!" Ben exclaimed, puffing his chest out like a pigeon attempting to intimidate a dragon.

"Though I'll point out," Elara interjected, her voice cutting through the air sharper than any blade, "this 'sense' does seem to flirt dangerously with outright lunacy."

"Outright lunacy is my middle name," Ben declared, though it wasn't, it was actually Herbert, but that was hardly inspirational.

"Ben 'Outright Lunacy' Herbert," Roran mused, nodding thoughtfully. "Has a certain ring to it."

"Focus!" Ben snapped, slapping Roran's shoulder with the flat of his hand. "Oak Isle needs us. We'll fight off Zalathor's cronies, protect these people, and then—"

"Find a miraculous way to track down the Descendant of Eclipse without getting ourselves turned into decorative undead topiaries? Sounds delightful," Elara drawled, already nocking another arrow.

"Right! Now let's show these boneheads that Oak Isle isn't just going to roll over and play dead," Ben rallied, drawing his sword with a flourish that he hoped looked at least half as heroic as it felt.

"Too bad we can't say the same for half the city..." Roran quipped as they prepared to meet the next wave head-on, their laughter echoing amidst the chaos as they charged into battle, fully aware that they were possibly making the worst—and most heroic—decision of their lives.

Ben parried a decaying arm that swung towards him with an enthusiasm that belied its rot, sending it flying into the abyss of battle. The undead assailant paused, seemingly confused about where its limb had gone before Roran dispatched it with a swing of his axe, adding insult to dismemberment.

"An excellent time for a strategic discussion," Elara shouted over the din, dodging a flailing ghoul as she made her way toward Ben. Her sarcasm was as sharp as the arrowheads in her quiver.

"Couldn't agree more! Anyone seen a conference room around?" Ben yelled back, punctuating his question with a thrust that sent another animated corpse toppling.

"Enough!" Elara's anger sliced through the chaos, and for a moment, even the undead seemed to pause. "We cannot lose sight of our true mission. Zalathor is but one head of the hydra. The Descendant of Eclipse and the Staff of Tomorrow—"

"Are certainly not going to waltz up to us here," Lila interjected, spinning with an elegance that sent heads, quite literally, rolling.

"Indeed." Elara brushed off some stray vertebrae from her shoulder. "We need the staff, and we need the descendant. Without them, this is all just an elaborate dance of death."

"Can we at least agree on a tango then?" Roran chipped in, cleaving through another opponent.

"Must you always make light of—" Ben began, but the look in Elara's eyes stopped him cold.

"Roran may jest," she said, "but he's not wrong about our predicament. We can't let Zalathor's parade of putrescence blind us to our ultimate goal."

"Fine," Ben conceded, panting as he sidestepped a zombie whose legs didn't get the memo it was dead. "Splitting up makes my stomach churn worse than the three-day-old fish stew at The Groggy Goblin, but I see your point."

"Then it's settled!" Roran declared, almost cheerily. "Some stand their ground, others seek the eclipse. What could possibly go wrong?"

"Everything," Lila said flatly, "which is precisely why we must be precise in our folly."

"Right." Ben squared his shoulders, looking each of his comrades in the eye. "You know what they say: divide and hopefully not get conquered."

"Who says that?" Lila asked, arching an eyebrow.

"Let's just pretend it's an old Oak Isle adage," Ben said, waving off the question as he readied himself for the split. "Now, let's carve out a path for both teams. May the winds favor us all."

"Or at least blow the stench away," Roran muttered as they grouped together, preparing to part ways in the heart of pandemonium. The decision weighed heavily, yet somewhere between the concern and the quips, their camaraderie shone like a beacon—a ludicrous, laughing light against the dark fantasy unfurling around them.

With a final, exaggerated salute that would've made the staunchest of generals giggle, Roran bid farewell to the half of their fellowship destined to become Zalathor's immediate problem. Elara, her eyes shimmering with unshed tears and the sheen of determination, clasped hands with those staying behind, her grip speaking volumes of promises to return triumphant or perhaps not at all.

"May your swords be swift and your wits swifter," Lila intoned, offering a solemn nod devoid of her usual sarcastic lilt. Their allies, in turn, responded with an assortment of thumbs-ups, hearty back-slaps, and the kind of teary-eyed grimaces that suggested they'd rather be having a root canal than facing an undead horde.

"Alright, enough of this sappy goodbye business," Ben declared, his voice cracking just a little as he turned towards the path less traveled—or more accurately, the path littered with bloodthirsty revenants. "To the Descendant of Eclipse!"

"Shouldn't we have a catchier battle cry?" Roran quipped as they jogged away from the relative safety of their parting point. "Something like, 'Onward, to glory and indigestion!' since we're clearly about to bite off more than we can chew."

"Quiet, Roran," Elara chided, though the corners of her mouth twitched upwards. "We need to stay focused."

"Focused on what? The battalion of skeletal warriors playing hopscotch with our intestines?" Lila interjected, drawing her twin blades with a flourish that somehow managed to be both deadly and droll.

Their banter was cut short by a guttural roar that echoed through the twisted trees of Oak Isle. Out from the shadowy underbrush emerged a ghastly sight—a pack of ghouls gnashing teeth that hadn't seen dental care in centuries.

"By the hairy toes of the Great Bard!" Roran exclaimed. "Do these fiends never tire?"

"Apparently not," Ben said, unsheathing his sword with a metallic ring that seemed to mock the gravity of their situation. "But we've got an eclipse to catch and a staff to secure, so let's make this quick."

The ensuing skirmish was less a display of martial prowess and more an interpretive dance of dodges, jabs, and the occasional accidental self-inflicted wound. Elara's magic crackled in the air, sending bolts of energy into the ranks of the undead, while Lila's blades sang a duet of death. Roran, somehow managing to trip over absolutely nothing, inadvertently discovered that a well-placed faceplant could also take down an approaching zombie.

"Who knew your greatest weapon would be clumsiness?" Ben laughed, parrying a skeletal swipe with a deftness that surprised everyone, himself included.

"Laugh it up," Roran retorted from the ground, wrestling with a particularly persistent ghoul. "I'm inventing new combat techniques here!"

"Let's hope that's not one of them," Elara said dryly, extending a hand to help him up.

"Can we agree to never speak of this again?" Roran asked, dusting himself off with as much dignity as he could muster.

"Agreed," Lila said with a smirk. "Now come. Our date with destiny awaits, and she's notoriously impatient."

With that, the quartet resumed their quest, their steps lighter and their spirits buoyed by the comic relief that had just saved their skins. They knew the path ahead was fraught with peril, but for now, they reveled in the small victory against Zalathor's minions, their laughter echoing through the ominous forest.

As Ben and his motley crew of would-be saviors plodded through the once vibrant market square of Oak Isle, they stumbled upon a scene that was equal parts tragic and absurd. A group of survivors, huddled together in what remained of an overturned fruit cart, were fending off a trio of skeletal warriors with nothing but overripe melons and a particularly pungent wheel of cheese.

"Take that, you boneheaded fiends!" shouted a sprightly old woman, lobbing a mushy apple with surprising accuracy at an undead's hollow eye socket. The skeleton, momentarily disoriented, flailed its arms comically before collapsing into a pile of calcium-rich debris.

Ben paused, torn between horror and hilarity. "I never thought I'd say this, but thank the gods for senile strength and spoiled fruit!"

Elara, her face streaked with soot and determination, conjured a whip of blue flame, snaring another assailant by its ribcage and yanking it towards a fiery demise. "Keep your wits about you! This is no time to be distracted by the eccentricities of combat!"

Lila, meanwhile, danced between the improvised projectiles, her twin blades dispatching foes with elegant sweeps. "I must admit, there's a certain... artistry to their madness."

"Artistry?" Roran huffed, vaulting over a crate with less grace and more luck. "This is sheer lunacy! But if it works, who am I to judge?" He then promptly slipped on a squashed banana, inadvertently careening into the last skeleton and reducing it to a heap of disjointed bones.

"Impeccable form, Roran," Ben quipped, offering a hand to his prone companion.

"Didn't you agree to never speak of my combat... mishaps again?" Roran grumbled, accepting the help up.

"Consider it a compliment," Lila chimed in, sheathing her swords. "You're consistently consistent in your inconsistency."

"Enough," Elara interjected, her gaze sweeping over the weary survivors. "Your resilience is inspiring, but you must find safety. We have a tyrant to topple, and with each fallen foe, our resolve hardens."

"Go," said Ben, nodding to the survivors. "We'll cover your retreat. For every soul saved today, we strike another blow against Zalathor."

With renewed vigor, the group of ragtag defenders scrambled to safer ground, leaving behind a battlefield strewn with fruity carnage and bony remnants.

"Forward!" Ben declared, leading the charge through the decimated streets. Their mission was clear, their purpose unwavering. They trudged through the desolation, their hearts heavy with the weight of responsibility, yet buoyed by the unyielding spirit of those they fought to protect.

"Remember, my friends," Ben said as they navigated the treacherous remains, "our tale is not one of tragedy but triumph. We will reclaim Oak Isle, one laugh at a time!"

"Here's to hoping the next undead horde has a weakness for slapstick," Roran added with a wry grin.

"Or at least a distaste for dairy," Lila mused.

Together, they pressed on, laughter mingling with the echoes of battle cries, a reminder that even in the darkest of times, hope—and humor—could still flourish.

As the cacophony of warfare rang through the once-tranquil avenues of Oak Isle's capital, a motley crew of defenders rallied to its defense, their arms laden with an arsenal that was as bizarre as it was unexpectedly effective. Led by Sir Cedric, whose armor clinked with every gallant stride, they prepared to face Zalathor's undead minions with a peculiar blend of valor and vaudeville.

"Brace yourselves!" Sir Cedric bellowed, his voice echoing off the city walls. "Remember, we fight with the ferocity of dragons and the wit of court jesters!"

"Sir," piped up a squire holding a catapult loaded with ripe tomatoes, "are you sure about this?"

"Absolutely!" Cedric exclaimed. "Nothing disheartens a skeleton like a squashed tomato to the cranium!"

With the fervor of a man who believed wholeheartedly in the power of produce, Sir Cedric signaled the attack. Tomatoes soared through the air like red comets, splattering against bone and armor with satisfying splats. The skeletons, momentarily stunned by the unconventional assault, hesitated, their hollow eye sockets seemingly widened in surprise.

"Ha-ha! Take that, ye boneheaded fiends!" shouted Dame Agatha, who wielded a bagpipe with a ferocity unmatched by any highland warrior. She squeezed the instrument with such force that the drones emitted a sound so dreadful, so discordant, that several of the undead clamped their skeletal hands over where their ears once were.

"Is it music or is it torture?" mused a young archer as he loosed an arrow adorned with a buzzing kazoo. It whistled through the air before finding its mark, and the resultant drone added to the eerie symphony.

"Both!" Cedric hollered back. "And it's working!"

Indeed, Zalathor's forces, unprepared for the comedic onslaught, began to falter. Skeletons tripped over rinds and peels while others recoiled from the incessant din of what could only be described as 'bagpipe warfare.'

"Bring forth the rubber chickens!" a knight called out, and from a wagon, a heap of the floppy fowl was distributed amongst the fighters. With a battle cry that would have made any minstrel's lyrics ludicrous, they charged, wielding the poultry with the might of Excalibur itself.

Skeletons clacked and clattered under the relentless barrage, bones shattering under the absurd might of rubbery wattles and comically long necks. Each impact was accompanied by a squeak that somehow inspired more terror in the undead than any blacksmith-forged blade.

"By the jesters of yore, we're winning!" Sir Cedric laughed, ducking as a skull soared overhead, ejected from the fray by the judicious application of a chicken leg.

"Take heart, my brave buffoons, our humor is our strength!" He rallied the troops, his voice rising above the melee. "For today, we prove that even in the darkest of shadows, laughter shines brightest!"

As the sun dipped below the horizon, casting the scene in a golden glow, the defenders of Oak Isle stood amidst the remnants of the most unusual battleground—fields littered with fruit, feathers, and the disjointed remains of an army that had met its match in the form of slapstick bravery.

"Zalathor will think twice before attacking a land protected by the shield of satire!" Sir Cedric declared, his chest swelling with pride beneath his dented cuirass. And with that, the defenders let out a triumphant cheer, their spirits undimmed by the setting sun, their laughter echoing into the encroaching night.

The ragtag band of adventurers, more resembling a walking infirmary than a fearsome group of heroes, limped their way to the foreboding gates of Zalathor's den. Ben, leading this parade of the pitiful, had a helmet that was dented in new and interesting ways from their last escapade. His normally bright armor was tarnished with the grime of battle, and his cape—which he insisted added a dramatic flair—was now a tattered rag flapping in the wind like the world's saddest surrender flag.

"Right," Ben said with forced bravado that fooled absolutely no one. "Zalathor won't know what hit him! Probably because we look like a troupe of traveling beggars, but still!"

Their cautious approach was marred by the clanking of their gear and the occasional grunt as someone tripped over their own feet. It wasn't the stealthiest entrance, but when your rogue was nursing a twisted ankle, and your mage had singed off half her eyebrows, standards tended to drop significantly.

As they crossed the threshold into Zalathor's lair, the atmosphere shifted palpably. A void of silence engulfed them, and it was so thick you could practically slice it with one of the many blunt swords their warrior was currently juggling in his arms, having lost all his scabbards.

"Ah, nothing quite says 'home' like the damp acoustics of dripping water and distant cackling," Ben quipped, trying to ignore the goosebumps forming on his skin. "Really brings out the rustic charm of the undead aesthetic."

They paused, straining their ears against the quiet. There it was—the soft plink-plink of water echoing through the cavernous space, accompanied by the unsettling soundtrack of Zalathor's laughter bouncing off the walls. It sounded as though he'd found the concept of impending doom absolutely hilarious, or perhaps he'd just heard one of Ben's jokes.

"Cheer up, everyone," Ben continued, with a grin as wobbly as their moral compass. "We've faced worse than a bit of sinister giggling. I mean, just last week, we survived that tavern brawl with nothing but our wits and an inexplicably angry badger. We can handle old Zally."

His attempt at lightening the mood fell flat, much like the expression of their healer who seemed to be questioning several of her life choices at that very moment. Nonetheless, they pressed on, because if there was one thing this group was good at, it was stubbornly refusing to acknowledge when they were outmatched, outwitted, and potentially out of their minds.

Ben's heart hammered in his chest like a blacksmith too stubborn to admit he was using the anvil all wrong. He led the way, each footfall a silent testament to his burgeoning career in stealth—if one could ignore the clattering of gear and the occasional curse from someone stepping on a particularly pointy rock.

"Keep your eyes peeled, folks," Ben whispered, though it came out more like a hiss as he tried not to trip over his own boots. His grip on his sword tightened, knuckles whitening around the hilt. The blade hadn't seen this much action since that time he mistook it for a skewer during a particularly dire shortage of cooking utensils.

"Peel your own eyes," muttered their mage, whose idea of 'stealth' was only casting the loudest spells when absolutely necessary. "I've seen less tense string quartets."

"Shh!" Ben insisted, despite knowing full well that subtlety had abandoned them at the first whiff of necromancer's lair mold. They crept onward, with the grace of a herd of cats attending a water ballet.

Then, without so much as a courteous forewarning, the ground decided it had had quite enough of being stepped on, thank you very much, and promptly gave way beneath them. There was a collective yelp—less a battle cry and more the sound of dignity evacuating the premises—as they tumbled headlong into darkness.

"Trap!" someone managed to shout, rather unhelpfully, as they were already well-acquainted with the sensation of falling.

They landed with a series of thuds, groans, and one suspiciously musical clang. Ben lay sprawled atop a pile of his comrades, blinking in the gloom, trying to determine if he still possessed all his limbs or if some had opted to take early retirement.

"Everyone alright?" he called out, hoping the response would be more than just pained groaning. It was mostly pained groaning.

"Define 'alright,'" the healer grumbled from somewhere to his left, her voice tinged with the kind of sarcasm usually reserved for mocking the accuracy of weather predictions.

"Alive, preferably," Ben replied, extricating himself from the human jigsaw puzzle they'd become.

"Could we land on something soft next time?" suggested the thief of the group, who prided himself on never getting caught—except by floors, apparently.

"Let's add it to the suggestion box," Ben retorted, finally hauling himself upright. He dusted off his pride before it could get too sullied by the fall. "Now, let's find those captives and show Zalathor what happens when you mess with a group that's too stubborn to know when they're beaten!"

Amidst the scattered laughter and groans, the echoes of the necromancer's mirth seemed to grow louder, chilling the air around them. They had fallen right into Zalathor's bony hands—or at least, the part of the lair where he probably kept his spare bony hands. The adventure, as ill-advised as it was, continued.

As Ben regained his footing, an unsavory stench wafted into his nostrils, a blend of decay and defeat. His eyes snapped open to a grotesque panorama: Zalathor's minions encircled them, their flesh hanging in tatters, red eyes flickering with unholy light like cheap tavern lanterns.

"Is it just me, or does anyone else feel ridiculously underdressed for this zombie soiree?" quipped the thief, brandishing his daggers with a flourish that was entirely inappropriate for the occasion.

"Focus!" Ben barked, though he couldn't help but admire the undead's commitment to their aesthetic. He raised his sword, its blade glinting with the faintest hope in the shadowy chamber. "Prepare yourselves!"

The group rallied, forming a back-to-back circle as the horde lurched closer. Spells sizzled through the air from the mage's fingertips, bursting against rotting flesh. The healer chanted incantations, her hands glowing with ethereal energy that mended wounds as quickly as they were inflicted.

"Remember, aim for their heads!" Ben reminded, as if offering directions to a particularly confusing buffet. "Or whatever passes for a head on these things!"

"Pretty sure that one's waving its spleen at me," the thief noted, dodging a swipe from a particularly enthusiastic ghoul.

"Less commentary, more stabbing, please!" Lila yelled, her twin blades a silver blur as she danced between their attackers. Beside her, Roran's axe sang a song of defiance, each swing an ode to stubborn survival.

Alas, for every minion dispatched, two seemed to take its place, like the world's most horrifying multiplication problem. Despite their valiant efforts, Lila was soon grappling with skeletal arms that grasped with the persistence of the last guest at a party. Roran fought to reach her but found himself ensnared by a bevy of bone-clad assailants.

"Can we get a raincheck on the heroics?" the thief called out, even as he parried and thrust.

"Bit busy at the moment!" Ben retorted, cleaving through the sea of undead with determination. But it was no use; the tide was against them.

With a final, desperate push, Lila and Roran were torn from their comrades, dragged into the suffocating dark by the relentless dead. Their determined cries faded, swallowed by the cavernous depths of Zalathor's lair.

"Looks like our invitation to this party just got revoked," the mage muttered, blasting away another wave of minions as the group formed a tighter knot, ready to fight until the bitter end—or at least until happy hour.

Ben's jaw clenched as he watched, powerless, the ghastly procession of undead dragging Lila and Roran into the abyss. Their cries for help reverberated off the cold, damp walls of Zalathor's lair, a morbid chorus accompanied by the clinking chains and the shuffling of decayed feet.

"Come back with my friends, you ambulatory compost heaps!" Ben roared at the retreating backs of the minions. His sword, which had seen better days and cleaner battles, was now a makeshift conductor's baton, orchestrating a symphony of frustration against the stone floor.

"Guys, I'm open to suggestions that don't involve being captured or turned into walking jerky!" he shouted over his shoulder to his remaining companions, who were busy tending to cuts that oozed something that definitely wasn't in the approved adventurer's handbook.

"Perhaps a tactical retreat?" suggested the mage, dodging a poorly-aimed swipe from an overly enthusiastic skeleton. "I hear the outside world has excellent wound-healing properties. Like not being surrounded by necromantic energy."

"Retreat? That word is not in my vocabulary!" Ben exclaimed, even as he took a strategic step back. "But it might be in the index under 'prudent life choices.'"

As they backed away from the horde, their spirits sank like a lead balloon in a pool of despair. The minions seemed content to let them go, perhaps having reached their quota of captives for the day.

"Next time we're RSVPing 'no' to dungeon invites," the thief quipped, wrapping a piece of torn cloak around a particularly nasty bite. "Especially if the host is an undead overlord with control issues."

"Agreed," Ben grunted, helping to support a warrior whose armor had seen too much action and not enough maintenance. "But mark my words; this isn't over. We'll come back for them with a plan so cunning you could pin a tail on it and call it a weasel."

"Ben's right," the mage said, mustering what little cheer he could. "Let's lick our wounds, sharpen our wits, and prepare for an encore performance. Preferably one where we aren't the opening act for a zombie jamboree."

So off they went, their footsteps heavy with defeat but hearts stubbornly ablaze with the kind of hope that only the truly desperate—or the comically optimistic—could muster. They would return, for their honor, for their friends, and for the chance to kick necromantic butt in the most epic—and laughable—comeback tour Oak Isle had ever seen.

The charred remnants of the evening sun dipped below the horizon, casting elongated shadows across the group as they huddled just beyond the gnarled reach of Zalathor's lair. Ben, his face a mosaic of grim resolve and soot, stood at the center, brandishing a map that had seen better days. "Alright, team," he declared, with the dramatic flair of a bard on his third ale, "it's high time we snatch our friends from the bony clutches of old bone-bag himself."

"Bone-bag?" The thief raised an eyebrow, nursing a wound while simultaneously pilfering through a pouch of questionable powders and potions. "Is that the best you've got? Because I was partial to 'Zalathor the Zany Necromancer.' It's got a certain... zing to it."

"Focus!" Ben snapped, but couldn't suppress the snort of laughter that escaped him. "We need to be swift and smart. Like foxes. But bigger. And with swords."

"Like bears with swords, then?" the mage chimed in, conjuring a small flame to light the battered map.

"Exactly." Ben nodded appreciatively at the mage's literal spark of genius. "Now, here's the plan: We'll use the secret passages marked here. They should lead us right to where Lila and Roran are being kept."

"Assuming they haven't been turned into decorative tapestries or something equally disturbing," the warrior mused aloud, his voice a deep rumble akin to distant thunder—or perhaps a mildly upset stomach.

"Decorative tapestries can't fight back," the thief pointed out with a wry smile. "We'd have the advantage."

"Enough!" Ben brought his hand down on the map with a slap. "We move out at dawn! Rest up, sharpen your blades, and for the love of all things bright and beautiful, someone please fix that armor. It sounds like a tavern brawl every time you take a step."

With a collective nod that was part determination, part resignation, and entirely comedic given their bedraggled state, the motley crew dispersed to prepare for their rescue mission.

As dawn broke with the subtlety of a sledgehammer to the senses, Ben led his allies back towards Zalathor's domain. Their strides were uneven—a symphony of limps, clanks, and the occasional jingle from the thief's overladen pockets—but their eyes shone with the kind of reckless hope only found in storybooks and songs sung off-key by drunken minstrels.

"Remember," Ben whispered, his voice cutting through the morning mist like a knife through room-temperature butter, "stay sharp, stay silent, and if all else fails—"

"Make 'em laugh?" the thief suggested with a grin.

"Sure," Ben replied, the corner of his mouth twitching upward. "Let's give them a show they'll never forget."

And with that, they vanished into the depths of the stronghold, their fears intertwined with their unyielding determination to save their friends—or go down in history as the most entertaining failure Oak Isle had ever witnessed.

The stronghold of Zalathor was a labyrinthine monstrosity, its walls lined with more tricks and traps than the thief's ledger had tallies of "borrowed" goods. The dimly lit corridors were a gauntlet designed by a madman—or a necromancer with too much time on his undead hands.

"Watch your step," Ben murmured as he narrowly sidestepped a tile that looked more suspicious than a two-headed troll offering free hugs. A second later, an axe swung down from the ceiling, missing him by a hair's breadth—a haircut by any other name.

"Ha! Is that all you've got, Zalathor?" the mage quipped, her voice echoing through the halls with bravado only matched by her extravagant hat. "My grandmother has scarier knitting needles!"

Their journey through the maze-like stronghold was less a stealthy incursion and more a slapstick routine of near-misses and absurd luck. At one point, the warrior tripped over his own feet, inadvertently triggering a barrage of darts that would have made a porcupine jealous. Miraculously, they all missed, embedding themselves into the wall with a sound like rain on a tin roof.

"Maybe we should keep him up front," the archer suggested, notching an arrow with a smirk. "He's got the instincts of a startled cat in a room full of rocking chairs."

"Hey!" the warrior protested, but there was no bite to it—only the sheepish acknowledgment of being the butt of the joke.

As they tiptoed past statues that eyed them with stony suspicion, their camaraderie was the torch that held back the darkness of uncertainty. When a hidden pitfall yawned open beneath them, it was the thief's nimble fingers (and even nimbler footwork) that saved them from becoming an impromptu adventurer stew.

"Would you look at that," he said, dangling from a rope he'd somehow already secured above. "I'm quite the catch."

"Can we throw you back?" the mage asked, deadpan, as she floated across with a flick of her wrist and a spark of magic.

Finally, after what felt like a lifetime spent dancing on the knife-edge of disaster, they reached the chamber where Lila and Roran were bound, gagged, and looking about as happy as minnows in a shark tank.

"Subtle as ever, I see," Lila mumbled through her gag, her eyes rolling so hard they could have powered a mill.

"Untie them quickly," Ben said, his heart hammering in his chest like a blacksmith shaping destiny on an anvil. The door before them loomed, heavy as the weight of their task.

"Ready for the grand finale?" the thief asked, wiggling his eyebrows as he freed Roran, who promptly punched him in the arm—probably harder than necessary.

"Let's make it unforgettable," Ben declared, stepping toward the door with purpose burning in his veins. This was it—the moment where they'd face Zalathor and change the fate of Oak Isle forever.

"Remember, folks," the mage said, brandishing her wand with a flourish, "laughter is the best spell in any book."

With a collective nod that was part bravery, part lunacy, and entirely in character for this band of misfits, they prepared to confront their foe. They were not just rescuers; they were entertainers, and if nothing else, they would give Zalathor a performance befitting the end of the world—or at least the end of his reign.

Ben's fingers curled around the doorknob, forged from the bones of Zalathor's vanquished foes—or so the legends claimed. As he twisted the knob with a dramatic flair worthy of a stage play, the door creaked open to reveal a grand chamber that screamed 'Necromancer Chic.' Skulls grinned from alcoves in the walls, and the ambient lighting was courtesy of soul-siphoning flames flickering in braziers.

"Talk about overcompensating," murmured the mage, her wand twirling like a baton in a parade.

"Shhh!" Ben hissed, though his voice carried the unmistakable tremble of suppressed giggles. "The fate of Oak Isle is at stake! No time for interior design critiques."

"Ben, look!" Lila pointed to the far end of the room where Zalathor hovered above a dark altar, his robes billowing as if caught in an otherworldly wind machine designed for maximum sinister effect.

"Ah, the prodigal pests arrive!" Zalathor's voice boomed through the hall with the echo effect of a bad villain monologue. "Do you like what I've done with the place?"

"Needs more cowbell," quipped Roran, earning him a glare from Ben and a snicker from the thief.

"Silence!" Zalathor raised his arms, and from the shadows crept an army of undead creatures, their red eyes glowing like discount rubies in a tacky necklace.

"Okay, team," Ben said, gripping his sword as if it were a comedian's microphone, "it's showtime! Remember, stick to the choreography!"

The minions charged, each step thudding in sync with the hearts of Ben's troupe. The clash of steel rang out, the sweet symphony of impending doom—or slapstick salvation.

"Take five!" the thief yelled as he ducked a decaying arm, rolling away with acrobatic finesse usually reserved for circus performers.

"Break a leg," the mage muttered, casting spells that sent skeletons into a frenzied tap dance before crumbling into bony heaps.

"More like break theirs!" Roran bellowed, snapping femurs with the enthusiasm of a child popping bubble wrap.

"Enough!" Zalathor descended, surrounded by a swirling vortex of dark energy. "You think this is some kind of game?!"

"Life's a game, Zalathor!" Ben called out, parrying blows left and right. "And we're here to win the boss level!"

"Prepare to meet your maker!" Zalathor sneered, extending his hands toward them, dark magic crackling at his fingertips.

"Joke's on you, pal," replied Ben, standing tall amidst the chaos, "our maker's got a wicked sense of humor!"

The chapter ended there, freezing the scene like a tableau vivant at the height of its suspense. Ben and his ragtag band stood encircled by undead monstrosities, the air thick with the promise of a battle that would either be their greatest victory or their most hilarious defeat. With the final showdown upon them, the fates held their breath, and readers were left dangling off the cliff, laughter and trepidation mingling in their throats.

Embers pirouetted into the twilight like deranged fireflies, performing a ludicrous ballet around Ben and Elara. They sat in a clearing hemmed in by trees so tall they seemed to be gossiping with the stars above. The pair huddled by a campfire whose crackles pierced the silence with the subtlety of a dragon playing hopscotch on a tin roof. Their faces, illuminated by the flickering light, were canvases of worry, doubt, and perhaps an unspoken longing for a comfy bed and a less apocalyptic itinerary.

"Ben," Elara began, her voice quivering like a jelly on a high wire, "do you ever feel like we're just two jesters in a play penned by a particularly sadistic playwright?"

"Only every second of every dreadfully long minute," Ben replied, poking the fire with a stick as if trying to provoke it into giving them better odds of success. "Why do you ask?"

Elara took a deep breath, the kind that usually precedes announcements of impending doom or the confession that one has accidentally shrunk the other's favorite tunic in the wash. "It's just that... I find myself riddled with the sort of fears that would make a haunted house feel like a cozy cottage." She pulled her cloak tighter, as though bracing against a storm of her own making. "Can we truly save Oak Isle, Ben? Are we heroes or simply out of our league?"

Ben gazed at her, his expression as serious as a mime at a silent retreat. "Elara, my dear comrade in this tragicomic caper, I too am stricken with trepidation. And while I'm not exactly sure what 'league' we're supposed to be in, I have a sneaking suspicion we might need to invent our own."

"Perhaps," Elara said, her eyes reflecting the dance of the flames, "but even jesters can slay dragons in the right tale." Her hand unconsciously went to the hilt of her sword, a gesture more reassuring than a teddy bear armed with nunchucks. "We may not know all the steps to this particular dance, but we've got rhythm, and I'll be damned if we don't sashay our way through this."

"Ah, Elara, your words are as comforting as the thought of a feather bed after a hundred-year sleep," Ben chuckled, his heart feeling a touch lighter. "Let's face it, we've tangled with more nightmares than a sleep-deprived bard and lived to tell the farce."

"Indeed," she nodded, her chuckle mingling with his. "And who's to say we won't pen the punchline to this joke ourselves?"

As laughter ebbed and the night drew its curtains tighter, the pair sat side by side, their doubts momentarily set aside like unwelcome guests asked to leave through the nearest window. The quest ahead loomed, but for now, the embers of their resolve glowed as brightly as the campfire before them.

Ben tossed a twig into the fire, watching it surrender to the flames with an enthusiasm he envied. "You know, Elara," he began, his voice carrying the weight of a thousand unwritten pages, "I understand your trepidation. I've penned enough tragedies to fill the Great Library of Sorrow itself."

"Tragedies?" Elara raised an eyebrow, her curiosity piqued despite the grim mood.

"Indeed," Ben sighed. "Once, I wrote a hero so woeful, he tripped over his own sword and impaled his foot before even facing the dragon. And let's not speak of the time I mistook a goblin for a leprechaun. The creature was less than amused by my limericks about pots of gold."

Elara stifled a giggle, though the shadows in her eyes remained. "But those were just stories, Ben. This—this is painfully real."

"Ah, but who's to say my blunders as a scribe haven't foreshadowed our fate?" His brow furrowed deeper, each line a chasm of doubt. "What if I'm more suited to chronicling farces than being the gallant hero Oak Isle needs?"

The flickering light of the campfire seemed to mock them, casting long, grotesque shadows that danced like sinister puppets around the clearing. They both stared into the heart of the blaze, lost in their own reflections, as the heat did little to warm the growing chill of despair.

"Perhaps we're merely jesters in a play written by the Fates, destined to caper at the edge of doom," Ben mumbled, his fingers tracing patterns in the dirt, as if he could rewrite their destiny on the forest floor.

"Jesters," Elara echoed hollowly. "I used to think that even in the direst of circumstances, humor would be our blade against the darkness. But now," she paused, her voice quivering like the last leaf clinging to a wintry branch, "now I fear our laughter might be but the prelude to a requiem."

They sat there, two souls adrift in an ocean of uncertainty, feeling the tide of hopelessness washing over them. It was a quiet invasion, a creeping fog that slithered through their armor and quenched the fires of resolve. Each thought of their past triumphs now seemed a fluke, a cosmic joke at their expense, and the laughter they had once shared became a distant echo swallowed by the void.

It was in this bleak tableau that the true test of their mettle began—not against the dark sorcerer Zalathor or his legions of nightmarish creatures—but against the most insidious of foes: the doubt within.

A lively zephyr, as if on a frolicsome errand from the gods of mirth themselves, swept through the somber grove with the gusto of a court jester tumbling into a royal banquet. Leaves, stirred from their solemn watch, danced a capricious jig above Ben and Elara's heads, their whispers sounding like the tittering audience of an invisible pantomime.

Ben's gaze snapped upward, following a particularly audacious leaf that twirled with the grace of a prima donna before landing with a delicate plop on his nose. He crossed his eyes, beholding the verdant interloper, and for a fleeting moment, the absurdity of it all tickled the edges of his mouth into an involuntary smirk.

"Ha! Even nature has conspired to jest at our expense," Ben exclaimed, plucking the leaf from his face and watching it rejoin the revelry above.

Elara, too, found herself entranced by the spectacle, her worries momentarily eclipsed by the enchantment of the forest's impromptu carnival. A chuckle escaped her lips, as bright and clear as the crystalline brook they had stumbled upon earlier in the day. She glanced at Ben and saw the reluctant amusement dancing in his eyes—a balm to the sting of their shared despondence.

"Perhaps," Elara began, her voice buoyed by a newfound levity, "we ought to take a cue from these leaves. They've weathered storms aplenty, yet here they are, waltzing in the wind without a care."

"Indeed," Ben agreed, the ghost of a smile still playing upon his lips. "They do not lament the gusts that shake them, nor do they dread the fall that awaits. They simply dance."

"Exactly!" Elara said, her eyes glistening with the spark of determination rather than the sheen of uncertainty. "We've braved the labyrinthine caves of the Gorgon Sisters, bested the riddles of the Sphinx—albeit with some highly questionable puns—and even outdrunk a horde of dwarven ale-masters, which I must say, is no small feat."

"Small feat, you say?" Ben quipped, arching an eyebrow. "Dwarves, small? Oh, what towering heights of wit!"

"Quiet, you," Elara retorted with a playful swat. "My point is, we've scaled mountains of adversity higher than the Tower of Babel and lived to tell the tale. Each trial, each tribulation, has forged us not into jesters, but into heroes. Heroes who occasionally enjoy a good bit of slapstick, I'll grant you."

"Heroes, then," Ben mused, feeling the weight of his self-doubt lighten. "With a penchant for theatrics and the occasional pie to the face."

"Indeed, heroes." Elara nodded resolutely. "And our next act shall be our grandest yet. We shall pen the final stanza in Zalathor's vile verse and close the book on his reign of terror—with or without custard pies."

"Then let us plot our daring rescue," Ben said, the flame of purpose rekindled in his heart. "For Lila, for Roran, and for every soul on Oak Isle who yearns for the light beyond the shadow."

"Agreed," Elara declared, standing up with a flourish that would have made the most seasoned bard blush with envy. "To victory or vaudevillian defeat! The stage is set, and the audience awaits."

Hand in hand, they turned their faces toward the morrow, hearts lighter and spirits clad in the unshakeable armor of camaraderie and comedy. For what was a quest, if not the greatest performance of their lives?

Ben hoisted a charred stick from the fire, the tip glowing like a dragon's eye in the waning light. He etched into the earth a clumsy map of their trials, each line a road traveled, each curve a friend gained.

"Remember Sir Reginald?" Ben chuckled, marking a stout line beside a mountainous squiggle. "The knight who thought his armor was enchanted to make him invisible when he sang?"

Elara snorted, her laughter mingling with the crackle of the fire. "How could I forget? He bellowed ballads while battling bandits, convinced his 'cloak of invisibility' shielded him."

"Yet it was not magic, but the shock of his terrible voice that stunned our foes long enough for us to strike!" Ben grinned, reveling in the absurdity of the memory.

Elara scooped a handful of earth, letting it cascade through her fingers like sands of time. "And the Battle of Bleakmoor Bog, where we fought back-to-back against the Mud-Monsters. Covered head to toe in sludge, we were—unrecognizable even to each other!"

"Indeed!" Ben exclaimed, drawing a wide circle that represented the bog. "But we triumphed, using wit as our weapon, luring them into the very quagmire they emerged from."

"Ah, and don't forget the sacrifice of the great wizard, Whizzlebang," Elara sighed, her tone softening with reverence. "His last spell saved us, sealing the portal and keeping the Shadow Swarm at bay."

"Whizzlebang," Ben murmured, bowing his head, marking a star on the ground for the fallen mage. "May his spirit soar beyond the stars."

"Each ally, each laugh-laden skirmish, has brought us closer to this moment," Elara mused, gazing into the flames, seeing not just fire but the faces of those they had met along the way.

"True, we've outwitted ogres with riddles, tricked trolls with treats, and made merry with minstrels under moonlit melodies," Ben recited theatrically, flourishing the stick as if it were a conductor's baton.

"And now, as we stand on the precipice of our final act," Elara continued, rising to her feet with a dramatic flair, "we must remember what drives us: the lives of every man, woman, and child in Oak Isle."

"Each victory, a testament to our cause! Each chortle and guffaw, a defiance of darkness!" Ben proclaimed, standing alongside Elara, their shadows dancing wildly against the trees.

"By the power of every punchline and pratfall, we shall preserve these people!" Elara declared, her fist punching the air with gusto.

"Let us forge ahead, not with the heaviness of doubt, but with the lightness of laughter," Ben added, a gleam of mischief in his eyes reminiscent of their most ludicrous escapades.

"Indeed, for it is the heart that chuckles in the face of fear that triumphs," Elara affirmed, her determined gaze piercing the veil of night.

"Then let our hearts be buoyant—as balloons at a carnival!" Ben cheered, feeling the spark of inspiration fan into a roaring blaze within their souls.

"Unto dawn we march, jesters turned guardians, bearing the banner of hope and hilarity!" Elara's voice rang out, clear and confident, echoing through the forest.

"May our humor be our herald, and our courage the crescendo in this symphony of salvation!" Ben bellowed, casting the stick back into the fire, where it belonged.

Together, they watched as the embers ascended towards the heavens, tiny beacons signaling the rebirth of resolve in their quest to protect the heart of Oak Isle.

Ben leaped to his feet, brandishing a half-eaten leg of some curious forest creature as if it were the fabled Sword of Silliness itself. "Elara, stalwart comrade in capers and comedy, we stand upon the precipice of punchlines and peril!" he declared, his voice echoing through the trees like a madcap minstrel.

"Indeed, Ben, my partner in puns and protector of the puny," Elara replied with a dramatic flourish, tossing her fiery locks back with a hand that had thrown many a pie in the face of danger. "For too long have our friends languished in the loathsome lair of that lugubrious lout, Zalathor!"

"Then let us tarry not!" Ben exclaimed, crushing the remains of his meaty prop underfoot with absurd determination. "We shall concoct a caper so cunning, so craftily composed, that it would confound even the confederation of court jesters!"

"Ha! A plan so preposterous that it just might pierce the very pallor of despair!" Elara chimed in, her eyes twinkling with a mischievous light. "We'll rescue Lila and Roran with such a ruckus that the bards will sing of it until their throats are sore and their lutes lament from overuse!"

"Ah, but how shall we embark upon this daring deliverance?" Ben pondered aloud, stroking his chin in an exaggerated gesture of contemplation. "Might we disguise ourselves as traveling salesfolk, peddling potions of laughable potency?"

"Or perchance," Elara added with a sly grin, "we infiltrate Zalathor's foreboding fortress as entertainers, ready to juggle and jest our way past his gormless guards?"

"Brilliance befits you, brave Elara!" Ben cheered, clapping his hands with enough force to startle a nearby squirrel into comedic contortions. "We shall bewilder them with buffoonery, baffle them with balderdash, and liberate our companions amidst a labyrinth of laughter!"

"Then it is settled," Elara nodded, rising to join Ben in a stance of ludicrous resolve. "To mirth, to madness, and to a mission most merry! We shall reclaim our comrades and crash Zalathor's calamitous carnival of cruelty!"

"Let the winds whisper of our whimsical warfare," Ben proclaimed, puffing out his chest with pride. "For by the break of dawn, we shall either stand victorious or fall amidst a fanfare of folly!"

With a hearty handshake that transformed into an impromptu jig, Ben and Elara sealed their pact, their laughter mingling with the crackle of the campfire, a melodic prelude to the pandemonium they were poised to unleash. The quest for Oak Isle's salvation was about to take a decidedly droll turn, and woe betide those who underestimated the power of a perfectly placed pratfall.

Ben, whose usual stoic demeanor had been usurped by an almost maniacal merriment, slapped a rolled parchment against his palm with every word he spoke. "And thusly, we shall deploy the decoy ducks of destiny!" he declared, his face alight with a hope so bright it could have lit the darkest dungeon in Zalathor's realm.

"Decoy ducks?" Elara echoed, her eyebrow arching in amusement as she sketched a circle in the dirt, marking their entrance point in the fortress. Her lips curled into a playful smirk. "Quacking their way to quell quivering quarry?"

"Exactly!" Ben chortled, twirling the parchment like a baton of buffoonery. "Our feathered friends shall flap forth, creating such a cacophony that even the most steadfast sentry shall succumb to the stupor of sheer silliness!"

Elara chuckled, the sound as clear and joyful as a bell in springtime. She watched as Ben theatrically donned a hat made from the hide of the hog-snouted ballyhoo—a creature known more for its comedic appearance than any practical use—and positioned it atop his head at a jaunty angle.

"Indeed," she said, mirth twinkling in her eyes as she mirrored his optimism. "Our strategy is as unorthodox as a dancing dragon, and thrice as entertaining."

"Ah, but dear Elara, remember the adage of ancient antics: 'The most preposterous plans perplex the pernicious!'" Ben proclaimed, flourishing the parchment which, upon unfurling, revealed a ludicrously complex diagram of their scheme.

"Perplexing our foes with the profound power of the preposterous—I do adore alliteration," Elara admitted, her voice brimming with glee and confidence. The doubt that had once clouded her gaze now dissipated entirely, replaced by the sparkle of a rejuvenated spirit.

"Then let us proceed with the audacity of jesters at the gallows!" Ben hooted, extending his hand towards her with dramatic flair.

Elara reached out, slipping her fingers between his with a grip that bespoke both camaraderie and courage. They stood together, side by side, resembling less the archetypal heroes of old and more a vaudevillian duo poised to prank a pantheon of gods.

"May our laughter lead us to triumph," Elara intoned, lifting their clasped hands as though bearing a standard into battle.

"Or at the very least," Ben added with a conspiratorial wink, "may it grant us a grand exit!"

They faced the treeline, where the shadows whispered of danger and the unknown, yet before them lay the path to adventure—an adventure that would be inked into legend with the quill of quirkiness.

"Forward, to folly and beyond!" Ben cried out, releasing Elara's hand only to strike a ludicrously heroic pose, one foot set upon a log as if he were conquering a miniature mountain.

"To victory or vaudeville!" Elara cheered, matching his pose with one of equal absurdity.

Their laughter melded with the night, a defiant declaration that they would face whatever perils awaited with wit as their weapon and whimsy as their shield. And so, the chosen ones of Oak Isle pressed on, united in purpose and fortified by the unyielding bond of shared laughter, ready to reclaim their home—or at the very least, go out with a gag.

In the musty clandestine chamber tucked beneath Oak Isle's oldest inn, Ben and his motley crew huddled like a pack of sardines with secrets. Cobwebs played tickle-tag in the corners of the room, while the flickering torches cast more shadows than light, lending the gathering an air of deep, profound, and—considering Ben's inability to stand still—increasingly fidgety suspense.

"Would you quit pacing, Ben?" Lila hissed, her eyes rolling so hard they could've bowled a strike in the adjacent alley. "You're making the floorboards nervous."

"Sorry," Ben mumbled, coming to a halt. He looked as if he was trying to solve a riddle wrapped in an enigma, swaddled in a vest of question marks.

Roran, meanwhile, stood stoic, like a statue that had seen too many battles and far too few barbers; his bushy eyebrows knitted together in concentration—or perhaps consternation at being in such a confined space with Ben's jittery antics.

The chamber itself seemed to hold its breath, the dust motes in the air ceasing their lazy dance as if even they sensed the gravity of the moment. Then all eyes turned to Elara, who stood before them with the composure of a queen about to declare war on boredom itself.

But then she hesitated, lips parting but no words forthcoming, and it was as if time decided to take a leisurely stroll. Ben's eyes widened, Roran's posture stiffened (if that was even possible), and Lila leaned forward, her curiosity piqued to near-lethal levels.

"Spit it out, Elara!" Ben finally blurted, unable to contain himself. "Before the tension in here gets so thick we could slice it and serve it with cheese!"

Elara, however, remained silent, a slight smirk tugging at the corner of her mouth as she let the suspense simmer to a slow boil, her eyes twinkling with the knowledge that she was about to flip their world upside down—as casually as one might flip a pancake.

Elara planted her boots firmly on the cool stone floor, a smirk still playing about her lips. With an air of high drama, she took a deliberate step forward, her cloak billowing behind her like the dark wings of fate itself. Her eyes, sharp as the edge of a scimitar, glinted with an unyielding resolve that could bend the wills of gods and men alike.

"Friends," Elara began, her voice resonating through the chamber with the authority of a war-horn, "the time for secrets lies slain at our feet, like so many hapless goblins after a tavern brawl. Behold!" She threw her arms wide as if embracing the very essence of the cosmos. "I am Elara, Descendant of Eclipse!"

Ben's mouth fell agape, an invisible apple of sheer astonishment lodged in his throat. His eyes bulged, comically mirroring the roundness of his dropped jaw, as if someone had just told him his beloved trousers were woven from unicorn mane—by unicorns.

"Descendant of—what now?" he managed to sputter, the words colliding into each other like clumsy dwarves on a slippery floor.

Beside him, Lila's gasp was sharp enough to cut through the silence that had fallen like a heavy tapestry. Her hand flew to her chest, fingers clutching the fabric of her tunic as if trying to keep her heart from leaping out and making a run for it. "By the Whispering Woods," she breathed, her eyes round as dinner plates.

Roran, ever the stoic mountain of muscle, stood frozen, his usually impassive face giving way to a look of such profound shock that one might think he'd just discovered his beard was infested with talking mice. "Eclipse," he echoed, the name rolling off his tongue slowly, laced with a cocktail of awe and disbelief.

The chamber seemed to echo back their reactions, the walls reverberating with the weight of the revelation, as if they too were struggling to comprehend the gravity of Elara's claim. The air crackled with energy, and for a moment, the hidden room felt less like a secret refuge and more like a stage set for the most grandiose of farces, where destiny itself was the punchline.

Ben's mind did cartwheels and backflips, a gymnast tumbling through the absurdity of the moment. Descendant of Eclipse? He might as well have been told Elara was an undercover mermaid with a penchant for yodeling. Trust, that invisible thread woven through their shared trials and monstrous encounters, now felt like a cobweb—delicate and liable to snap.

"Elara," he said, his voice stumbling over itself like a drunk pixie, "when you said you had secrets, I thought maybe you stole extra biscuits at breakfast, not that you're some sort of... of prophesied heroine."

His thoughts were a jamboree of chaos, a festival of doubts with jesters juggling his emotions. There was betrayal, yes, but also admiration. Annoyance waltzed with awe, and suspicion sashayed with respect. How many times had she saved their hides with her quick thinking? How often had her laughter brightened the gloom of their quest?

"Ben, it's still me," Elara insisted, her tone steady as a mountain yet warm as a freshly baked pie.

"Right, you just happen to be the one destined to wield the Staff of Tomorrow," Ben retorted, trying to keep his tone light despite the tempest inside. "No big deal. Just another Tuesday."

"Staff of Tomorrow?" Lila interjected, her voice rising like dough in an oven. "The legendary staff that's been missing since the Age of Whimsy?"

"Indeed," Elara nodded, her eyes twinkling with the kind of resolve usually reserved for epic ballads or particularly dramatic theater productions. "It's been my charge to protect it from Zalathor's grimy clutches. And it is our destiny to use it to save Oak Isle from his reign of terror."

"Of course! Why wield a regular old stick when you can swing around a fancy staff that determines the fate of the realm?" Ben quipped, his humor a shield against the onslaught of revelations. "So where is this mythic weapon? In your pocket? Or is it more of a 'sword in the stone' situation?"

"Patience, Ben. All will be revealed," Elara replied with a knowing smile that suggested she found his bewilderment as amusing as a court jester's antics.

"Patience," he echoed mockingly, though a part of him couldn't help but feel a surge of pride. They weren't just a band of misfits anymore; they were at the heart of a story that would be told for generations to come, assuming they survived long enough to tell it.

"Alright then, Descendant of Eclipse," Ben sighed theatrically, offering a mock bow. "Lead on to our destiny. May the bards sing of our valor, or at least our ability to fumble through this mess with some semblance of dignity."

Despite himself, despite the doubts and the world-turned-upside-down sensation gnawing at his gut, Ben couldn't deny the spark of excitement, the flicker of hope that maybe, just maybe, they were about to do something truly extraordinary.

The chamber, hewn from the very heart of the mountain, seemed to hold its breath, as if the ancient stones themselves sensed the gravity of Elara's revelation. Dust motes danced like mischievous sprites in shafts of light that spilled from cracks in the ceiling, and the walls, encrusted with gems that glinted like tiny eyes, bore witness to the unfolding drama.

"By the crooked teeth of the Under-Gnomes," Lila gasped, her voice awash with a blend of reverence and incredulity that echoed off the cavernous walls. Her hands clutched at the air as if trying to grasp the concept that Elara, their unassuming companion, was now revealed as a hero of legend.

Roran's eyes bulged, his expression one of a man who had just been told his favorite ale was brewed by a society of teetotaler pixies. "The Descendant of... What in the seven hells?!"

Ben, still grappling with the notion that Elara was more than just a peerless pickpocket with an affinity for trouble, blinked rapidly, his mouth working soundlessly. The air itself seemed to shimmer with the weight of destiny, the energy so palpable that he half-expected it to materialize into a gaudy, overbearing mentor character who'd slap them on their backs and offer cryptic advice.

Then Elara stepped forward, every inch the fabled Descendant of Eclipse. A cape of shadows seemed to flutter around her, although that could have just been Roran's cloak which he had accidentally dropped in his shock.

"Friends, comrades, assorted tagalongs," Elara began, her voice laced with the kind of thunderous gravity usually reserved for prophets or those afflicted with severe indigestion. "We stand on the brink of history, the cusp of a tale so epic it would make the most verbose bard beg for brevity."

"Defeating Zalathor is no mere errand, no simple jaunt through the woods to pluck daisies and chase after rabid unicorns," she continued. "It is our destiny, our burden. We are the only hope for

Oak Isle, and I—by some cosmic jest or twist of fate—am your leader in this endeavor."

"Great," Ben muttered under his breath, unable to resist a jab despite the solemnity. "No pressure then, just the usual doom of an entire realm riding on our shoulders. And here I thought we were going to play a friendly game of 'Who Can Stab the Ogre.'"

Elara's gaze swept across her companions, fierce and unyielding as an iron golem's poker face during a high-stakes bluff. "I am unwavering, unflinching, and possibly allergic to failure, though I've never stuck around long enough after a mishap to find out. Together, we will strike at the heart of darkness and reclaim the dawn for Oak Isle!"

"Reclaim the dawn," Roran repeated, his voice a mix of awe and the realization that he might have left the oven on back at their last hideout.

"Indeed," Elara nodded, her silhouette outlined by a dramatic flair of light that probably warranted its own theme music. "Now, steel yourselves. We embark on a quest so daunting that even the bravest heroes would soil their chainmail at the mere mention. But fear not! For in the face of certain doom, we shall laugh, we shall love, and most importantly, we will likely bumble our way to victory or an amusingly heroic end!"

"Yay for potentially humorous deaths," Ben quipped, offering a salute with an imaginary cap that he wished was real and brimming with magical evasion skills. "Onward to destiny, or at least a memorable footnote in the annals of 'Quests That Seemed Like a Good Idea at the Time.'"

In the charged silence that followed Elara's bold declaration, the hidden chamber seemed to hold its breath, waiting for someone, anyone, to shatter the moment with a sneeze or an ill-timed giggle. But none came. Instead, there was Ben, his fingers drumming an erratic rhythm on the hilt of his sword as if it were a lute out of tune.

"Right," he said finally, jolting like a puppet whose strings had been yanked by an overeager child. "Questing. Heroic deeds. Potentially humorous deaths. Got it."

Elara turned to him, and in the flickering torchlight, her eyes found his. It was one of those gazes that could have melted glaciers—or at least made them seriously reconsider their life choices. For a heartbeat or two, they simply looked at each other, the kind of look that was a whole conversation in itself. It said, 'We're probably going to regret this,' coupled with a resounding, 'But we'll do it together.'

"Ben," she said, her voice steady despite the storm of possibilities swirling in her eyes, "we've laughed in the face of absurdity, tripped over our own feet into danger, and now..."

"Now?" Ben repeated, his mouth dry as the wit at a dragon's tea party.

"Now we become the punchline that saves the world," Elara finished with a smirk, her hand reaching out to rest briefly on his arm—a touch lighter than a pixie's wing, yet laden with the weight of destiny.

"Ah, perfect," Ben breathed out, grinning. "I've always wanted to be a well-timed joke."

The moment stretched between them, a bubble of camaraderie ready to pop at the slightest nudge of reality. And reality, as it so often does, came crashing in with all the subtlety of a minotaur in a porcelain shop.

A sudden, ear-splitting screech tore through the chamber, like the sound of a banshee who had stubbed her toe on the corner of eternity. The four companions whirled toward the source, weapons drawn, hearts hammering a frenetic beat that could've woken the dead—or at least prompted them to complain about the noise.

"Was that...?" Lila began, but her question hung unfinished in the air, choked by the thickening tension.

"An omen?" Roran offered, brandishing his staff with the confidence of a man wielding a very large and particularly pointy stick.

"Or perhaps," Ben mused, his eyes narrowing as he peered into the dark corridors beyond, "the dinner bell for something with far too many teeth and a taste for hero tartare."

"Either way," Elara declared, her voice slicing through the uncertainty, "it seems our next chapter begins with a cliffhanger. Literally. I'm fairly certain there is an actual cliff involved."

"Of course, there is," Ben sighed, exchanging one last conspiratorial glance with Elara. "Wouldn't be a proper quest without the risk of plummeting to our comedic demise."

As the screech echoed once more, now accompanied by the distant rumble of something vast and undoubtedly unpleasant awakening, the companions steeled themselves for what lay ahead. With the Staff of Tomorrow their secret weapon and laughter their shield, they would face whatever came next—be it beast, battle, or the most epic of punchlines.

"Ready?" Elara asked, her eyes alight with the thrill of the unknown.

"Ready as I'll ever be," Ben replied, his smile that of a man who fully embraced the ludicrousness of their fate.

"Then let's—" Elara started, but another sound cut her off, a deep, ominous voice that rolled through the chamber like thunder.

"Heroes of Oak Isle," it boomed, sending shivers down their spines. "Zalathor awaits."

And with those foreboding words, the chapter slammed shut, leaving readers teetering on the edge of their seats, craving the chaos that was sure to come.

The walls of the hidden chamber seemed to pulsate with the rhythm of their racing hearts. Ben tugged at the collar of his tunic, an attempt to free himself from the clutches of the heat that was not entirely due to the torches flickering along the stone walls.

"Alright, Elara," he said, his voice a hushed whisper against the thick air, "drop the stone on us."

Elara's lips quirked into what might have been a smirk or a prelude to a battle cry; with Elara, it was often a toss-up. She stepped forward, her boots echoing a solitary beat on the hard ground. She was a silhouette wrapped in authority and secrets, and as she drew a breath, the chamber held its own in suspense.

"Friends," Elara began, her gaze sweeping over Ben, Lila, and Roran like a conquering hero surveying her realm, "I am the Descendant of Eclipse."

The proclamation hung in the air, weightier than the ancient stones that encased them. Ben felt his jaw slacken, his usual quips and jests scurrying away like mice before a storm. Beside him, Lila's gasp was a sharp intake, a punctuation in the silence, while Roran's eyes grew wide, reflecting the torchlight as if they were portals to another, more astonished world.

Ben wrestled with a cacophony of thoughts. Trust and doubt clashed within him, a tango of emotions where every step was misplaced. How could he not have seen? But then, Elara was a mystery swathed in enigma's clothing – it made sense, in a way that twisted his brain into knots.

"Protecting the Staff of Tomorrow," Elara continued, her voice imbued with a gravity that pulled at their very souls, "is my birthright. It is the key to defeating Zalathor and freeing Oak Isle from his reign of terror."

There was awe in Lila's wide-eyed stare, disbelief etched into Roran's furrowed brow, and a dawning respect in Ben's eyes as he beheld Elara. The air seemed to crackle, charged with energy, anticipation...and a hint of dread for what lay ahead.

"Oak Isle will be free," Elara declared, her resolve a blade unsheathed. "Peace will be restored. This I vow."

Ben met Elara's gaze, and in that silent exchange, words were unnecessary. They shared a nod, a fleeting smile, and an unspoken agreement that their path, however strewn with obstacles and potential pratfalls, was one they would walk together.

"Then let's—" Elara started once again, only to be interrupted by the ominous voice that had ended the previous chapter. It rolled through the chamber, sending ripples through the tension-laden air.

"Heroes of Oak Isle," it boomed, causing the torches to flicker as if afraid. "Zalathor awaits."

The message was clear, the challenge undeniable. The moment of truth loomed like a shadow ready to devour the light of their courage. As the echo of the voice died away, leaving a heavy silence, their destiny beckoned with a sardonic grin.

"Good thing I've always wanted to meet a celebrity," Ben quipped, his humor a thin veil over the rapid drumbeat of his pulse.

Elara raised an eyebrow, her stance unyielding. "Let's give him a grand entrance he won't forget."

And on that note, the scene sliced to black, the next page as yet unwritten, the laughter and valor of our heroes a beacon in the darkness of uncertainty.

The chamber's stony silence shattered under the weight of Elara's announcement, and yet, amid the gravity of the moment, Roran couldn't help but waggle his eyebrows theatrically. "Descendant of Eclipse? Is that like being the heir to an interstellar coffee chain?"

"Quiet, Roran," Lila chided, smothering an inappropriate giggle as she clutched the hem of her cloak. "This is serious."

"Right, because nothing says 'serious' like a villain named Zalathor," Ben added with a smirk, nudging an ancient vase with his boot, which wobbled ominously before settling back into place. "Sounds like he should be peddling cosmic life insurance."

"Ben, this isn't the time for..." Elara trailed off, her lips curving into a reluctant smile. "Actually, never mind. We could use a bit of levity."

"Levity?" Roran scoffed, puffing out his chest. "I've got enough levity to float us all to Zalathor's lair on a cloud of laughter."

"Please don't," Lila muttered, eyeing Roran as if he might actually attempt it.

"Floating aside," Elara cut in, the torchlight casting dancing shadows over her determined features, "we have the Staff of Tomorrow. And tomorrow, we face Zalathor."

"Staff of Tomorrow?" Ben quirked a brow. "Is it going to predict next week's lottery numbers or just poke our enemies with mystical precision?"

"Both, if you're lucky," Elara retorted, hoisting the staff with a flourish that sent sparkles scattering around the chamber, "and don't forget, it's also a handy backscratcher."

"Handy," Roran echoed, nodding sagely. "Multitasking tools for the multitasking hero."

"Can it multitask us right into Zalathor's fortress then?" Lila asked, eager despite the sarcasm lacing her words.

"Patience, my intrepid companions," Elara said, her voice dropping an octave in mock solemnity. "For now, let us bask in the afterglow of shock and awe."

"Shock, awe, and a side of snark," Ben supplied, stepping closer to Elara. Their eyes locked, a silent exchange of mirth mingling with resolve.

"Indeed. Now, let's—" Elara began, only to be cut off by a sudden rumble that shook the chamber.

"Oops," Roran said, patting his stomach. "That was me. Note to self: Never trust a goblin's cooking, no matter how convincing the sales pitch."

"Are we sure he's not the true Descendant of Eclipse?" Lila deadpanned, rolling her eyes at Roran's sheepish grin.

"Let's focus," Elara urged, though her eyes twinkled with shared amusement. "We have a realm to save, a villain to thwart, and apparently, some goblin cuisine to avoid."

"Add 'avoid culinary disasters' to the quest log," Ben declared, brandishing an imaginary quill.

"Quest log updated," Roran chimed in, pretending to scribble in the air.

"Let's make this grand entrance one for the history books," Elara said, lifting the Staff of Tomorrow high. "And let's hope the history books have a sense of humor."

"Agreed," Lila nodded, her face alight with excitement. "Because if we're going down, we're going down laughing."

"Then onward!" Ben exclaimed, as they moved towards their destiny, footsteps synchronized, hearts buoyant with jest, and spirits armed with the deadliest weapon of all—laughter.

Ben's heart was a drumroll of paradoxical emotions—thunderous yet somehow in tune with the ludicrous symphony that was their quest. He took a deep breath, letting the dusty air of the chamber coat his lungs like icing on a dubious goblin cake.

"Alright, team," he said, a crooked smile playing on his lips, "we're going up against Zalathor armed with the most unexpected weapon—Elara's heritage. And possibly Roran's indigestion."

"Indigestion?" Elara raised an eyebrow, her posture a mix of regal and ready-to-rumble. "I thought we agreed to call it 'the gaseous gambit.'"

"Right, how could I forget?" Ben feigned a slap to his forehead. "The gaseous gambit: Zalathor won't see it coming."

"Neither did we," Lila quipped, fanning the air dramatically.

"Focus," Roran interposed, though his smirk betrayed his appreciation for the banter. "We've a dark lord to dethrone, and I've got just the trick up my sleeve."

"Is it your other sleeve?" Ben teased, leaning in to inspect Roran's suspiciously bulging cloak.

"Ha! As if I'd reveal my secrets before the final act," Roran declared, puffing out his chest with mock pride.

"Enough about sleeves and secrets!" Elara clapped her hands together, sparking a tiny but impressive shower of mystical light. "We have a realm to save. Remember, every joke we crack is a strike against Zalathor's gloom. Our laughter is our shield, our wit, our sword!"

"Speaking of swords, are we sure we can't just tickle him into submission?" Lila mused, twirling a lock of hair around her finger. "I mean, has anyone actually tried?"

"Alas, dear Lila, if only defeating ancient evils were so simple," Ben sighed theatrically. "But worry not! With Elara's Eclipse blood running hotter than dragonfire, we stand more than a chance."

"Plus," Elara added with a grin that could light the darkest dungeon, "I've been practicing my dramatic monologues. By the time I'm through, Zalathor will be begging for mercy—or at least a decent playwright."

"Bravo!" cheered Lila, clapping her hands. "Now let's set forth, lest the suspense kill us before the villain gets a chance!"

"Forward!" Ben cried, leading the way as they poured out of the chamber, each step a staccato beat in their march toward destiny.

"Remember," Elara called over her shoulder, her voice ringing with valor and a hint of mischief, "stay sharp, stay sassy, and above all, stay silly!"

"Those are words to die laughing for," Roran agreed, striding alongside his companions, his previous unease now replaced by a bubbling anticipation.

"Or live chuckling," Ben corrected, the old stone corridors echoing with their collective resolve—and the occasional snicker. "To victory or vaudeville!"

And with that, they stepped into the unknown, their spirits buoyed by bravado, their path lit by the flickering torch of hope, and their journey soundtracked by the relentless rhythm of their own irrepressible humor.

In the gloomy embrace of a room where light itself seemed too frightened to linger, Ben and Elara sat shoulder to shoulder, their silhouettes mere whispers against the encroaching shadows. The flickering candle between them was a lone star in an otherwise desolate cosmos, its glow battling valiantly against the darkness that sought to claim every corner.

"By the hairy toes of the Elder Trolls, Zalathor's going to wish he'd never crossed paths with us," Ben grumbled, his voice a mix of gravel and fire. His fingers curled into fists, knuckles popping like the chorus of a vengeful goblin orchestra.

"Indeed," Elara chimed in, her features set in a mask of stoic fury that could make even the most impudent of imps reconsider its mischief. "Lila and Roran might be in his clutches, but we've faced worse than his parlor tricks. Remember the Bog of Eternal Stench? We emerged smelling like roses... well, roses dredged in swamp muck, but nonetheless victorious."

Ben snorted, a smirk tugging at his lips. "That's one way to put it. And let's not forget the time you charmed that ogre with nothing but your wits and a sock puppet."

"Ah, Sir Sockington the Brave," Elara mused with a wistful sigh. "Who knew ogres were so susceptible to poorly constructed theater?"

"Or the time I convinced a band of marauding trolls that I was their long-lost king returned from exile." Ben puffed out his chest, mimicking the grandeur he had feigned that day. "I still don't know whether to attribute our escape to my acting skills or their sheer stupidity."

"Bit of both, I reckon," Elara said with a laugh that held the echoes of a dozen battles fought side by side.

"Every scar, every narrow escape, they've all been leading to this moment," Ben said, his eyes glinting with a resolve that matched the steel of his sword. "We're not the same naïve adventurers who started this quest. We're seasoned, cunning, and, dare I say, attractively rugged."

"Speak for yourself on the last one," Elara teased, though the pride in her gaze was unmistakable. "But you're right. We've grown stronger, more resilient. Zalathor's reign of terror ends with us, and we start by bringing our friends home."

"Agreed. It's time to show that dark-hearted tyrant that he's picked a fight with the wrong heroes. We'll rescue Lila and Roran, and then," Ben paused dramatically, "we'll liberate the land while cracking jokes so sharp they'd put the edge of any blade to shame."

"Let's hope our humor proves as effective as our swordplay," Elara replied, rising to her feet with a fluid grace that belied the weight of the armor adorning her frame.

"Even if it doesn't, we'll go down in history as the duo who died laughing," Ben declared, standing beside her, tall and defiant.

"Then it's settled." Elara extended her hand, which Ben clasped with fervor. "For friendship, for freedom, and for the sheer joy of ruining a villain's day."

"Especially that last bit," Ben added, as they both shared a grin that would have sent lesser evils scurrying for cover.

With hearts ablaze and spirits buoyed by the countless trials they had overcome, Ben and Elara stepped forth from the shadowy refuge, ready to carve their path through legend and into the very annals of comedic heroism.

Ben and Elara stood at the precipice of Zalathor's lair, a labyrinthine fortress carved into the malignant heart of Mount Gloomspire. They exchanged a knowing glance; their shared history of battles won and lost was etched into the silent communication between them.

"Right," Ben muttered, retrieving a crumpled map from his pocket. "If we can slip past the Gorgon Gatekeeper using the Medusa Mirror I lifted from the Bazaar of the Bizarre, we'll have a clear shot to the dungeons."

Elara nodded, unfurling a scroll of her own. "And once inside, we exploit the old catacombs beneath the East Wing. It's said that Zalathor's minions avoid it due to superstitious dread—something about spectral janitors."

"Ha! Ghostly mop-wielders are the least of our worries." Ben chuckled, stashing away the map as they crept forward. The Gorgon Gatekeeper, a mass of serpentine tresses and a gaze that promised petrification, loomed ahead. With the grace of a pair of synchronized swans, Ben and Elara brandished the Medusa Mirror just as the creature's eyes glowed with a baleful light. Reflected upon itself, the monster stiffened into stone, a permanent fixture of its own domain.

"Score one for the home team," Elara whispered, flashing Ben a victorious smirk as they sidestepped the newly formed statue.

"Home team's on a roll," Ben replied, leading the way into the pulsating shadows of Zalathor's inner sanctum.

As they ventured deeper, a corridor lined with runes presented itself, each glyph thrumming with arcane power. "Trap runes," Elara cautioned. "One misstep and we're likely to be turned into a pair of decorative toads."

"Or worse, sent on an involuntary dimension-hopping vacation." Ben surveyed the patterns, taking a deep breath. "Follow my lead." With the precision of a maestro conducting an invisible orchestra, Ben danced across the corridor, leaping and twirling around each glowing sigil. Elara mirrored his movements, a step behind but equally adept, until they reached the other side unscathed and unmistakably not amphibious.

"Nice footwork," Elara commended, brushing a stray lock of hair from her face.

"Thanks, I've been practicing in case we ever crash a royal ball," Ben jested, winking at her as they pressed on.

Their next challenge emerged in the form of a phalanx of guards clad in armor that clanked like a cacophony of kitchen pots in a windstorm. But these were no ordinary soldiers; they moved with an eerie synchronicity, controlled by a sorcerer hidden within the ranks.

"Marionette men," Ben observed, drawing his sword—a blade that seemed to hum with eagerness. "I say we find the puppet master and cut some strings."

"Agreed," Elara replied, summoning a glow to her hands that promised a swift and dazzling application of spellcraft.

They charged into battle, a symphony of steel and sorcery. Ben deflected blows with a parry that could only be described as cheekily flamboyant, while Elara's spells burst forth in radiant arcs, severing the magical threads that bound the guards. One by one, the armored foes collapsed, reduced to nothing more than heaps of enchanted scrap.

"Remind me to never get on your bad side," Ben quipped as they navigated through the fallen guards, Elara rolling her eyes at his jest.

"Focus. We're not out of the woods yet—or rather, the very non-wooden, oppressively gothic corridors of doom," she retorted.

"Ah yes, the scenic route to heroism," he mused, and together they advanced, ready for whatever lay ahead in the dark depths of Zalathor's lair.

Ben and Elara stood before a door that whispered threats in ancient tongues, its surface writhing with shadows that seemed eager to leap at their throats. They exchanged a glance that held the weight of unspoken fears and unsung ballads of bravery.

"Seems like Zalathor's interior decorator was going for 'early malevolent,'" Ben remarked, eyebrow arched as he eyed the door. "Maybe we knock and ask if they've heard about our lord and savior, sheer dumb luck?"

Elara snorted, a smirk playing on her lips. "Or maybe we let them sample the delightful taste of 'surprise arcane fireball.' That usually gets a warm reception."

"Speaking of warm receptions," Ben retorted, reaching into his satchel and pulling out a tiny silver bell. "Remember this little chime of chaos from the Witches' Market?"

Elara's eyes lit up with recognition. "The one that turns everything upside down? Literally?"

"Exactly." Ben winked and rang the bell thrice. The shadows shrieked as the room flipped vertically, throwing off the door's enchantments. Now hanging from what used to be the ceiling, they giggled at their own disorientation.

"Gravity is overrated anyway," Elara quipped, casting a spell that allowed them to walk along the new 'floor' with ease, leaving the door far above, utterly bewildered by its own redundancy.

"Next up: the corridor of ten thousand whispers," Ben announced as they approached a hallway lined with stone faces, each murmuring curses. He reached into his bag again, withdrawing two pairs of outrageously fluffy earmuffs. "Shall we?"

"Subtle," Elara chuckled, fitting the muffs over her ears. "Fashion and function."

They strutted through the corridor, the muffs rendering the sinister susurrations into something that sounded suspiciously like a goblin choir singing off-key. Ben mimicked conducting an orchestra while Elara pretended to be moved to tears by the performance, wiping away mock tears.

"Encore, encore!" Ben bellowed in faux appreciation, bowing deeply to the stony-faced audience as they left the corridor behind.

"Bravo indeed," Elara agreed, grinning broadly. "But let's not give them the satisfaction of an actual encore."

"Agreed, my dear Elara," Ben said, flourishing a dramatic bow. "Onward, to the Labyrinth of Lost Limbs!"

"Ah, sounds... inviting," Elara deadpanned, though her eyes sparkled with the thrill of their next challenge.

"Who names these places?" Ben mused. "I'm going to start calling our hideout 'The Snug of Cuddles and Hot Cocoa.'"

"Only if I get to name our weapons," she replied. "I shall dub my staff 'The Stick of Snuggly Doom.'"

"Perfect! And my sword shall henceforth be known as 'The Blade of Bedtime Stories.'" Ben drew his weapon, giving it an affectionate pat.

"May it lull our foes into eternal slumber," Elara concurred with a mock-serious nod.

Together, armed with wit and whimsy as much as steel and sorcery, they wove through Zalathor's lair, turning peril into punchlines and danger into daring jests. The dark fantasy world had never seen such a blend of heroism and hilarity as the tale of Ben and Elara, the duo that laughed in the face of doom.

In the gloom of Zalathor's lair, where shadows clung like cobwebs and the air was thick with malevolent whispers, Ben and Elara skulked with the stealth of a pair of pickpockets at a bankers' ball. Their hearts pounded a rhythm of resolve as they crept closer to the chamber where Lila and Roran languished in chains. But unbeknownst to them, their every step was watched by eyes as dark as the void itself.

"Are you sure we took the right turn? This corridor looks exactly like the last seventeen we've passed," muttered Ben, squinting at the walls that seemed to flicker with an eerie sameness.

"Unless Zalathor's minions are remarkably fond of repeating décor, I think we're on the right—"

Elara's words were cut off by a sudden chill that swept through the corridor like a winter gust through a keyhole. The duo froze as a low growl echoed, bouncing off the stones with menacing intent. A cadre of spectral hounds, their eyes glowing like embers from the deepest furnace of hell, materialized before them, baring ghostly fangs.

"Ah, the welcoming committee," quipped Ben, drawing 'The Blade of Bedtime Stories' with a flourish that would have made a swashbuckler swoon. "I suppose Zalathor got our RSVP."

"Seems he spared no expense on the party favors," retorted Elara, her fingers dancing over 'The Stick of Snuggly Doom'. A shimmering aura wrapped around the staff, its soft glow belying the raw power within.

"Shall we dance?" Ben asked, winking at Elara as the spectral beasts lunged.

"Thought you'd never ask," she replied, twirling into action.

Like a choreographed ballet of blades and blasts, they dove into battle. Ben's sword carved arcs of silver light, each swing a lullaby whispered sharply enough to slice through spirit flesh. Beside him, Elara's staff hummed, its tip alight with arcane fire that seared the incorporeal fur of their attackers.

"Your left!" shouted Elara, as one of the hounds snapped at Ben's flank.

"Good catch!" he said, ducking under the gnashing jaws and delivering a swift kick that sent the beast dissipating into mist. "How about a little teamwork?"

"Always," she replied, spinning her staff above her head. With a deft flick, she launched a bolt of energy that ricocheted off the walls, creating a dazzling light show.

"Follow my lead," Ben called out, his blade now a blur. He leaped into the air, using the wall as a springboard, and came down hard, driving his sword into the ground. The impact sent a shockwave rippling through the stone, disorienting the pack of phantom hounds.

"Nice move, but watch this!" Elara channeled her magic, and the floor beneath the hounds turned slick as if coated with the finest banana peels of the underworld. The creatures scrambled, their paws finding no purchase on the treacherous terrain.

"Slippery when hexed, eh?" Ben chuckled, as the last of the hounds lost its footing and slid into its brethren, knocking them into a heap of vanquished vapors.

"Looks like that's the last of them," said Elara, brushing a strand of hair from her face, her eyes scanning for more foes.

"Indeed," Ben agreed, sheathing his sword with a satisfied click. "But let's not dally; Lila and Roran won't rescue themselves."

"Right behind you," Elara responded, setting off once again into the murky depths of Zalathor's stronghold, their laughter fading into echoes as they faced the darkness together.

Ben's foot caught on an uneven flagstone, sending a jolt of surprise through him. The ground beneath them was shifting, the stones of Zalathor's lair rearranging themselves like pieces of a monstrous puzzle.

"Trap or tantrum?" Elara quipped, leaping nimbly aside as a stone wall emerged from the floor with a groan, aiming to separate them.

"Both," Ben replied, grasping her hand. With a grunt, he pulled her towards him just as the wall sealed shut, barely avoiding their separation.

"Talk about moving house," Elara said, dusting off her cloak with exaggerated care. "Zalathor really should consider a career in interior design."

"Maybe after we've redecorated his face," Ben retorted, eyeing the new maze-like layout before them. They had been prepared for battle, not a labyrinthine puzzle that seemed to pulse with malevolence.

"Let's not get lost in home improvements," Elara suggested, pointing towards a narrow corridor that hadn't been there moments before. "That way looks promising... if you fancy a stroll down Creepy Corridor Number Five."

"Lead on, MacDuff," Ben said, drawing his sword once more and following her into the dim passage.

They hadn't gone far when a figure stepped out from the shadows ahead—a silhouette they knew all too well. It was Grindle, the old sage who had guided them through the Enchanted Forest, his eyes now glinting with something cold and unfamiliar.

"Grindle?" Ben asked, lowering his weapon slightly. "What are you doing here?"

"Ah, the prodigal pupils return," Grindle sneered, his voice dripping with sarcasm. "Did you really think I'd side with such... amateur enchanters?"

"Betrayal? Really, Grindle? That's so last season," Elara scoffed, though her heart pounded at the realization of his treachery.

"Enough!" Grindle bellowed, raising his staff. A shimmering barrier sprang up around them, trapping them in a magical cage.

"Didn't see that coming," Ben muttered, pressing against the barrier with his shoulder, only to be repelled by a force that felt like a thousand rubber bands snapping back.

"Neither did I," Elara admitted, her mind racing. "But let's bounce back from this setback, shall we?"

"Always," Ben affirmed, meeting her gaze. Together, they focused their wills against the barrier. Where once they might have faltered, the bond between them now surged strong and clear. They could almost hear Lila's laughter and Roran's steady voice, urging them on.

"Remember the time we turned that ogre's club into a bouquet of flowers?" Elara asked, a mischievous glint in her eye.

"Hard to forget," Ben said with a grin. "Ready for a repeat performance?"

"Always," Elara echoed. They channeled their power, weaving strands of magic that twisted and sparked against the barrier. Slowly, the walls began to wilt like petals, transforming from impenetrable shield to a shower of harmless, fragrant blooms.

"Looks like your betrayal is wilting, Grindle," Ben taunted, stepping through the remains of the spell.

"Never underestimate the power of a good floral arrangement," Elara added cheerily, brushing past the deflated sage.

"Come on," Ben said, his voice firm with resolve. "We've got friends to save and a tyrant to topple."

"Right behind you," Elara nodded, her spirits unshaken. "And after that, maybe we'll teach Zalathor a thing or two about loyalty—and interior design."

"Elara, do you think that's supposed to be his face?" Ben whispered as they crept through the shadowy corridor, gesturing at a garish tapestry depicting Zalathor in all his brooding menace.

"Only if he was aiming for 'constipated gargoyle'," Elara stifled a laugh, ducking under a low-hanging cobweb. They had navigated Zalathor's labyrinth of a lair, each room more ostentatiously evil than the last. The latest décor featured an abundance of black velvet and skulls with questionable taste in candle placement.

As they neared the heart of the dark fortress, the air grew thick with a sense of impending doom—or was it just the overbearing scent of brimstone and incense? They found themselves standing before an ominous door, its surface etched with runes that screamed 'final boss room' louder than a banshee at a silent retreat.

"Ah, the would-be heroes arrive!" boomed a voice that could only belong to Zalathor. The door swung open with a dramatic creak, revealing their nemesis perched atop a throne that looked suspiciously like it was carved from the petrified remains of lesser villains who didn't read the memo on minimalism.

"Zalathor," Ben said, stepping forward with a determined glare. "We've come for Lila and Roran."

"Of course you have," Zalathor smirked, twirling what appeared to be a mustache made of living shadows. "But did you really think I wouldn't anticipate your little rescue attempt?"

Behind him, shackled to the wall, were Lila and Roran, looking decidedly unimpressed by their captor's theatrics.

"Let them go, Zalathor," Elara demanded, her hand inching toward the hilt of her sword. "This ends now!"

"Ah, but the fun is just beginning!" With a snap of his fingers, ghostly chains rattled, and spectral guards materialized around them. "Welcome to the grand finale of my reign of terror—where your story ends, and my eternal dominion begins!"

Ben and Elara exchanged a glance; this was it—the moment they had been fighting for. They couldn't afford to lose, not when so much was at stake. Taking a deep breath, they prepared to face the horde, their hearts thundering with the weight of their destiny.

"Last chance to surrender, Zalathor," Ben called out, his voice steady despite the rising tension.

"Please," Elara added with a smirk. "You wouldn't want to miss your appointment with defeat. It's terribly rude to keep catastrophe waiting."

"Bold words for the soon-to-be vanquished!" Zalathor laughed maniacally, the sound echoing off the walls.

As the first wave of apparitions lunged, Ben and Elara sprang into action, their weapons dancing in the dim light, a symphony of steel and sorcery. They fought back-to-back, their banter as sharp as their blades.

"Remember when we thought infiltrating a dragon's tea party was tough?" Ben grunted, parrying a ghostly strike.

"Those were simpler times," Elara quipped, dispatching another specter with a flick of her wrist. "At least the scones were decent!"

The battle raged on, the duo carving a path toward their friends. Just as they began to gain the upper hand, the ground beneath them shuddered. The chamber shook violently, dust cascading from above as a deafening roar filled the space.

"Is that...?" Ben started.

"Yep," Elara confirmed, eyes wide but sparkling with mischief. "He's summoned his pet wyrm."

"Of course he has," Ben sighed. "Because why have a fair fight when you can bring a colossal, fire-breathing cheat code?"

"Ben! Elara!" Lila's voice cut through the chaos. "The amulet! Use the amulet!"

Glancing at each other, realization dawned on them. Amidst laughter and spellfire, they grasped the amulet that hung around Elara's neck, a trinket they'd picked up from a fallen foe, with powers yet unknown.

"Here goes nothing!" Elara shouted, activating the amulet. A blinding light erupted, enveloping them in a protective bubble just as the wyrm unleashed a torrent of flame.

The chapter closed with the inferno raging outside their magical shield, the heat pressing against their safe haven like the breath of a monstrous oven. As the light slowly dimmed, Ben and Elara stared out at the scene before them, their faces set with grim resolve.

"Guess we're adding 'wyrm taming' to our resumes," Ben quipped, gripping his sword tighter.

"Right after 'tyrant toppling,'" Elara added with a grin, her eyes alight with the fire of determination.

With the fate of their friends hanging in the balance, and Zalathor's victory within reach, the stage was set for a showdown that would either be their greatest triumph or their final act. And as the amulet's glow faded, the only certainty was that the next chapter would begin with a bang—or in their case, possibly a roar.

The earth quaked under the thunderous charge of Ben and his valiant comrades, their steely gaze fixed upon the grotesque visage of Zalathor, the Flatulent King. With weapons brandished like the shining teeth of a starved wolf pack, they descended into the fray, a symphony of clashing steel scoring their entry.

"Forward to glory!" Ben roared, his sword slicing through the air as if it were an extension of his indomitable will. The pungent stench of Zalathor's infamous gaseous emissions battled against the scent of determination that wafted from our heroes. It was the opening scene of battle, where every warrior's mettle would be tested.

Elara, her eyes shimmering with the arcane, channeled her mystical might into a dome of shimmering energy that enveloped their ranks. "Shield of Aetherius, protect us!" she bellowed, her voice rising over the cacophony of war. Her fingers danced in the air, weaving patterns that pulled at the very threads of reality.

"Nice bubble, Elara," Ben chuckled amidst the chaos, even as his own hands crackled with barely contained power. "Now watch this!"

With a flourish that would have made any stage magician green with envy, Ben unleashed a tempestuous barrage of lightning bolts. The arcs of electricity jagged across the sky, a spiderweb of searing vengeance that struck down foe after foe. Their bodies juddered and smoked, the scent of singed villainy briefly overpowering even Zalathor's noxious presence.

Not content with just one display of pyrotechnics, Elara conjured balls of fire that careened through the enemy lines like comets with particularly bad tempers. Each impact blossomed into a fiery flower of destruction, sending Zalathor's minions scurrying like ants in a child's sadistic game.

"Take that, you flatulent fiend!" Ben hollered, his bravado echoing over the battlefield as he lobbed a particularly large bolt of lightning, which sizzled towards the enemy with the enthusiasm of a lightning bug on its first date.

"Your wind-breaking days are numbered, Zalathor!" Elara added with a smirk, launching another salvo of fireballs that painted the twilight with streaks of orange and red.

As the two mages wove their spells together, a dance of destruction played out before them, their allies safe within the cocoon of their combined magic. The tide of battle ebbed and flowed, but under the relentless assault of spellcraft, it seemed as though the day would soon belong to the forces of good, humor, and considerably better hygiene.

Amidst the chaos of clashing steel and explosive sorcery, Lila scaled an ancient ruin with the agility of a mountain cat. Her quiver bristled with arrows fletched with the feathers of the elusive snicker-snatch bird, known for their ability to tickle enemies to madness. Finding her perch atop a crumbling wall, she nocked an arrow, drew back her bowstring, and squinted one eye with comedic precision.

"Time to pluck some poultry," she muttered, releasing the deadly missile. It soared through the air, whistling a jaunty tune before embedding itself in the rear of a goblin who yelped and leaped into the embrace of his unsuspecting comrades. One by one, her arrows launched forth, each finding its mark amid the enemy ranks with the punctuality of a tea-time invitation. The soldiers fell in slapstick succession, creating a domino effect that sent helmets and swords flying like an overzealous jester's props.

Below, Roran bellowed a war cry that sounded suspiciously like the mating call of the wild yodeling yak. With a sword as hefty as a tavern keeper's tab on ale night, he charged headlong into Zalathor's minions. His blade swung in arcs that would make a rainbow jealous, glinting with the reflection of Elara's fireballs that lit up the battlefield like a festival bonfire.

"Make way! Comin' through!" Roran roared, his voice carrying over the din. Enemy soldiers scattered before him like bowling pins at the hands of a giant. His muscular arms bulged with each swing, a testament to years of training—or perhaps just lifting too many tankards in the local mead hall.

A particularly rotund ogre loomed ahead, brandishing a club the size of a young tree. Roran met the creature's charge with a dancer's grace and a bull's force, sidestepping at the last moment and delivering a blow that sent the ogre twirling in a pirouette before collapsing in a heap. Roran winked at an imaginary audience, acknowledging their silent applause.

"Who says warriors can't be graceful?" he mumbled, before plunging back into the fray. His swordplay was a whirlwind of bluster and brute force, and with every fallen foe, Roran carved a path of hilarity and heroism, inspiring his allies to push forward into the belly of battle.

The clatter of swords and the cries of battle faded to a sinister silence as Zalathor raised his arms, a twisted grin creasing his face. From the earth arose a shambling tide of decay—skeletons clacking in macabre rhythm, zombies moaning like lovelorn cats, and ghouls whose stench outdid even Zalathor's notorious flatulence.

"Undead minions!" shouted Ben, his voice tinged with both horror and annoyance. "Why does it always have to be undead minions?"

"Because necromancy is terribly in vogue this century," Elara quipped, twirling her wand with flair. "Now let's blow them away!"

With a flick of her wrist, Elara summoned a wind that howled like a banshee with a stubbed toe. The gust swept through the ranks of the undead, lifting zombies off their feet and tossing skeletons about like leaves in an autumn storm. Bones rattled and skulls rolled, bowling over their less fortunate comrades in an undead farce.

"Strike while the iron is hot—or, in this case, while the zombies are airborne!" Lila called out, notching arrow after arrow, each one whistling through the air with deadly intent.

"Hot? I'll show you hot!" Elara declared. With another dramatic gesture, she conjured a wall of fire that blazed into existence, its flames leaping eagerly toward the sky like acrobats in a fiery circus act. The inferno crackled with laughter, or so it seemed to the assembled heroes, as it danced between them and the approaching horrors, singing the eyebrows of any undead foolish enough to get too close.

"Looks like Zalathor's minions just got... fired!" Roran bellowed, unable to resist the pun, as he cleaved through a particularly persistent zombie that had managed to dodge both wind and flame.

"Roran, your humor slays me more than your swordplay," Elara chuckled, shaking her head at the warrior's incorrigible jesting even as she maintained her magical barrier.

"Then my work here is done!" Roran grinned, swinging his sword with gusto, sending limbs and rotting flesh flying in a grim ballet of destruction. "But I suppose I can spare a few extra swings for our decomposing friends."

As the wall of fire held back the main force of the undead, the heroes fought with renewed vigor, knowing that Elara's sorcery had given them the upper hand in a battle that had taken a decidedly eerie turn. With every undead minion dispatched, their resolve hardened—not even Zalathor's grotesque surprises could dampen their spirits.

"Comedy and carnage make excellent bedfellows!" Roran exclaimed, his laughter echoing across the battlefield as the heroes pressed on, undaunted by the darkness that surrounded them.

Ben, eyes alight with the fires of Elara's incantation, felt his pulse thrum to the rhythm of battle. The air crackled with arcane energy, and the scent of singed undead tinged every breath. He stood amidst the chaotic waltz of war, a steadfast conductor ready to unleash his own symphony of destruction.

"By the saggy undergarments of the ancients," Ben muttered, his voice barely audible over the clamor of clashing steel. "It's time to tap into the ol' mystical keg." With a dramatic flourish that would've made a theatre actor blush, Ben extended his arms, fingers splayed wide.

"Magic, don't fail me now!" he cried, as if commanding an unruly hound. The very fabric of reality hesitated, quivering under the weight of his command. Then, like a dam bursting forth, Ben's latent powers surged through him—a torrential flood of raw, unbridled energy.

"Behold, the Whirlwind of Walloping Wonder!" Ben roared, as a spiraling vortex of luminous force erupted from his being. It swept across the battlefield, an iridescent wave of pure comedic wrath. Armor buckled, bones shattered, and foes were sent cartwheeling through the air like ragdolls in a tornado—all to the sound of Ben's maniacal laughter.

"Take that, you decomposed devils!" he whooped, the thrill of victory coursing through his veins. "You've just been Ben-nihilated!"

But as the dust settled, and Ben basked in the glory of his magical onslaught, a foul wind began to stir. It was not the sweet zephyr of triumph, but rather the harbinger of a most odorous doom.

"Friends!" Zalathor bellowed, his voice echoing with malice and a hint of indigestion. "Behold my royal secret weapon: the 'Gust of Gastrointestinal Grievance'!"

With an unceremonious lift of his regal robes, the Flatulent King released a miasma so vile, so horrendously putrid, it could only have been brewed in the bowels of the abyss itself. A greenish haze enveloped the heroes, its stench a blend of rotten eggs and the despair of a thousand unwashed trolls.

"By the cologne of calamity, what fresh hell is this?" Roran gasped, his face contorting in disgust as he clumsily swung his blade, slicing through more air than enemy.

"Elara! A little help here? I think my nostrils are melting!" Lila coughed, her precision faltering as she fired a volley of arrows into the fog, hoping for the best.

"Can't... breathe..." Ben wheezed, his bravado deflating like a punctured balloon. His movements slowed to a nauseating crawl, each step a herculean effort against the pungent assault on their senses.

"Very well, King of Stink," Elara spat, her voice laced with both fury and a hint of mint—her desperate attempt to mask the smell. "Two can play at this game!"

With teary eyes and a resolve steeled by the foulest of fumes, the heroes rallied. They may have been temporarily incapacitated by Zalathor's noxious tactics, but they were far from defeated. For in the world of high-stakes hilarity and dark fantasy, not even the most stomach-churning of gaseous gambits could dampen the spirits of those destined for legend.

Hoisting her longbow with the grace of an elven ballerina caught in a pirouette, Lila squinted through the miasma that Zalathor had conjured. Her eyes, honed by years of spotting rabbits in thicket and men in tavern shadows, flickered like twin beacons of predatory focus. There! A gap as inviting as a keg at a dwarven wedding lay bare in the enemy's ranks.

"Roran!" she hissed, gesturing with a subtlety that would make a mime feel clumsy. "To the left of the three-headed ogre with the underbite!"

"Underbite?" Roran blinked, momentarily puzzled before his gaze followed her pointed finger. "Ah! The one picking its ear with a club?"

"Exactly!" Lila nodded, already notching an arrow with a flourish that sang a silent death lullaby. "On my mark, we split their attention like a cheesemonger's cleaver."

"Cheesy tactics for a cheesy foe," Roran quipped, his grin flashing briefly before he hunkered down, muscles coiled like springs in a trickster's box.

"Mark!" Lila barked, her voice slicing through the chaos. With the precision of a maestro conducting a symphony of slaughter, her arrows danced toward their targets. One, two, three—each whistle of feathered death finding purchase in the flesh of the unsuspecting.

"Whoopsie-daisy!" Roran chimed, leaping into the fray with the enthusiasm of a child plunging into a puddle. His sword became a blur, a silver streak that reaped enemies like a farmer in a frenzy of harvest. They fell to his might, creating a domino effect of dismay within their disorganized lines.

Amidst the fracas, Ben summoned the remnants of his willpower, shaking off the lingering malaise from the royal flatulence. He glared at Zalathor with the intensity of a man who has found a worm in his apple—a particularly nasty worm that wore a crown and spouted sonnets of stench.

"Time to end your reign, Your Highness of Horrors!" Ben roared, charging forward like a bull that had taken umbrage to a matador's ostentatious outfit.

Zalathor, bloated with bluster, met him head-on, their swords clashing with a cacophony that could wake the dead—if the dead weren't already joining the party courtesy of Zalathor's necromancy. Sparks rained down as steel kissed steel, each exchange a testament to Ben's burgeoning wrath and the Flatulent King's indigestible arrogance.

"Have at thee, you gasbag!" Ben taunted, swinging with the ferocity of a tempest in a tavern. His blade carved arcs of defiance, each strike punctuated by the ringing song of metal and the sputtering curses of his foul foe.

"Thou art but a pebble in my shoe, a tick upon mine arse!" Zalathor retorted, his ripostes as laden with hot air as his belly was with ill winds.

Their duel spiraled into legend, a tale to be told with guffaws and groans around campfires and alehouses. For when the dust settled on this most pungent of battlefields, it would be said that even the mightiest of stenches could not quell the fervor of a true hero—or the sharp aim of a witty archer and the hearty swing of a stalwart warrior.

Elara, perched atop a mound of vanquished foes like a queen upon her throne, watched Ben and Zalathor with the intensity of a hawk eyeing a field mouse. Her fingers danced in arcane patterns, weaving the very fabric of magic into a tapestry of undoing for the Flatulent King. A corona of mystical energy flickered around her, casting otherworldly shadows upon her determined visage.

"By the winds of Woe-Be-Gone," she intoned, her voice slicing through the clamor of combat, "let thine inflated ego meet the pinprick of humility!"

The air crackled and shimmered as she unleashed her spell, a beam of sapphire light that spiraled towards Zalathor with the inevitability of doom. It struck him squarely in the chest, where his heart—if such a thing existed within his malodorous mass—would be. The impact was silent but profound, as if hope itself had given the king a swift kick in the nethers.

Zalathor's eyes widened, the color draining from his puffed-up cheeks. He faltered, his ripostes slowing, the certainty of his swings replaced by the flailing of a man suddenly aware he was caught in a whirlpool of his own making. Ben, seizing the moment like a cat lunging at a particularly saucy mouse, rekindled the fire in his limbs.

"Your reign ends here, oh Sultan of Stink!" Ben bellowed, raising his sword high. With all the grace of a poet penning the final verse to an ode, he brought his weapon down in a mighty arc, cleaving through both the stench and the desperation that filled the air.

Zalathor, the Flatulent King, let out a final, wheezing gasp—a swan song squeezed from bellows no longer grand. His corpulent form crumpled like a puppet whose strings had been snipped by an overzealous child. Thud! The sound echoed, resonating with a finality that seemed to say, 'Thus passes the windbag.'

For a heartbeat, the battlefield held its breath, the clash of arms pausing as if time itself stood still to mark the fall of flatulence. Then, chaos resumed anew, but this time as a frantic scramble of retreat. Zalathor's forces, their spirits deflated, scattered like leaves before an autumn gale.

"Retreat! Retreat!" they cried, tripping over one another in a mad dash for safety, leaving behind armor and dignity in equal measure.

"Fly, you fools, lest you wish to share in your master's fragrant fate!" Elara called after them, her laughter ringing clear above the din of cowardice.

Ben stood there, amidst the disarray, his sword dripping defiance, his chest heaving with the exertion of victory. The day was won, the battle ended, and though their journey was far from over, the heroes of Oak Isle could now glimpse the future—a future scoured clean of tyranny and terrible smells.

Ben staggered through the thick of warriors, each step a conquest over his own exhaustion. He slumped down next to Elara, who was already conjuring a glittering tapestry of healing energy above a line of the wounded. The light from her spellwork made her eyes glisten like twin sapphires in a sea of mud and despair.

"Good fight?" he asked between gulps of air, as if they had just finished a spirited game of tug-of-war rather than a battle for their very souls.

"Decent," Elara smirked, winking at him. "Your swordplay was almost as impressive as my incantations. Almost."

"Ha! I'd like to see your spells cleave a zombie's head in two," Ben jested back, clutching his side where a bruise was surely blossoming.

As they shared a brief respite, Lila appeared, her quiver empty but her spirits full. She flopped down beside them with a grace that belied the carnage around. "I'll need new arrows," she announced triumphantly. "Seems I've sent all mine on a one-way trip to enemy skulls."

"Make sure the next batch has ribbons," Roran boomed as he joined the circle, a grin splitting his grizzled face. "It'll add flair to your lethal deliveries."

"Or perhaps little flags that say 'Farewell from Lila,'" Ben suggested, earning a chuckle from the group.

"Or 'Express from Oak Isle,'" Elara chimed in, raising an eyebrow playfully.

"Enough about the archery fanfare," Lila said, rolling her eyes. "Let's not forget the undead chorus line you banished with a gust of wind, Elara. They were quite literally blown away by your performance."

"Indeed," Roran added solemnly, though his eyes danced with mirth. "Never have I seen such graceful disintegration."

The laughter they shared was a balm, soothing the abrasions of war if only for a moment. It stitched them closer together, a patchwork of camaraderie upon the torn fabric of battle.

But as the din of celebration petered out, a somber silence took its place. They rose, turning to behold the grim aftermath that stretched before them. Craters pocked the earth, and the once verdant fields were now a tableau of reds and browns, painted with the broad strokes of conflict.

"Too many have fallen," Roran murmured, his voice a low rumble of thunder, distant yet foreboding.

"Then let us ensure their sacrifices were not in vain," Elara declared, her gaze sweeping across the horizon where the first timid stars began to twinkle.

"Oak Isle will bloom anew," Lila promised, nocking an imaginary arrow and firing it skyward—a silent salute to those who would not return.

"Stronger, braver, and perhaps with less flatulence," Ben added, earning him a round of subdued snickers.

"Here, here," Elara agreed. "To our comrades, our home, and the future we will forge from the ashes of this day."

"From the ashes," they echoed in unison, a quartet of voices that rose to the heavens, mingling with the whispers of the departed.

In the fading light of dusk, they stood shoulder to shoulder, a band of heroes undaunted by the specter of loss. Together, they pledged their resolve to honor the memories of the fallen, to heal the wounds of the land, and to craft a dawn filled with laughter and life. A tomorrow where the tales of their valor would be sung with gusto, and where the stench of tyranny would be replaced by the sweet scent of hope.

As the sun dipped below the horizon, casting a fiery glow that danced over the still-smoldering ruins of the battlefield, Ben squinted into the distance. He could feel the pulse of his magic, a tangible buzz beneath his skin, a reminder of the power he had unleashed and the potential yet untapped.

"Did anyone see where Zalathor's crown landed?" Ben asked, scratching his head. Around him, the charred remnants of the battlefield seemed to echo back his question with a mocking snort.

"Looking to add another feather to your cap, oh vanquisher of the flatulent?" Elara teased, her eyes twinkling with mischief as she conjured a small orb of light to illuminate the growing evening gloom. It hovered above them like a miniature sun, banishing the shadows and perhaps, symbolically, the darkness of their recent trials.

"More like hoping it's not cursed with eternal odor," Ben replied with a grin, waving his hand in front of his nose for emphasis. "I'd rather not have our victory commemorated by the stench of Zalathor's legacy."

"Speaking of legacies," Roran interjected, clapping Ben on the shoulder with a force that would've felled a lesser man. "We've got a whole island to rebuild. And I say we start with the taverns. A sturdy table is the cornerstone of civilization!"

"Roran has a point," Lila chimed in, already sketching imaginary blueprints in the air with her fingers. Her bow, though absent from her hands, was ever present in her poise—straight-backed and unyielding. "We'll need strong foundations. Not just for ale and camaraderie, but for the future generations who'll look back at what we accomplish next."

"First, though, a feast!" declared Elara. "One without the fear of poison or... explosive desserts." She glanced at Ben knowingly, who nodded solemnly, all too aware of past culinary mishaps involving enchanted pastries.

"Agreed," Ben said, a soft chuckle escaping his lips. "But let's also toast to those who can't join us. To the memories that will never fade and the stories that will be told."

"Stories that'll likely get taller with each telling," Lila added, her smirk suggesting she'd be the first to embellish the tales.

"Then let's live lives worthy of such tales," Elara proposed, her voice steady and sure, a beacon cutting through the uncertainties of the road ahead.

"May our enemies quake at the mere rumor of our return," Roran proclaimed, raising an imaginary goblet to the stars.

"May our laughter ring louder than any war horn," Ben continued, his heart feeling lighter despite the weight of responsibility.

"May our arrows fly true, our spells astound, and our swords never dull—unless it's from slicing too many celebration cakes," Lila concluded, the twinkle in her eye reflecting the last rays of daylight.

The four of them stood together, a tableau of resilience amidst the ruins. Their journey had been arduous, marked by battles won and loved ones lost, but the bonds forged in the crucible of conflict were unbreakable. They were united, a fellowship tempered in fire, ready to meet whatever challenges lay ahead with courage, wit, and an unwavering spirit.

And as the evening star emerged to claim its place in the firmament, the heroes of Oak Isle faced the twilight, their silhouettes etched against the canvas of a world they had saved—and would continue to protect. The laughter and banter echoed around them, a melody of hope that promised new adventures, new legends, and a future crafted by their own hands.

"Tomorrow, we build," Ben stated with resolve, his friends nodding in agreement.

"Tonight, we feast!" Roran boomed, and even the heavens seemed to pause in anticipation of the revelry to come.

"Let the tales begin," whispered the wind, and the heroes' laughter was the reply that carried it onward.

Ben stood amidst the chaos of what had once been the grand hall, its vaulted ceilings now hung with tattered banners and the air thick with the stench of sulfur and defeat. The marble floor was littered with the remnants of a fierce battle, scorched earth mingling with shattered armor. At the far end, upon a throne that seemed to emit a dull groan under his weight, lounged the source of Oak Isle's suffering: the Flatulent King.

"Ah, the whiff of fear," the king bellowed, a smirk creasing his corpulent features as he eyed Ben from across the room. "Or is that just me?"

The air trembled as the king shifted, his voluminous robes straining against the immense girth of his belly. With a casual flick of his bejeweled fingers, the Flatulent King conjured an ominous green mist that coiled around him like serpents preparing to strike.

"Prepare yourself, young whelp," the king taunted, his voice a rumble deep within his cavernous chest. "For I have dined on the beans of Beelzebub, and my powers are at their peak!"

Ben squared his shoulders, clutching the hilt of his sword with a resolve that belied the queasiness in his stomach. As the first wave of malodorous miasma rolled towards him, he could taste the tang of rotten eggs and spoiled cabbage on his tongue.

With a flourish of his royal rump, the Flatulent King unleashed a barrage of noxious blasts, each one a symphony of grotesque sound and fury. They roared through the air, invisible yet undeniably present, seeking to envelop Ben in their putrid embrace.

"By the winds of destiny, that reeks!" Ben coughed, feeling his eyes water and his knees buckle under the sheer force of the olfactory onslaught. He knew he must not let the stench cloud his mind or dampen his spirit; otherwise, he'd be as good as dead, or worse—enslaved by the tyranny of toxic fumes.

"Your scent-sational attacks won't break me!" Ben shouted back, finding strength in defiance, his words slicing through the fetid fog like a beacon of hope for all of Oak Isle. "I will not falter in the face of flatulence!"

The Flatulent King laughed, a sound that rumbled ominously like thunder foretelling a storm of gas. "We shall see, hero. We shall smell!" he declared, punctuating his threat with another gust of ghastly wind.

Ben steadied himself, his heart pounding in his chest not just from exertion but from the knowledge that the fate of his kingdom rested on his ability to withstand this aromatic assault. The battle between the valiant and the vile had truly begun, and only one would emerge victorious from this pungent predicament.

Ben, his nostrils assailed by the gastronomic monstrosity of the Flatulent King's onslaught, clutched the Staff of Tomorrow with a grip that could crush stone. The ornate artifact pulsed with an otherworldly glow, its arcane runes shimmering like a discotheque of destiny amidst the dreary gray stones of the grand hall.

"Enough of your colon-curdling capers!" Ben roared, defiance flaring in his chest like indigestion after a dubious stew. With a flourishing twirl of the staff, he summoned forth a cascade of magical energy, each burst popping and crackling through the air, an extravagant fireworks show countering the invisible waves of stench.

The grand hall became an arena of competing spectacles; on one side, the lurid lightshow of Ben's spellcraft, on the other, the putrescent puffery of the Flatulent King's unnatural abilities. Colorful beams ricocheted off walls, casting prismatic shadows that danced along with the rhythm of battle, while foul fumes sought to smother them in their malodorous miasma.

"Try and catch me, your gaseousness!" Ben taunted, his feet finding purchase where others would slip on the treacherous terrain of soot and debris. He darted forward, the staff leaving streaks of brilliance in its wake as he leaped into the air, somersaulting over a particularly dense cloud of noxious gas.

With the grace of a swallow evading a flatulent storm, he twisted mid-air, his cloak billowing around him like the sails of a ship braving the tempestuous winds. Landing with the poise of a cat—or perhaps more aptly, a cat avoiding a particularly smelly litter box—Ben narrowly escaped the green-tinged tendrils that snapped at his heels.

"Oooh, what's wrong, my liege?" Ben chided, his voice laced with mockery as he bounded from fallen banner to toppled throne, "Can't your royal rear end keep up?"

His jest was met with a low growl from the king, who seemed decidedly unamused by the display of acrobatics. Yet, for all his flatulence and fury, the monarch of methane could not land a single sulfurous strike upon the agile hero. Each bound and leap Ben executed was a testament to his tenacity, a ballet performed in the face of biological warfare.

And so, the grand hall bore witness to a most peculiar battle—a clash of might and mirth, where valor vied against vapor, and the fate of Oak Isle hung in the balance, teetering on the edge of laughter and lunacy.

Ben ducked as the Flatulent King, his face reddening with exertion and frustration, abandoned the fruitless volleys of his infamous gas attacks. The king's swollen midsection swung forward with the force of a trebuchet, aiming to crush Ben beneath its immense girth. But the self-proclaimed monarch had underestimated his adversary.

"Really? Belly bumps?" Ben snorted, dancing aside as the King's stomach lumbered past, stirring the air with the scent of a dozen spoiled feasts. "What's next, Your Highness, death by doughnut?"

The King's eyes narrowed, and he pivoted on one foot—a move that would have been impressive had it not been accompanied by an involuntary flatulent fanfare. With the agility of a man half his size and three times less gaseous, he launched another corporeal strike, his belly leading like the hammer of an angry god.

But Ben was a blur, his movements a symphony of dodges and weaves. He could feel the breeze from each near miss, the displaced air tinged with the aroma of defeat—or perhaps that was just the lingering stench of the King's earlier offenses.

"Come on, you can do better than that!" Ben egged on, his voice carrying the taunt of a jesters' jibe as he parried the fleshy onslaughts with the ease of a seasoned duelist.

Then, seizing a momentary lapse in the King's attack pattern, Ben struck. His enchanted sword hummed with power, slicing through the air with the precision of a surgeon and the flair of an artist. Silver flashes of steel targeted the sovereign of stink where his armor chafed, at the joints and underarms—each spot known to be tender from the royal habit of overindulgence.

"Tickle, tickle," Ben chuckled, darting in and out, his blade kissing the King's side with a chime of metal against metal. The King howled, not in pain, but in sheer irritation, his temper flaring hotter than dragonfire chili on feast day.

"Insolent knave!" roared the King, his voice booming through the hall like thunder rolling over fetid marshlands. "I'll squash you like—"

"Like a grape under a dancing elephant?" Ben interjected, nimbly avoiding another ponderous swing. "You'll have to catch me first!"

And the chase continued, with Ben's laughter echoing off the walls, mixing with the grunts and growls of the increasingly irate Flatulent King. Each time the King thought he had cornered the spry hero, Ben would slip away, leaving behind nothing but his taunts and the faint whiff of victory.

Ben, now a blur of motion and mockery, danced around the grand hall, his blade a whispering death to the Flatulent King's pride. The king's face turned the color of spoiled plums as he puffed and panted, each breath a labored wheeze.

"Enough!" bellowed the king, his voice cracking with fury. "Minions, arise! Engulf him in your gaseous embrace!"

From the shadows of the battle-scarred hall, a cacophony of pops and squeaks announced the arrival of the farting minions. They were an unholy assembly of creatures, each more grotesque than the last—a choir of stench with a single purpose: to overwhelm Ben with their repulsive fumes.

But Ben, whose nostrils had already been tested by the king's own aromatic assaults, stood undaunted. He raised the Staff of Tomorrow high, its crystal top catching the light of the torches that still burned along the walls.

"By the winds of yore," Ben incanted, his voice steady despite the encroaching stink, "I summon thee, Gust of Freshness!"

A whirlwind sprang forth from the staff, spiraling like a dervish unleashed. It swept through the hall, gathering force and purpose. The minions, caught in the tempest's path, spun helplessly, their flatulence no match for the cleansing zephyr. Their vile chorus was drowned out by the howling wind, their presence scattered like leaves in a storm.

Ben watched, a grin plastered on his face, as the gust carried away the remnants of the flatulent horde. Their defeat was as swift as it was fragrant, leaving behind nothing but the echoes of their embarrassing exit.

The path to the Flatulent King now lay clear, the air purified by Ben's magical might. The king, stripped of his malodorous minions, stood alone—his eyes wide with disbelief at the resilience of the hero before him.

"Your move, your Gassiness," Ben quipped, twirling his sword with a flourish and readying himself for the next phase of this most odorous battle.

Ben squared his shoulders, the light from the Staff of Tomorrow casting an ethereal glow over the battlefield's carnage. The Flatulent King, once a figure of terror and comedic disgust, now faltered before him, the stench of fear mingling with the perpetual odor that clung to his royal robes.

"Time to end this noxious nightmare," Ben muttered, the staff pulsing in his grip as he drew upon its ancient power. With a defiant cry, he swung it forward, releasing a torrent of radiant energy that sliced through the fetid air like a scythe through overripe cabbage.

The beam, bright as the first dawn, struck the Flatulent King squarely in the chest, eliciting a belch of surprise from the beleaguered monarch. He staggered backward, his corpulent form shimmering with the effort to ward off the magical onslaught. His usual green-hued miasma wavered, dissipating under the relentless assault of Ben's spell.

"Curse you, Ben!" the Flatulent King wheezed, his voice a gasp amid the sputtering of his own failing powers.

But the despot was not yet spent. With a guttural groan that seemed to emanate from the very depths of his bloated belly, the Flatulent King summoned every ounce of his remaining strength. His face reddened, veins popping, eyes bulging with the strain of conjuring his most feared weapon: the Ultimate Fartnado, a vortex of villainous vapor capable of leveling cities and suffocating the souls of the brave.

"Behold my final gust!" the king roared, lifting his arms as the ominous rumble of digestive doom built within him.

Ben watched, grimly amused, as the corners of the grand hall began to swirl with the telltale signs of the coming storm. It was a desperate move, one that reeked of defeat, and the hero knew that if he could withstand this last, flatulent fury, victory would be his—and Oak Isle's for the taking.

"Let's spin this wind," Ben quipped, tightening his hold on the staff, prepared to face the ultimate test of his mettle and his nostrils.

The grand hall reverberated with the impending doom of the Flatulent King's ultimate gambit, the very air pregnant with anticipation and a hint of brimstone. Ben stood resolute, his eyes narrowed in focus as he drew from the Staff of Tomorrow's endless wellspring of power. His fingers danced along its runes, which glowed with an ethereal radiance, casting prismatic reflections upon the tattered banners of Oak Isle.

"Whirlwind Shield!" Ben bellowed, thrusting the staff forward. A cyclone of magical force spiraled into being around him, a shimmering barrier against the miasmic onslaught that was to come. The ceiling groaned, stones weeping dust, as the king's cheeks puffed to the brink of bursting.

With a thunderous eruption that shook the very foundations of the castle, the Flatulent King unleashed his torrential Fartnado. It collided with Ben's whirlwind shield in a cacophonous symphony of wind and stench, a battle of gales that threatened to tear the world asunder. Yet Ben's shield held fast, repelling the toxic tempest with a resonance that sent the adversary staggering back on his heels, gasping for air amidst his own fetid creation.

"Impossible!" the Flatulent King gasped, his voice aghast with disbelief.

"Improbable, maybe. But never impossible," Ben retorted, his quip slicing through the tension like his sword through warm butter.

Seizing the moment as the king reeled, Ben leapt into action, his feet finding purchase on the marble floor slick with the remnants of their magical melee. He sprinted with the grace of a gazelle in a meadow—albeit one chased by the most malodorous lion imaginable.

"Time to puncture your bloated reign!" Ben cried out, brandishing his enchanted sword with a flourish that would have made any swashbuckler green with envy—or perhaps it was just the lingering effects of the king's gases.

He closed the distance between them with the inevitability of destiny itself. The Flatulent King, still winded from his exertion, swung his pendulous belly in defense, but Ben was faster, nimbler, a dancer amidst the chaos of combat. He ducked beneath the gelatinous arc of royal gut and thrust his sword forward with all the might his weary arms could muster.

The blade sang a high-pitched note as it cleaved through the air, striking true. It pierced the tyrant's corpulent form with a squelchy thud, an anti-climax to the bombastic symphony of their duel. The Flatulent King's eyes bulged, his mouth agape in silent shock, as he teetered like a felled oak before collapsing onto the ground with a quake that might have rivaled his own noxious powers.

"Long live the fresh air!" Ben proclaimed triumphantly, even as he fought the urge to pinch his nose. The battle was won, the day was saved, and not a moment too soon—for the aroma of victory was far sweeter than the scent of defeat that now lingered in the grand hall.

With the Flatulent King now sprawled across the grand hall's floor, his reign of reeking terror concluded, a collective gasp turned to cheers among the people of Oak Isle. They emerged hesitantly from behind tapestries and under banquet tables, their noses twitching as they tested the air for any lingering miasma. The smell of sulfur and brimstone was quickly replaced by the sweet aroma of freedom. The citizens flung open the windows with dramatic flair, inviting in the crisp sea breeze to cleanse their once befouled castle.

"Breath deep, my friends!" Ben bellowed, standing atop the defeated king's girth like a conqueror of old, his chest heaving with fatigue. "The only winds that shall blow through Oak Isle are those of change!"

A minstrel, who had been cowering behind a particularly robust suit of armor, seized the moment. He struck up a jaunty tune on his lute, one that spoke of fresh starts and even fresher air, a melody so catchy it made the crowd forget their recent trials. They joined in song, their voices rising in a chorus of celebration, punctuated by the occasional uncontrollable giggle at the situation's absurdity.

"Ben! Ben! Ben!" they chanted in rhythm with their dancing feet. Children did cartwheels, women twirled with abandon, and even the most grizzled warriors couldn't help but caper about with uncharacteristic joviality. In the midst of it all stood Ben, his smile wry beneath the exhaustion etched on his face.

"Today we have proven," he paused to drape the king's own royal cloak—a bit too fragrant for his liking—over a nearby chair, "that no force of flatulence can stifle the spirit of this great land!"

They hoisted him onto their shoulders then, a hero not because he sought glory but because he'd dared to stand against the gusts of tyranny. They paraded him around the hall, his name echoing off the stone walls, each cheer a brushstroke painting him into the colorful canvas of their history.

"May the ballads sung in your honor never be as winded as the foe you've vanquished!" cried an old woman as she tossed a garland of flowers around his neck.

"Let our children's children breathe easy, knowing it was Ben who deodorized our destiny!" declared a blacksmith, raising his hammer high.

And so, amidst laughter and song, the legacy of Ben—the brave, the bold, the slightly bemused—was sealed. His tale would be told in every corner of Oak Isle, from the highest tower to the humblest hearth, a story to inspire and entertain for generations to come. And as the last echoes of mirth reverberated throughout the land, the sunset painted the sky in hues of victory: a brilliant palette of purples, oranges, and golds, untainted by the shadow of the Flatulent King.

Ben heaved a sigh, the kind that untangled the knots in his weary muscles and unraveled the lingering stench from his nostrils. With the Flatulent King now just an unpleasant memory, the grand hall of the castle no longer echoed with the sounds of battle or the odorous evidence of his reign. It was time to roll up his sleeves—both metaphorically and literally—and rebuild what had been lost.

"Alright, you magnificent masons, whimsical woodworkers, and plucky plumbers," Ben boomed, addressing the motley crew of allies who'd stood by him through thick and thin (and through thick, unbreathable air). "We have a kingdom to refurbish!"

The blacksmith, still riding the high of victory, swung his hammer into action, transforming twisted metal back into useful tools with merry clinks and clangs that sang out like a hopeful tune for the future. The carpenters, armed with saws and chisels that danced in their hands, began repairing the splintered thrones and shattered tables, each shaving of wood a step towards normalcy.

"Careful with that tapestry!" Ben called out as townsfolk hoisted a vibrant piece of fabric depicting the Battle of Breezy Bluffs. "It's not just a wall covering; it's a lesson in 'what not to eat before a fight.'"

Laughter bubbled up around him, the sound far sweeter than any of the Flatulent King's emissions. Children scampered about, carrying messages and small tools, their faces smeared with soot but alight with enthusiasm. They were like little sparks flitting through the shadows of the past, igniting hope for the years ahead.

"Look at this, Ben!" A young girl tugged at his tunic, pointing toward a newly erected statue. It was a rather... generous interpretation of Ben himself, complete with an exaggeratedly heroic stance and a suspiciously bulging bicep. Above the statue's head, a plaque read: 'Ben, the Windbreaker.'

"Ah, a monument to my strength," Ben chuckled, scratching his head. "Although, I do hope they've captured my good side."

"Both sides are your good sides when you're the hero, Ben!" the girl giggled, her laughter joining the chorus of reconstruction.

As the sun dipped lower in the sky, painting the clouds in shades of triumph, Ben realized that the true foundation of Oak Isle was its people. Their resilience was the mortar, their unity the bricks, and their shared flatulence-free future the roof over their heads.

"Tomorrow," Ben proclaimed, resting his hand on the hilt of his sword-turned-shovel, "we plant gardens where once there were gaseous graveyards. We'll grow roses that need not compete with the scent of sulfur, and we shall dine on beans without fear!"

"Long live Ben, the Harbinger of Fresh Air!" the crowd cheered, raising tankards of mead and cups of mint tea.

And so, amidst the absurdity and mirth, the seeds of a new Oak Isle were sown. It would be a place remembered not for the darkness it endured but for the light-hearted spirit it embraced, a land where the only thing more robust than its walls was the laughter ringing through them.

The world was a mosaic of charred earth and fractured stone, the once-majestic Oak Isle now resembling the aftermath of a dragon's temper tantrum. As Ben trudged through the smoldering remains, his boots kicked up a cocktail of ash and defeat. The allies who had stood by him—those who weren't decorating the battlefield with their eternal slumber—rallied around him like a bunch of mismatched chess pieces left on the board after a furious game.

"Look at this," grumbled Sir Reginald, whose armor was dented in so many places he looked like a walking metal raisin. "My grandmother hits harder than those fiends, and she's been dead for a century."

"Your grandmother could probably still take them," snorted Mage Melinda, waving her wand absentmindedly, accidentally setting a nearby bush back on fire.

"Too soon," chided Archer Annabelle, as she plucked an arrow from the ground, inspected it, and shrugged before slotting it back into her quiver. "But yeah, Granny Reg was legendary."

Ben couldn't help but smirk, despite the heavy stone of grief lodged in his throat. They stood in a loose circle, each lost in thought as they remembered friends who had fought valiantly, whose jokes would no longer fill the night air, whose laughter would no longer ease the tension before a skirmish.

"Remember when Sir Lancelittle charged the enemy yelling about how they'd never take his favorite ale?" chuckled Ben, his voice breaking the silence.

"Or when Lady Eliza used her 'fearsome' battle cry, which sounded more like a kitten's yawn?" added Reginald, the hint of a smile tugging at his battered visage.

"Good times," sighed Melinda, her wand now creating a series of mournful sparkles that fizzled out like their hopes of a casualty-free victory.

Amidst the shared stories and bittersweet laughter, Ben's heart grew heavier with each passing moment, the weight of survival pressing down on him like a monstrous golem. He looked around at the faces of his remaining companions, their eyes shadowed with similar pain, and wondered if triumph came at too steep a price.

"Are we the lucky ones or the cursed?" he pondered aloud, his gaze lifting to the darkened sky where dragons might have roamed in less apocalyptic circumstances.

"Bit of both," Melinda responded, her voice soft as the last glowing embers of a dying fire.

"Definitely cursed," muttered Annabelle, twanging her bowstring in a melancholy tune.

"Let's just say we're... uniquely fortunate," offered Reginald, trying to straighten his helmet, only to have it comically spin around, obscuring his vision.

"Uniquely fortunate to carry the burden of the fallen," Ben mused, his mind awash with the faces of those who lay still amidst the destruction. Survivor's guilt gnawed at him, an insidious worm in the apple of their victory.

"Hey, at least you've got new material for your books, eh Ben?" Annabelle nudged him with an elbow, a weak attempt at lightening the mood.

"Indeed," Ben forced a chuckle, knowing his quill would be stained with more than just ink when he next set it to parchment.

"May our fallen comrades inspire tales of valor," said Reginald, finally managing to right his helmet. "And may our future battles be... less fatal."

"Here's to hoping," they all murmured, raising an assortment of battered weapons toward the heavens, a silent salute to those who had given everything.

As laughter and tears mingled in the sooty air, Ben realized the tale of Oak Isle would be one of darkness and light, of despair and humor—a story only they could tell, and one that must be told.

Ben hefted a shovel, its blade dulled from use, and thrust it into the earth. Around him, the people of Oak Isle, from the wizened baker to the young pageboy who dreamt of knighthood, joined in. They dug graves as if each spade of dirt was a step toward healing their wounded hearts.

"Oy, careful there!" bellowed Sir Harold, the knight whose armor never quite fit right. He had accidentally unearthed a particularly disgruntled mole. The creature, wearing a minuscule helmet, shook a tiny fist at the interruption before scurrying away to less disturbed grounds.

"Seems even the moles wear armor in these parts," quipped Ben, allowing a brief smile to cross his lips despite the somber occasion.

The funeral procession was a cavalcade of mismatched sorrow. A bard, plucking a lute with broken strings, led them on a woefully off-key dirge. The air filled with the scent of roses and regret, roses because they were thought to guide spirits to the afterlife, and regret because, well, everyone had some regrets, especially about the bard's musical talents.

"Here we lay our brave heroes to rest," intoned Grand Mage Elric, whose once majestic robes now sported burn marks and an inexplicable number of spoons sticking out from various pockets. "May they find peace and a distinct lack of epic battles in the great beyond."

"Or at least a spell of silence for that lute," whispered Annabelle, her eyes glistening with unshed tears.

"Shh," chided Reginald, trying to maintain decorum but failing to suppress his own snort of laughter.

Following the ceremony, the townsfolk gathered amongst the ruins, hands ready and hearts determined. Ben, taking charge with an earnestness born of shared loss, pointed to the crumbled walls of what used to be the library.

"Alright, team," he announced, "let's turn this rubble into a castle! Err... again."

"Perhaps this time with fewer secret passages that lead to certain doom?" suggested Annabelle, dusting off a stone and placing it onto a growing pile.

"Agreed. We'll leave those to the professionals—like us," Reginald added, while trying to negotiate with a stubborn piece of timber that seemed more interested in playing dead than being useful.

"Let's just make sure the foundations are strong," said Ben, his voice steady, a contrast to the chaos around them. "We build not just for ourselves, but for the memories of those we've lost."

"Speaking of strong foundations," piped up Sir Harold, "I think I found the mole's new fortress." He gestured toward a hill of fresh soil, the disgruntled mole standing atop it like a conqueror.

"Let the rebuilding commence!" exclaimed Ben, raising his shovel like a standard. "For Oak Isle, for our fallen, and for the hope that one day, our biggest problem will be negotiating land rights with militant moles!"

Laughter rose amidst the clinking of tools and the shuffling of feet, a testament to the resilience of the human spirit—and perhaps a bit to the absurdity of life itself. Together, they worked, building not just a kingdom, but a future where their tales of valor, sacrifice, and the occasional comedic mole could thrive.

Ben's quill danced furiously across the parchment, each stroke a defiant battle against the silence that threatened to swallow him whole. In his lamp-lit chamber, far from the cacophony of construction, he wove words like spells, stitching together the fabric of his grief and the heroism of his fallen comrades into an epic tapestry of fantasy.

"Lo! And there stood Sir Reginald, his armor dented, his spirit indomitable, wielding the mighty Hammer of Hilarity to smite the Gloom-Goblins with jests so potent, they exploded into fits of unwilling laughter," Ben wrote, a half-grin tugging at his lips. Each memory was a balm and a blade—soothing yet slicing anew the wounds of loss.

Outside, the clamor of rebuilding echoed up through the open window, the rhythmic hammering a heartbeat for Oak Isle's resurgence. Laughter rang out with the clang of metal, a symphony of resilience as the people—blacksmiths, bakers, and bookbinders alike—formed a motley brigade of reconstruction.

"Thou shalt not place thy bricks askew!" boomed the voice of Annabelle, now dubbed the Masonry Maestro, her commands peppered with dramatic flair as she directed a line of citizens balancing stones atop their heads.

"Verily, we are constructing a fortress, not a funhouse!" someone retorted, eliciting chuckles and a spirited volley of mock insults that flew as freely as the mortar being slapped between stones.

"Attention! We have a Code Red!" Sir Harold announced, marching into the square with a wheelbarrow full of chickens. "The feathered fiends hath claimed yon grain silo as their sovereign cluckdom!"

"By the Beard of the Ancients, not the Cluckpocalypse again!" groaned a villager, already running towards the chaos with a broom in hand.

Ben paused, listening to the absurdity below, and felt a warmth spread through him. These were the moments—the ridiculous, unexpected trials—that forged the essence of Oak Isle. Their ability not just to endure, but to do so with a stubborn streak of humor, was the true magic he sought to capture on the page.

"Today, I pen our tale," Ben murmured, dipping his quill once more. "A story of unity, of mirth amidst mourning, and the unyielding spirit of Oak Isle, where even the shadows fear to tread lest they be tickled into the light."

With each word, he immortalized their collective strength, crafting a narrative that would outlast them all. For in the end, it wasn't just about rebuilding stone and timber—it was about weaving the very soul of their community into a legend that would echo through the ages, a beacon of hope and hilarity for generations to come.

Ben stood atop the remnants of a crumbled wall, his silhouette stark against the dawn sky. He surveyed the bustling crowds below with a mix of pride and solemnity. His voice boomed across the square, bolstered by the acoustics of half-toppled structures and the natural amplification of necessity.

"Friends, countrymen, lend me your shovels!" he cried out, striking an unintentionally comedic pose as his foot slipped on a loose stone, nearly sending him tumbling into the motley assortment of builders, bakers, and candlestick makers turned amateur architects. He caught himself, flashing a grin that was equal parts sheepish and endearing. "We build not just homes but hope! We forge not merely walls, but will!"

A cheer erupted from the crowd, laced with the irony only those who have danced with darkness could truly appreciate. Sir Harold, clad in an apron adorned with egg stains—souvenirs of the morning's Cluckpocalypse skirmish—raised a hammer high. "To hope and hammers!" he shouted, then added under his breath, "And to not falling off walls, eh, Ben?"

As laughter rippled through the assembly, Ben descended, joining the throng. He passed among them, doling out encouragement like a jester distributing jests at a feast. Yet beneath the levity, a palpable determination pulsed—the heartbeat of Oak Isle, resilient and unbreakable.

"Remember, we rebuild not for the morrow alone," Ben said to a group solemnly patching a bakery's façade, "but for the countless breakfasts to come, with pastries aplenty and nary a chicken in sight unless it's stuffed with cheese and herbs!"

"Ah, to dream of quiches instead of conquests!" one baker exclaimed, wiping a tear of mirth from his eye.

Later, within the safety of the great hall's still-standing walls, Ben gathered with his closest allies. A circle of mismatched chairs cradled warriors and wizards, each bearing scars seen and unseen. They shared tales not of battles, but of dreams, fears, and the occasional ludicrous nightmare involving poultry-led uprisings.

"Last night," confessed the mage Myrella, "I dreamt I was a duck, serenely floating upon a pond. Upon waking, I realized it was no duck I embodied, but hope itself—buoyant and untroubled by the ripples of our past strife."

"Quack on, sister," Sir Harold responded with a solemn nod, the absurdity of the statement wholly embraced by the group.

"Let us be ducks together," Ben proclaimed, eliciting a round of gentle quacks and heartfelt laughter. It was this, the sharing of even the most bizarre burdens, that wove them tighter than ever.

"Tomorrow," Ben announced, rising from his chair and donning an invisible mantle of leadership, "we host a feast. A grand table set amidst the scaffolding! For nothing says 'recovery' like eating roasted goose under a half-built roof!"

"May the geese forgive us," Myrella murmured, and they all understood. For in their hearts, each knew the true feast was not of food, but of fellowship; a banquet of shared healing, where every chuckle and guffaw served to mend the tattered edges of their spirits.

As the moon crept high, casting a glow over the reconstructed silhouettes of Oak Isle, Ben retired to his quarters, his heart full. He inked fresh words onto parchment—a testament to their collective journey through sorrow and absurdity, toward a horizon where laughter rang louder than lamentations, and where hope was served daily, with a generous side of whimsy.

Ben trudged across the cobbled streets of Oak Isle, his boots kicking up dust where once there had been only rubble. Each step was a staccato in the symphony of reconstruction around him, the clamor of hammers and saws playing the most raucous of melodies. His latest mission: to deliver solace as one might distribute bread—a meager sustenance for the soul.

"Good morrow, Mistress Witherbloom," Ben greeted, tipping his hat—a floppy thing that seemed to wilt under the gravity of its task—to a matronly woman whose eyes were twin lakes of sorrow.

"Sir Ben," she sniffed, dabbing her eyes with a handkerchief as flamboyantly purple as the blooms that used to grace her garden. "Come ye with words or with wine?"

"Both," Ben replied, brandishing a bottle with such flourish it might well have been Excalibur itself. "For what are words without wine but dry letters on a parched tongue?"

They shared a drink, a toast to her fallen son, who had wielded jokes like daggers and laughter like a shield. "He would've liked this,"

Mistress Witherbloom chuckled through tears, "a toast so grand it'd make the heavens blush."

"Blush they shall," Ben proclaimed, "for your son's bravery has painted them in hues of valor!"

Leaving Mistress Witherbloom with a promise—a vow etched in the vault of his heart—Ben continued his pilgrimage, weaving through the tapestry of the town's rebirth. Where despair had clawed deep furrows, now sprouted seeds of hope, watered by the sweat and tears of its people.

At the site of a new library, where scrolls and tomes would soon whisper tales of magic and myth, Ben couldn't help but chuckle. The building rose lopsided, as if trying to lean away from the soot-stained smithy across the lane. "A testament to our resilience," he quipped to the architect, "and to the fact that even in construction, Oak Isle cannot resist a good lean."

"Indeed," the architect agreed, squinting at the skewed edifice as if it held the secrets of the universe—or at least the secret to standing straight. "We build as we live, slightly askew, but always reaching upward."

The sun dipped low, casting long shadows that danced merrily around the growing structures. Children played tag among the beams and bricks, their laughter echoing off walls that promised tomorrow would be brighter than today. Ben stood amidst it all, a chronicler of chaos turned architect of amity.

"See how we rise," Ben declared to no one and everyone, arms spread wide as if to embrace the burgeoning skyline. "From ashes to aspirations! From ruins to rapture!"

And as the stars blinked awake above, winking at the absurd spectacle below, Oak Isle did more than rebuild; it reinvented itself—brick by whimsical brick—into a kingdom not just restored, but reborn. A land where memories were honored with jests as well as jousts, and where strength was measured not just by stone, but by the unstoppable surge of collective mirth.

"Tomorrow," Ben whispered to the moon, a conspiratorial twinkle in his eye, "we forge ahead with more than mortar. We build with belly laughs and bold hearts. For what is a kingdom without its spirit, but a castle made of cards?"

The last stone was set, the final brushstroke of paint applied. Oak Isle stood not just restored, but bedazzled with the glory of tenacious survival. Ben, clad in a tunic so vibrant it could guide ships home on the darkest nights, wove through the throng of revelers like a bard in search of a rhyme.

"Feast, my friends!" he bellowed, raising a goblet that looked suspiciously like a repurposed chamber pot, albeit one studded with an improbable number of jewels. "Today, we eat, drink, and be merry, for tomorrow we... continue to be merry!"

Laughter bubbled up from the crowd as they gathered around tables groaning under the weight of roasted meats, exotic fruits, and pies—so many pies. Each pastry crust was an edible monument to their perseverance. The ale flowed like a river of golden hopes, and the wine sparkled like the twinkling eyes of mischievous sprites.

"Look at us!" Ben cried out, standing on a table, defying both decorum and balance. "We are the people who patch our walls with determination and our roofs with sheer stubbornness!"

Music struck up, a lively tune played on lutes and drums made from the armor of vanquished foes. It was a melody that seemed to tickle the very soul, prompting even the most reserved scholars to jig with joyful abandon.

"Sing!" Ben urged, and the kingdom sang. They sang of lost heroes with smiles instead of tears, turning mournful dirges into ditties that had feet tapping and hearts lighter than a pixie's whisper.

As dusk settled, torches flared to life, casting a glow on faces flushed with laughter. Ben leaped down from his makeshift stage, landing with a flourish that would have impressed the most acrobatic of court jesters.

"Come now," he beckoned, leading a procession to the base of the newly erected tower—a spiral of ambition that soared high above the treetops, its tip tickling the belly of the sky.

"Let us ascend!" Ben declared, the first to place a boot upon the spiraling stairs. The climb was dizzying, not just in height but in hilarity, as each step was engraved with a joke or riddle, ensuring that breathlessness came from chuckles as much as exertion.

At last, they spilled onto the open-air platform atop the world, gasping between guffaws. Ben strode to the edge, casting his gaze over the kingdom that pulsed with a vibrancy only possible through shared trials and triumphs.

"Oak Isle," he addressed the twilight, "you have been cracked, but never shattered. You have been scorched, but never consumed."

He raised his arms wide, inviting the horizon into his embrace. "We have built more than towers and houses. We have constructed a testament to the unbreakable spirit—the kind that laughs in the face of darkness."

His voice grew soft, but no less firm. "To those we've lost," he murmured, the wind carrying his words like seeds of promise, "your memory will be the cornerstone of every joyous moment henceforth."

"Let this tower stand as a guardian," Ben vowed with the solemnity of a knight pledging fealty, "a sentinel against sorrow, a beacon of belly laughs. As long as I draw breath," he turned, meeting the eyes of each of his companions in turn, "I shall protect this island and its indomitable spirit."

A cheer rose from below, climbing the tower to swirl around them, and Ben knew. He knew that as long as there were stories to be told and songs to be sung, Oak Isle would remain unbroken, its people united under the banner of mirth and majesty.

Ben's cloak billowed behind him as he descended the spiraling staircase of the tower, each step a drumbeat in the anthem of renewal. The scent of fresh mortar and timber wafted up to greet him, the perfume of progress that only a recently besieged fantasy realm could appreciate.

"Behold!" he exclaimed with grandiose flair, sweeping into the bustling square where the townsfolk worked with a symphony of hammers and laughter. "The phoenix of Oak Isle arises, not from ashes, but from excessive amounts of elbow grease and an alarming quantity of turnip wine!"

A murmur of amusement rippled through the crowd. Ben had always found that humor was as necessary as swordplay in the healing process. It fortified the soul against the lingering shadows of loss.

"Look at this," he said, picking up a brick with exaggerated care. "This is no ordinary brick. It's the very embodiment of resilience! And just like you," he pointed at a strapping young lad with a wheelbarrow, "it's incredibly dense and nearly impossible to move emotionally."

The townspeople erupted into hearty guffaws, their spirits lifted by Ben's relentless jesting. Even in the midst of reconstruction, Ben knew the power of a well-timed jape could fortify hearts as surely as walls.

"Come now, let us link arms and stand shoulder to shoulder!" Ben cried, drawing closer to a cluster of villagers. They linked arms, forming an unbroken chain around the newly erected fountain at the heart of the square—a monument featuring a cherub spouting water from its mouth, and if one looked closely, sticking out its tongue.

"United," Ben proclaimed, "we are more impenetrable than the most complex tavern riddle. Forward, with the strength of a thousand overfed minotaurs and the resilience of a cockroach bard who simply refuses to leave after last call!"

Laughter rang out again, echoing off the newly raised structures, infusing the air with vitality. Oak Isle was not merely rebuilding; it was reimagining itself as a haven where sorrow would be drowned in waves of mirth, where every stone laid was a joke shared, and every timber hoisted was a toast to the enduring spirit of its people.

And so, as the sun dipped below the horizon, painting the sky with hues of victory and promise, the chapter drew to a close. There stood Oak Isle, a beacon of hope in a world that too often forgot to smile. Its people, arm in arm, faced the future not as survivors, but as triumphant architects of joy—undaunted, unyielding, and uproariously alive.

The battle had left Oak Isle looking like the aftermath of a particularly nasty goblin frat party. Turrets were toppled, walls crumbled, and here and there, a smoldering heap that might once have been an ogre lay smoking gently in the morning sun.

Ben picked his way through the rubble, carefully avoiding a still-twitching tentacle—remnants of the Kraken skirmish. He scribbled notes onto a parchment with a quill that had seen better days. "Hmm, 'Kraken Carnage'? No, no... 'Tentacle Troubles in Tumbledown Town'? I'll workshop it," he mumbled to himself, ever the author even amidst chaos.

Lila was nearby, engaged in an animated discussion with a stone gargoyle that had lost its perch. "You're not fooling anyone, Gerald," she chastised the stone creature. "We all know you can move when you want to." The gargoyle stayed infuriatingly inanimate, though Ben could've sworn he saw a wink when Lila turned her back.

"Can't believe the cheek of some enchanted stonework," Lila muttered, dusting off her hands as she walked back to the others. Her ability to talk life into anything was legendary, but even she seemed at a loss for words to rally the scattered bricks back into wall-form.

Roran, sporting what looked like the beginnings of an epic bruise under one eye, was attempting to straighten a flagpole. The banner, now reading 'Oak Isl' after the 'e' had taken flight, was caught in a half-mast tangle.

"Any luck with the flag?" Ben called out, ducking as a rogue spell zoomed past, turning a pile of debris into a rather surprised-looking rabbit.

"Flag? Ha!" Roran laughed, giving up on the pole. "I'm just trying to keep my balance! The ground's more uneven than a dragon's bedtime story."

"Maybe we should plant carrots instead of flags," Ben suggested, watching the rabbit twitch its nose indignantly before bounding away.

"Or write books about rabbits," Lila chimed in, her eyes twinkling with mirth despite the destruction surrounding them. "Seems they're all that will survive this mess."

"An epic tale of hares and havoc," Ben pondered aloud. "Actually, that's not half bad."

"Focus, you two," Roran interjected, though the smirk on his face belied his stern tone. "We've got a kingdom to un-crumble first."

"Ah yes, the great un-crumbling," Ben said with a dramatic flourish, almost dropping his quill. "It shall be our finest hour—or at least a moderately decent one, considering the circumstances."

Together, the trio surveyed the scene, a once-proud kingdom now resembling a patchwork quilt sewn by drunk pixies. They knew the road to restoration was long and fraught with the risk of splinters, but armed with unyielding spirit and the occasional burst of inappropriate laughter, they were ready to face it head-on.

"First order of business," Lila declared, stepping over a moat that was now more puddle than perilous. "Let's convince the statues that playing dead won't get them out of helping."

"Second order," Roran added. "Find out where that rabbit went. It owes us a new 'e.'"

And so, with humor as their shield and camaraderie as their sword, Ben, Lila, and Roran set forth to piece together their beloved, bedraggled Oak Isle.

The sun rose over Oak Isle like a weary actor, hesitant to face an audience after a particularly unforgiving act. The once-majestic towers and spires now lay in jumbled heaps of stone, but amid the rubble, the heart of the kingdom beat with a stubborn tempo.

"Hand me that plank, will you?" called out a burly blacksmith, his voice ringing against the clatter of reconstruction. A woman, her apron stained with the soot of ten hearths, hoisted a wooden beam onto her shoulder with a grunt that would've made the minotaurs of lore nod in approval.

"Careful, Martha!" a man chortled from atop a half-rebuilt wall. "Wouldn't want you to throw your back out and be stuck in bed while there's fun to be had!"

"Fun? If this is your idea of a good time, Gerald, remind me to skip your next birthday bash," she retorted, the twinkle in her eye belying her gruff words.

Everywhere one looked, the people of Oak Isle buzzed like a hive of bees drunk on hope rather than honey. They hammered, they sawed, and they lifted, each task punctuated by laughter or a jest that seemed to weave the very air together with threads of camaraderie.

Amidst this ballet of determination, Ben found himself at his trusty desk, which had miraculously survived the chaos with nothing more than a slightly charred leg. He settled into his chair with the grace of an ogre at a tea party, quill poised above a fresh scroll. His gaze flitted across the inkwell, then to the window overlooking the diligent townsfolk.

"Come on, Ben," he muttered to himself, "time to spin gold from this mess. Hmm... 'The Chronicles of Clumsy Knights: The Great Un-Crumbling'? Too on the nose?"

He dipped the quill into the ink, the tip hovering over the parchment as if afraid to mar its pristine surface. With a deep breath that puffed out his cheeks, he let the quill dance across the page, each stroke a testament to the resilience he witnessed outside.

"Ah, got to include the bit where Sir Roderick tripped over his own sword belt and took out three goblins," Ben chuckled, scribbling furiously. "And the part where Lady Eliza used her lute to whack that troll on the noggin. Now that's what I call a hit single."

Just as he was rounding out a particularly thrilling paragraph involving enchanted turnips and a duel of wits, a soft knock rapped on his door.

"Enter, oh knocker of wood," Ben called out with a flourish usually reserved for wizards revealing hidden realms.

"Ben, you wouldn't believe it," Lila said as she peeked inside, her face flushed with excitement. "Old Man Cedric just chased a chicken around the square claiming it stole his dentures!"

"Ha! That's going straight into chapter twelve," Ben exclaimed, his eyes sparkling with delight. "This tale shall be my masterpiece, full of bravery, buffoonery, and—"

"Chickens?" Lila offered with a smirk.

"Especially chickens," Ben affirmed, dipping his quill once more.

Behind him, through the open window, the symphony of Oak Isle's rebirth crescendoed, a chorus of laughter and clanging tools serenading his thoughts. And though the road ahead was long and littered with unexpected poultry, Ben knew one thing for certain: the story of their great un-crumbling would be nothing short of legendary.

Ben's fingers danced across the parchment with the same fervor as a minstrel's over lute strings, his quill flicking in a rhythm that seemed to mock the very notion of writer's block. The ink swirled and twirled into letters, words, sentences—a tapestry of tales spun from the very essence of Oak Isle's spirit.

"Ah, my dear friends," he mused aloud, though none but the whispering shadows kept him company, "how you've unwittingly authored the grandest adventure of them all." His mind wandered back through the annals of chaos and heroism, each memory etching itself into his work, painting scenes with strokes of daring escapades and the unavoidable snicker of mishaps.

Once upon a time, his stories had been forged in the somber depths of solemn quests and battles grim. But now? Now they teemed with the lifeblood of unbridled hilarity and heart, much like Roran's ill-fated attempt to mount a steed, only to grace the dirt with an impromptu interpretative dance.

"Comedy," he whispered, "thou art the unexpected hero in a narrative of doom and gloom."

A stolen glance at the stacks of filled pages brought forth a satisfied nod—only for his brow to furrow as he faced the blank space awaiting a title. A title to encapsulate the essence of this newfound fusion of laughter and legend. He tapped the quill against his chin, pondered, then scribbled a possibility:

"Chronicles of Courage: A Compendium of Capers and—No, no, too encyclopedic."

He scrunched the paper, tossed it over his shoulder, and tried again.

"Oak Isle Oddities: An Epic of Errors and—Argh, sounds like a cookbook for disaster!"

With each failed attempt, he crumpled the parchment into a ball, aiming for the wastebasket as if it were a hoop in some grand sport of literary accuracy. The pile grew, a testament to his struggle.

"Ben's Bedazzling Banters and Battles?" he muttered, immediately groaning. "By the beards of the ancients, I might as well call it 'Ben's Big Book of Blunders!'"

The room echoed with his laughter, a solitary yet full-hearted sound that bounced off the walls and mingled with the distant clamor of reconstruction. He wiped a tear from his eye, still chuckling at the absurdity.

"Perhaps," Ben conceded, speaking to the quill as if it were his most trusted advisor, "the perfect title is a quest in itself—one that requires a touch more rumination, or perhaps a flagon of ale."

With a resigned sigh, he leaned back in his chair, eyes twinkling with amusement. The book would find its name in due time; of that, he was certain. For now, there was joy in the journey, laughter in the telling, and a kingdom of eager ears awaiting the next page-turning delight born from the quixotic quill of Ben the Bard.

Ben plucked another quill from the cluster in his inkwell, as if selecting a sword for a duel. The latest volume of his adventures lay open on the desk, the blank page staring at him with expectant hunger. He dipped the quill tip into the dark pool of ink and pressed it against the parchment, the scratching sound akin to the skittering feet of a beetle over stone.

"Ah!" he exclaimed triumphantly, inscribing a character that seemed to dance with life upon the paper. "That's how you'll do battle, Sir Rumbletum!" The name emerged from his memories, a tribute to Roran's boisterous laughter that often rumbled like distant thunder during their late-night strategy sessions.

"Your belly-laugh will be your war cry," Ben mused aloud, imagining Roran's persona embellished within the stout and fearless knight he had just penned. He could almost hear Lila's voice, light and teasing, chiding him for turning their harrowing experiences into comedic escapades.

"Wouldn't want to make light of our near demise by dragon fire, now would we?" Ben chuckled, recalling the time Lila had single-handedly doused the flames with a concoction of her own making, leaving them smelling of tar and roses for weeks.

As the morning sun crept through the window, casting long shadows across the room, a soft knock interrupted his reverie. Ben turned toward the door just as a young page slipped inside, bowing awkwardly while presenting a sealed envelope on a silver platter.

"From a reader, Master Ben," said the page, his voice cracking like a minstrel hitting a high note.

"Thank you, lad," Ben replied with a grandiose wave of his hand, dismissing the boy. His hands trembled slightly with anticipation as he broke the wax seal, unfolding the letter with the same care one might use to unravel an ancient scroll.

"Dear Master Ben," he read aloud, adopting the dramatic tone of a town crier, "your tales have woven themselves into the very fabric of my soul." Ben paused, eyebrows raised high enough to threaten his hairline. "You inspire me to grasp the quill and dare to dream upon the parchment."

"By the whispering woods of Wistful Woe," Ben gasped, genuinely touched by the words. "To think my humble musings could give rise to such fervor!"

He continued reading, each line of the letter a testament to the power of storytelling and the unseen bond between writer and reader. The fan spoke of characters they had come to love as friends and adventures that sparked a flame within their heart to create worlds of their own.

"Mayhap there is magic in madness," Ben murmured, a smile playing on his lips as he placed the letter on the desk, vowing to pen a response posthaste. He glanced back at his manuscript, feeling a fresh surge of inspiration.

"Right, onward!" he declared, flourishing the quill with renewed zest. "Our next adventure awaits, and I shall be its faithful scribe. For every chuckle earned, every gasp drawn, and every tear shed, we forge ahead!"

With that, Ben leaned forward, his quill dancing across the page once more, spinning tales of valor and whimsy, where even amidst the darkest of times, a spark of laughter could ignite hope in the hearts of many.

With a flamboyant swish of his cloak, Ben burst through the double doors of the publishing house like a hero entering a dragon's lair. The musty scent of ink and parchment, pungent as a witch's brew, filled his nostrils. Fingers still ink-stained from his morning's work, he navigated the maze of cluttered desks and towers of manuscripts.

"Ben! The scribe whose pen is mightier than the Sword of Sorrow!" boomed Gregory, his publisher, emerging from behind a stack of books that teetered like the Tower of Trepidation. Gregory's eyes sparkled with the kind of fervor usually reserved for discovering lost tomes of ancient lore.

"Gregory, steadfast steward of my scribbles!" Ben greeted with equal gusto. "I bring tidings of the next tome, which I have titled—"

"Wait, let me guess," interrupted Gregory, leaning forward, "'The Giggling Goblin's Guide to Gargantuan Giants'?"

"Ha! You jest, but nay," Ben chuckled, shaking his head. "It shall be named—"

"'The Perilous Plight of the Pouting Pixies'?"

"Close, but no quill strike," Ben retorted with a wink. "It is 'The Jester's Joust with Jaded Juggernauts'. And it promises laughter amidst lament, as always."

"By the Beard of the Befuddled Bard! That will sell faster than firewater at the Festival of Fools!" exclaimed Gregory, clapping his hands together. "We await with bated breath, Ben. Your tales have brought light to these dark times."

"Then let us not keep the masses in suspense," Ben said with a flourish, producing his latest manuscript from his satchel.

"Indeed! To the book signing! Where your adoring audience awaits!" Gregory declared, ushering him toward the exit with grandiose gestures.

—-

The bookshop was a cacophony of chaos, a veritable carnival of literary delight. Fans formed a snaking line that wound around shelves stacked with spell books and biographies of bygone heroes. Ben took his place at the signing table, which was adorned with quills as extravagant as the feathers on a peacock knight's helmet.

"Sir Ben!" squealed a woman clad in a gown stitched with images of Ben's characters, clutching her copy of 'The Rogue's Rollicking Romp' to her chest. "Your stories are like a tickling enchantment upon my soul!"

"Madam, your words honor me as much as your dress dazzles," Ben replied, dipping his quill into an inkpot shimmering with glittering dust. He scrawled his name across the title page, adding a small doodle of a grinning imp.

Next came a young lad, barely taller than the pile of books he carried. "M-Master Ben," he stammered, "your books make even the gloomiest of goblin-filled nights bright with mirth!"

"Then let this signature serve as a beacon against the darkness," Ben proclaimed, bestowing upon the pages a flourish so elaborate it would put the most ostentatious of wizards to shame.

Hours passed, filled with laughter and tales shared between writer and reader. Ben listened to each fan, their praises and jests fueling his spirit like a feast fit for a famished fable-spinner. As the final book was signed, and the last reader left with a spring in their step, Ben sat back, his heart brimming with the joy of shared stories.

"Another successful conquest, Sir Ben," Gregory said, appearing beside him with a satisfied smile. "You've penned another chapter in the legacy of laughter."

"Indeed," Ben agreed, his own smile broadening. "And as the sun sets upon this day, we look to the morrow, where more adventures await to be written and relished!"

With a shared nod to future follies and fantasies, they exited the bookshop, the echoes of jovial banter accompanying them like the end credits of a bard's ballad.

Ben stumbled through the cluttered streets of Oak Isle, his steps buoyant despite the weight of exhaustion. He'd been signing books until his fingers were as gnarled as the ancient oaks themselves, and yet his heart was light, fluttering like a quill caught in a merry breeze.

"Ben, you old scribbler!" The voice belonged to Elara, her tone as bright as the glinting sun on polished armor. With arms wide and a smile that could outshine the moon, she swept towards him, her presence a balm to the tired writer's soul.

"Elara! By the quills of Quorinthian scribes, I've missed your effervescent charm!" Ben declared, opening his arms for an embrace that would surely be sung about by poets in taverns for eons to come.

They collided with the force of two comrades who had weathered storms of ink and parchment together. When they finally parted, Elara produced a bottle of sparkling elixir, its contents shimmering like liquid magic.

"To us, Ben," she toasted, her eyes sparkling with mischief and memories. "To our adventures in the written word, and to the unwritten epics that await!"

"May our tales be as boundless as the Endless Eastern Expanse, and our spirits as undaunted as the heroes within them!" Ben replied, clinking his glass against hers with a chime that seemed to sing of new beginnings.

The bubbly potion fizzled down their throats, tickling them with flavors of adventure and hilarity. As they laughed, the very air around them seemed to thrum with the pulse of creation, each chuckle weaving into the tapestry of Oak Isle's renewal.

"Look at them, Elara," Ben gestured broadly to encompass the bustling workers, the rebuilding stone by stone, the determined faces smeared with soot and smiles. "Our stories have kindled fires in hearths and hearts alike. Oak Isle isn't just rising from the ashes—it's being reborn as a kingdom of dreamers and doers!"

"Indeed," Elara nodded, her gaze sweeping across the horizon where the first pillars of a new hall rose towards the sky. "It's as if every laugh from your pages has planted a seed, now blossoming into hope for the morrow."

"Then let us continue to plant seeds of joy and jest," Ben proclaimed, his voice swelling with a passion that rivalled the most dramatic of thespians. "For as long as there is breath in my body and ink in my well, I shall script sagas to stir the souls of the young and the young at heart!"

And so, amidst the clatter of construction and the symphony of survival, Ben and Elara stood side by side—a duo united by the unbreakable bond of friendship and the unwavering belief in the power of laughter.

As dusk settled upon Oak Isle, a sense of hope enveloped the land. The kingdom, bolstered by the strength of its people and the enchantment of Ben's tales, began to heal and thrive once more. Stories became the mortar binding the stones of the past with the bricks of the future, and the laughter shared between pages became the anthem of a realm reborn.

The End.

Don't miss out!

Visit the website below and you can sign up to receive emails whenever Aaron Abilene publishes a new book. There's no charge and no obligation.

https://books2read.com/r/B-A-YOIP-FZROC

BOOKS 2 READ

Connecting independent readers to independent writers.

Also by Aaron Abilene

505
505: Resurrection

Balls
Dead Awake

Carnival Game
Full Moon Howl
Donovan
Shades of Z

Deadeye
Deadeye & Friends
Cowboys Vs Aliens

Ferris
Life in Prescott

Afterlife in Love

Island

Paradise Island

The Lost Island

The Lost Island 2

The Lost Island 3

The Island 2

Pandemic

Pandemic

Prototype

The Compound

Slacker

Slacker 2

Slacker: Dead Man Walkin'

Texas

A Vampire in Texas

Thomas

Quarantine
Contagion
Eradication
Isolation
Immune
Pathogen

Virus

Raising Hell

Zombie Bride

Zombie Bride
Zombie Bride 2
Zombie Bride 3

Standalone

The Victims of Pinocchio
A Christmas Nightmare
Pain
Fat Jesus
A Zombie's Revenge
505
The Headhunter
Crash
Tranq
The Island
Dog
The Quiet Man

Joe Superhero
Feral
Good Guys
Devil Child of Texas
Romeo and Juliet and Zombies
The Gamer
Becoming Alpha
Dead West
Small Town Blues
Shades of Z: Redux
The Gift of Death
Killer Claus
Skarred
Home Sweet Home
Alligator Allan
10 Days
Army of The Dumbest Dead
Kid
The Cult of Stupid
9 Time Felon
Slater
Bad Review: Hannah Dies
Me Again
Maurice and Me
Breaking Wind
The Family Business
Lazy Boyz
Sparkles The Vampire Clown
She's Psycho
Vicious Cycle
Romeo and Juliet: True Love Conquers All
Hunting Sarah
Random Acts of Stupidity

Born Killer
The Abducted
Graham Hiney
Zartan
The Firsts in Life

Milton Keynes UK
Ingram Content Group UK Ltd.
UKHW010811220424
441551UK00001B/143